Dead Man's Island

David McDine

First published by Endeavour Media Ltd in 2018.

———

Table of Contents

1

A Watery Grave

Dead Man's Island in the rain was as God-forsaken a place as you could find anywhere on earth.

In a steady downpour, four bedraggled Frenchmen in the tattered remnants of their sulphur-yellow prisoner-of-war uniforms shuffled forward carrying a plain wooden coffin.

On the order of a British naval captain, who lifted his bicorn hat in salute, they lowered the tricolour-covered box into a shallow, watery-bottomed grave.

Three members of the burial party moved back, leaving their comrade standing alone beside the grave, his long lank hair soaked through and clinging to his shoulders. He leaned forward, muttered some words, made the sign of the cross, paused for a moment and stepped back himself.

A corporal called four sodden, red-jacketed marines to attention. They discarded the canvas covers protecting their flintlocks from the rain, raised their muskets and on his barked order fired over the grave.

But it was only a three-shot volley and the marine whose weapon misfired winced at the corporal's hissed curse.

The Frenchman who had spoken the words over the coffin that no-one else but his maker could have heard, stepped forward again. He bent to retrieve the flag, folded it and tucked it under his arm. No doubt it would be called into service again before long.

Without needing orders, his three companions began shovelling mud into the grave, abandoning their task as soon as the coffin was covered.

*

A tall, dark-haired naval lieutenant standing beside the captain replaced his own hat and turned up his collar against the elements. But it was a losing battle.

It was one of those dark, depressing days of low cloud, a biting wind off the North Sea and continuous rain that to Lieutenant Oliver Anson felt as if it were soaking him through to his very soul.

Wishing he had worn a boat cloak like the captain, he was wondering what the hell he was doing there anyway. Why, he asked himself, had he been summoned from his Sea Fencible command on the coast to this sinisterly named islet at the junction of the Swale and the Medway – the river that divides the Men of Kent from the Kentish Men?

Island was a misnomer for what was in truth little more than a miserable stretch of sub-tidal mudflats, frequented only by wildfowl and the occasional burial party from the nearby prison hulks.

Shelduck, ringed plover, lapwing, oystercatcher and redshank probed the shallow waters for lugworm and other sustenance, and to the superstitious sailors manning the oars of the captain's barge the plaintive *crooee, crooee, crooee* cries of curlew that haunted this dismal place sounded like the uneasy spirits of the dead.

*

An urgent message from Commodore Home Popham had brought Anson to the dockyard but when he arrived there had been no sign of the enigmatic senior officer known in the navy as 'a damned cunning fellow' owing to his unconventional, inventive way of thinking.

The curiously named commodore was in overall command of all the Sea Fencible detachments from Beachy Head in Sussex to Deal in Kent – the area likely to be first stop on the invasion route when the French decided the time was right.

It had been Home Popham himself who came up with the idea of establishing the Sea Fencibles, a kind of naval militia made up of boatmen and fishermen – and no doubt a good many smugglers – whose role was to man shore batteries and gunboats to oppose enemy landings.

In return for their service they were granted an exemption from full-time naval service – or servitude, as they thought of it.

Many – including Anson – had thought of this rag-bag force of harbour rats as an ineffective bunch of man-of-war dodgers, but he had changed his tune since his Seagate detachment's capture of a Normandy privateer. They had proved their worth then, sure enough.

When Anson was appointed to the Seagate unit, Home Popham had hinted strongly that there would be an extra dimension to his duties – the gathering of intelligence and possibly what the commodore had called 'tip-toeing around France' on clandestine missions.

Certainly Seagate was well positioned for such activities, being a little over twenty miles from the enemy coast. And Anson's recent escape from

France following an abortive cutting-out raid fitted him well for such a role.

So far he had not been called upon to perform such additional duties and the summons to Chatham had filled him with expectation. But when he arrived at the dockyard the commodore was nowhere to be found.

Instead, Anson learned that he was required to attend the funeral of a Frenchmen from one of the hulks who, he was told, had fallen ill and died ashore in hospital.

And although he had racked his brains he could not think of a reason for being called to witness the interment of a Frenchman he could not have known from Adam.

Without any explanation he had been ordered to take his place in the launch carrying the coffin and burial party out to Dead Man's Island, and, having witnessed the pathetic ceremony, he was still none the wiser.

No doubt Captain Matthew Wills who had presided over the burial would put him in the picture later.

Anson had passed this way three years earlier during the Nore Mutiny. Indeed, the 64-gun third rate HMS *Euphemus*, the ship he had been called upon to prise away from the mutinous fleet, had stuck fast on mud-banks not far from here and had to be kedged off while under fire.

It had been a hazardous time, when the red flags of mutiny had flown from almost every masthead in the great anchorage and Anson had thought his time had come, staring down the barrel of a pistol levelled at him by a ruthless revolutionary.

But against the odds he and the loyal hands had managed to break free and take the ship into the safety of Sheerness dockyard, their defection spelling the beginning of the end for the mutiny.

So he knew the captain from that time when he had been able to render a vital service at a perilous moment.

The brief funeral over, the marines formed up and stomped through the mud back to the boat, followed by the four prisoners.

Anson took step beside Captain Wills and as the two walked slowly away from the grave he asked: 'I'm not entirely sure why I'm here, sir. Can you enlighten me?'

The captain indicated the Frenchmen plodding ahead of them towards the boat, so that Anson could now see the letters T.O. stamped on the back of their ragged yellow jackets. He knew this stood for Transport Office, the organisation responsible for administering prisoners-of-war. 'You make a reliable witness, Anson. These fellows don't—'

'I'm afraid I don't follow your drift, sir.'

Wills spoke quietly, for Anson's ears only. 'Commodore Home Popham wanted you to witness the burial of Lieutenant Hurel for a particular reason that will soon become apparent.'

'So when will the commodore see me?'

'He won't. He's left.'

'Left?' Anson was taken aback.

'Yes, posted. He's been given command of HMS *Romney* and a small squadron and is due to sail any minute – something to do with throwing the French out of Egypt, I hear, and then on to India. It was all rather sudden.'

'Good grief!' Anson had known that if Home Popham had been involved then whatever lay behind the summons to witness the funeral must be of a clandestine nature. Although the commodore had been in overall command of Sea Fencible units along the invasion coast, his role had encompassed intelligence too.

'So now that he's gone will *you* be briefing me as to what all this is about, sir? I must admit that at the moment I am totally mystified.'

'Of course – once we're away from this dreadful place and are drying out back at Chatham.'

Anson asked: 'But perhaps you can tell me now, sir, who was this Lieutenant Hurel and what did he die of?'

'Just one of the prisoners, and you could say it was gaol fever that carried him off, although after he …' The captain hesitated. 'After he was, well, taken ill, he was brought ashore to spend his last hours as a prisoner in some comfort. The hulks are not the most salubrious lodgings.'

Anson nodded. His own brief period as a prisoner of the French had been a push-over compared to what he had heard of life in the hulks and he resolved to give the French burial party a few of the coins in his purse.

He was well aware that even a small amount could make the difference between survival and going under in an environment where some men sold or gambled even their last rags of clothing and went naked to obtain food.

More than one thing about his summons to the funeral bothered Anson – not least how long the Frenchman's body had been awaiting burial.

'May I ask, *when* did he die, sir?'

Captain Wills, his prematurely grey hair now thoroughly soaked and clinging to his forehead, hesitated. 'Hmm, just last night I believe.'

Anson frowned, trying to fathom it out. 'But, sir, I came in answer to a message sent two days ago – and yet you tell me he died only last night?'

'Let's say that a few days ago he exhibited signs of a contagious disease, so he had to be removed immediately from his fellow prisoners. It could be assumed he was about to, shall we say, pass on ... so you were sent for in anticipation.'

Anson's bewilderment was obvious and Wills smiled. 'I appreciate this is all a little mysterious, but come, my boy, and all will be revealed.'

Carefully negotiating the already deeply puddled salt marsh, they made their way back to the launch, where the coxswain was holding the painter tied to an ancient mooring post to steady it against the current and the rowers were cradling their oars between their knees, blades upright.

The prisoners and marines embarked, Anson climbed on board and lent an arm to Captain Wills who boarded last according to strict naval custom – senior officer last in, first out.

The coxswain untied the rope and on his order to 'Shove off!' the rowers dipped their oars as one. He barked: 'Give way!' and they pulled away strongly, relieved to leave the sinister atmosphere of this desolate place.

A teenaged midshipman leaned forward over the prow calling instructions aimed at avoiding the treacherous series of mudflats off Queenborough that were fast being covered by the incoming tide.

Anson shielded his eyes with his hand to look back through slanting rain, but already Dead Man's Island had faded from sight almost as if it had never existed.

2

Angels of Mercy

Phineas Shrubb, Baptist preacher, apothecary, sometime surgeon's mate in the Royal Navy during the American War of Independence and now of the Seagate Sea Fencibles, had set up surgery at the detachment building and was awaiting his patients.

He had made the eight-mile journey from his cottage in a fold of the North Downs to tend to the wounded from last week's battle against a Normandy privateer.

The 12-gun *Égalité* had caused mayhem along the Kent and Sussex coast for many months past, snapping up small merchantmen and coasters as prizes. But at last the raider been lured into a trap, set by Lieutenant Anson, the detachment's commander, overwhelmed and taken.

The feat was still the talk of the town and was already being dubbed somewhat grandiosely as the Battle of Seagate, although most – including the mayor – had been led to believe that the divisional captain was the hero of the hour rather than Anson.

Indeed, the social-climbing Captain Arthur Veryan St Cleer Hoare, whose pretentious name reflected his claimed kinship with West Country aristocracy, was still showing off the privateer captain's sword to all and sundry. It had been surrendered to him, he boasted, at the end of the battle.

The French had lost a good many men thanks mainly to a well-aimed carronade shot from one of the detachment's gunboats and the ferocity of the boarders.

Sea Fencible casualties had been light and the more serious of them were now being ferried to the detachment building in Tom Marsh's pony and trap.

The bosun, Sam Fagg, had organised this rather than home visits so that each man would qualify for his shilling a day for turning up. To him it meant that the men would not have to aggravate their wounds by scratching around for their daily bread – a kindness appreciated by all.

'Anyways,' the bosun rationalised, 'I reckon good old King George 'as got more'n enough and can afford to give our boys a shillin' or two arter what they've done.'

Shrubb, a white-haired, kindly, smiley man, had been recruited by Lieutenant Anson to vet new recruits, weeding out only complete imbeciles and those with rickets, consumption, ruptures and the like.

Otherwise the policy was to allow pretty well anyone in – keenness being seen as more important than being totally sound of wind and limb.

Anson himself had allowed young Tom Marsh, patently a cripple who hopped around on crutches, to slip through Shrubb's net. The lieutenant justified this on the grounds that the youngster was keen to a fault, had considerable upper body strength due to handling his crutches that made him a superb oarsman – and owned a pony and trap which was currently the detachment's only form of land transport other than shanks' pony.

Now that the detachment was almost up to strength and had seen action against the Normandy privateer, Shrubb's role had changed from vetting recruits to repairing fencibles wounded in the fight.

It was a skill he had learned well during his service in the proper navy and had not forgotten in the two decades since the American war, but he looked more preacher than medical man, severely dressed as he invariably was in black from top to toe except for the white of his shirt showing at his neck.

His daughter Sarah, who had volunteered to help with the wounded after the privateer action, was also attired in almost puritanical fashion – in a long, plain black dress with white bonnet that completely hid her hair.

But Anson himself, and no doubt many of the fencibles, had noted how friendly, confident but gentle she was – and how attractive in a wholesome way.

Fagg had summed her up as: 'Not one as I'd marry meself on account of not being keen on prayin' an' all that. More of a girl what you'd like yer son to marry if you 'ad a son, which I ain't, thank Gawd, so far as I know, that is. Whatever, 'er and 'er father are right bleedin' angels of mercy, they are.'

Shrubb and his daughter were in the detachment building examining the wounded men's injuries when Sergeant Tom Hoover walked in, asking: 'How's it going?'

The pair looked up and Shrubb told him: 'Pretty well. I need some hot water, but it would not be fitting for Sarah to fetch some from the inn on her own. Perhaps …?'

'Sure, I'll go with her. My pleasure.'

*

Both Fagg and Hoover had been wounded and captured along with Anson during the raid on the port of St Valery-en-Caux in Normandy by the frigate HMS *Phryne* the year before and during their prolonged and arduous escape back to England they had bonded closely.

Anson had hoped to be reappointed to his ship along with his fellow escapers but instead was posted against his wishes to run the then shambolic Sea Fencible detachment that had been poorly led and bullied by a corrupt bosun.

He had enlisted the aid of Fagg and Hoover, had them promoted and appointed as bosun and master at arms, and together the three had cleaned out what Anson called 'the Augean stables' – a reference to one of the Labours of Hercules – and turned the Seagate detachment into a force capable of taking on, and capturing, the Normandy privateer.

The cheeky, wise-cracking former foretop-man Sam Fagg had been dragged up on the mean streets of Chatham and was an ace procurer of whatever the unit needed, albeit not always strictly according to the rule book.

Rules, he reckoned, were made to be bent – as long as no-one's looking. But although that was his personal philosophy, he knew every trick in the book so the rest of the Seagate fencibles could get nothing past him.

But Tom Hoover was altogether a different kettle of fish. Fully recovered from the wound he suffered in the Normandy raid, he was fit, smart and dependable – a first class trainer of men in the use of small arms, cutlass and half pike.

It had been many years now since his widowed mother had brought him and his sisters from the newly independent United States to Portsmouth. And as soon as he was old enough he had joined the marines rather than go into his mother's tailoring business.

Now his accent and use of words only occasionally revealed his New England upbringing. Mostly, others mistook him for an East Anglian and Hoover was content for them to do so rather than have to answer the inevitable question about what was an American, who must therefore be a rebel, doing in a red coat.

*

Sarah found a jug and together they walked across to the Mermaid inn where Hoover cadged some water from the giant soot-blackened kettle kept simmering in the open inglenook fireplace.

As they walked back Sarah asked: 'Do I understand, sergeant, that you are from America?'

He sighed but with the ghost of a smile. Others who asked usually got short shrift, but he did not mind telling *her*. 'I can't deny it, Miss Shrubb. I was born there true enough, but I have been in this country – *your* country – for a good long time now. I'm kind of, well, almost British now.'

'Did you know that my father was a surgeon's mate in the navy and served there during the American war?'

'I did know that and I admire him for it.'

'But would you not have been enemies then?'

He laughed. 'Bless you, no, Miss Shrubb. I was just a child but my father was a loyalist. Loyal to the British crown, that is. We didn't support the rebels and as a matter of fact my father was killed *by* them at the Battle of Brandywine in Pennsylvania. There was nothing left for us in the States once they'd won their independence, so my mother brought me and my sisters to England.'

'I'm so sorry. I did not mean to open old wounds.'

'Not to worry ma'am. It was a good while ago. My mother died a few years back and my sisters are married and gone I don't know where. Now I owe my loyalty to the marines, and my friends here. *They* are my family now.'

'But you are still an American?'

'I was born there and will ever be an American. I love America and one day I hope to return. I pray the day will come when we don't think of people as being rebels or loyalists – just Americans.'

She smiled understandingly. 'My father has told me about the Bill of Rights and of all men being equal, with unalienable rights to life, liberty and the pursuit of happiness. Those are declarations I find I could subscribe to, just as I do the truths of the Sermon on the Mount. They are sentiments few could dispute.'

Hoover smiled. 'I find myself much in accord with you, Miss Shrubb, *much* in accord, but for now back home I'd be seen as a loyalist lackey.'

'But one day you may return?'

Hoover nodded. 'Could be – could very well be … some day …'

'My father tells me that it is not unusual for Americans to serve in our navy.'

'That's true, although most have been pressed.'

'But to wear that red coat?'

He conceded: 'To volunteer? Yes, I guess that *is* a mite unusual.'

'From what I hear of your escape from France with Lieutenant Anson, you *are* an unusual person, sergeant.'

'Ma'am, Miss Shrubb, I'd reckon it real friendly if you'd drop the sergeant and call me by my proper first name.'

She blushed. 'Thomas, isn't it?'

'Well, them that's close call me Tom, but I'd happily settle for Thomas from you. It's what you might call an improvement on sergeant.'

As they re-entered the fencible building she asked: 'Do you have religion, sergeant ... Thomas?'

'I was brought up in the Baptist way, ma'am, much like yourself. But I'm not exactly what Lieutenant Anson calls a God-botherer, if you'll excuse my language.'

They were interrupted by her father. 'Ah, there you are, and you've managed to find some hot water. Well, sergeant, I'm pleased to report that all is well with the casualties. Ned Heale's missing fingers are still absent without leave of course, and will remain so, I fear. However, the wounds are healing nicely, as is his shoulder – very clean and not in need of treatment by maggot.'

Hoover grimaced. 'Glad to hear that. Don't relish the thought of seeing those grubs chewing away at a wounded man.'

'But it works.'

'How about Joe Hobbs?'

'His thigh wound is also clean and healing well, as is Tom Hogben's face. The stitches from temple to jaw have not improved his looks and have given his right eye a somewhat droopy look, but his mates have been telling him all will be well if he confines his courting to the hours of darkness.'

'So all in all we came out of that scrap with *Égalité* pretty well?' Hoover asked.

'Very well indeed, when compared to the French. Now, I just need Sarah to bathe these wounds with salted water and put on fresh dressings. Then all will be shipshape. Oh, by the way, Jacob Shallow heard I was here and turned up with a nasty head cold so I have dosed him with a tincture of garlic and milk. That should do the trick.'

Hoover grinned. 'It'll sure keep the rest of us well away so with luck we won't catch it off him!'

Leaving Sarah with the patients, Shrubb and Hoover went outside to find Tom Marsh waiting with his pony and trap.

On the way Shrubb confided: 'Please don't tell him so, but I am gratified that Lieutenant Anson sought me out to help with the fencibles. It has taken me back to my own navy days and given me much more of a purpose than prescribing cures for villagers' backaches and bowel disorders.'

'Glad to hear it, Mister Shrubb, and I can tell you that we all appreciate what you and Sarah ...' he hesitated, 'I mean what you and your daughter, do for us.'

'Good, good! So when Lieutenant Anson returns kindly report to him that on the whole everything is very satisfactory concerning the wounded.'

'That I will, Mister Shrubb.' Hoover hesitated again. 'By the way, your daughter ...'

'What about her?'

Hoover hesitated. 'I was just wondering ... but no, it's nothing.'

Phineas Shrubb looked puzzled, but kept his peace.

3

A Mysterious Mission

Back in the Commissioner's House at Chatham Dockyard, Anson followed Captain Wills into his office and they both took off their jackets and hung them beside a pot-bellied stove to dry.

'Thank God that's over!' Captain Wills exclaimed as he waved his visitor to a chair and filled two glasses from a decanter on his desk.

Fixing Anson with a penetrating but not unkindly stare, Wills was apparently noting that, since they had last met, the small scatter of powder burns on the lieutenant's right cheek had been joined by a livid V-shaped scar above his left eye.

'Well, my boy, I hear, and indeed I can see that you had a torrid time of it over that cutting-out raid by HMS *Phryne* on the Normandy coast – hit in the head, captured, escaping from France and all, eh?'

The attempted cutting-out of a privateer from the heavily defended harbour of St Valery-en-Caux the year before had ended in disaster, leaving several dead and Anson, Fagg and Hoover stranded ashore, wounded and taken prisoner. Their eventual escape had been some feat, but nevertheless the whole episode had proved a setback to his naval career.

'Torrid is a pretty good word for it, sir, and it cost me my place in the ship – any ship.'

Missing, presumed dead, he had been replaced as second lieutenant of the frigate and on his return from France all the Admiralty had seen fit to offer him was pen-pushing, the impress service or a Sea Fencible appointment.

The thought of being a glorified clerk had appalled him. Nor could he stomach leading gangs pressing unwilling men for naval service. So a fencible command had been his reluctant choice.

The captain, himself serving ashore while others were winning glory, prize money and promotion afloat, was sympathetic. 'But from what I hear since then you have been earning your keep down at Seagate.'

'Thank you, sir. It was not my choice but I must say it's had its moments!'

The captain laughed. 'I believe that's what they call an understatement. I was referring to the capture of that French brig.'

'*Égalité?*' Anson was pleased to learn that news had spread of how his fencible unit had taken the troublesome Normandy privateer that had been wreaking havoc along the south coast.

Wills stroked his chin. 'Yes, quite a coup capturing that blighter. I hear your divisional captain is claiming it as his personal triumph. But those who know him, well ...' Captain Wills stopped himself from speaking ill of one of equal rank in the presence of a junior, but his hesitation spoke volumes.

'I've not seen his report, sir. He chose not to let me have sight of it before he sent it to the Admiralty.'

'Well, I'm told that Hoare's report belittles the part you played in the affair. And you've obviously not seen that it's just been published in the *London Gazette*, so it's now gospel.'

This came as no surprise to Anson. 'I'm not concerned sir. My men know what happened. They were there—'

'And the district captain was not, I hear.'

Anson smiled ruefully. His senior officer, Captain Hoare, was a self-seeking poser who had arrived on board the privateer *after* she had been taken but had immediately set about convincing the powers that be and anyone else who would listen that the glory was *his*.

But Anson had lost no sleep over it. 'I am happy for it to be seen as a team effort, sir, and I am proud of my Sea Fencibles. They may be thought of by some as a bunch of harbour rats, but in taking *Égalité* I believe they performed in the best traditions of the service.'

He well knew that many in the navy proper, notably Hoare, were dismissive, contemptuous even, of the fencibles, largely because they were exempted from sea service at a time when men-of-war were undermanned. And, to add insult to injury, they were paid a shilling a day when undergoing training of dubious worth.

But Captain Wills was clearly not among the doubters. He waved his hand dismissively. 'What you have shown, Anson, is that when properly led, these "harbour rats", as you call them, are perfectly capable as a second line of defence should the Frogs elude our men-of-war.'

'That may be, sir, but of course no-one can be sure how they would perform in the event of an invasion. They've yet to be properly tested. Like swallows in spring, one Frenchman does not a summer make. However, our secondary role *is* to attack and annoy small privateers or retake any vessels that may have fallen into the enemy's hands, and in that they *have* been thoroughly tested and, I trust, not been found wanting.'

Wills banged a fist on his desk and declared: 'Wanting? Certainly not! I hear you and your Seagate men certainly attacked that Normandy privateer with great spirit and annoyed the hell out of him, so there's no need whatsoever to apologise for your fencibles – on the contrary!'

'Thank you, sir. I must confess to being rather proud of them myself.'

The captain raised his glass in salute. 'Excellent, Anson, excellent! We'll drink to that.' He took a swig. 'And then I have arranged for you to visit the hulk where the officer whose funeral we have just attended was incarcerated.'

Anson was mystified. 'Sir?'

'Yes, I wish you to return the few belongings he had to the senior French officer, personally, and for you to make sure that his fellow prisoners know that the perfidious English gave their comrade as decent a burial as possible, with the appropriate military honours.'

'But won't those Frenchmen who helped bury him take his possessions back and tell them that, sir?'

Wills shook his head and produced a canvas bag. 'They were from a different hulk. In any event the prisoners are in such dire straits that there's no guarantee that these few possessions would ever reach those he wanted to have them. Those fellows at the funeral would doubtless have converted his belongings, pathetic though they may be, for their own use.'

'But how will I know who to hand his things to?'

'I understand the man accepted by the other prisoners as their leader is a fellow named Bardet. He's listed as a lieutenant but apparently chooses to be known as Citizen Bardet, or Citoyen Bardet as the Frogs call him. The Transport Office people and the hulk's staff have to deal through him.'

'So I am to hand the bag to him?'

'Yes, to him and him alone. It's important that he receives it from a British officer, and a sea officer at that, as I'm told he is a naval man himself. And you will do well to tell him that you were not long since a prisoner yourself – and that the French treated you well, as I hope they did. They tell me he speaks pretty good English.'

18

'That's a relief, sir. I tested my schoolboy French to the limit after the Normandy raid and was found wanting. None of the Frenchmen I encountered mentioned la plume de ma tante ...'

'Ah, yes! I, too, learned useless phrases like that at school. It'd have been much better if we'd been taught how to call upon the Frogs to strike their flags and useful stuff like that! Anyway, here's Lieutenant Hurel's kit, such as it is.'

Taking charge of the bag, Anson couldn't help looking puzzled and the captain could see that. 'Look, my boy, I am not at liberty to put you fully in the picture at present. The reason for all this will be made known to you later.'

'Very well, sir.'

Retrieving his by now merely damp jacket, Anson put it on but as he made to leave Captain Wills held up his hand.

'Sir?'

'By the by, Anson, meant to ask you before, I noticed you giving something to the French burial party and shaking their hands ...'

Anson paused with his hand on the door handle. 'As you said, I was a prisoner myself, sir, and by and large the French behaved decently to me. I gave the prisoners some coins because I imagine they will use them to make their lives a little more comfortable for a few days at least.'

Noting the captain's quizzical look, he added: 'War is war, sir, but I take the view that we are not savages, and nor are the French.'

Wills smiled, his opinion confirmed. 'Young man, you are indeed one of a kind!'

4

Damned With Faint Praise

The Reverend Thomas Anson, distant kinsman many times removed of the late, great, circumnavigator and reformer of the navy, Admiral Lord Anson, paced his shingled driveway impatiently awaiting the arrival of the local carrier.

The rector of Hardres-with-Farthingham, a large, remote and scattered parish nestling high up in the North Downs, had a particular reason for wanting to intercept Hezekiah Dale's cart today. As well as carrying anything from occasional passengers to pots and pans ordered from Canterbury shops by the local farmers and smallholders, and taking their produce to market, he brought the mail and the newspapers three times a week.

It had been Hezikiah who brought the rector's wounded and exhausted son Oliver home from Dover after his escape from France. But today the rector was expecting not his son but the latest edition of the county newspaper, the *Kentish Gazette*.

He was nigh on certain it would contain a report, copied from the official *London Gazette*, of Oliver's capture of the Normandy privateer *Égalité* off the Kent coast.

The Reverend Anson would have liked to have gone to sea himself, but family tradition dictated otherwise and sent him into the church. He liked to say that he was *pressed* into the church rather than the navy and that his own parents had led the press gang.

His eldest son, Augustine, named after the saint who had come to Kent from Rome in 597 AD to Christianise Britain, had followed him into the church, and was now a minor canon at Canterbury Cathedral – an ambitious man already well practised in church politics. A bishop's crozier could be within his grasp one day.

Truth be told, although gratified at his eldest son's blossoming career in the church, the rector could not bring himself to like the man – however much he tried. Gussie, as he had been known as a boy, was too fond of himself, too self-seeking and too much of a prig to endear himself to anyone.

Other than his mother – and the archdeacon's thin-lipped and angular daughter, whom he intended to marry – Gussie was disliked by most, especially the servants whom he brow-beat and bullied.

The rector's youngest son, Abraham, was still at school but destined for the army, and as for his daughters Elizabeth and Anne, well, if he had been honest with himself he would admit that he would be happy if they stopped becoming a drain on his purse and married well.

However, there had been nothing to stop his second son fulfilling his frustrated dream as a sea officer. And so it was apt, the rector thought, that he should take a vicarious interest in his son's naval career.

As a distant kinsman of *the* Anson, the rector had been thrilled at Oliver's early appointments in ships of the line and then a frigate.

But he had been hugely disappointed when his son, through no fault of his own, was put in charge of a Sea Fencible detachment down at Seagate following his daring escape from France.

Commanding a bunch of man-of-war-dodging harbour rats was not exactly the stuff of naval legend. But then came the *Égalité* affair and the armchair sailor was enthused once again.

So far all he had been able to glean was that the privateer was cruising the coast picking off small merchant vessels when lured into a trap, attacked, boarded and taken by the Seagate Sea Fencibles.

But although the exploit was the talk of the county, the rector was anxious for details – and the *Gazette* would provide them.

At last Hezikiah's cart rounded the bend and made its way slowly down towards the rectory.

As it approached, the carter touched his whip handle to his old pointy hat. 'Good day t'ye, your reverence. Waitin' for the paper, is it? Wantin' to read all about that son of yourn's hexploits?'

'Good morning, Hezikiah. Do I take it that you know what's in the *Gazette*?'

'That I do, sir. Mind you, I 'aven't read it meself. I can read orlright but not to understand it, like.'

'Hmm, well perhaps you'll be good enough to let me have my copy and I'll read out the gist of it to you so you'll be able to spread the good news even wider, as it were.'

The rector was very well aware that by telling the carrier one would in effect be spreading the news in an ever-increasing circle, as the man was well known for exchanging news and gossip with everyone he met along the way.

Hezikiah nodded enthusiastically. 'That'd be kind of you, your reverence. Now, let's see, 'ere's your copy, marked wiv your name, ain't it?'

The Reverend Anson laid the paper on the back of the cart, quickly scanned the front page columns of advertisements and turned the page.

'Ah, here it is! A letter written by my son's divisional captain, Captain Hoare, to the Admiralty and reprinted in full by the look of it ...'

He cleared his throat and read:

"To inform your Lordships of the successful taking of a French privateer off the port of Seagate by gunboats of the Special Sea Fencible Detachment under my command."

'That's my son's command of course. This chap is merely the figurehead, as it were. It wouldn't do for Oliver to sing his own praises.'

He read on:

"The privateer Égalité, of twelve guns, out of Normandy, has been a regular raider along the coasts of Kent and Sussex for some months past, boarding, taking or robbing and sinking a number of small craft and causing disruption to trade."

'That's true. According to what fellow clerics have told me this wretched Frenchman had been causing mayhem for a good while. And it was the same privateer that my Oliver tried to cut out in Normandy, you know, when he was wounded and made prisoner.'

Hezikiah nodded. 'I remember that well enough, your reverence, on account of me bein' the one what brought him 'ome from Dover ...'

'So you were, so you were. Anyway, to return to the captain's report:

"The operation, which I had been planning for some time in line with intelligence gathered by me from westward, was timed to coincide with the privateer's predicted appearance in the area of our Channel ports. It was carried out by two of the new gunboats currently being trialled by the said detachment under my command, and it is respectfully suggested that its success was largely due to the manoeuvrability and armament of these craft and of the determination and high level of training of my Sea Fencible crews."'

The rector looked up, a cloud of doubt on his face. His understanding was that his son had trained the detachment, but perhaps praise for his part in all this was yet to come … He read on again, but silently now:

"The privateer which was in the act of attempting to capture a merchantman was herself taken by surprise in a carefully-planned operation, fired upon by my gunboats, boarded and taken after a stiff action following which the master of Égalité, *styling himself Capitaine Lapraik, surrendered his sword to me. Fifteen of my men were wounded, some seriously. Of the French, some thirty were killed or wounded, and the remaining thirty-five, including their captain, taken prisoner and handed over by me to a military detachment I summoned from Shorncliffe for escort to the Medway hulks."*

Now the rector *was* astonished. This was nothing like the version that had been relayed to him by fellow clergymen in Seagate and Folkestone. It was *Oliver* who had planned and led the operation, yet he received no mention!

But then his eyes fell on the faint praise of Captain Arthur Veryan St Cleer Hoare's penultimate paragraph before his plea for prize money:

"I have the honour to commend to your Lordships the steadiness and resolve of the S F and mention the support I received from Lieutenant Anson, of the Seagate Special Detachment, and Lieutenant Coney, of the Impress Service, under my command."

Working himself up into a rage, the rector shouted: 'Support? *Support*! It's outrageous! He's damned Oliver with faint praise – humiliated him. God damn the man!' and he tore the newspaper into shreds and flung them into the air.

Never having heard a man of the cloth utter an oath before, and certainly not one invoking his maker, Hezikiah looked askance, asking nervously: 'I take it Master Oliver's boss 'as claimed all the credit for hisself, rector?'

But he got no answer. The rector of Hardres-with-Farthingham had already turned on his heel and was striding back up his driveway kicking stones this way and that as he went and muttering angrily to himself.

5

A Floating Gin Palace

The prison hulks lay closely anchored along the river below the village of Gillingham in line of sight of one another. Anson presumed that was so that from each one a watch could be kept on those either side to spot any trouble and render mutual support if required.

He recognised once-proud British warships – *Bristol*, *Hero*, *Eagle*, *Camperdown* – and noted a couple of captured ships he did not know. All masts, rigging and sails had been removed and apparently haphazard superstructures, erected to house prison staff and stores, cluttered the top decks.

The hulks were bedecked overall but with washing rather than flags hanging from lines slung all over the deck, and Anson mouthed a phrase his father had often used in his sermons: 'How are the mighty fallen …'

He knew of the hulks only by ill repute – as overcrowded hell-holes often accommodating far more than twice as many men as they were supposed to and with a correspondingly high death rate.

It was rumoured that poorly paid guards were susceptible to bribes and that the chaos resulting from such large numbers of prisoners made it relatively easy to conceal escapes for some time – time that enabled determined men to make a complete get-away.

The boat's crew were used to carrying visitors to and from the hulks and when they reached the third in line they shipped oars, the coxswain grabbed the painter and jumped for the wooden jetty that had been constructed at water level amidships.

Once the boat had been secured, Anson clambered onto the jetty carrying the canvas bag over his shoulder. Two militiamen standing guard there with muskets came to attention and the coxswain knuckled his forehead. 'We've to wait and take you back once you've finished with these here Frogs, sir.'

'Very good, coxswain. I'll not keep you too long. No doubt these guards will prevent any prisoners from taking my place while you wait …'

The coxswain grinned. 'Aye, aye, sir!'

Anson turned and made his way over the creaking jetty to the long stairway that led up to the top deck. This was a novelty – he had never gone on board ship up a rickety stair like this before.

He noted that a galleried walkway had been built around the outside of the ship, just above the high tide water-line, he supposed to allow patrolling guards to inspect for escape holes.

As he climbed the stairway, Anson saw that the open gun ports were covered with iron grills and at several of them he glimpsed wan faces staring out: French prisoners.

A vile smell that appeared to emanate from the rotting gash encircling the hulk, moulding timbers, boiled cabbage, urine and worse engulfed him and almost made him retch. He paused for a split second with his hand to his mouth before continuing.

At the top of the stair he stepped on deck, touching his hand to his bicorn hat and looking round for the officer of the watch who would have welcomed visitors aboard a proper warship in commission. But only the sergeant of the guard awaited him. Noting Anson's uniform he snapped to attention, saluted and enquired: 'Lieutenant Anson, sir? I'm to show you around this floatin' gin palace.'

Anson had a great respect for the marines but could not help feeling a little miffed that the commanding officer had not seen fit to greet him when he had clearly been informed by Captain Wills in advance of his visit.

'Thank you, sergeant. Obliged to you, but I'd like to make my number with the captain first. Lieutenant Packham, is it not?'

'That's him orlright, but no can do, sir. He's bin ashore since yesterday on what he calls business and we ain't sure when he'll be back. P'raps one of the midshipmen will do instead, like?'

Anson could imagine what the calibre of officer appointed to command a floating prison must be like and guessed that Packham's business ashore might be less than official. But he held his tongue and nodded curtly.

The sergeant acknowledged by touching hand to hat and called to a nearby seaman: 'Double along and fetch one of the mids!'

While waiting, Anson clasped his hands behind his back and looked around him at the higgledy-piggledy structures on the hulk's once-immaculate upper deck.

After a few minutes a dishevelled and spotty midshipman emerged from one of the hut-like buildings looking as if he had just been roused from a deep sleep, which no doubt he had.

He hurried over to Anson, raised his hand to salute and appeared startled to discover that his hat was missing.

Anson, normally of a tolerant nature where youngsters were involved, was growing a trifle irritated.

'Mister ...?'

'B-blair, sir.'

'Is it customary to appear hatless when on duty on board, Mister Blair?'

The boy answered hesitatingly and with the faint trace of an Edinburgh accent: 'No, sir, sorry, sir! It had slipped my mind that we were to expect a visitor, sir ...'

On board a proper navy ship the youngster would have been mast-headed, but this hulk *had* no masts, so Anson treated him to a withering stare instead.

'I suggest you take immediate steps to reunite yourself with your hat, Mister Blair, and make a note to yourself not to be parted from it again, visitors or no.'

'Yes, sir, I will, sir ...'

'And meanwhile the sergeant here will show me around this, er, ship, he being in possession of his hat.'

Anson registered an amused grunt from the sergeant as the quivering midshipman made to touch his absent hat, faltered, and hastened away.

Catching the marine's eye, Anson raised his eyebrows in mock exasperation.

When they were alone he quizzed the sergeant about the crew and the make-up of the guard force. He learned that apart from the absent captain there was a master's mate, young Blair and another midshipman, fifteen seamen and four boys.

Normally a lieutenant of marines commanded the guard force of a handful of marines backed up by a platoon of militiamen from the Midlands, the sergeant told him, but his officer was ashore in hospital with some sort of fever he had picked up aboard the hulk. That sounded ominous and Anson wondered how many Frenchmen went down with such illnesses in this malodorous floating prison.

'Are the prisoners compliant?'

'Most of them, yes, sir, but there's more than eight hundred and you can be sure there's plenty of awkward squads among 'em. The ones you'll see are pretty much civilised, as Frogs go. But down on the bottom deck there's the lowest of the low.'

Anson asked: 'How so? Who are they?'

'They're the real dregs. Gamblers who've lost everything – any possessions they had when they were captured, their bedding, clothes. Even their food – not just today's ration, but tomorrow's, next week's. You name it, those wretches will gamble it away.'

'Good grief!'

'Total loonies … they don't give a shit, excuse my French, sir. Should 'ave said they don't give a *fig* for the rules or anything else. They ought to be put down, if you ask me. But lying around mostly naked and without food a lot of them won't last long anyway.'

'But the rest conform?'

'Pretty much. They choose from among themselves who they want to be in charge of this and that – like the cooks who take over the rations and do all the messing.'

'Very democratic.'

'Whatever, sir, but the real guv'nors are the bloke they call Citoyen Bardet – that's "Citizen" to us Brits – and his committee. They pretty much say what goes on board this floatin' paradise and there's not a lot the captain and the guard force can do about it.'

Anson mulled over what he had been told before ordering: 'Let's proceed, sergeant. The boat will be waiting for me and I'd sooner not delay it too long.'

'Right, sir, this way!'

He motioned two of the militiamen to follow and they stepped out smartly and descended a ladder to what had once been the spotless main gun-deck where they were greeted by an overpowering stench of unwashed human bodies, ordure, urine – and a din of jabbering voices that made Anson think of the Tower of Babel.

It was dark down there and it took a few moments for their eyes to adjust to the gloom.

Where once rows of great guns had dominated, Anson was confronted with an extraordinary scene of scores of prisoners, many seated on benches around the wooden walls, most wearing tattered remnants of mustard-coloured uniforms or scarecrow-like ragged clothing of every sort imaginable.

Many were chattering, reading, playing cards, sewing, working at handicrafts or painting. He spotted one man busily stitching an old boot and another surrounded by a small attentive group apparently holding a lesson of some sort. Anson was astonished to see a dancing class and a fencing lesson with wooden foils in progress in the middle of the deck.

But other prisoners were stretched out apparently asleep on or under benches and a few sat alone, heads bowed and pathetic as if overcome by melancholy.

There was a brief lull as many of the inmates paused to clock their visitors, but, evidently satisfied they were not worth further attention, the buzz broke out again and they turned back to their pursuits.

The sergeant took in the officer's amazed look. 'Incredible, ain't it? You just don't credit all the things they get up to, do yer?'

Anson shrugged. 'Chiefly I am here to see the French officer recognised by the others as their commander – this Bardet you mentioned – but I also wished to see how the prisoners live, and I confess I find the whole scene down here quite extraordinary.'

'They live like what you see, sir. They're crowded, right enough, and 'tis much the same on the other decks, except those dead-beats down below that I told you about, but this lot ain't dead and they gets fed, so it can't be all bad, can it? As to Citizen Bardet, well, he'll surely be here on the main gun deck – that is if he ain't on a run ashore, heh, heh!'

'Will this Bardet or any of the others be willing to talk to me?'

The sergeant put a hand up as if to shield his ear. 'Not a problem, sir. It's trying to stop the beggars talking that's the problem!'

He pointed to a heavily-bearded, coarse-featured individual with thick curly hair, who was holding forth to a small group of fellow prisoners.

'There he is, over there, Citizen Bardet surrounded by what he calls his committee havin' yet another meeting I expect. Gawd knows what they find to rabbit on about dawn to dusk. Anyhow, he speaks pretty good English so you won't have to resort to Frog-speak.'

He led the way across to the group calling: 'Oi, you, Frenchie! Have a word with this orficer, will you? He proberly wants t'know what you'd like fer yer birthday ...'

The man held up his hand to pause the meeting and turned to look Anson up and down.

He asked in heavily-accented English: 'What can I do for you, lieutenant?'

'You are Lieutenant Bardet?'

'The men call me *Citoyen* Bardet. Did you not 'ear that we 'ad a revolution?'

'I did, indeed. In fact I was lately in France as a prisoner myself, but I formed the opinion that all that revolutionary stuff had by now given way to using proper military parlance again. Do you tell me I am wrong?'

'You were exchanged?'

'No, I was wounded so had not given my parole and was able to escape with a clear conscience.'

Bardet spat on the deck. 'Parole, pah! It is for cowards. You were right not to give it. I 'ave refused to give mine and so they keep me 'ere in this floating pigsty. But I, too, will escape when I am ready.'

He said it with such certainty that Anson had no doubt that's *exactly* what he would do when the opportunity arose. It was, after all, what he would do himself if their places were reversed.

'So lieutenant, why are you 'ere and what do you want with me?'

Anson cleared his throat. 'Earlier today I attended the funeral of one of your comrades, a Lieutenant Hurel ...'

The man thought for a moment before nodding. 'Yes, I remember 'im. He was on this deck, a, 'ow-do-you-say, *solitary* man without especial friends, although 'e did give fencing lessons to some of the other prisoners – for a few coins. A few days ago 'e fell ill and the guards took 'im away. I am sad to 'ear that he 'as died, but not surprised. Death is never far away in the 'ulks.'

'Yes, dead and buried, I'm afraid. We gave him an honourable funeral. Your tricolour was draped over his coffin, some words were spoken over him by one of the French burial party, and marines fired a salute over his grave.'

The Frenchman shrugged. 'Ça ne fait rien. The words were wasted. There is no God, but at least you could say he 'as escaped the 'ulks.'

Although he was the son of a clergyman himself, Anson was not entirely sure there was a God either, but this was not the place for a philosophical discussion.

Instead he offered the canvas bag. 'I have been asked to bring you this. It was Lieutenant Hurel's.'

'And what is in it?'

'I have no idea, I have not looked in it, but I understand that it contains a few possessions he wanted you to dispose of, as you see fit.'

Bardet laughed. 'You are very trusting, monsieur. Suppose 'e had left me a pair of pistols?'

Anson shrugged and allowed himself the ghost of a smile.

The Frenchman took the bag. 'I doubt 'e had much to leave, but yes, I will see that 'is pitiful possessions go where they are most needed.'

'Thank you. That was my mission and now I will leave you in peace. My apologies for interrupting your committee meeting.'

Citizen Bardet appeared surprised, and amused. 'As you can see and 'ear, there is little peace in a 'ulk. But I thank you for your ... politesse. It is something we are not accustomed to from the English.'

'Please don't mention it. Now, is there anything I can do for you?'

'Nothing, unless you can set us all free or perhaps arrange for a shipment of good French wine ...'

Then, as an afterthought, he added: 'But maybe you would like to buy a souvenir of your visit?' He waved towards the craftsmen. 'Time 'angs 'eavy on the 'ulks, so the men with skills pass the day making things with bone, wood – whatever they can find ...'

Anson nodded. 'I noticed them at work and I admire their industry.'

'The things they make are sold to the guards, visitors and dealers who sell them on ashore. Guillotines are especially popular with our English customers, although, regrettably the models are made from bones of animals rather than aristos ...'

'I see,' Anson smiled at the black humour. 'I suppose for republican Frenchmen aristocratic bones would be more appropriate!'

'Bien sûr! But they are difficult to come by in the 'ulks. Nevertheless, every purchase by visitors 'elps the economy of our little world. If you buy something, the craftsman who sells it to you then pays a comrade to perform some service, in turn he may purchase some extra food, and so it goes ...'

'I see. Yes, I would be delighted to buy a souvenir. He held out his hand and for a moment the Frenchman hesitated, looking round as if gauging the reaction of his fellow prisoners. Then, mind made up, he took Anson's hand.

'Au revoir, Citoyen Bardet, et bon chance.'

The Frenchman grinned. 'A bientôt, monsieur. But if we meet again I very much 'ope our positions will be reversed!'

The guard sergeant led Anson to where the craftsmen were busily engaged in producing items for sale to make life in the hulk more bearable – and, not least, to keep themselves occupied.

As they approached, a large rat scurried past pursued by two half-naked prisoners armed with pointed sticks. Anson glanced at the sergeant but he appeared oblivious. No doubt such hunts were commonplace here.

Pinned to a bulkhead beside the craftsmen was a poster promoting a boxing match to be held on board several days hence, pitching a powerful-looking Breton against a scar-faced bruiser of similar hefty build from Marseilles.

The sergeant noted his interest and grinned. 'Quite some fight, that'll be, sir. They 'ate one another, that pair do. Both reckon they're the hulk's champion, so this'll be a decider. A lot of money will be riding on this match ...'

He paused, no doubt wondering if the visiting officer might be too regimental to trust with such information, tapped his nose and added conspiratorially: 'Of course, they ain't *supposed* to gamble but 'ow can you stop 'em? Anyway, I fancy a bit of a flutter meself.'

Anson was non-committal. 'Really?'

'Yeah, my money'll be on the Breton. Tough as a brick-built shite-house, he is. Mind you, the other bloke's supposed to 'ave learnt 'is trade in the drinkin' dens of Marseilles where they'll duff you up soon as look at you, so it could go either way. But the Breton hasn't got so many scars on his face as the other bloke so I reckon that's a good sign.'

Anson raised his eyebrows. Gambling didn't interest him and he had no great wish to see a couple of Frenchmen beat the living daylights out of one another. But he reckoned it was not for him to interfere with the running of the hulk. That was down to the absent-on-business Lieutenant Packham, wherever he might be.

Nodding to the craftsmen, Anson examined their work: beautiful ships, houses and a great variety of other models made from bone, exquisite marquetry boxes and straw-work mats and baskets.

There were also paintings for sale – some landscapes, apparently of remembered French scenes, and others showing the hulks themselves. There were portraits, too. Some were of famous people including France's First Consul, General Bonaparte and his wife Josephine, presumably painted from memory, and there were others, both of prisoners and members of the guard force.

Spotting a potential customer, one of the prisoner-artists offered to paint Anson's likeness there and then, assuring him: 'Monsieur, I will make you look almost human!'

But he declined, telling himself he must not keep the boat waiting any longer. In any event he was not keen to have his scarred features recorded for posterity, and, since he had no wife, who would he give such a painting to anyway?

Nevertheless, after a careful perusal of what was on offer he left the hulk carrying two neatly-wrapped packages. He knew exactly who would appreciate such mementos.

6

Back from the Dead

Back ashore, Anson reported to Captain Wills on the success of his assignment.

'You were well received, I hope?'

'The captain was not on board, sir. Ashore on, er, official business, I believe, and the officer of marines is sick in hospital. But his sergeant proved a perfectly competent guide.'

Captain Wills raised his eyebrows. He was clearly well aware of the type of business Packham was likely to have been pursuing ashore.

'And you managed to meet the senior prisoner, Bardet?'

'I did, sir. He was holding a meeting with his committee but he received me respectfully and I reported on Lieutenant Hurel's funeral …'

'Did you return his belongings?'

'I did, sir, as instructed.'

'In front of them all?'

Puzzled, Anson nodded.

'Excellent! And you were believed?'

Anson frowned. 'Why would I not be believed, sir? I'm afraid I don't follow …'

'It is of the greatest importance that they believed your version of events.'

'But why would they not, sir? Naturally they accepted what I told them. After all, I merely reported what I had observed myself on Dead Man's Island.'

Wills laughed. 'Capital! But I have to tell you that you have successfully sold them a pup, a perfect lie!'

Anson was shocked. 'How can that be, sir?'

The captain put up his hands. 'Now at last I can let you in on a closely guarded secret – the reason why you were summoned to attend that mock funeral and why you were sent on board the hulk to report back to the Frogs.'

'*Mock* funeral?' Anson queried.

'Yes, *mock*.' Wills got up, opened the door to a connecting office and added theatrically: 'I think it's time you met the late lamented Lieutenant Hurel ...'

Anson's astonishment could not have been greater.

He stood open-mouthed as the captain ushered in a lank-haired young man of medium height, dark, gaunt good looks, wearing a coarse, ill-fitting cutaway blue brass-buttoned jacket, check shirt, red neckerchief, loose off-white trousers and a pair of once-black shoes that had clearly seen far better days – and long ago at that.

'Lieutenant Anson, meet Lieutenant Hurel, former inmate of the prisoner-of-war hulks!'

'Good grief!' Anson exclaimed. 'I thought I had just attended your funeral!'

'Most kind of you, monsieur, and you have reported my death and burial to my fellow countrymen I understand?'

Suddenly Anson could see things clearly. He turned to Captain Wills. 'Am I to understand that you wished to make this officer disappear from the hulk without making his comrades suspicious, sir?'

'Correct!'

'So his death and the funeral were staged?'

The captain nodded. 'Using a pretended fever and a coffin filled with flints.'

'And I was duped into believing it all so that I could convince the French he really was dead ...?'

Captain Wills clapped his hands. 'Spot on, my boy, spot on! But to say you were duped is coming it a bit heavy. To make sure you were entirely convincing I was obliged to keep you in the dark ... until now.'

'But why have you gone to all this trouble? Not wishing to insult Lieutenant Hurel, but what is it about him that makes all this subterfuge necessary?'

The Frenchman had seated himself at the captain's desk, folded his arms and assumed a slightly supercilious smile.

Wills waved Anson to another chair. 'He is of the greatest importance to our cause because he has indicated his willingness to undertake a clandestine mission. He is a royalist, you see.'

Anson looked questioningly at the Frenchman, who nodded. 'It is true, monsieur. I owe the republicans nothing. They are my enemies. You

British are their enemies, too, so it follows that you are my friends. I 'ave what I believe you call a score to settle ...'

'And may I ask what this mission is and what part I am expected to play, other than to attend fake funerals?'

Hurel made to answer, but Captain Wills hushed him. 'Look, suffice it to say that it will involve a return to France. But it is not for me to say more. In fact I know very little more myself. This whole business was the brain-child of Home Popham and now that he has left—'

'It will still go ahead?'

'Yes, although not quite as originally planned. Now that the French have signed a peace treaty with the German states they can concentrate all their efforts on having a go at us. Home Popham had envisaged a general reconnaissance of invasion preparations in the French ports, but now I gather a more specific mission has arisen.'

'But why all the play-acting you asked me to do on the hulk? Surely his fellow prisoners cannot have any influence on such a mission?'

'Ah, Anson, you are wrong there. What with exchanges of prisoners, escapes, and the presence of spies or traitors, bribed or no, connected with the hulks ... well, to put it simply, wooden walls have ears.'

That, Anson knew, was only too true. His sea service had taught him that it was next to impossible to keep something hidden from others' ears in a warship.

Captain Wills assured him: 'What's more, believe it or not, we know that the prisoners are able to communicate not only between the hulks but with people ashore – even to and from France itself.'

'Good grief!'

'So you can see why it is vital that Hurel is believed dead, and by returning his possessions so publicly I very much hope you have convinced his fellow prisoners of that. Your task will be to get him back to France, clandestinely, so that he can pursue *his* mission.'

Anson asked: 'What's to become of Lieutenant Hurel in the meantime?'

'You will have noted that he has assumed the appearance of a common sailor?'

Anson was forced to acknowledge that the Frenchman *looked* the part.

'I had first proposed that he dress as a pregnant woman, posing as the wife of an officer away at sea, but—'

'Non, absolutely non!'

'Calm down, Hurel, you have already won that argument.'

'Dressing as a woman would 'ave been an affront to my 'onour.'

'Yes, yes, but no-one would have known.'

'*I* would have known, monsieur. To me, 'onour is everything. I feel I should remind you that one of my female ancestors was the mistress of a king!'

'Forget all that, Hurel. You won your point, but now you must pose as a common sailor and when anyone else is around you must carry Lieutenant Anson's kit.'

'That will be preferable to becoming a woman.'

Close to exasperation, Captain Wills turned to Anson. 'So now Hurel must do another disappearing trick. He needs to harbour up well away from here until he's been well and truly forgotten by one and all, and until certain other plans are in place, but somewhere convenient for his coming mission.'

'And you wish me to help him disappear, sir?'

'You are a Man of Kent, are you not, so you would appear to be the ideal person to conceal him within striking distance of the coast. He must vanish off the face of the earth, mind. Can you make that happen?'

Anson thought for a moment. 'I could take him to Seagate ...'

Captain Wills shook his head. 'Not yet. That would be too public and what with the smugglers going back and forth, well, the Channel ports leak like sieves.'

During his escape from France Anson had learned how the Kentish smugglers were tolerated over the other side because of their free trading despite the blockades. Indeed, they were more or less free to come and go whenever it suited them, especially via the port of Dunkirk.

And it was well known in the service that they carried not only the gold the enemy needed to fund the war in return for smuggled goods, but no doubt escaped prisoners, spies – even the latest English newspapers. No, it would not do to risk exposure by taking Hurel to the coast until the last moment.

Captain Wills toyed with his side whiskers and asked: 'Your father is a clergyman is he not?'

'Yes, he's the rector at Hardres Minnis, near Canterbury. I suppose we could go there.' But then another thought struck him. 'No, better still, I have friend who lives near Faversham. We'll go there.'

'Is this friend discreet?'

'None more so, sir.'

'And his house?'

'Spacious, and well away from the nearest village. He is a retired banker, unmarried, but his orphaned niece lives with him.'

'Servants?'

Anson's mind went back to those peaceful days he had spent as the guest of Josiah Parkin at Ludden Hall just before he had helped HMS *Euphemus* break away from the mutinous fleet at the Nore anchorage three years earlier.

'It was where I was convalescing when you sent for me during the mutiny, sir. There's just a butler-cum-groom and his wife who is his housekeeper and cook, two live-in maids, a gardener who tends the grounds several times a week. Oh, and a woman from the village helps sometimes.'

He smiled at the recollection of Emily, the large middle-aged lady with work-coarsened hands and a noticeable moustache who had been his ministering angel when he had been laid low with fever.

'And you are confident they are all trustworthy?'

'Absolutely, sir! Without question.'

Wills nodded. 'Good. Then I suggest you hole up there and when Lord Nelson is ready you will be sent for and the faceless ones at Dover Castle will brief you fully. But that will not be for at least a couple of weeks.'

Anson knew the captain was referring to those who looked after intelligence matters on the invasion coast, but he was taken aback by the mention of the great naval hero. 'Did you say *Nelson*, sir?'

Wills smiled. 'Did I? Must have been the slip of the tongue. I merely meant to say that you'd be summoned and fully briefed once the admiral is in the Downs and certain other preparations are ready.'

Anson knew that there was a mishmash of warships gathering in the great Downs anchorage off the fishing town of Deal, and it could most likely mean some sort of action was pending against the French whose ports just twenty or thirty miles across the Channel were reputed to be full of invasion barges.

But for the moment Captain Wills was clearly not willing – or able – to impart anything else.

A smarting sensation from Anson's tender backside reminded him: 'I rode here, sir, so if we are to get to Faversham, Monsieur Hurel will need a horse.'

The Frenchman laughed. 'I fear that thanks to the less than adequate rations the English serve on the 'ulks I am now all skins and bones and I will not be able to sit a 'orse for very long, gentlemen. On the 'ulk I could 'ave eaten one, but I would prefer not to ride one at present!'

The captain deliberated for a moment before announcing: 'Neither of you need ride. It would make you too conspicuous in any case. Sailors on horseback? No, I don't think so. I'll arrange for a private carriage to take you.'

'And my horse?'

'It can take a make and mend, Anson, and trot along behind. All I ask is that you both disembark a few miles from your friend's house and send the coach back. It is of the utmost importance that no-one else must know where you are. Is that clear?'

'Perfectly clear, sir.'

7

Return to Ludden Hall

Near a familiar fork in the Dover road Anson called for the coachman to stop and motioned to Hurel to disembark.

They climbed down, Anson unhitched Ebony and watched as the driver turned the coach slowly with much fussing and chivvying of the horses. He was forced to stop the manoeuvre to let a mail coach speed by at some eight miles an hour, but then completed the turn and with a wave of his whip set off back towards Chatham.

Anson looked after the retreating mail coach wistfully, recalling the journey he had made in – or rather clinging to the top of – just such a vehicle three years earlier after the guard had been wounded during an attempted robbery.

At the time Anson had been on his way to deliver important papers to the admiral at the Nore anchorage, but he had arrived to find red flags flying from every masthead signifying that mutiny was already under way.

It was on his way home for a spot of enforced leave that he had succumbed to a fever and been brought by an elderly retired banker, active antiquary and avid naturalist, Josiah Parkin, to recover at his secluded home near Faversham.

Leading his horse, Anson beckoned to Hurel, who had slumped on to a milestone, to join him, calling: 'You'd best carry my dunnage, sailor!'

Hurel gave him a look of disgust but picked up Anson's bag nevertheless and they left the Dover road and set off down the lane.

After barely half a mile they came upon the familiar iron gates at the end of the drive that led to Ludden Hall.

Anson lifted the latch and led Ebony through, Hurel waiting behind to shut it after them.

Ludden Hall was just as Anson remembered it: the long, gravel driveway curved round past a small willow-fringed lake and led up to the broad paved steps fronting the iron-studded oak doors framed by large Doric columns.

The imposing stone-built house stood in several acres of gardens, lawns, flower beds and a walled and gated plot for vegetables and beehives. The whole was well kept but not over-manicured; Josiah Parkin was too keen a naturalist to opt for the clinical geometric styles favoured by some.

They crunched up the gravel and as they passed the lake Anson thought it wise to tell Hurel to take a seat in an arbour so that he could approach the house alone. To spring a French prisoner-of-war on his friend without some prior explanation could prove something of a shock.

Although there had not been time to warn the old gentleman of his arrival, Anson was nevertheless greeted with great enthusiasm.

During his convalescence he had formed a lasting attachment to his host and on his last night there before returning to the Nore they had been joined by Parkin's orphaned niece Cassandra and enjoyed a most convivial dinner.

It was a happy memory that had sustained him on many an arduous and boring watch in the Mediterranean and then on blockade duty off the Brittany coast.

Parkin called for his butler-cum-coachman Dodson to take charge of Ebony and then he and his guest adjourned to the old gentleman's study where Anson apologised for not being in touch since his escape from France, confessing: 'It has been most remiss of me, sir, but I have been rather occupied.'

Parkin dismissed his apology with a wave of his hand. 'I met your father at a gathering of Kentish antiquarians. He told me you had been a prisoner of the French and that since your remarkable escape you have been exceptionally busy sweeping the enemy from the Channel coast.'

'All grossly exaggerated!' Anson protested.

'Nevertheless, making contact with an old fogey like me must have been furthest from your mind. Suffice it to say that I, and Cassandra of course, are proud to know such a heroic former guest!'

Anson blushed. He was embarrassed that he had not made contact with Parkin and his niece since his escape from France and hearing that they had been following his adventures, vicariously, rubbed it in.

Nor did he enjoy praise or notoriety, and again he protested: 'My father, being a clergyman, does tend to over-egg the pudding, sir. I can assure you that the French would no doubt have been only too delighted to be rid of me and since then I have merely been messing about in boats with as disreputable a bunch of scallywags as you'll find in any fishing port from here to Cornwall ...'

Amused, Parkin countered, smiling: 'If your goodly father exaggerates then I am quite certain that you do the complete opposite. The last I heard from *you* was the most welcome letter you sent from Gibraltar just before your ship was due to sail to join the Channel blockade, and no doubt you played down your Mediterranean adventures in that, too.'

'Not in the slightest ... and, by the by, I hope the stuffed specimens I sent with it arrived safely, were to your liking and are now part of your collection of natural history and antiquarian objects?'

A pained look crossed Parkin's face. 'Stuffed ...?'

'They *did* arrive, I hope – the stuffed hoopoe, blue-cheeked bee-eater and greater short-toed lark?'

Parkin paused before answering, almost apologetically: 'Oh? So *that's* what they were! Such are the wonders of Mediterranean avians, but—'

Puzzled, Anson ventured: 'But, what, sir?'

The old gentleman sighed. 'Look, I can think of no easy way of breaking this sad news to you. I fear that despite the assurance you received that they had been prepared for display by the master bird-stuffer Louis Dufresne, they did not, how shall I put it ...?'

'Did not, *what*?'

'I am afraid they did not survive the voyage.'

Anson was mortified. 'Oh, what a shame! My abject apologies. Was the box not strong enough?'

'Not strong enough for that ingenious creature *Rattus rattus*, alias the ship rat. One or more of his tribe gnawed their way into the box, perhaps during the sea passage—'

'Rats!' Anson exclaimed indignantly.

'Exactly. I detected the tell-tale marks of their incisors. And although when they got into the box even they must have noticed that the birds were demonstrably long dead, they nevertheless consumed all but a few feathers, bones and glass eyes.'

'I am so sorry, dear sir. I blame myself entirely. I should have had the foresight to have the specimens packed in a lead-lined box.'

'No, no. Not your fault at all. It was merely nature at work. I console myself that Monsieur Dufresne's use of arsenical soap to preserve the skins will have given the culprits an extremely bad stomach ache, even supposing it did not prove fatal.'

Suddenly realising that he had not yet enquired the reason for Anson's visit, Parkin added: 'I do hope you have come to stay for at least a few days. You will recall how starved my niece and I are for agreeable company.'

'Indeed I have, sir, if that is acceptable to you. But first I have an enormous favour to ask of you ...'

Parkin was all smiles. 'Ask away, my dear fellow, ask away, and if it's within my power of course I will grant it.'

'Well, you see, I have brought a Frenchman, from the hulks.'

'Good heavens, a specimen for me to examine and add to my collection? Now that *would* be a first!' And he added mischievously: "Has he, too, been stuffed?'

'No, I'm afraid not. Well, not recently at any rate. This specimen is still very much alive and currently sitting in the arbour beside your driveway, concealed against wagging tongues.'

Somewhat ruefully, Parkin ventured: 'Then *not* a corpse for dissecting, I surmise?'

'Not just at present, sir.'

Sensing that something far more serious was afoot than bantering about stuffed creatures, Parkin kept silent as Anson explained as much as he felt he could about the fake funeral, the reason for bringing a Frenchman to Ludden Hall and why they needed to stay out of the public gaze for a while.

The old gentleman was delighted to accommodate them. 'As you know,' he told Anson, 'the most exciting thing that occurs here is when the gamekeeper calls with some dead creatures for dissection, or when I am forced to play-act at being ill when my odious banking cousins come calling, so to have a live Frenchman here – and you, of course – will be a real treat!'

Their stay at Ludden Hall duly arranged, Anson wrote a note for the old gentleman to send to Seagate requiring spare clothing to be collected from his room at the Rose and brought to him by young Tom Marsh in his pony and trap.

*

Hurel, now bathed, his lower deck disguise abandoned, and dressed rather more respectably in an old bottle green tail coat of Parkin's, with white Nankeen breeches and silk stockings, appeared for a pre-dinner drink with Anson and their host. The Frenchman's disreputable holey footwear had

42

been discarded in favour of a pair of his host's silver-buckled shoes that were obviously far too big for him.

He may have been fitted out to look like a common sailor before he left Chatham, but now at first glance he could be taken for a country gentleman like his host, whose clothes he was wearing.

Wine glasses in hand, Parkin and his two guests stood together in the library where the Frenchman paid close attention to the framed prints of Roman ruins and the cases of stuffed birds and mammals.

Hurel showed particular interest in a fox and the badger in a nearby case. 'I 'ave seen reynard – the fox – many times, but this creature ...'

Parkin offered: 'You perhaps mean *Meles meles* – the badger?'

'Ah oui, le blaireau! A creature of the night, is he not?'

'Nocturnal, yes.'

And Anson interjected: 'Just as you must be, Hurel, if we are not to give the game away ...'

'What game is this? Not something like that ridiculous English game of cricket, I 'ope! No-one but the English can begin to understand the rules, if indeed there are any!'

They laughed and Hurel turned to his host. 'It is so very gentil of you to allow me to stay 'ere at your charming 'ome, monsieur. The use of your clothes and the delightful room you 'ave made available to me is most kind – most kind indeed. My sojourn as a guest of your King on the 'ulks was a little less comfortable, despite the extensive views of the river.'

Parkin waved aside his compliment. 'Perish the thought that we would not welcome a gentleman like yourself, sir, no matter what his nationality. As my particular friend, Anson here, well knows, we country mice are deprived of salubrious company and seize the opportunity of entertaining guests whenever they pop out of the woodwork!'

Hurel was puzzled. 'I 'ave noticed various animals in glass cases, monsieur. Perhaps they include these mice you speak of? But I 'ave not seen any, as you say, pop out of the woodwork – so far.'

'A treat to come, perhaps,' Anson interjected. 'But I should explain, Hurel, Mister Parkin is using the vernacular when he refers to country mice. His meaning, I believe, is that whereas town mice see many visitors, those who live in the depths of the country see relatively few. Hence his enhanced pleasure at receiving guests – and as circumstances have temporarily reduced you to being as poor as a church mouse, I am sure you are doubly welcome!'

Now Hurel was totally bewildered. 'My boyhood tutors assured me after years of study that I spoke English passably well, apart from the dropped "haitches", whatever they are. But now, well I can see there are depths to the language that I will never fathom! Town mice and country mice coming out of the woodwork ... and now you say I 'ave become a church mouse – *extraordinaire*!'

Parkin reassured him. 'Even those of us born to it trip up sometimes and muddle up our mitigates with our militates – and our principals and principles. But may I venture to say, monsieur, that you speak this most difficult language very well – very well indeed, apart from the dropped aitches your tutors spoke of – and many a Man of Kent and Kentish Man shares *that* habit, or should I say 'abit?'

Their laughter was interrupted by the arrival of an extremely good-looking young lady wearing a striking blue satin gown with elbow-length frilled cuffs and a kerchief covering her décolletage.

She paused at the library door. 'You appear to be having a very jolly time, gentlemen.' And, turning to Parkin, she teased: 'I hope you have not been forcing too much wine on our guests this early in the evening, uncle dear!'

Parkin smiled affectionately. 'Not at all, my child. Monsieur Hurel, here, has just made a most amusing remark – hence the laughter.'

He took her hand. 'Gentlemen, allow me to present my niece, Cassandra. Sadly my brother and his dear wife died of the typhoid fever when she was just a child and she has lived with me ever since. She is like a daughter to me.'

Anson did a double-take. When he was last at Ludden Hall, Cassandra was a pretty dark-haired girl just turned sixteen, but now, some three years on, she was stunning.

Despite the enveloping gown she clearly had a most handsome figure and her raven hair and pure, English rose complexion made her a natural beauty, a very attractive woman indeed.

He had taken to her when they first met, drawn to her enquiring, enlightened mind – so refreshing after the many vacuous females of his acquaintance. She had been pretty then, in a girlish way, but now she had blossomed – and he was riveted.

Hurel appeared similarly dumbstruck, but only for a moment.

Anson bowed, but the Frenchman bowed lower, took her hand and kissed it, muttering: 'Charming, charming ...'

Well, Anson, thought to himself, Hurel had been at sea for some time before being captured and locked up aboard a hulk, so no doubt *any* female from eight to eighty would charm him – and there was no doubt that Cassandra *was* charming.

Fearing that this show of, what to him, were immoderate mawkish French manners might embarrass their hosts, Anson caused a diversion by producing the parcel he had concealed behind his back.

'I have a present for you, sir, er, that is a present for each of you.'

He noticed that Cassandra used the distraction to free her hand from Hurel's eager grasp.

She asked coquettishly: 'Not, I trust, the remains of more stuffed birds, Mister Anson?'

'Oh no,' he reassured her. 'And when the parcels were wrapped on board the hulk there was no sign of rat infestation!'

'The hulk?'

'Yes, I had occasion to go on board the hulk where Hurel, here, had been confined, and there the prisoners run a sort of market where they sell souvenirs they have made to the guards and visitors.'

She looked concerned. 'I do hope people do not go along to stare at the poor prisoners as if they were animals in some zoological gardens.'

Hurel saw another opening for complimenting her. 'If they were all as charming as you, ma'amselle, we would not 'ave minded the stares at all! In fact …'

'May I? The old gentleman took his pocket knife to the string securing his parcel and pulled back the brown paper to reveal a beautiful model of a frigate, intricately carved out of bone, with rigging made from hair, and flying French colours.

Anson explained: 'It was created on board the hulk by poor prisoners out of the animal bone left over from their meagre rations and sold to raise money for a few comforts.'

Parkin was marvelling at the model. 'Such craftsmanship, and no doubt using basic tools. Exquisite! It will take pride of place in my collection.'

'I could have bought a model guillotine, also made of bone, but I thought the ship was perhaps, well, less gruesome …'

The old man chuckled. 'I trust the guillotine you saw was not made from the bones of some unfortunate who had been decapitated by one!'

Cassandra had opened her parcel containing what at first appeared to be a volume of poetry but upon examination proved to be a jewellery box with hinged lid and various interior compartments – the whole made out of fine marquetry straw work.

She was enthralled, murmuring: 'Thank you so much, sir. This is truly a work of art and I shall treasure it always.'

Lightening the mood, she teased Parkin: 'You must find a glassblower to make a dome to protect your frigate from ships' rats, uncle!'

They laughed, and, touched by their obvious delight in his gifts, Anson explained: 'Although the ship is wearing French colours, she closely resembles HMS *Phryne*, the frigate I joined in the Mediterranean after my earlier visit here. But then, that is only natural, because *Phryne* was French-built and captured by our navy.'

Suddenly conscious that he might have offended Hurel, he quickly added: 'No doubt due to superior force and after a stout defence ...'

But Hurel merely shrugged and laughed. 'It is of no account to me, mon ami. Please do not forget that I am not a republican, but a royalist. You may capture as many *republican* Frenchmen as you like. 'Ow do you say, the more the 'appier?'

'Merrier. It's the more the merrier – and you have dropped another aitch or two, monsieur!' Parkin corrected him gently. 'But hark – there goes the gong. Dinner is served.' And Cassandra took his arm and they led the way into the dining room.

8

Careless Talk

Within minutes of taking their places at the dining table, Hurel had chosen to reveal his true name and pre-Revolution title: Gérard, Baron Hurel de Pisseleu-aux-Bois, to their hosts.

No doubt, Anson thought, it was in an effort to impress Cassandra. In truth, this was a young woman *anyone* with blood in his veins would wish to impress.

He could not mask a slight smirk at the thought that when rendered in an English accent the Frenchman's surname sounded like a urinal in the woods.

But Anson quickly dismissed the unkind thought when Hurel, close to tears, spoke falteringly of the loss of his family, estate and title during the French Revolution – The Terror.

Sensing the sadness overwhelming his guest, Parkin tried comforting him. 'Very sad, monsieur, so very sad. Permit us to share your sorrow with a minute of silence in memory of your dear family ...'

All four bowed their heads and Anson thought he detected a quiet sob from the Frenchman but he did not look up until their host tapped a glass with a spoon.

'Now, gentlemen – and you, my dear, of course – this must be the first dinner Monsieur ...' He hesitated before continuing: 'Forgive me, the first occasion that you, Baron, have dined in what I hope you will find is civilised company for many a month. On such an auspicious occasion we are all forbidden to be gloomy and may I wish you joy of what I think I can accurately call your resurrection!'

Another tap on his glass summoned Dodson to fill their glasses and the maids, dressed in their best and blushing whenever the two young male guests so much as glanced at them, brought in the first course.

During dinner Parkin and Cassandra recalled for Hurel's benefit their memories of Anson's first visit to Ludden Hall, at the time of the Nore mutiny when he had been brought there to convalesce after being taken ill on the coach while on his way to stay at his father's rectory.

Quizzed by Hurel, Anson revealed that he had then been summoned back to Chatham and tasked with helping to break HMS *Euphemus* free from the mutinous fleet.

But he was reluctant to discuss the mission in detail, protesting: 'I played only a very minor part.'

Parkin protested: 'Nonsense, my dear Anson. In reality the small part you claim to have played actually led to the collapse of the whole mutiny, did it not? At least, that is what your father led me to believe.'

Anson spread his hands in protest. 'Let us talk of happier things than mutinies …'

But Hurel had clearly seen a way to steer the attention away from Anson and reveal more about himself to their hosts.

Clearly forgetting that his host had tried his best to confine conversation to happier things, he spoke vehemently: 'Your mutinies were no doubt inspired by the republicans who infest France. They are the same people who murdered my father, mother and elder brother.'

He explained that he had served in the navy of the ancien régime, but escaped when his family were taken – and when he learned of their fate changed his appearance and rejoined under an assumed – or at least abridged – name.

'The republicans were glad enough to recruit any experienced sea officer not to bother with making too many enquiries. As far as they were concerned I was willing to serve the new *régime* under the tricolour and that was sufficient.'

Anson asked: 'How did you come to be captured?'

'It is quite easy to be captured by you English, mon ami. All you need to do is to go to sea and they will find you—'

'And send you to the hulks?'

'Just so, but that was my wish. As soon as I could after I was made prisoner I whispered in the right ear who I really was and that as a royalist I was willing to undertake any mission that might 'elp undermine the republic.'

'But nevertheless you were sent to the hulks?'

'Certainly. It was part of what I believe you call a cover plan. I have been acting the part of a revolutionary fanatic since I rejoined the navy and while a prisoner in the hulks. But what motivates me is revenge – revenge for the assassination of my parents and brother – and the restoration of our family estate. Now I 'ave the chance to strike back!'

There was fire in his eyes as he spoke and any initial doubts Anson may have had about the Frenchman's motives evaporated.

*

On the third morning Emily appeared from the village having heard via that unseen miracle of local communication that her former patient had returned.

She greeted Anson effusively and he flushed at the memory of her administering to his every need at the time of the mutiny – including giving him a bed-bath – when he had been laid low with the fever.

To allay his embarrassment she had told him she'd had two husbands, brought up five boys, *and* laid out the dead in this parish, so he didn't have anything she hadn't seen a hundred times before.

He had been far from reassured at the time, but the recollection amused him now.

'How did you hear I was back, Emily?' he asked.

'Why, Mister Anson, the word's round the village that you'd come back with a foreign gent. Some say 'e's a Dutchman and some says 'e's a Frog – sorry, I mean a Frenchie. Anyhow, they say as he spoke some foreign lingo – not one as we've heard of round here.'

'Good grief! But how did the word get round?' He turned to Parkin. 'No-one from Ludden Hall has been down to the village since we arrived, have they?'

His host shook his head. 'No, but in the country news has a habit of spreading, perhaps a chance sighting on the road, who knows?' And he added, mysteriously: 'It's rather like jungle drums without the drumming.'

A thought occurred to Anson. 'Hurel, have you spoken to anyone since we arrived here, apart from our hosts and the servants, that is?'

'No, mon ami, no-one except for the man with the gun …'

'Good grief! What man with a gun?'

'The man who arrived when you went into the house with Monsieur Parkin and left me sitting beside the little lake. The man with dead animals 'anging from 'is belt …'

A gamekeeper! No doubt bringing more creatures for the old gentleman to dissect.

'Did you speak to this man?'

'Merely to wish him bonjour …'

Anson winced. So that was it. News of a foreigner, possibly a Frenchman, staying at Ludden Hall would spread like ripples on a pond when a pebble was thrown in.

They were compromised and would have to move on. But when he explained the situation to Parkin, the old gentleman persuaded him to stay for one more night and make an early morning start.

And at the prospect of another evening with his host – and especially with his niece – Anson was happy to concur.

Meanwhile, as Cassandra showed Hurel around the Ludden Hall gardens, in which he had expressed great but suspect interest, Anson joined Parkin in the summerhouse to take morning coffee and peruse the newspapers – just as they often had three years before.

*

Next day the old gentleman and his niece bade farewell to their guests with some reluctance and Anson assured them he would be back for a longer stay at the earliest opportunity. They had enjoyed another pleasant evening together although Anson had found he was becoming increasingly irritated with the close attention the Frenchman was paying Cassandra.

After downing a considerable amount of wine le Baron, as he had started styling himself, burbled on about his family's estates, lost to the revolutionary tyrants. He invited Parkin and his niece to visit him there 'as soon as the war is over' as if winning back his land was a simple matter, which Anson doubted.

And as they took their leave Hurel drooled over Cassandra's hand for far too long for Anson's taste, mouthing 'Au revoir' over and over again with some fervour before he could be shepherded into Parkin's carriage.

The coachman-cum-butler Dodson had already attached Ebony's head collar to the coach so that the gelding could trot behind and off they set with Hurel monopolising the window calling: 'Au revoir, à bientôt!' as they crunched down the gravel drive.

Anson was feeling more than a little annoyed with his companion. If Hurel had not foolishly addressed the gamekeeper in French they could have stayed with Parkin and his niece for as long as it took.

But move on they must and Seagate was out of the question. He would never be able to keep Hurel out of the public eye there – certainly not at the Sea Fencible detachment or his room at the Rose Inn.

Now the only place he could think of going where they could hope to keep a low profile was his father's rectory.

There was no time to warn his family, but so be it. The important thing now was to prevent Hurel from compromising them again once they got there.

And so he resolved to spend the journey coaching the Frenchman on the importance of security. Judging from the man's performance at Ludden Hall things did not augur well.

9

A Cunning Plan

Back on board the hulk Anson had visited in the Medway, the prisoner known to one and all – including the guard force – as Citizen Bardet, thought over the visit from the English naval lieutenant who had brought him a dead man's possessions.

There had been something unusual about it, something he could not quite put his finger on. Why hadn't the few pathetic items simply been left with the guard commander? Why had the Rosbifs bothered to return them at all?

Perhaps the English lieutenant had deliberately sought him out to size him up, but why? Bardet was certain the authorities could not possibly know of the escape he planned to make imminently.

His daring and, he hoped, foolproof plan, was known to only those he was taking with him and a few others sworn to secrecy on pain of death. In any event, the support team had a vested interest in keeping the escape plan under close wraps, because if he succeeded – when he succeeded – they could use the same means to spirit themselves away from this hell on water.

He had been surprised at the respect shown him by the visiting lieutenant and could have grown to like him if he had not been English. But had his apparent humanity hidden some ulterior motive?

Bardet shrugged. 'Ça ne fait rien.' By the time the English got their act together he and his companions would be long gone. And he smirked at his own audacity in telling the lieutenant to his face that he intended to escape whenever he chose.

The two he was taking with him were men he had served with since hostilities began: the Parisian Girault, a butcher in civilian life; and the Corsican known as Cornacchia, the crow, who looked as if he might cut your throat as soon as look at you – and probably would.

When elected as their leader by his fellow prisoners, Bardet had appointed these two as his bodyguards and he trusted them completely.

Their loyalty, if ever in doubt, was ensured by the perks of their office – the extra food and privileges that came their leader's way.

One loudmouth who had the temerity to question Bardet's authority had disappeared one stormy night. Some believed he had escaped. Others thought he had been murdered and thrown overboard, but that would have been next to impossible owing to the sentinels' walkway around the hull. And so the rumour grew that he had been chopped up by Bardet's butcher henchman and fed to the starving wretches on the lower deck.

The truth was that the missing man had been an informer and when the authorities feared that his cover had been blown they had spirited him away for his own safety and replanted him in a land prison many miles away to continue his treachery.

Not knowing this, Bardet was content to allow the rumour that the man had ended up as dinner for the lower deck to continue to circulate because it strengthened his authority. The meat that *had* been fed to them that night had in reality come from a visitor's dog which had been lured below deck by artful miscreants offering it scraps.

There had been a minor hoo-ha when it disappeared, but the search for it was called off when a saintly-looking elderly prisoner assured its owner he had witnessed it jumping over the side trying to catch a seagull and it had last been seen swimming ashore. The owner had been misguided enough to press a few coins on the prisoner for his honesty ...

Bardet's bodyguards had been captured with him when their ship had been out-run, boarded and taken a year earlier when trying to evade the Channel blockade. That meant that that he had spent twelve long months in this floating pigsty and he did not intend to waste another day here.

For the umpteenth time he thought over his escape plan. His preparation had been detailed, thorough, and conducted in great secrecy.

He had employed two former ship's carpenters to saw a round hole – just big enough for a man – in a secluded compartment just above the low tide water-line.

Despite the relative ease of obtaining – or making – the necessary tools, the work had taken many weeks. Small saws used in model-making were regarded by the authorities as legitimate craft tools, no-one dreaming that they could be used to cut a hole in the side of a warship, however old and decrepit.

But Bardet knew about the long-term effect of dripping on a stone and had been prepared for slow progress. If his team had been able to do the work during the day it would have only taken a relatively short time. But Bardet insisted that they work only at night, on low tides – and in silence.

Whenever the carpenters set to work one of his henchmen was always on hand to keep others at bay. Other trusted lookouts were posted and ready to cause a diversion if ever guards showed signs of coming near. The lookouts were wise enough not to poke their noses too far into what was going on, accepting – as the carpenters had – that they would have their own chance to escape when the hoo-ha had died down after Bardet had got away.

Although the timbers were massive they were spongy and gradually a circular furrow appeared, to be disguised with a mixture of tar and glue at the end of each shift. A plank bearing hooks was secured to the ship's timbers each side of the escape hole with iron nails. This was done at a time when many of the model-makers on the main gun deck were told to make as much noise as they could for ten minutes to disguise what was going on below. But the nails were not fully knocked in. That would be done later. For the moment it was sufficient that they could hold the bar in place.

The sawyers had made their cut sloping inwards, and the reason for this finally became clear when water began to seep in. Work stopped but was resumed during the ebb and in the meantime the bar was sufficient to keep the circular escape hole in place. The furrow was again filled with the mixture of tar and glue and filthy old rags were then draped from nails above to disguise it. Anything better would not have lasted long in a hulk where clothing was gambled away or exchanged for food as a matter of course.

The final cut had been made the night before and, if Bardet ever prayed, it would be to ask that the filling of glue and tar inserted into the cuts would stop water seepage during the coming high tides. Not being a believer, he did not pray. But the water did not come in.

The roundel was just big enough for the bulkiest man – the Corsican – to slip through. They had measured it carefully.

Bardet called his escape team together and ran over the plan for the last time. 'Tonight, after we have eaten, Girault and Cornacchia will get our escape kit ready and go down to the hole with the carpenters. The ship's committee have agreed to stage a diversion which will involve a boxing match. The English love their sports so they will be watching that, too.'

His companions exchanged a grin at the prospect of fooling their guards.

'I will make myself seen around the ring. In fact I will announce the match. Then I, too, will slip away and make my way below. At the height of the fight, which will be staged carefully, others will enter the ring and start a general brawl with plenty of noise. That will be our moment.'

There was nodded agreement.

'Meanwhile the carpenters will take out the panel and we will climb through and emerge under the walkway. It will be low tide and we will cling to the walkway while those inside seal the escape hole up again. Simple, is it not? Then, using our inflated pigs' bladders for flotation we three will paddle for the shore just below Gillingham. What happens after that is secret. Suffice it to say that there is a plan ...'

While the other prisoners and a number of their guards gathered on the main gun deck ready for the match, Bardet's escape team slipped quietly away and, singly, so as not to attract attention, made their way down the companionway to the lower deck.

He remained until last and entered the chalked area that was to be the boxing ring. There was mounting excitement as he held up his hands for attention and announced the match, loud cheers greeting the two boxers as they stepped forward. A burly petty officer acting as referee held up a neckerchief, dropped it, and the adversaries waded into one another throwing punches.

*

Bardet pushed his way through the excited prisoners and followed his escape team below.

They had brought with them some left-overs from the evening meal and threw them to the naked wretches who infested this noxious place.

While the down-and-outs fought over the scraps the carpenters quickly removed the tarry paste from the rim of the escape hole and lifted the wooden roundel free. A little water spilled in at the bottom but Bardet had judged the tide right.

He stripped swiftly, was greased with lard by one of the carpenters, climbed on the man's back and disappeared through the hole. His prison clothes would be put to good use by the support men – and he had more suitable attire in his canvas bag.

Girault threw off his yellow jacket and trousers, was similarly greased around the shoulders, chest and back and slipped through the hole, followed moments later by Cornacchia.

After him went a narrow canoe-like craft, not big enough for the escapers, but fashioned by the carpenters to carry and keep dry the clothes they would put on once ashore.

Last of all the canvas kit bags containing their escape gear was pushed through the hole after them and within minutes the back-up team had secured the roundel in place and resealed the rim.

Satisfied that the escape hole was well enough disguised, the carpenters and lookouts made their way back up to the main gun deck and joined the excited spectators as the boxers punched, butted and shoved one another around the ring.

Once outside the hulk, hidden under the sentinels' walkway, Bardet took stock.

He waited for a while listening for the thud of boots above, but could hear nothing but the lapping of the water and the loud din emanating from the barred but open ports on the main gun deck above.

Satisfied that there was no sentinel close by, he gripped the staging overhead and made his way to the edge of the walkway where he again checked for footsteps above.

Still there were none, and he imagined, correctly, that most of the guard force had found reasons to be at the boxing match.

Hanging on to the edge of the walkway, he called softly to the others and they joined him, Cornacchia, the strongest swimmer, pulling the canoe-like raft now carrying their escape kit behind him.

Once again Bardet checked for activity above, but still there was none – and then, on cue, the noise level emanating from the gun ports increased to a crescendo.

By the watery moonlight his companions could see the flash of his teeth framed by his bearded mouth and they grinned too. The diversion had started as planned, bang on time.

*

The match was already in full swing when the escape back-up team, carpenters and lookouts arrived, unnoticed, back on the main gun deck.

The burly Breton appeared to have the upper hand over the Marseilles bruiser, who had already been down twice, but the two boxers, amply bribed by Bardet, were merely putting on a show. Blows were connecting sure enough, but there was little if any power in them.

To unknowing spectators, especially members of the ship's crew and guard force, it looked as if the Breton was handing out a real battering and bets were being laid at increasingly changing odds.

Pushing his way through the crush of spectators to the front, Chambon the carpenter waited for the right moment and then deliberately and openly shoved the Breton from behind so that he stumbled forward awkwardly, took a blow to the head from his apparently surprised opponent and fell to his knees.

This was the signal for those in the know about the plan to create a diversion to make sure that all hell broke loose. But it was hardly necessary to simulate disorder. Those, unaware of the trick, who had placed bets on the Breton, were outraged that their man had apparently been sabotaged and within seconds the circle had been broken and the boxers sank beneath a wave of bodies as rival supporters waded in, fists flying.

The sergeant of the guard, who had already placed a sizeable bet of his own on the Breton, shouted for order, but in vain. The noise was too great.

Frustrated, he grabbed a militiaman by the shoulder and shouted in his ear: 'Find your orficer and gather your mates – we've got to stop this afore these crazy Frogs kill each other orf!'

*

Girault pulled the already-inflated pigskin flotation devices from the kitbags and handed them to the others. Bardet took his and tied it round his hairy chest. But the Corsican refused his with a shake of his head as if it were an insult to offer such a thing to someone like him who had learned to swim in the choppy waters off Ajaccio almost before he could walk.

Shrugging, Girault tied the Corsican's float to his own and looped them under his arms. There had not been much opportunity for swimming in the back streets of Paris and he was grateful for any help he could get for what to him was going to be some ordeal.

As the noise above increased, the escapers heard running feet on the walkway above their heads and then the *clip-clop* of boots ascending the stairway leading to the top deck. The remaining sentinels had deserted their posts to help quell the disorder.

Checking that his companions were ready, Bardet listened again for any sign of the guards, but there was none and the noise from above was still raging.

Then, supported by the pigskins, he kicked away from the walkway towards a few pinpricks of light on the south bank of the river – the lights of the village of Gillingham.

The water was cold but as Bardet and his companions swam away from the hulk he could already see what he hoped was a pinpoint of light from a lantern being swung to and fro by someone on the river bank only fifty yards away. That was what he had paid for – a lantern that focused the light via a long spout with a bull's-eye glass at the end to avoid throwing out a wide arc. It was a device well used by smugglers both sides of what to all Frenchman was La Manche – that stretch of water the Rosbifs arrogantly insisted on calling the *English* Channel.

The needle of light told Bardet that his contact ashore had heard the boxing match kerfuffle and was guiding them in.

Bardet hoped the man would extinguish the lantern the moment he spotted them. Otherwise there was a real danger that, despite the diversion, a member of the guard force aboard the hulk might remain alert enough to see the light. And if the alarm was raised, support would come from the other prison ships strung out in line of sight, for'ard and astern.

It would be unforgivable if their escape was thwarted after so much time and effort had been put into it.

Now, as the three neared the bank, the light suddenly went out. Their contact had spotted them at last.

Cornacchia was first to touch bottom. He stood unsteadily and cautiously made his way ashore through the thick Medway mud, dragging the raft with their clothing behind him.

10

A Copybook Exercise

Nestled in the back of a hay cart with his two fellow escapers, Citizen Bardet enjoyed going over in his mind how well his plan had come together.

Everything had gone exactly as planned: putting together their escape kit, the cutting of the roundel in the side of the hulk, the diversion at the boxing match, getting safely ashore – and the rendezvous with their Kentish contact.

A bribed militiaman with the guard force had acted as his go-between with smugglers who hung out in the pubs ashore and put him in touch with the escape network based down the coast around Whitstable. It was run by men who cared not for King and country, but nor did they help Frenchmen escape because of any revolutionary fervour. They were in it solely for the money.

It had been a copybook exercise and he grinned to himself as he speculated that even now their disappearance had probably not been noticed. Taking his place at the centre of the coming morning's session of the ship's committee would be an equally hirsute prisoner dressed in his discarded clothes – and suitably rewarded for agreeing to fool *les* Rosbifs.

The escapers had waded ashore chilled and smeared with filthy mud, looking like some fantastic creatures emerging from the primeval swamp.

Even from the riverbank they could hear a loud din from the hulk and Bardet had supposed that the diversion had by then turned into a genuine riot. Whatever, it kept the guard force – and the attention of their counterparts on the nearby hulks – busy long enough for him to complete his getaway.

Although at first they could not see him, their waiting contact had called softly to them and they followed his voice to where a large shape loomed out of the darkness.

Approached stealthily, they saw that it was a hay cart, drawn by a heavy horse. Again, just as planned.

'Everyfink orlright, monsewers? You're in safe hands now. It's all bin arranged for you.'

Bardet faced their contact, a scar-faced unshaven man wearing a pointy hat and a heavy smock. 'All went trés bien, but for this disgusting mud ...'

He had not reckoned on getting so filthy and they would need to clean the worst off before putting on their escape clothes.

Girault and the Corsican were trying to scrape the mud off themselves with their hands, but the contact held up his hand.

'Not a problem, gents. Get it orf with hay.' And he handed Bardet a handful.

The Frenchman began wiping the mud off and his companions followed suit.

Finally satisfied that they could get no more off without soap and water, they donned their escape clothes – countrymen's apparel, a mixture of tattered old jackets, trousers, leggings, battered round hats and holey shoes.

The only items Bardet had retained from his old life on the hulk were his sea boots that he had worn since he first became an officer. They were past their best now, but, as he was fond of saying, they were as comfortable to slip on as a plump and willing woman.

He gave his companions the once-over and concluded that at least in semi-darkness they could pass for poor Kentish labourers – as long as they didn't open their mouths.

Their contact indicated that it was time to get under way and they climbed up on the wagon and buried themselves among the hay.

'All set? Then we'll be orf, gents. We'll be holin' up in a barn by the marshes when it starts gettin' light and the 'oss needs a rest. You won't be disturbed there and the next man down the line will come there and fix you up with summat to eat. He's in on it all so nuffink to worry about. Then it'll be on to a boat.'

As he prodded the horse forward he turned: 'If by chance I get stopped along the way I'll say I picked you up out of the goodness of me 'eart while you wus walking and found you wus loyal Guernsey men on yer way to Whitstable to catch your ship.'

Bardet nodded. 'That's correct, we're Guernsey men, *bien sûr*. And these two don't speak the English.'

'Good, now if I wus you I'd 'ave a nap while y'may.'

Exhausted by their night's labours, the escapers were happy to oblige.

Bardet dozed off with a smile on his face. They had made good their escape and, as planned, were now well and truly in the system.

11

An Unwelcome Caller

Sam Fagg, bosun of the Seagate Sea Fencible detachment, was sitting back with his feet on the table, long clay pipe in hand, contemplating whether or not to go for a wet at the nearby Mermaid.

He was startled out of his reverie when the door banged open and a plump, pink-faced naval officer with extravagant side whiskers known in the service as "buggers's grips" entered unannounced – Captain Arthur Veryan St Cleer Hoare.

Fagg groaned inwardly. The divisional captain was one of his least favourite people.

*

Hoare's behaviour after the taking of the Normandy privateer had disgusted those who had taken part in the real action. They had seen him for what he was: a lazy, pompous glory-stealer who cared nothing for those serving under him and was solely interested in advancing himself and climbing the social ladder.

The man's early naval career had been pretty much of a doddle, as befitted an *almost* aristocrat with a silver tongue and a ready pen devoted to ensuring his personal success.

This idle streak in his makeup had soon been detected by the captain of the frigate HMS *Seraphim*, when Hoare was appointed as his first lieutenant.

The captain had disliked his pretentious attitude and tendency to neglect his duties to the point that he had decided to get rid of him at the earliest opportunity.

But then by chance *Seraphim* had encountered a French fifth rate and in the resulting skirmish in the Bay of Biscay a cannon ball had neatly removed the captain's head.

With command thrust so suddenly upon him, the terrified Hoare had wisely broken off the engagement and fled, his gunners managing to get off a couple of balls from the stern-chasers as he manoeuvred out of danger.

His report on the incident was a masterful example of his literary talent. He was able to claim, truthfully, that despite their patent inequality, he had damaged the Frenchman and avenged his unfortunate headless captain. And the way in which he used false modesty and apparent understatement to describe the event made him appear to be the reluctant hero of the hour.

Promotion to post captain was immediate but, unfortunately for Hoare, *Seraphim* went almost straight off into refit and the only appointment available was what he himself described as 'divisional captain for a clutch of south coast Sea Fencible detachments and signal stations, commanding half a dozen lieutenants, assorted human flotsam and jetsam of the Channel ports, and temporary owner of the scruffy huts that serve as their bases.'

However, he had consoled himself that at least he would not be called upon to risk life and limb – unless the French invaded, of course. But in the meantime he could leave all the work to his lieutenants and devote his own more valuable time to embellishing his social life and keeping him, and his minor fame as the *almost* aristocratic, self-proclaimed hammer of the French, in the eyes and ears of the county's movers and shakers.

Civic dinners and his busy round of social events were beginning to take their toll on the gallant captain's waistline and this very morning he had reminded himself to complain to his tailor about his shrinking uniform. Clearly the wretched needle-pusher had used inferior cloth or had scrimped on the amount he had used of it.

*

Despite his game leg – a legacy of the raid on St Valery-en-Caux when he, Lieutenant Anson and the marine Tom Hoover had been wounded and captured – Fagg moved with the alacrity of the foretop-man he once was and leapt to his feet as Captain Hoare entered.

'Bosun, I am here to see Lieutenant Anson.'

Fagg knuckled his forehead. 'Ain't 'ere, sir.'

'Wherever he's idling, kindly fetch him.'

'Orders, sir. Away on orficial business.'

'Orders, whose orders? He takes his orders from *me*, and I have given him no orders! And *where* is he away?'

'Chatham, I fink, sir. Sent for—'

'Sent for? *I* am the only one who can send for him. Who sent for him and when did he leave?'

Fagg pondered. 'Some commodore I fink, sir, Poporf or some such name. And he left at the end of last week or thereabouts.'

'So you are left in charge?'

'I am, sir.'

'Are you pursuing training? One privateer does not a summer make, you know. There are Frenchmen aplenty and we must not rest on our laurels.'

'Laurels, sir? Never 'eard of 'em. Some kind of flowers, are they?'

Hoare ignored the near insolence. 'And where, pray, is the master-at-arms?'

'Tom 'oover? He's gorn off with Mister Shrubb, sir, checking up on the wounded.'

Hoover and Shrubb had indeed gone off in Tom Marsh's pony and trap to visit the injured men now recovering at home, and to save them coming in the sergeant had taken each of them one of the King's shillings that Fagg made free with, reckoning that their wounds entitled them to a day's pay.

Hoare sniffed. 'I wouldn't have thought that would take long, given that only a few were hurt.' This was not what the divisional captain had indicated in his official report on the "battle" in which he'd made the casualty list sound like the butcher's bill after a fleet action.

Fagg assured him: 'Mister Shrubb's very particular about them as was wounded, sir. Doesn't want 'em to turn sceptical, nor nuffink.'

Even the humourless Hoare could not hide a smile. 'So he's making sure their wounds don't turn septic, eh?'

'That's right, sir, he's what Mister Anson calls "a bit of a God-botherer." But that don't put a man like Mister Shrubb orf treatin' us lot what ain't exackly keen on church and chapel-going. He's a proper Christian, he is.'

'Tell me, the master-at-arms, Sergeant what's-'is-name, he's an American, ain't he – a rebel?'

'Tom 'oover? Don't fink he'd like being called a rebel, sir. His lot was on the other side to the rebels – our side.'

'I'll call him what I damn well please. You can't trust Americans. Mark my words: all those colonists are tarred with the same brush, babbling on about the rights of man and such. I'd have 'em all flogged!'

Tired of being on the receiving end of Hoare's verbal broadsides, Fagg went on to the attack. 'About that prize money what you said as you'd get for the boys for taking that Froggie privateer, sir?'

'Yes, well, I have it on good authority that prize money *will* be forthcoming to encourage the rest of the Sea Fencibles around the country to do the same should the opportunity arise …'

'Can you tell me 'ow much we'll get? The boys are askin', see.'

'You'll find out soon enough, though the wheels of Admiralty Courts grind exceeding slow.'

'So, 'ow much will *you* get, sir?'

Hoare flushed. 'You are on the verge of being insolent, bosun. It is sufficient for you to know that *I* will get my just desserts for taking the French captain prisoner and accepting the surrender of his ship. *You* will get your just desserts. The men will get theirs.'

Fagg pursed his lips, musing, and confessed: 'Whenever I've 'ad money, the pusser's snatched it back on account of some kit I'm supposed to 'ave 'ad, or I've pissed it away in pubs, treatin' tarts and whatnot.' He smiled at the recollection of the tarts. At least *that* had been money well spent.

'But I've what they call matured since them days. This time it's gonna be different. If I get enough I'm 'angin' on to it and maybe I'll set meself up in a pub. Free drink, see? Or I might buy meself a chicken farm. Always liked chickens, I 'ave—'

Hoare snorted: 'I haven't got time to stand here listening to your ramblings, man! But, come to think of it, you've got me thinking. Sea Fencibles are the dregs. If these harbour rats of yours are suddenly given a wodge of prize money it'll go straight to their heads—'

'Well, a few will piss it away, I s'pose—'

'A few? The men will run amuck! Harbour rats to a man. Not to be trusted with money. I'll make Anson personally responsible for their behaviour once the prize money comes through. Make sure you tell him that!'

'Aye aye, sir!'

'And while you're at it, tell him that the capture of the privateer has given a golden opportunity to get the detachment up to full strength.'

'Already in 'and, sir!' Fagg assured him.

*

Captain Hoare had been right – news of the capture of the Normandy privateer and with it the promise of prize money had by now spread far and wide and created a fertile recruiting climate.

There had been little problem finding recruits since the ousting of the detachment's brutish and corrupt bosun, Billy MacIntyre – known as Black Mac to those he had tormented and blackmailed.

But now, as his replacement, Sam Fagg was swamped by would-be recruits.

'I'm 'avin' to beat 'em orf wiv sticks,' he complained later to the master-at-arms.

Tom Hoover was sympathetic. 'Can't you weed some of them out on medical grounds?'

'Good idea, but I'd need old man Shrubb to do the weedin', so's it's all fair and above board, like.'

Hoover saw a chance of progressing his acquaintance with Sarah Shrubb and asked innocently: 'How about I go fetch him?'

Shrubb was duly fetched and, leaving him with the bosun, Hoover volunteered to accompany Sarah into town for sewing articles she required, using the pretext that the place was full of militiamen, who, being from Essex, were inclined to pester unaccompanied females.

Fagg explained his dilemma to the apothecary-cum-surgeon's mate. 'This is 'ow it is, Phin. I got a dozen blokes 'ere what wants to join the fencibles, but I can only take a couple, well, four at most. So p'raps you can weed 'em out, so it's sort of legal, like, an' so's they can't keep on pesterin' me. Orlright?'

*

His examination duly completed, Shrubb reported back to the bosun. 'Well, Samuel, of the twelve potential recruits I've looked over, nine are sound of wind and limb and suitable for enrolling as fencibles.'

'But, like I told you, we can only take four at most.'

'Yes, yes, brother, but the five spares can be sent off to the Folkestone detachment. Several of them live nearer there than here anyway.'

'Oh, orlright, I 'adn't thought of that. But which of 'em should I get rid of altogether, then?'

'Well, you obviously can't take Pearse.'

'For why? A good old seaman, 'e is. Served for years and only come out on account of wounds.'

'But that's the point. You noticed his awkward way of walking?'

Fagg nodded. 'That I did, but there's a good few of us old sailors what limps, meself included. Mine comes on account of that there cuttin'-out raid, along of Tom 'oover and Mister Anson. Them Frog doctors wus rubbish at settin' me ankle. So what's wrong wiv a limp if you're a right seaman like George Pearse?'

'A limp's one thing, but a wooden leg's another.'

Fagg registered astonishment. 'Are you tellin' me George's only got one leg?'

'I'm afraid so. Didn't you notice when he volunteered?'

Fagg thought for a moment. 'I met 'im in the Mermaid and 'e put 'imself across as a right good seaman, but, come to think on it, 'e did keep 'is feet under the table ...'

'Well, in his case, his foot.'

Fagg pulled a face. 'The cheeky beggar, puttin' one over on me like that! Any'ow, what was wrong wiv the other two?'

'Wright, despite the facial hair, has other physical attributes that indicate he – *she* – is a female.'

'A female? You mean a woman? Now 'ow did he, er, *she*, pull the wool over me eyes, eh? I reckoned I could tell the difference – even on a dark night down a back alley ...'

Shrubb pushed aside the dark alley image. 'I have come across this sort of thing in the navy during the American war. Some disguised themselves so as not to be parted from their sweethearts – others for patriotic reasons. I have some sympathy with her. Why shouldn't women be allowed to serve King and country? Perhaps one day, but for the present I fear it rules her out.'

'But 'ow about Gladwish? You ain't goin' to tell me 'e's only got one leg or tits!'

'Oh, no. His case is quite dissimilar. He's perfectly physically fit, has retained all his body parts and is definitely male, but—'

'So what *is* wrong wiv 'im?'

'I am very much afraid he believes he is King George the Third in person and that the man sitting on the throne is an impostor. He cannot be persuaded otherwise and if you take him on I fear he will disrupt the detachment and refuse to take orders from anyone but himself – as King, you see?'

Fagg grimaced but, remembering that Shrubb was a man of God, muttered under his breath so as not to be heard: 'Jesus Christ!'

But Shrubb had heard and countered: 'No, King George ...'

12

An Unwelcome Guest

Hurel was jerked awake as Tom Marsh turned the pony and trap off the road into the rectory's tree-lined drive.

'Nous sommes ici?'

'Yes, but English now, please.'

'D'accord!' Hurel tapped his nose to signify complicity before pulling an anguished face as he realised his faux pas. 'Excusez moi … I mean yes!'

Anson smiled indulgently. It was going to be nigh impossible to stop the Frenchman giving himself away at every twist and turn.

Ahead, young Jemmy Beer, the butler's son, appeared, waiting to take the pony in hand.

'Good day to you, Jemmy. This is Tom Marsh, one of my Sea Fencibles, and this is his trap. Be good enough to take care of him and his pony – and Ebony of course.'

The diminutive groom put his hand to his forehead. 'Right-ho, Master Anson.'

Anson grabbed his kit, jumped down, and beckoned Hurel to join him.

The Frenchman stretched himself and took stock of the immaculate rectory grounds dotted with rose beds and shrubs, announcing sotto voce, 'Very beautiful – and very English.'

Anson gestured to the iron-studded door and together they mounted the wide steps just as it swung open to reveal the butler.

'Good day t'you sir, sirs,' George Beer welcomed them. 'If you'll be staying I'll take your bags to your room, Master Anson, and how about this gennelman?'

'We will indeed be staying Mister Beer, and will need a room for my guest.'

Hurel grinned inanely, but said nothing. Anson's insistence that he must not tell his life story to the world and his wife had shut him up – for the present at least.

'Are my parents at home?'

'They are, Master Oliver, and your brother is here, too.'

'Gussie?'

'Mister Augustine, sir?' Beer smirked at Anson's use of the nickname his unpopular brother hated so. 'Yes, come to talk about 'is weddin' I believe, to that harchdeacon's daughter.'

Anson grimaced. He regarded Gussie, recently appointed minor canon at Canterbury Cathedral, as a pompous, self-seeking prig. But in front of a servant – and a guest – he held his tongue.

Hurel was shown to a guest room and Anson sought out his parents, taking tea in the library.

'I apologise for springing my friend upon you father, mother, but there are reasons.'

'Reasons?'

'He is on, what shall I say, a sensitive mission and must not allow himself to become the subject of gossip.'

His mother protested: 'Gossip? I never gossip!'

'But in a house like this, mother, what with my sisters and the servants, why, just as in a warship I doubt anything remains private for long.'

While his wife was spluttering her way to an appropriate response the rector asked: 'Who is this mysterious friend?'

'He is an officer, a foreign officer, but prepared to help us fight the French republicans, and most certainly a gentleman of good family, but I cannot elucidate further …'

Augustine Anson entered, clearly having heard the last exchange. 'Foreign? Heaven forfend. He's not a papist, is he? Don't tell me he's a papist!'

Anson considered for a moment. 'Now you come to mention it he may well be, but it's not a topic uppermost in my mind when I meet someone, especially an ally. I prefer not to give them ridiculous religious labels, but rate them on their personal merits or otherwise.'

'So he is a papist! Well, clearly he cannot be allowed to stay under this roof. Why, how would I explain to the archdeacon that my own parents were harbouring a papist?'

Anson laughed. 'Didn't some biblical cove say something about "judge not, that ye be not judged?" What if God is a Roman Catholic, or even a Baptist?'

His brother was apoplectic. 'Blasphemy! How dare you say such things in our father's rectory of all places – a bastion of the Anglican Church!'

'Anyway, wasn't that cathedral of yours originally Roman Catholic until Henry the Eighth wanted a divorce? And aren't you named after a papist?'

Gussie was indeed named after the saint who brought Christianity to England from Rome. But, intensely proud as he was of his appointment as a minor canon, this was too much for him and he left the room in a huff, grumbling: 'I will not stay here to be insulted by this ... this ...' he groped for a non-Anglo Saxon word to describe what he thought of his younger brother but could not find one that would not offend his mother's sensitivities.

At the door he turned to hiss at his parents: 'I sincerely trust that you will have the good sense not to give shelter to someone who is most likely an enemy alien – and a left-footer at that!'

*

Alone again with his parents, Anson apologised. 'I did not wish to cause trouble, but Gussie is so bigoted. He has a habit of getting under my skin.'

His father shook his head. 'It takes two, I fear, and it seems at times that you deliberately set out to provoke him. The quotation about judging comes from Mark, by the way. You would do well to remember that it continues: "And why beholdest thou the mote that is in thy brother's eye, but consider not the beam that is in thine own eye."'

Shrugging, Anson offered: 'If it is going to embarrass you, my friend and I will go elsewhere. He *is* a Frenchman, but a royalist who, as I said, is going to aid us in the war against the republicans. I just thought a country rectory would be the perfect place to harbour up for a while.'

To his surprise it was his mother who came to his support. 'If this friend of yours is an ally and a gentleman, well, as it appears that Augustine will not now be staying to dinner, I have no objection to your staying for a few days at least.'

The rector waved his hands in mock surrender. 'Gussie, I mean Augustine, will not thank me for it, but I agree. I must say that I am most intrigued by our mystery guest and hope for stimulating conversation while he is at our table ...'

'Thank you both. However it will be necessary to swear all the family – and the servants – to strict silence about Hurel outside the rectory. He may dine with the family and walk in the gardens, but talk of his stay here must be kept under wraps. It is a matter of life and death – and of the greatest importance to the national interest. And that is no idle claim.'

His father nodded: 'Very well, I will talk to your sisters and the servants. And I look forward to meeting our mysterious guest at dinner.'

*

Anson was confronted by his sisters. 'We hear you have brought a guest. Is he a brother officer? When can we meet him?'

'Well yes, he is an officer.'

'So, is he a soldier?'

'I'm afraid he does not wear a red jacket, and at the present, being on, er, leave, he wears plain clothes.'

'Is he, then, a fellow sea officer?'

'He is not in our navy, but I can tell you no more.'

'Not an army officer and not in our navy, then what?'

'Please don't ask. You will meet him at dinner when we will reveal as much as we can – as long as you keep everything you learn strictly to yourselves.'

'How thrilling! Will he speak to us?'

Anson recalled what the sergeant of the guard had said of the French prisoners in the hulks and repeated: 'The trick is to stop the, er, French talking ...' He reasoned his sisters would find out Hurel's nationality as soon as they met him, so they might as well know now.

'So he's French? Brother, how very exciting!'

*

When Anson took Hurel down to meet the family, Augustine was hovering in the hallway, leather bag in hand preparing to leave.

Despite the earlier clash, Anson attempted to introduce him, but his brother interrupted rudely: 'Our apologies monsieur, but I'm afraid we are fresh out of frogs' legs for your dinner. However, I daresay cook could rustle up some snails from the garden.'

Hurel frowned, puzzled over the remark for a moment and then laughed. 'Ah, I see it now! You are making an English joke about French food. Very amusing, *Father*, but for myself I do not like the frogs legs or the snails. But at this moment I am so 'ungry that I could surely devour a 'orse!

Gussie recoiled at being addressed as if he were a Catholic priest and retorted: '*Canon* Anson is my preferred title, monsieur, and we will notify you when one of our horses dies, but until then we shall continue to ride them rather than eat them.'

Anson held up his hands. 'Come now Gussie. That's no way to welcome a guest—'

But his brother spun on him angrily. 'I don't know what you were thinking, bringing an enemy alien into our midst. Have you no sense of social proprieties at all? This is the last you'll see of me while *he* is here!'

Without waiting for an answer he flounced out, turning at the door to hiss: 'And you can stop calling me by that childish nickname!'

Anson laughed and shouted after him, 'Of course, Gussie, whatever you say, Gussie!'

Alone again with Hurel, he asked the Frenchman: 'I hope my brother's ill manners have not offended you?'

'Not at all, mon ami. I take it this is what in England is known as brotherly love?'

'Touché! And now I believe supper awaits us. Will beefsteaks suit you?'

Hurel smiled. 'After the 'ulks, beefsteaks will suit me very well!'

As if on cue the dinner gong sounded and Anson and Hurel made their way through to the dining room where his parents and sisters were waiting with glasses of sherry in their hands and only partially restrained expectancy.

'Mother, father, sisters, may I introduce my good friend and ally Lieutenant Hurel, or perhaps I should say, Gérard, Baron Hurel de Pisseleu-aux-Bois.'

His parents and sisters were open-mouthed and Hurel bowed low. 'Enchanté, and my 'eartfelt thanks for your 'ospitality in allowing me to stay in your lovely 'ome.'

The rector returned his bow. 'We are delighted to welcome you, Baron ... delighted! May I present my wife and our daughters Anne and Elizabeth?'

Hurel bobbed his head and kissed the hands of each in turn. 'Doubly enchanted, Madame Anson, Mademoiselle Anne, Mademoiselle Elizabeth ...'

Both girls were still open-mouthed and staring. Clearly the thought of being in the company of a real live titled gentleman had impressed them beyond measure. At this moment the fact that he was from an enemy nation mattered to them not one jot.

Anson warned him. 'Beware, mon ami, both my sisters are actively seeking husbands.'

They pretended shock and Anne rebuked him: 'Really, Oliver, your attempts at humour are pathetic. It comes no doubt from mixing with common sailors.'

During the meal Hurel dominated the conversation, regaling his hosts with stories of his upbringing in the family chateau – before the revolution – and flirted openly with the awe-struck Anson sisters.

They were so engrossed that only Anson noticed the crunch of hooves and iron-shod wheels on gravel as his brother Gussie made his departure.

Anson left it to his parents to quiz the Frenchman on everything from The Terror to his prospects of regaining his lost estate when the war was won.

His sisters were desperate to ask about the latest Paris fashions, surely a futile exercise considering that their guest had spent the past year or more at sea or in the hulks. But to hear Hurel's views on the matter you would have thought he had spent that time in the salons and drawing rooms of France's new élite.

It all went far better than Anson had expected, but the more he heard le Baron burbling on the more concerned he grew at the man's garrulity. The family and the staff could be sworn to secrecy, but if Hurel wore his heart on his sleeve and told his life story to all-comers there would be little prospect of keeping their coming mission under wraps.

It was a relief when his father broke up the post-dinner port session on the pretext of having to deal with some parochial business in the morning, and the Frenchman was at last persuaded to retire for the night.

13

Down the Swale

The horse and cart had disappeared by the time Bardet and his companions awoke, but someone else had entered the barn.

The man was framed in the doorway, the early-morning light silhouetting him. He looked like a fisherman – heavily bearded and wearing a canvas smock and trousers tucked into muddy sea boots, with an old sou'wester hat hanging behind his head from a length of cord. He was carrying a half-filled sack over his shoulder but appeared to be unarmed.

The escapers were hidden in the hay and at first the newcomer could not see them.

Quietly Bardet reached for the pitchfork he had found when they arrived. He pulled it to him and rose suddenly from his covering of hay brandishing it like Neptune emerging from the waves.

The newcomer near jumped out of his skin. 'Gor'blimey! You near frightened the shit outta me! Put that thing down for Gawd's sake. If you're the Frenchies, I'm your guide, friend, ami, orlright?'

The escapers remained on the alert and staring at him.

'Look, the password I was told to give yer is "fraternity", orlright? Now d'you believe I'm on yer side?'

Bardet lowered his weapon.

'You mean fraternité …'

'That's what I said, didn't I? Whatever, I don't do Frog-speak meself. Anyway, you got to follow me now, across the marshes, see? I'm to take yer to where I've got a boat hid up and row yer down the Swale.'

Bardet knew something of the geography, learnt from the hulk guard he had bribed to communicate with the escape route organisers ashore. The Swale estuary was the waterway that cut the Isle of Sheppey off from mainland Kent. To the north it led into the Medway, south and east to the open sea.

'We are ready. But we are 'ungry. Do you 'ave food? Water?'

'Better'n that mate. I got bread and cheese, but I got wine too. That's what you Frenchies drink, ain't it?'

They fell on the food as if half-starved, which they were.

Their watching guide reassured them: 'There's more vittles in the boat, mates, but we got to leave now, afore there's anyone about.'

They set off in single file behind him down a narrow path that led off into the marshes.

Bardet was used to the bleak and depressing view of the shoreline from the hulks, but this was something else. The desolate coastal marshes were everywhere intersected by dykes and stretched for miles, the only notable feature being the rising ground of the Isle of Sheppey, now to their north.

It was as dismal a sight as you could find, but the escapers were far from downcast. They were en route to freedom – and home.

They saw no other human beings and only a few sheep grazing the higher land, but a flock of plovers rose at their approach and there were a great many waders – curlews, redshanks and oystercatchers – probing the marshier mud. And as they neared the water they disturbed pintail, widgeon and teal.

The guide motioned the escapers to crouch down while he went forward alone to check that all was well with his boat and that there was no-one else around.

Satisfied, he beckoned them on and they waded the last few yards to where it was hidden among the reeds.

They climbed aboard and made themselves as comfortable as they could while he unshipped the oars, fitted them into the rowlocks and pulled away.

Bardet found the other promised sack of victuals and they set to as the guide rowed slowly but strongly out into the estuary.

As they progressed Bardet took the opportunity to quiz their new guide, asking who had sent him to their aid.

'I don't know 'cos I don't *need* to know. What you don't know yer can't tell. I just got a message to pick yer up and take you to the next stop, like. Them as fixes all this is clever. They ain't bin caught yet and if we all keep our gobs closed and do just what we're told they won't ever get caught, right?'

Bardet shrugged. The man was right, bien sûr.

They passed Milton Creek to starboard and by noon were off Oare and the ancient town of Faversham where they first encountered other craft, mostly fishing boats.

The guide had suggested that one of the prisoners should make use of a fishing rod he had in the boat to allay suspicion and Cornacchia, a keen angler, was happy to oblige. Bardet and Girault dozed in the thwarts, unseen from passing vessels.

Another long stretch of empty, flat, marshy shore came into view to the south and to the north Shell Ness, marking the extremity of Sheppey, could be seen – and beyond it the North Sea.

The guide rested on his oars. 'There yer are mates, that there's the open sea and what we're headin' for now is what we calls the platform. The sea 'ereabouts ebbs two miles or more from the shore, see?'

'So?'

'Well, we'll be reachin' the platform when the tide's out so I'll land yer on it. It's where us fishermen land our catch and clean it. The market boats can load oysters, fish and whatnot at any time or tide, see?'

The platform was now clearly in view and a few oyster and cockle gatherers could be seen around an old wreck further inshore.

'What will 'appen after we land on this platform?'

'Another guide'll walk you ashore. See that 'ulk of an old brig? That's where the oyster people used to live. Line that up with the platform and you can see a buildin' just a few yards up on the beach. It's a pub called the Blue Anchor and that's where you're ' eaded next.'

'And there is no-one else about? No military?'

The guide laughed. 'Bless me no, what'd sodgers be doin' down 'ere, gettin' their boots all muddy? No, no – all you get hereabouts is the fisherfolk and wild-fowlers using punts or the half barrels sunk in the mud as hides. But I don't reckon any of 'em's about today.'

'And this Blue Anchor?'

'Don't worry about the landlord there or his customers. They do well out of the escape business, and I reckon some of 'em would be revolutioners themselves given half a chance!'

*

Daylight was fading and the new guide waited while the escapers cleaned themselves up and had a meal at the Blue Anchor before mounting his heavy horse and leading the way to Seasalter Cross and on along a narrow lane with high protective banks.

The pub landlord had explained to Bardet that a man going ahead on horseback would be best able to warn the escapers of any likely trouble ahead.

On the way they met only a couple of workmen trudging their way home. The guide nodded to them but carried on without speaking – and the two showed no interest in the Frenchmen, escapers evidently being a common sight hereabouts.

It was not long before they came upon a crossroads. The guide raised his hand and waved it to right and left – the signal to get off the path while he trotted forward to check that all was well.

After a few minutes he returned, leaned down and told Bardet: 'That's Pye Alley Farm the other side of the crossroads. I think all's clear but you'll know if you see a light from a little window over the door when you get up close. The farmer here will fit you up with any clothes you need and feed you. Then you'll be shown where to hide up until they're ready to send you across to France. Au revoir, messieurs!' And the horseman touched his horse's rump and trotted off back towards the Blue Anchor.

The escapers approached the crossroads and, looking ahead, Bardet could clearly see the square of light from the farmhouse ahead: it was the all-clear signal.

He nodded to himself in satisfaction. His escape had gone exactly as planned and in a few days he and his companions should be back in France.

14

Arranging a Bunfight

So much had happened since Anson had been summoned to Chatham – the mock funeral, his visit to the hulks, the brief stay at Ludden Hall, and now holed up with Hurel at his father's rectory. Small wonder, he told himself, that he had given little thought to running his Sea Fencible detachment.

Leaving Hurel in the care of his family he set off on Ebony for Seagate where Fagg and Hoover soon brought him up to date and he told them as much as he was able of the mission he was likely to have to undertake with the Frenchman.

Fagg warned him: 'That there Captain 'oare's bin asking after you, sir. I told 'im you'd been summonsed, like, by that Commodore Poporf bloke, but 'e seemed a bit miffed.'

'When was he here?'

'Well, soon after you left and agin just a couple of hours ago.'

Hoover offered: 'Yeah, he said he was going to see the mayor. Something about a presentation?'

Anson shrugged. 'Very well, I'll seek him out.'

He made his way to the Rose where he found Captain Hoare in the dining room with the mayor and three of his cronies, all local tradesmen when not engaged in busy-bodying around the town on corporation matters.

The remains of what had obviously been a substantial lunch were on the table and all five were tucking into cheese and port wine.

'Ah, Anson, my dear fellow! Back from Chatham, are you? You must tell me about that. Meanwhile, you've missed a splendid lunch but do join us and help yourself to some of this cheese. There's plenty for all, is there not Mister Mayor?'

The mayor adjusted his paunch so that a little more of it hung over his belt and laughed. 'Indeed there is, sir, and all paid for courtesy of our grateful townsfolk!'

Anson cringed inwardly. He had no wish to join this group and the thought of impoverished townspeople footing the bill for these parasites revolted him.

Not least, he was put out because Hoare had successfully convinced the mayor and his henchmen that *he* had masterminded and led the operation to capture the Normandy privateer although in reality he had nothing to do with the planning and arrived on the scene only after *Égalité* had been taken.

Anson excused himself. 'Most kind of you, gentlemen, but I have already eaten.'

'Well, take a pew anyway. His Worship the Mayor here was just telling me that he's proposing to invite the town council to grant me a presentation sword in honour of my ...' He hesitated, remembering that Anson had been there – indeed had been the true victor – before continuing condescendingly: 'I of course meant *our* victory over the Frogs.'

Anson remained standing and managed to stifle a gasp at his superior officer's bare-faced effrontery, muttering: 'A presentation sword? Good grief!'

Hoare appeared not to register the sarcasm, reading it as awe rather than incredulity. 'Yes, I was a bit taken aback myself. It's the same sort of thing as the swords of honour presented to people like Nelson by the City of London, although not quite so ornate, eh, gentlemen?'

Equating himself to Lord Nelson was breathtaking even by Hoare's standard, Anson thought. There would be no honour about *this* sword, and the local coffers would probably only run to a cheap version anyway; but then cheap would be fitting in this instance.

The mayor took another lump of cheese and refilled his glass from the decanter before passing it to his left. 'Not quite so ornate, sir, but I daresay we can run to a handsome ceremonial weapon, suitably inscribed – perhaps something like: "To the victor of the Battle of Seagate, the date, your name, Captain Hoare, and from the grateful Mayor, Corporation and townsmen." That kind of thing ... oh, and various patriotic symbols of course.'

Anson took a deep breath and said nothing, not trusting himself to hide his disgust.

But Hoare was enthusiastic. 'Capital, Your Worship! Handsome of you, but just be sure the engraver spells the full name correctly: Captain Arthur Veryan St Cleer Hoare. You may not be aware that I am closely related to a number of prominent, indeed aristocratic, West Country families ...' He pondered and then added: 'I think perhaps you should add Royal Navy after my name to indicate that I am not a lowly *army* captain, eh?'

The mayor scribbled a note: 'Never fear, it shall be done exactly as you've suggested, sir.'

'Good, good. Now, allow me to suggest that you hold a presentation ceremony at the town hall after one of your council meetings followed by a civic dinner for the top people here at the Rose. Once we've vacated the town hall it can be used for a bun-fight that all the hoi polloi and Sea Fencibles can attend. Then you can all bask in the reflected glory, eh Anson?' The imputation was clear: Anson would not be at the civic dinner.

But when Hoare turned to see his subordinate's reaction, Anson was no longer there.

*

Back at the detachment, Anson was in a huddle with Hoover and Fagg discussing the training programme for the fencibles when Hoare turned up, red-faced, perspiring and a little unsteady on his feet. His three-hour lunch with the mayor had clearly taken its toll.

'Ah, Anson, I was just telling you about the bun-fight when I receive my presentation sword but you disappeared ...'

'Duty called, sir.'

'Now you come to mention duty, your bosun tells me you were summoned to Chatham. What was that all about and why wasn't I consulted?'

'I fear you were busily engaged in, er, fostering good relations with civic leaders at the time.'

Hoare reflected. 'Fostering, eh? Good word, that. Yes, yes, an onerous task but someone has to do it.'

'Quite. It's fortunate that you are able to relieve us mere detachment commanders of such duties.'

The divisional captain nodded appreciatively at what he mistook as a compliment, but then recollected that he had not got an answer to his question. 'But *why* were you summoned, behind my back, ignoring the chain of command?'

'It concerned some matter which will involve me in carrying out a reconnaissance in due course, but as yet I know not what. I am to hold myself in readiness and will be called to Dover Castle to be briefed about it when the powers that be have their ducks in a row.'

Hoare tapped his nose conspiratorially. 'Hmm. More than likely connected to my own summons to advise Nelson on Sea Fencible matters for some operation he's planning. They would have known I'd be busy advising the great man, so looks as if you're going to be lurked for some minor task connected to that.'

Relieved at not having to elucidate about his summons to Chatham, Anson quickly switched to the attack. 'May I enquire, sir, about where the men stand regarding prize money for the Normandy privateer?'

'Prize money? Your wretched bosun was on to me about the same thing.'

'Yes, the men have been asking about it.'

Hoare searched his wine-befuddled brain. 'Yes, yes, I recall that I put up the case, quite forcibly, and am hopeful of a satisfactory outcome, but these things take time. Tides may wait for no man, but Admiralty prize courts grind precious slow.'

Anson was aware that the Admiralty Prize Court, part of the King's Division of the High Court of Justice, had the authority to consider whether a ship had been lawfully captured – to evaluate claims and condemn prizes. It could also authorise head money of £5 per enemy sailor captured. It ruled on disputed prize cases and either condemned the ship, cargo, or both as lawful prizes or found in favour of the owners as "not lawful prize" although that was extremely unlikely given the circumstances. The court could also order the sale or destruction of the ship and distribution of the proceeds. All ships in sight of the capture qualified as their presence was deemed to have encouraged the enemy to surrender rather than fighting on until they were sunk.

That great oracle of law, the late Lord Mansfield, the Lord Chief Justice, had famously said: "The end of a PRIZE COURT IS TO SUSPEND THE PROPERTY TILL CONDEMNATION; TO PUNISH EVERY SORT OF MISBEHAVIOR IN THE CAPTORS; TO RESTORE INSTANTLY ... IF UPON THE MOST SUMMARY EXAMINATION, IF THE GOODS ARE REALLY A PRIZE, against everybody, giving everybody a fair opportunity of being heard. A captor may, and must, force every person interested to defend, and every person interested may force him to proceed to condemn, without delay."

Anson ventured: 'I am led to believe that the captured privateer is now down at Portsmouth ready to be put up for sale, so may we expect to know of the outcome soon?'

Hoare stroked his chin. 'Yes, come to think on it, I could do with my eighth share. I'll put a ferret into the system. But surely you are not hard up, Anson?'

'No, sir, I ask merely for the sake of the fencibles, most of whom are more than hard up, to put it mildly. But since you mention it, may I remind you that I am still considerably out of pocket as a result of your instruction to me to obtain uniforms for my detachment so that they would not disgrace the service at the Lord Lieutenant's royal review?'

Anson had acquired uniforms of dark blue jackets, red-striped trousers, straw hats and sea boots for his detachment from a Chatham tailor who had blamed wartime shortages for his high prices.

The men had worn them to the recent royal review at Mote Park, Maidstone, where they had upheld the pride of the service against the gaudily uniformed militiamen, volunteers and the peacocks of the yeomanry.

But Hoare was clearly irritated to be quizzed on such a matter by his junior officer and asked waspishly: 'So?'

'As you are aware, sir, I obtained the uniforms according to your instructions and settled the not inconsiderable bill myself.'

'Very noble of you, I'm sure, but what's the point you are making?'

'The point, sir, is that I passed my claim to you some time ago but it has not been paid and I am considerably out of pocket. Put simply, I wish to be reimbursed.'

'Very little hope of that, Anson! When you have been in the service for as long as I have you will learn that it is extremely unwise to shell out on behalf of their lordships without squeezing the money out of the hammock-counters first. Otherwise the chances are that at best you'll whistle for your money for a long, long time, and at worst you'll never see it again!'

'But, sir, you instructed me—'

'*Advised* you, I think you'll find. Look Anson, I'm a growing a little tired of your wittering on about money allegedly owed you and that sort of thing. Ain't gentlemanly – ain't *officer*-like. Just put it down to experience and crack on …'

15

A Fairlight Interlude

Fuming, Anson gave thought to how he could best spend the time before he was summoned to present himself at Dover Castle for instructions on the mission he and Hurel were to carry out.

He had no wish to sit around at the rectory watching his sisters throwing themselves at le Baron, putting up with his mother's match-making – or risking bumping into Charlotte Brax if he ventured out of the grounds. He feared he had compromised himself as far as Squire Brax's voluptuous, husband-hunting daughter was concerned and dreaded meeting her again.

Nor would staying at his room at the Rose in Folkestone and overseeing basic training for the fencibles hold much interest for him. Fagg and Hoover were perfectly capable of looking after that.

There was only one agreeable possibility – a visit to his particular friend Commander Amos Armstrong at Fairlight Signal Station on the windswept South Downs above the Channel fishing port of Hastings.

Having assured himself that Fagg and Hoover had everything well under control at the detachment and that training was going well, Anson made up his mind to go.

He wrote a note to be delivered to Hurel at the rectory explaining that he would be away for a day or so and reminding the Frenchman that he must keep a low profile.

Still sore from his ride, he did not feel obliged to set off to Fairlight on horseback, so left the good-natured, but – for Anson – uncomfortable Ebony with the ostlers at the Rose and took passage in young Tom Marsh's pony and trap.

*

As before, the – he hoped – temporary custodian and master of all he surveyed, Commander Amos Armstrong was delighted to welcome his brother officer to his inhospitable signal station looking out over the Channel.

Most of the time, he claimed, he was bereft of agreeable company.

With only what he called his "moon-faced young midshipman", two lower-deck signalmen and a couple of dragoons to share his lonely eyrie, he lacked like-minded companionship to share his vigil monitoring ship movements, especially any Frenchmen, and relaying the occasional signal.

Nor was there anyone with whom he could share a glass of wine or brandy, undoubtedly supplied by the very smugglers he was meant to keep an eye out for.

It was from this outpost of empire that Armstrong had recorded the movements of the Normandy privateer that preyed on English merchantmen and his carefully kept log had enabled him to predict the Frenchman's return so that Anson could lure the raider into a trap.

'Mon vieux!' Armstrong enthused, helping Anson down from the cart. 'How very good to see you! I do hope you will be able to stay a while?'

'I can and will, but allow me to ask you, why do you always call me "mon vieux" when it's patently obvious that I am neither French nor old?'

'Ah, mon vieux, sorry, I should say my dear fellow, I fear the expression has stayed with me since I spent a year in Paris as a youngster well before the revolution got under way and heads started to roll.'

'What on earth were you doing there when the likes of me were dozy young midshipmen trying to learn the mysteries of navigation and so forth?'

'Ah, well, it was decided that it would be best for me to learn something of the ways of the world before cutting myself off from it and settling for a life at sea ...'

'But why Paris?'

'Well, the grand tour would have taken too long. I'd have been almost in my dotage if I did that before becoming a midshipman. So I was sent by my most amenable father to Paris to learn the language and, well, certain other life skills of a romantic nature ...'

Having joined Armstrong for a run ashore in London, Anson could guess what those skills were.

'Yes, my father thought that when I joined the navy the ability to speak French would come in handy, taking surrenders and that kind of thing ...'

Anson was amused at such foresight.

'Sadly the old boy's reduced to being pushed around in a Bath chair by a sturdy maid these days, God bless him.'

'No doubt your father *is* old, but why do you call me "mon vieux"?'

'Well, you see, the crowd I ran around with in Paris were mostly aristos of a sort and although we were only in our early teens everyone called everyone else "mon vieux".'

'Even the girls?'

'Oh no, they were always mon amour! Anyway, these things stick, which is more than I can say for my young French friends' heads. I suspect most of them will have lost theirs to the guillotine during The Terror ...'

Anson nodded understandingly.

'Oh, talking of the fair sex, do you think it would be in order for me to write inviting your two charming sisters to visit Fairlight? Elizabeth did show quite an interest in it when I stayed at the rectory for the Brax ball.'

'Certainly you should write. After all, Elizabeth sent you a note via me when I came here before to plan the *Égalité* affair, did she not? Both girls are on the hunt for husbands, you know, and you are clearly in Elizabeth's gun-sights.'

Armstrong spluttered: 'You're a touch ahead of the clock, mon vieux, but yes, I will compose an invite for you to take back with you, if you will.'

Anson thought he detected a blush on his friend's cheeks, but then that could have been due to the prevailing westerlies.

Remembering his duties as a host, Armstrong hurried to change the subject: 'Anyway, *mon vieux*, a warm welcome. My dragoons and signalmen will look after young Marsh and his pony, so let's get out of this wind and take a glass or two in my so-called abode.'

But Anson halted him for a moment. 'While we are still alone I should tell you of something that I have been strictly ordered to keep under wraps.'

'Even from me?'

'From the world, but then I trust you more than anyone I know, and I would welcome your opinion on it all. I am dying to tell someone. You see, it concerns my attendance at a funeral that never was and a clandestine mission of some kind that I am apparently going to be called upon to undertake.'

'Tell all, *mon vieux,* and it will be a secret shared.'

*

Once Anson had told Armstrong all he knew about the Hurel affair, they agreed to say no more about it lest any of the men overheard.

Instead, over a few more than two glasses and their mutton chops – the best his host could muster and one of the few things his signalman-cum-cook could produce on the station's small stove without ruining it – Anson filled Armstrong in on the details of the capture of *Égalité*.

The last Armstrong had seen of the privateer was the Frenchman giving chase to the *Kentish Trader* as the small merchantman fled eastward towards Seagate with Anson disguised as the skipper and a party of his Sea Fencibles hidden below deck.

But he knew the gist of the outcome because Anson had written to him immediately after the battle that ensued thanking his friend for the vital part he had played in predicting the privateer's return to the Sussex coast.

Characteristically, Anson had played down his own role in taking *Égalité*, but now he was able to give Armstrong, hungry for detail, a blow-by-blow account.

And, as the wine did its work, he revealed to his astonished friend how the divisional captain had arrived on board when it was all over but nevertheless demanded the French captain's sword that Anson had already accepted when the privateer struck, but had handed back.

Taken aback, Armstrong asked: 'You had handed it back because ...?'

'Because the Frenchman had ordered his men to lay down their arms to avoid further bloodshed. Therefore I thought it the honourable thing to do.'

'But Captain Hoare felt otherwise?'

'It appears so. What's more he claimed the victory, lording it in front of the local bigwigs, and gave me a severe dressing down as if I were some wet-behind-the-ears midshipman ...'

Armstrong was incensed. 'I trust you have complained and demanded redress?'

Anson shook his head. 'To me, such a course would not be honourable. In any event, Hoare insisted on reporting the capture of *Égalité* to the Admiralty himself, but did not see fit to show me his letter. Nevertheless, I've no doubt he painted himself the hero of the hour.'

Pouring another glass, Armstrong could not hide his fury. 'The wretched social-climbing Captain et cetera, et cetera Hoare, or whatever he calls himself, must be given his come-uppance and I'll not rest until he has!'

'No, no,' Anson protested. 'Don't concern yourself on my account. Those who were actually there know what happened and that's enough for me. Remember your Latin: Sibi quisque naufragium facit – each man makes his own shipwreck. Given time, Hoare is the kind of man who will fulfil that prophecy without any help from us.'

Armstrong could but agree and revealed: 'I've been summoned to the Admiralty, y'know—'

'Summoned?'

'Yes summoned. Usually, as you know, from time to time I go cap in hand seeking a posting to anywhere on God's earth except here, and get sent packing with a large flea in my ear. But this time *they* have sent for me, would you believe?'

'A posting a last?'

'Could be. I can't think of any particular offence I've perpetrated of late that warrants another dressing down. Mind you, whatever's behind it I'll find a way to say my piece about Hoare's outrageous claims about the *Égalité* affair.'

Anson shook his head. 'Please do no such thing. You will win no kudos wittering on about a senior officer. In any event, although you were heavily involved in the planning – and we could not have succeeded without the intelligence you provided – you were not actually there when the privateer was taken, so the Admiralty will completely ignore what you have to say and insert another black mark against your name.'

'Oh, very well! I am sure you're right as usual. I'll keep my mouth shut tight when I get to the corridors of power and go to listening mode for once.'

'Good, I'm sure that would be the best thing for both our sakes.'

*

As soon as the sun was over the yardarm of Armstrong's land-locked command, they drank to success for his visit to the Admiralty and the commander announced: 'After all that nonsense about the dreaded Hoare we need to cheer ourselves up. Now let's see what I can rustle up by way of some entertainment for our rare but honoured guest. Wait there. Don't move an inch!'

He disappeared into the outer room where his signalmen, dragoons and Tom Marsh were finishing their mutton supper.

Anson heard the buzz of conversation, then the scrape and screech of a fiddle being tuned.

Flinging the door open, Armstrong announced: 'Allow me to introduce the Fairlight ensemble, with Dragoon Dillon on the fiddle accompanied by the rest on percussion instruments of a somewhat improvised nature! Middy – break out some more bottles of the better red!'

'Bravo!' Anson clapped loudly. 'Let the music begin. Is it to be sea shanties?'

Dillon raised his bow. 'If you'll allow me, sorr, I'd like to limber up with an Irish tune in remembrance of my home.'

'Of course, Irish it shall be!'

The Irishman tried an experimental scrape with his bow, turned a peg to adjust a wayward string, and, tapping his foot to keep time, launched into a lively jig, with the signalmen, his fellow dragoon and Tom Marsh joining in on a variety of cooking utensils masquerading as percussion instruments.

His nod to his Irish heritage over, Dillon swung into a hornpipe that got the sailors' feet jigging and then *Heart of Oak*.

Inhibitions overcome thanks to the wine, Armstrong and Anson bellowed in unison:

"Come, cheer up, my lads. 'tis to glory we steer,
To add something more to this wonderful year,
To honour we call you, as freemen not slaves,
For who are so free as the sons of the waves?"

Then, holding both hands aloft to halt the entire orchestra, Fairlight's commander called upon all present to join in the chorus:

"Heart of oak are our ships, jolly tars are our men,
We always are ready; steady boys, steady!
We'll fight and we'll conquer again and again ... "

To cries of *Spanish Ladies*! Dillon and the percussion team struck up again:

"Farewell and adieu to you, Spanish ladies
Farewell and adieu to you, ladies of Spain
For we're under orders
For to sail to old England
But we hope in a short time to see you again."

They ranted and roared through the chorus like true British sailors and the wine and singing continued with great vehemence into the night such that any passing shepherd must have thought there was an entire warship lying just off the coast with its crew celebrating some famous victory.

For once, Armstrong and his men were not 'watch on, stop on'. They had let the end go, and looking out for enemy shipping was forgotten.

And with no Revenue men about either, this night the Sussex smuggling fraternity could go about their importing activities without fear of interruption.

*

Next morning Anson awoke with a similar dull pain behind the eyes that he had last suffered many months before following a run ashore in London with the same Amos Armstrong.

He decided a pre-breakfast stroll in the bracing air on the Downs might clear his head, and left Armstrong at his desk, scratching his head and pondering how to continue his letter to his friend's sisters.

So far he had successfully completed only the salutation. But already he was having doubts. Perhaps he should address them alphabetically, in which case it should be "Dear Anne and Elizabeth". Or perhaps eldest first: "Dear Elizabeth and Anne". Either way, would they assume that he favoured whoever was mentioned first?

Truth be told, it was Elizabeth that he had been most thrilled to have on his arm at the Brax Hall ball. There was something about her dark good looks, cheerful demeanour and intelligent conversation that had captivated him – far more so than her slightly sulky and stuck-up sister.

Then there was the fact that both were sisters of his particular friend Oliver Anson, and he could think of no-one he would prefer more to be his brother-in-law as well as brother-in-arms.

But, he told himself, he was getting ahead of himself here. He had only briefly met the Anson sisters and had so much enjoyed dancing with them both at the Brax Hall ball.

Beyond knowing that they liked dancing and that Elizabeth showed a flattering interest in him and his career at sea, temporarily stalled thanks to this ghastly signal station appointment, he as yet knew little about them.

He knew that both enjoyed lady-like pursuits such as watercolour painting, embroidery and visiting the poor of their father's parish, but beyond that … well, *that* was the point of the letter. Since he could not abandon his cliff-top station he had determined that they should be invited to visit him.

Finally he made up his mind and wrote:

"To the dear Misses Anson,

Remembering with great affection the wonderful evening I enjoyed in your company at the Brax Hall ball and the interest you both so kindly

*showed in my signal station, I have the temerity to write suggesting –
indeed pleading – that you visit me here in my lonely eyrie at Fairlight.*

*Here I could offer extensive views of the English Channel, devoid, I hope,
of enemy warships, a guided tour of my humble station, such as it is, and a
demonstration of how such a telegraphic wonder operates.*

*When I tell you that a meal will be thrown in, I fear you could take that
almost literally as I am totally reliant on the culinary skills of my
signalmen who are more familiar with salt beef and plum duff than the
refined dishes prepared by the rectory cook!*

*As to travel arrangements, I am asking your brother Oliver, my
particular friend, to make the necessary arrangements so you can be here
and back within a day.*

Hoping that you will be willing and able to accept this invitation,
I remain
Your devoted friend and admirer,
A Armstrong
Commander, Royal Navy
Fairlight Signal Station
Sussex."

16

Pye Alley Farm

Bardet and his companions approached the farmhouse with some trepidation, despite the assurance by their guide that the light from the small square window above the side door meant all was well.

As they drew nearer, Bardet could see that this was a large, brick-built house roofed with the peg-tiles that he had noticed were common to this part of England. The window showing the light was small – just big enough to frame a man's head – and positioned under the eaves. The light from it could only be seen when approached, as they had, from Seasalter and the coast.

He motioned Girault and Cornacchia to stand either side of the door and tapped three times.

It opened immediately to reveal a thick-set, red-faced man he correctly assumed to be the farmer who looked them up and down and beckoned them inside.

'You're expected, gents. Fed up with life in the hulks, eh?'

Bardet nodded.

'D'you want anything to eat, drink?'

'No. We 'ave eaten, but we are very tired.'

'It's been a long day, eh? Take off your boots down here and I'll show you upstairs.'

They complied, glad to be rid of their boots after so long, and the farmer led them upstairs to a room with two single beds and a washstand, telling them: 'You can clean up and sleep here tonight, boys. But two of you will have to share, all right?'

Bardet, who would *not* be sharing, shrugged agreement. He asked: 'Are we safe 'ere, from soldiers, informers?'

'We're off the beaten track here. There's no military about and the locals don't dare rat on us. They know what would happen to them if they did. Anyway, most of 'em get some benefit or other out of the smuggling and escape trades. Mind you, best keep your boots close at hand just in case I have to move you sharpish.'

Bardet immediately claimed what appeared to him to be the most comfortable bed and indicated to the others that they would have to share the other, Girault with his head to one end, Cornacchia with his at the other.

The farmer sniffed the now-rancid air. With their boots off, he told himself, it wouldn't be surprising if the two sharing end to end fainted from the smell.

Smell or no smell, all three were asleep almost before their host had left the room.

*

After a good night's sleep, interrupted only by his companions' curses whenever one or the other's head encountered a foot, and a breakfast of ham and eggs, Bardet went into a huddle with the farmer.

'We'll fit you out with any more clothes you need and then you'll have to hide out in the woods during the day, alright?'

'When can we leave for France?'

'It could be a few days, could be weeks. Depends if there's what they call a hue and cry – and when there's a smuggling run we can get you on.'

Bardet shook his head and gave the farmer the kind of look he had used in the hulk to browbeat dissenters. 'I am not going to wait for weeks, mon ami. You must get me away as soon as possible. Is that understood?'

But the farmer was not to be intimidated. 'Steady, mate. What I'm telling you is for your own good. You can sleep here at night when all's clear, but it's too dicey for you to stay indoors in the daytime. As to getting you away, we'll do that the minute we can – when we reckon it's safe, right? We haven't failed to get escapers away yet and don't intend to mess things up now by jumping the gun.'

Bardet shrugged. 'Very well, but make it soon.'

'We will, we will. But by the by, we've heard there's another foreign gent hiding up near Faversham. Word is that he's a Frog, too – sorry mate, I mean a Frenchie. We're trying to find out if he's coming here to join your lot for the crossing.'

Bardet was puzzled. He knew all the escape plans for his hulk, but of course it could be someone who had got away from the *Bristol*, *Eagle* or one of the other prison ships.

Another possibility was that the mystery man was an officer who had given his parole but unless he had broken it and intended to escape there would be no need to hide.

The only other Frenchmen at large this side of La Manche would be royalists – traitors siding with the Rosbifs.

He stared at his host. 'I would like to know more of this man. Has he, too, escaped? If so, perhaps he can join us. If not, if he is a royalist, then …'

Slowly, Bardet drew his hand across his throat.

17

A Welcome Invitation

It was with still pounding head but lighter heart that Anson took leave of his friend. For once both had been able to forget the loneliness of command and relax in convivial company.

Nevertheless, the journey back from Fairlight was a silent affair, Tom Marsh suffering with a much worse headache having been plied with far more smuggled wine than was good for him by Armstrong's dragoons and signalmen until the early hours.

*

The arrival of Armstrong's message at Hardres Minnis rectory was greeted with barely suppressed excitement by the Misses Anson, to whom it was jointly addressed.

Elizabeth, the elder by little more than a year, used her seniority to seize it and break the seal, announcing: 'It is most likely in response to the note I sent him after the Brax Hall ball!'

Anne wrinkled her nose in distaste. She, too, had been somewhat taken by the commander and had enjoyed her share of dances with him at the ball. But since then, through their older brother Augustine, she had met one of his fellow clerics shortly to be inducted into a nearby parish and, despite his skeletal figure and abnormally loud speaking voice, quite fancied the life *he* could offer. However, these were early days, so she was keeping her options open.

'The letter is clearly addressed to both of us equally,' she sniffed, 'but you may read it out loud if you wish. No verbal editing, mind!'

They clucked and giggled over Armstrong's wording, savouring his blandishments and titivated by the picture he painted of his signal station.

Elizabeth confessed: 'I long to see him in his natural element, as it were, sweeping the Channel with his telescope and sending warnings of enemy ships. A telegraphic wonder? How thrilling!'

Anne was more down to earth. 'Do you suppose it's an imposing establishment? Like a mini-fortress, I mean? Oliver is only a lieutenant but has lots of men under him, so will Commander Armstrong have even more?'

Together they bearded their father in his study where he was relieved to be interrupted in his weekly chore of copying, mainly verbatim – and only slightly amending – an all-purpose sermon from a book of such exemplars.

It had been produced by a long-dead cleric who apparently knew everything there was to know about life and religion although he had not left the confines of his own rectory for more than half a century. Certainly he had been a past master at composing exceedingly boring sermons.

The Reverend Anson was keen to marry off both daughters as soon as possible to relieve some of the drain on his purse, so any approach from a likely suitor was welcomed.

He read the letter, sat back and smiled indulgently. 'A visit to Fairlight and Commander Armstrong? Oliver's friend?'

Elizabeth nodded enthusiastically. 'Yes father, you surely remember him staying at the rectory for the Brax Hall ball? The rather good-looking, gentlemanly officer ...'

Of course the rector remembered him – a sturdily-built, sandy-haired fellow with a smiley, weather-beaten face, from a landed Northumbrian family and with impeccable manners learned while completing his education among the aristocracy of pre-revolutionary Paris. Now, if one of his daughters could capture such a man of evident means who had much impressed him, why, then he'd be delighted.

He teased his daughters. 'Hmm, yes, I recall him vaguely and have no objection in principle, as long as you are both properly chaperoned ...'

Elizabeth protested: 'We would be chaperoning each other, father. And Jemmy would be with us.'

'Oh, so you would wish to travel in the carriage?'

'How else?' Anne asked petulantly.

'Hmm, well, your mother may well object. After all, it is a long way and we hardly know the fellow. I will put it to your mother and, as ever in all things, her decision will be final.'

*

Having learned his lesson the hard way, the rector deferred to his wife on all matters other than those directly involving his maker. Although he was nominally head of the household, she ruled the roost where he and their offspring were concerned.

Herself a clergyman's daughter, she had high ambitions for their sons and daughters.

Augustine was doing nicely, already a minor canon and well on the way, she hoped, to becoming a dean, bishop or even archbishop. He was soon to be married to the archdeacon's daughter – no beauty, but a sensible clergy daughter not unlike herself.

Oliver had slipped from her control when her husband persuaded her to let him join the navy. But she had no doubt that he would achieve flag rank, particularly if, as she dearly hoped, he married Charlotte who would bring a goodly part of the Brax fortune to the marriage bed.

Their youngest son, Abraham, was destined for the army, which was a pity, she felt, as it would mean mixing with a lot of rough fellows just as Oliver did with uncouth sailors.

But then there had not been a soldier in the family since great uncle Hannibal Anson was trampled to death by an elephant when tiger-hunting in Uttar-Pradesh. So if the youngest of her brood did well in the army, having a general in the family would be some compensation. It was early days, of course, because the boy was still at boarding school.

As for Elizabeth and Anne, well, it was vital that they made good marriages, and that meant finding wealthy and influential husbands. They had been expertly trained in parochial skills including arranging the church flowers and visiting the poor and sick whether they wanted to be visited or not.

When not on parish duty they painted in watercolours, embroidered and read poetry and romantic novels. But their education in affairs of the heart was sadly lacking, chiefly because their mother didn't have one – or, if she did, it had hardened over the years.

Both were pretty enough to attract men, but it was finding the right ones that was the problem. Anne, who took after her mother and Augustine in temperament, would make an excellent wife for an up-and-coming churchman. Indeed, Augustine had already introduced her to a likely prospect.

But Elizabeth, who was much more like the sometimes flighty rector and her impetuous brother Oliver, would be harder to match.

It was while the rector's wife was musing over such matters that her husband sought her out to show her Armstrong's letter and consult her as to how their daughters should respond.

'I am as keen as you are to marry the girls off, but we must only consider *suitable* suitors. And the question here is, would a mere sea officer be able to support one of them in the manner to which she has become accustomed?'

The rector agreed. 'But of course, my dear, all that's proposed at present is a mere visit – an outing for them, not a marriage market. I daresay that if he becomes attached to one or the other things might progress, but for the moment ...'

'As ever, rector ...' She only called him that when she was about to lay down the law or reprimand him, which was pretty often. 'As ever, you are prepared to think the best of people and agree to almost anything off the cuff. Has it not crossed your mind that this man is a sailor? Have you forgotten the expression: "a wife in every port"?'

'Actually I think it's a girl, dear – a girl in every port.'

'I rest my case! Kindly leave this with me. I will consult Oliver as to this man's prospects and give you my decision after that.'

The rector nodded obediently. She was right again, of course.

Nevertheless, the thought of having another sea officer – and a commander at that – in the family did have its attractions. Why, one day both Oliver and his brother-in-law might achieve flag rank with all the wealth and kudos that would flow from it ...

*

His mother was lying in wait for Anson when he returned to the rectory, and demanded: 'This friend of yours, the one you brought to the Brax ball – Captain Armstrong. Apparently quite gentlemanly, despite being in the navy—'

'*Commander* Armstrong. What about him, mother?'

'All these ranks are most confusing. Where is he from?'

'Well, at present he is at the Fairlight Signal Station, although itching to get back to sea.'

'No, no. I mean where does he hail from – originally?'

'Oh, Northumberland I believe.'

'Great heavens! That's somewhere near Scotland, is it not?'

'Nearer there than here, for sure, mother. I believe he is due to inherit an extensive estate up there, or "up north" as some call it.'

Her sceptical expression faded at that and she tilted her head and pursed her lips speculatively. 'Well, that is gratifying from an income perspective – as long as it consists of farms, forests, coal mines and the like and not just bleak grouse moors,' his mother mused. 'But no-one would wish to *live* in such a place, would they? So far north and devoid of civilised society ...'

'Mother, have I mentioned to you before that you are a dreadful snob? Anyway, why this sudden interest in Armstrong? Could it be to do with him inviting the girls to visit his signal station? Don't tell me, you are lining him up as a target for marriage aren't you?'

'Well, when he stayed here he did pay a good deal of attention to your sisters. He seemed quite taken with them, although it was difficult to tell whether it was Elizabeth or Anne who interested him most.'

He thought back to Armstrong's visit and the ball they had attended together at Brax Hall. It was there on that sultry night using the excuse of needing to take the air on the terrace that Squire Brax's voracious eldest daughter Charlotte had made such a play for Anson, and to his regret now, he had responded enthusiastically.

'Mother, any sailor home from the sea or stuck in a signals station and deprived of female company for months on end will take an interest in *any* woman.'

That, he thought ruefully, was how he had allowed himself to become entrapped by the over-ripe and pushy Charlotte, desperate to find herself a husband. How he regretted succumbing to lust and sleeping with her – and now the scheming minx had painted him into a tight corner.

His mother's protest brushed away his dark thoughts. 'Your sisters are not women! They are *ladies*. Yes, they need suitable husbands, of course, and I would be failing in my duty as a mother if I did not vet possible candidates with due diligence.'

Anson laughed. 'You make it sound as if Armstrong is about to sit the matrimonial equivalent of a lieutenant's examination! He has merely invited them to lunch ...'

'It is clearly a declaration of interest and an opportunity for him to decide which of them he favours.'

'Mother, I think you will find that Elizabeth has already aimed a cupid's dart at the gallant commander in the guise of a heavily-scented letter sent some time ago. I reckon this invitation to visit Fairlight is a direct response.'

'What! You tell me she is in correspondence with this man without my knowledge? I sincerely hope nothing improper has been said ... or occurred!'

Anson had helped his sister draft the note following the Brax ball so could vouch for its chaste nature, but chose not to put his mother's mind at rest and instead threw in provocatively: 'No doubt they're planning to run away together and Anne is merely invited along as cover …'

His mother almost choked but then noticed his sly smile and rebuked him: 'This tendency to the lowest form of wit is *not* what we are used to in church circles and you were most definitely *not* brought up to it. It clearly comes from spending too much time in the company of rough sailors.'

'Mother, I can think of no-one in the world less like a rough sailor than Armstrong. He is a well-mannered, educated, honourable man of good repute and good family. There is no-one – *no-one* – I would choose over him to call my brother-in-law. I hope that satisfies your examination board and that you consider due diligence done!'

Amused, he gave her an exaggerated bow and made his exit, thinking as he left that he would prefer the company of his rough sailors to the prim and prudish inhabitants of a rectory any day of the week, be they family or not.

*

'Brother?'

Anson looked up from the *Kentish Gazette* report he had been reading on the latest manoeuvres of the Kentish volunteers and sat back in his wicker-work chair as his sister swept into the rectory summerhouse. 'Yes Elizabeth, what can I do for you?'

She flopped into a chair beside him. 'I was just wondering about how ranks work in the navy, and, perhaps the marines too?'

Anson knew that Elizabeth had been attracted to his friend Armstrong and was itching to visit him at Fairlight. No doubt she was following the same line of enquiry as their mother.

He decided to indulge her. 'Well, you no doubt recall that I began life – my naval life, that is – as a midshipman?

She wrinkled her nose. 'I was very little, but I do remember you wearing your pointy navy hat and chasing us around with a dagger when you were supposed to be helping the servants to pack your trunk.'

'Dirk, not dagger. It was a midshipman's dirk.'

'Whatever it was, you terrified Anne and I with it and mother was very cross with you.'

Anson had never forgotten that time when, a day short of his thirteenth birthday, he had gone off on his own full of notions of adventure and glory to join his first ship at Chatham.

A lot of water had passed under the bridge since then. There had been years of being run ragged as a midshipman, seemingly endless boring hours on watch in all weathers on blockade duty off the French coast, and the many discomforts of life living hugger-mugger in the confined conditions of His Majesty's warships and existing at times on a less than wholesome diet.

But there had been plenty of adventure and comradeship, a sort of shared glory perhaps from exploits like the escape of HMS *Euphemus* from the Nore Mutiny, the successful prize-taking cruise of HMS *Phryne* in the Mediterranean and the capture of the Normandy privateer by his Seagate Sea Fencibles.

His sister brought him out of his reverie, asking: 'But how did you get to become a lieutenant? That's what you are now, are you not?'

'That's what I was the last time I looked. What did it take to become one? It took a great deal of sea time – a minimum of six years – and then I had to pass the examination. Ship-handling, navigational problems – ever a trial for someone like me, always struggling with mathematics. I still shudder at the memory of it. It was a far worse ordeal than escaping from France.'

'But you passed?'

'I suspect the three captains who examined me must have thought I had a closer kinship with *the* Anson than our family actually has.'

'So why is Commander Armstrong a commander, and is that better than being a lieutenant?'

'Ah,' thought Anson, 'so this *is* all about Armstrong, as I expected.'

Elbows resting on the arms of his chair, he clasped his hands and rested his chin on them as if deep in thought before looking up to find her waiting expectantly for his response.

'Well, you see, Armstrong is somewhat older than me so he has been in the service longer, and is no doubt considerably wiser. That's why he is senior to me in rank.'

'But if he is a commander why is he not given a ship to command, not just some building in Sussex?'

Anson laughed. 'It's not just a building, it's a signals station! But as to why he, and I, come to that, have not been given ships, well, you had best address that question to their lordships at the Admiralty. But I very much doubt that you will get a positive response.'

'So why don't you go and ask them? Surely they would listen to you after all you have done.'

'Armstrong and I have both gone hat in hand and pleaded for sea-going posts and slunk away ship-*less* with our tails between our legs. There are more than 2,000 lieutenants and commanders, around 500 captains and only 100 or so admirals of various hues and ranks. That's why in the navy we pray for a bloody war or a sickly season so that we can step into dead men's shoes. Other than that we patiently wait our turn, unless we have interest.'

'What do you mean by interest?'

'Influential friends in high places who can help advance one's career.'

'And the marines? Anne particularly asked me to find out about the ranks of the marines. Is it as difficult for one of them to become an officer?'

Anson frowned, wondering what lay behind *this* question. Could his younger sister have fallen for Lieutenant McKenzie at the memorial service?

But while he was still pondering his answer, George Beer appeared at the summerhouse door to announce that lunch was being served, giving Anson the excuse to escape further interrogation.

18

A Warning Signal

Amos Armstrong, the unwilling incumbent of Fairlight Signal Station on the gorse-studded headland high above the old fishing town of Hastings, was growing impatient and snapping at his underlings.

Dressed in his very best uniform – the one he wore for his visits to the Admiralty seeking a posting to a ship, or anywhere other than his present draughty command – he was anxiously awaiting visitors. And not just any visitors, but eligible females, rare as rocking horse droppings in his lonely eyrie.

His moon-faced midshipman was also in best fig, such as it was, and the youngster's face positively glowed from the good scrubbing he had been ordered to give himself earlier.

The two signalmen who, in the absence of a recognised uniform, which the navy had not yet got around to providing for inhabitants of the lower deck, were in new striped shirts, baggy white trousers and straw hats specially bought for them from a Hastings tailor by Armstrong himself. He was adamant that they would not disgrace him, certainly not in the matter of dress.

The two dragoons assigned to the station, Dillon and Hillman, were normally reasonably smart enough in their regimentals, but today they too had made an extra effort – and their horses had been favoured with a comprehensive wash and brush-up.

At long last Lloyd, the cheekiest of his signalmen, keeping watch from the roof, shouted: 'Deck there! Sail in sight approaching from the east.'

Armstrong responded: Most amusing, Lloyd. I take it you are referring to that carriage I can now see approaching.'

He raised his navy-issue telescope and focused on the carriage, hoping for an early sight of his guests, but at first he could only see the Reverend Anson's young groom at the reins.

As the rig drew closer he spotted an undeniably female face at the side window and he called his men to action stations, taking up his chosen position ready to take the salute. The moon-faced boy stood beside him ready to open the carriage door.

The signal station was a small wooden building, with two main rooms and a newly added extension that could quite easily have been taken for a poor cottage were it not for an eighty-foot mast with a thirty-foot gaff attached for running up flags and signal balls.

Armstrong had paid out of his own pocket to have the extra room built on as his private retreat, but it was furnished with plain deal tables and chairs much like the sailors' accommodation except that he had a cot rather than the hammocks they favoured – and a pair of comfortable armchairs that had cost him a week's pay.

He had described it to Anson as a dire place – day after day with naught but the whining midshipman, oafish signalmen, strait-laced dragoons, and occasional picnickers and dog-walkers for company.

The commander did not welcome these idle gawpers who made themselves a nuisance by trespassing on the site, giving him concerns for the security of the small arms, signal code book and logbook that he guarded with his life – and engaging the sailors with ridiculous questions, a favourite of which was: 'Can you see what they're up to in France from here?'

Lloyd, he knew, enjoyed telling them that through the glass he could see Frenchmen in their gardens gathering frogs and snails for their supper. And more often than not he was believed.

But today's visitors were something else entirely. His lonely vigil was about to be enlivened by his first-ever visit by ladies – and young and attractive ones at that.

The welcome on board the cliff-top station satisfactorily concluded, Armstrong showed the Misses Anson around his little empire, explaining: 'There was a beacon site at the time of the Armada – imagine that! And it remains an important location for keeping an eye out for our enemies.'

Elizabeth was clearly fascinated by it all and bombarded him with intelligent questions. How like her brother, he thought.

But her sister Anne was less enthusiastic and sniffed: 'I had assumed something dignified with the name of a signals station would be quite a grand affair, but this is … well, a hut …'

She was much more like her mother and her elder brother Gussie, Armstrong reflected.

Embarrassed by her sister's rudeness, Elizabeth hastened to get back on track, asking: 'Is your principal role to monitor French ships, sir?'

'Indeed it is. When the wind blows hard from the west, which is pretty often, our warships sail for the protection of Dungeness Bay, over towards Seagate. And that's when the French privateers grab the opportunity to swoop down and capture our merchant vessels. My main job is to spot enemy ships and signal warnings of their approach.'

'But there are other tasks?'

'We are also charged with keeping a look-out for French prisoners attempting to escape – and for smugglers unloading their cargoes. We have special signals for both eventualities and send them by hoisting different arrangements of balls and flags.'

'But how will the next station know what the signals mean?'

'Simple. They merely look in their copy of the code book that we are all issued with and all is revealed.'

Elizabeth laughed sweetly. 'How clever!'

Anne was far more interested in status and reward, asking: 'As a commander, are you above our brother Oliver, who is merely a lieutenant?'

'Bless you, no. In reality we rank equally in our present shore-bound situations. Like Sea Fencible detachments, coastal signal stations are normally commanded by lieutenants—'

'Yet you are styled as a commander?'

'Styled, but not paid as … It's a long, boring story. I was – am – a commander, but sadly there don't appear to be nearly enough ships to go round, and being without one on half pay did not appeal.'

Anne mouthed: 'Hmm, only *half* pay …'

'So rather than lounge around for the rest of the war I reluctantly accepted an appointment to a coastal signal station where I can at least see the sea. Their lordships at the Admiralty were kind enough to allow me to retain my rank while paying me as a lieutenant.'

'So, like our brother, would you prefer to be at sea rather than looking at it?'

'Prefer? I'd give my right, er, my eye teeth to serve anywhere but here. In fact I have gone hat in hand a number of times to plead with their lordships for a sea posting, but am always sent packing with my tail between my legs.'

'So you are here for the duration?'

'I pray not but fear so. However, enough of my career frustrations, ladies, let us move on to more pleasant matters, such as luncheon!'

He had apologised in advance for what he warned would be a ragamuffin meal, but it proved not to be.

The truth was that Armstrong had ordered the courses from a Hastings inn. In view of the distance from inn to signal station he had deemed a cold collage safest, as fewer things could go wrong with it.

He had arranged for the dragoons to serve it up, being less likely to drop it in the ladies' laps than his midshipman or the coarse-mannered sailors.

During the meal Elizabeth asked: 'Tell me, sir, you were involved in that Normandy privateer affair with Oliver, were you not?'

'I was indeed, Miss Anson. I was able to furnish your brother with intelligence of the privateer's movements as the Frenchman sailed up and down the coast annoying coastal traffic. Your brother was thus able to prepare a trap.'

Pointing to a rack in the corner, he added: 'Those are the very muskets we fired to alert him to the privateer's approach.'

'How very exciting! I should very much like to fire a musket, although I doubt I have the shoulders for it.'

Armstrong was on the point of telling Elizabeth that she had extremely attractive shoulders, when they were hailed from the duty look-out: 'Deck there! Sail, approachin' from the west!'

'Ah, this may be of interest to you ladies. Since we have more or less finished lunch, may I suggest we go outside and see what's occurring?'

He led the way, grabbing his telescope, and they gathered on the seaward side of the station. Armstrong shouted to the lookout: 'What's afoot, Lloyd?'

'Sail coming west to east just beyond the fishing boats. Looks quite big and a bit like a warship of some kind.'

Armstrong handed the telescope to Elizabeth. 'Perhaps you'd care to take a look through this glass. I'm afraid it's only one of Dolland's navy issue versions. Your brother has bought himself a superior model, you know, having been lucky with prize money.'

Elizabeth took the proffered glass and raised it awkwardly, turning to Armstrong to ask sweetly: 'It's awfully heavy. Could you ...?'

'Of course. Allow me to help you hold it up and adjust it for you.'

Their hands touched lightly and her head brushed his shoulder as they raised the telescope together and she peered into the eyepiece, exclaiming: 'Look at the fishing boats, how pretty they are, like little toy boats!'

He was enthralled himself and might have taken her in his arms there and then had it not been for her obviously disapproving sister watching like a hawk.

'Oh, how close they look through the glass! But that one's bigger and appears to have guns. It's flying a very pretty flag of some sort, red white and blue, so it must be one of our warships!'

Armstrong shielded his eyes and peered out to sea. 'No, by God! It's not ours – it's one of theirs – a Frenchman!'

Elizabeth laughed lightly. 'How thrilling to see the enemy – and so close I feel I can almost reach out and touch them!'

He almost snatched the glass from her and focused on the mystery ship. 'It's a privateer for sure, of twelve, no, fourteen guns, and heading east. I'm afraid our party is over, ladies!'

He had seen similar vessels used in the Mediterranean along the North African and Spanish coasts for transporting horses. This looked as if it had been converted – a fast, flush-decked, three-masted vessel of 300 or 400 tons and a single tier of guns, roughly equivalent to a British sloop.

'The crafty blighter … sorry ladies, I mean *devil*, is going right through the fishing fleet!'

Snapping the glass shut, he explained: 'There is work to be done! That Frenchman is heading towards Dungeness, Seagate and points east, no doubt intent on snapping up merchantmen just as the Normandy privateer did. I must send a warning signal forthwith.'

He called for the midshipman: 'Roust out the signal for enemy privateer off the coast, heading east – and look lively about it!'

The boy dashed to the store, but Lloyd and his mate had beaten him to it and were already putting the appropriate flags and balls together and attaching them to the ropes ready to raise up the yard-arm.

'When they're ready you may help hoist the signal if you wish, ladies, and help strike a blow for old England.' But, he noted, only Elizabeth took up his offer, her face shining with the thrill of it.

Excusing himself, Armstrong went off to compose a written message and Dragoon Dillon set about readying his horse. It was a clear day and the flag signal would be copied down the line, but the only way to get a fuller message away was by one of the specially-selected, well-mounted, light cavalrymen attached to the station.

Armstrong emerged with the written message and Dillon took it, saluted, mounted up and trotted off towards the next station at Dungeness. From there, Armstrong told his visitors as they made their departure, the procedure would be repeated eastward, with the added warning signal, Number 65: "Sea Fencibles are to embark and the boats be in readiness to act."

He raised his hat as the Anson sisters' coach followed Dillon down the track and wondered if the alert would be received in time for the fencible detachments along the coast to man shore batteries and gunboats and see off the Frenchman.

In particular, he hoped Anson would be alerted in time to bring off another coup as spectacular as the capture of the Normandy privateer.

19

A Clash at Seagate

Sam Fagg was relaxing in a chair outside the Sea Fencible building enjoying an afternoon pipe and chatting to Tom Hoover when news of the latest privateer threat reached Seagate via a dragoon galloper from Dungeness.

Immediately Hoover set off to gather as many fencibles as he could find, telling them to rendezvous at the gun battery.

With Lieutenant Anson on his way to Dover, Fagg reluctantly sent Tom Marsh to inform Captain Hoare that a privateer was heading east along the coast and was expected in the Seagate area imminently.

The gallant captain arrived huffing and puffing from another session of "fostering good relations with the civic authorities" – a phrase and concept he had adopted with enthusiasm.

'What's afoot? Another damned Frenchman, eh?'

Fagg knuckled his forehead. 'That's right, sir. Anuvver bleedin' Frog, and 'e's 'eadin' this way. In the habsence of Lieutenant Anson what's gorn orf to Dover Castle, on orders like, I told meself I'd better hinform you, sir.'

'Quite right, bosun. Now we must summon the men to man the battery.'

'Already sorted, sir. Tom Hoover's gorn orf roundin' up as many as 'e can find and sendin' 'em down 'ere. And as soon as I've got enuff I'll get *Striker* under way.'

Now, following the already near-legendary Battle of Seagate the two new gunboats trialled successfully by the detachment had been named *Striker* and *Stinger*.

To their own considerable amusement, their crews had proposed they be named *Flogger* and *Starter*. This was a reference to the assurance they had been given when first parading under Lieutenant Anson, that there would be no flogging of his men with a cat-o'-nine-tails or "starting" as customary in the navy with a blow from a rope's end to liven up dozy sailors.

But Anson, who preferred to lead by example and natural authority, drew the line at humour when it came to the naming of His Majesty's vessels, however insignificant in the scale of things nautical. And so he had decreed names that implied aggression against the enemy rather than internal discipline.

Hoare gestured acceptance to Fagg's assurance that the response to the latest privateer threat was in hand and, still perspiring from the effort of breaking away from his postprandial port and cheese, mopped his brow with a handkerchief.

The bosun asked cheekily: 'You coming wiv us in the boat, sir, to take command, like, you bein' what they calls the over-all big white chief ...?'

A momentary look of alarm registered on Hoare's puffy cheeks.

'I'll take charge ashore. There's the second boat's crew to organise and I'll need to get the battery into action as soon as we have enough hands.'

Fagg's opinion of the captain's leadership skills could not have been lower after the Normandy privateer affair. To him, Hoare was one of those officers, fortunately relatively rare in the service, of whom it was said that men followed more out of curiosity than anything else. So the bosun was determined to taunt his superior.

'Jacob Shallow 'ere can get the guns ready and there'll be plenty to man the second boat when the word gets round. So you won't be much use 'ere, will ye ... *sir*?' Fagg's years as a cocky foretop-man had made him a past master at delivering the insolent delayed "sir."

'Don't question me, man. Remember your place!'

A few fencibles had emerged from the pub and others around the town had been alerted and were gathering beside the battery. Fagg shouted: 'Get yourselves down to the 'arbour and get the canvas cover orf *Striker*. There's annuver Frog privateer 'eadin' this way!'

They turned to go, but he called them back: 'Nah, 'ang on, 'ang on! Don't go empty-'anded! You, Bishop, get powder and wads. There's shot an' whatnot in the boat. And the rest of you take oars.'

They disappeared into the detachment building to get the equipment and Fagg cursed at the delay. But oars would disappear if kept in the boats overnight.

He turned to Shallow. 'Jake, when Sar'nt 'oover gets 'ere tell 'im what's 'appening and that we'll need *Stinger* to back us up. Get the sar'n't to see if 'e can cobble enough rowers together.'

'Right-o, bosun!'

'But you stay 'ere, Jake, and get the battery into action once you've got enough bodies. At least get everything ready for when Sampson Marsh gets here.'

He made to leave, but turned to order: 'Once the Frenchman comes in sight, fire a gun. A bleedin' great bang might frighten the Frogs orf!'

Hoare stood back, taking no part in giving the orders, merely commenting: 'Very good, bosun. Carry on.'

Fagg gathered up the half dozen fencibles carrying oars and powder, and they set off for the harbour at a trot – or in his case a fast limp, his ankle broken during the failed cutting-out operation in Normandy still giving him trouble.

The canvas was already off the carronade when he arrived trailing after the rest and flung himself into the boat, breathing hard.

He noted with relief that Joe Hobbs, the detachment's best coxswain, was already at the tiller and a few more men had appeared.

'Right boys, let's get to it!' he shouted, and some elderly fisherman dropped the nets they were mending and helped shove the gunboat away from the harbour wall.

*

Through a borrowed glass – a fine three-foot model by Dolland, purchased at the princely sum of six guineas out his own pocket by Anson and kept in the detachment building – Hoare watched proceedings.

The privateer was now in plain sight heading directly for a coaster that had been caught unawares and wisely struck immediately after a single shot across her bows.

Hoare was joined by the mayor, who had heard the Frenchmen's warning shot and came hurrying from his shop in the High Street. He was wringing his hands. 'Oh dear, oh dear, Captain Hoare, another attack!'

'Ah, Mister Mayor. Fear not, all is under control. I have despatched some of my men in one of the gunboats to see off this Frenchman and I'll send the other boat as soon as I have enough hands to man it.'

'Thank heavens you're here, sir. What would we do without you?'

Hoare smirked. 'Merely doin' me duty. I'm about to get the battery into action so we'll soon send this pesky privateer packing.'

'Bravo, sir! Is there anything I can do?'

A brainwave struck Hoare. 'Why, yes, I do believe there is. You can join me and a few of our brave lads in manning one of the guns.'

The mayor looked doubtful.

'Just think: if you're seen to be helping us to get rid of this Frenchman you will be the talk of the town by nightfall. Why, they'll be making up songs about you in the pubs!'

The mayor liked the sound of that, but protested: 'I know nothing about gunnery whatsoever ... I'd be useless!'

Although Hoare privately agreed, he saw the value of involving the chief citizen and countered: 'Worry not – you'll be told exactly what to do.'

They moved over to where Jacob Shallow and a few fellow fencibles were busily uncovering one of the battery's 18-pounders.

Shallow had already sent two men off and now they came hurrying back, one with a swab and leather bucketful of water, the other with powder and wads.

Hoare pointed to a small pyramid of shot. 'Perhaps you'd care to select a ball to send to the Frenchmen, eh, Mister Mayor?'

'I would indeed, sir.' And, with a grunt at the effort, Seagate's chief citizen picked up one of the heavy balls and brought it to the gun.'

There was no time to obtain a slow match, but Shallow had a solution. 'You, Jacko!' he shouted at a newly arrived fencible who had a clay pipe clenched in his teeth. 'Keep that there pipe a-burning. We're going to need it!'

Hoare decided the moment had arrived to assume command but was unsure of what to do next, so tapped Shallow on the shoulder with the telescope. 'You, Swallow isn't it? Give the orders.'

'It's Shallow, sir. Aye aye, sir,' and, desperately trying to recall the drill he had learned from the detachment's chief gunner, Sampson Marsh, he yelled: 'Sponge!' and grabbed the sponge stick himself, dipped it into the bucket to wet it, plunged it down the barrel and wiggled it.

'Load cartridge!' The powder man obliged and rammed the cartridge home.

'Load ball!'

Hoare interjected: 'That's you, Mister Mayor.'

The mayor staggered forward and put the shot into the mouth of the gun as daintily as if he was presenting a bouquet to a lady and it, too, was shoved in with the ramrod.

'Load wad!' Again the powder man obliged.

Shallow cried: 'Point!' and looked around for someone to aim the cannon.'

'Then give the order to fire, Swallow!'

Shouting: 'It's *Shallow*, sir!' the greengrocer-cum-gunner snatched the pipe from the smoking Jacko's mouth, blew on it to make the tobacco flare and tipped some of the embers into the touchhole.

The makeshift gun crew flinched as the 18-pounder roared and lurched back, spewing forth the ball which flew well away from the privateer.

Nevertheless, it had startled the Frenchmen as well as the gun crew.

*

By the time *Striker* was rowed out, the French privateer had secured the coaster alongside. The master of the merchant vessel and his crew of three men and a couple of boys were crowded aft with hands raised while some of the Frenchman had already set about plundering his vessel.

With only half the oars manned, Sam Fagg was having trouble loading the carronade. The only chance he had of saving the day was getting off a shot and causing some real damage, but even when ready he dared not fire for fear of hitting the coaster or its crew.

As he rammed home the ball he shouted to the coxswain: 'See if ye can bring us round t'other side, Joe. There's no way I can 'it the effin' Frog from 'ere.'

Hobbs stuck his thumb up and ordered the starboard rowers to hold fast so that their opposite numbers could pull the boat round.

But with so little oar-power the manoeuvre took time – time Fagg could ill afford. He cursed his lack of preparedness. But then, he reasoned, it was hardly his fault.

Captain Hoare was constantly on the detachment's back bawling them out for paying out too many of the King's shillings, and no shillings meant no fencibles on permanent duty. It was as simple as that. The men had to earn a living rain or shine, not hang around the detachment without reward waiting for something that might never happen.

A loud crack from the Seagate shore battery turned all heads and the plundering Frenchmen looked around for the fall of shot. But when none could be seen they returned to the task of off-loading the coaster. She was too small for them to bother sailing away as a prize, so the intention was to sink her.

*

Back at the battery Captain Hoare peered through the glass trying to follow the ball but saw nothing but sea.

He turned to the gun crew. 'Just a touch wide, I think. Re-load Swallow!'

'*Shallow*, sir. Aye aye, sir!'

The crew repeated the swabbing and loading sequence, the mayor again being given the honour of selecting the ball destined, he hoped, to sink the Frenchman.

When all was ready, Hoare stepped forward and announced. 'I think we need some real navy expertise this time.' He took position beside the gun and squinted out to sea in the general direction of the drama being played out there, pronouncing: 'Port a bit, Swallow, and up a bit, I think.'

Shallow and his mates manhandled the gun so that it pointed slightly more to the left and elevated the barrel a smidgen.

'About right, don't you think, Mister Mayor?' Hoare asked.

The mayor shrugged. 'Looks near enough to me, sir, although gunnery isn't my ...'

The rest of the gun crew were muttering and Shallow spoke for them: 'Sir, sir! It looks like the coaster's in the way, like. If we fire we might 'it it!'

'Nonsense, man. You fencibles would spend half your lives arguing the toss given a chance. Just get on with it!'

'What, fire, sir?

'Yes, fire damn you ... *fire*!'

Again Shallow put his mate's pipe to the touch hole and again the gun roared and lurched back. The only difference this time was that there was no mistaking the fall of shot.

To cries of alarm from the privateer's crew and their English captives, the ball struck the coaster on the water-line amidships sending woodwork flying.

The coaster was already rocking and rolling in the heavy sea, and within minutes she was taking on a great deal of water and clearly about to sink.

The French boarders rushed to abandon the sinking vessel leaving their prisoners to their fate.

Barely able to keep his feet in the gunboat wallowing close by, Sam Fagg could hardly believe his eyes. 'Shit! Our own battery's gorn and blurry well sunk the effin' coaster!'

It took some moments for him to recover his wits and call to Joe Hobbs to swing *Striker* round so they could rescue the coaster's crew, now floundering in the water.

On board the privateer the French captain was even more astonished. And as he frantically urged his boarding party to speed up their return and ordered others to cut the ropes securing the sinking coaster he shook his head in disbelief. These crazy Rosbifs were clearly prepared to sink their own vessels rather than allow them to be taken – *'Encroyable!'*

*

Back at the battery, Hoare was already shifting the blame on others. 'Hmm, your gunnery was a bit awry there, Swallow. I do believe you've hit the coaster.'

'But, sir!'

Ignoring Shallow's protest, he raised the glass and focused on the drama being played out below, noting to his relief that the privateer was crowding on sail and leaving the scene.

Seagate's chief citizen was still registering shock, but Hoare reassured him: 'Never mind, Mister Mayor, we've frightened the Frogs off!'

'But what about *our* vessel?

Hoare waved a hand dismissively. 'Not to worry. We'll put the loss of the coaster down as due to enemy action.'

Swallowing hard, the mayor stammered: 'I, well, er, s-suppose—'

But Hoare interrupted him. 'Yes, yes. It's just as that fellow Bonaparte himself says: *"On ne fait pas d'omelette sans casser des oeufs"* – eh?'

The mayor was perplexed and Hoare translated: 'You can't make an omelette without breaking eggs. This is war!'

But despite his bravado, he knew that this was one privateer action that required playing down rather than up. However, he prided himself on being a past master at playing things up or down depending which best suited his career prospects.

He had famously played himself up after the *Seraphim* incident in which his captain had been decapitated – and of course the recent taking of the Normandy privateer.

But this one could be a trifle tricky. It was the first time he had actually presided over the sinking of a friendly vessel. No matter, he'd exaggerate the mayor's role so that the oaf would have his tongue in the mangle, so to speak.

And he'd use his false modesty ploy about his own part in it. It was a technique that had yet to fail the gallant divisional captain.

20

The Key to England

Dover Castle dominated the heights above the famous white cliffs and the port – imposing, seemingly impregnable and popularly known as the Key to England, at least to those with a shaky grasp of its history.

Anson knew *his* – and that a small party of Dover men had seized it for Parliament during the Civil War, proving to him at least that a clever plan carried out with determination could triumph over apparent might.

He made his way to the Keep, the castle's innermost stronghold, and checked in with the sergeant of the guard. 'Name of Anson, sir? You're expected by the officer in room three, down that passage there and third left.'

Rapping at the heavy oak door marked "3" he heard a faint voice from within call: 'Enter!' and did as he was told.

A familiar figure rose, smiling, from behind the large desk that dominated the cell-like office.

'Ah, Anson, we meet again! Come in and take a pew.'

'Colonel Redfearn! Good to see you again, sir. It's been quite a while since we met – at dinner at my father's rectory a while back.'

'Yes, it was something of a celebration of your escape from France and you were surrounded by a trio of extremely attractive young ladies, I recall.'

Anson remembered the occasion with a twinge of embarrassment. It was where he had first been hooked by Charlotte Brax stroking his thigh under the table, and Bosun Fagg had discomfited him by loudly referring to the caviar as "snail shit."

Not least, after a good deal of wine and port, Anson had, in hindsight, waxed a touch too lyrical when giving this very same colonel of engineers the benefit of his views on France and the French, the ease of going back and forth across the Channel unhindered, and the likelihood or otherwise of an imminent enemy invasion.

But he reckoned Redfearn was the kind of man he could level with. 'I fear that after rather too much wine I allowed my tongue to run away with me a little too freely that evening, sir. I hope I didn't make too much of a fool of myself trying to impress you with what little knowledge I had of all things French ...'

'Not at all, Anson. In vino veritas, as the Latins said, and all the male guests downed many a glass. I woke next day with quite a headache myself. Your father keeps a damn fine table – and cellar, thanks no doubt to a bit of help from the free traders!'

He smiled at the recollection. 'But let's get to the business in hand. I've been following your exploits closely since then.'

Anson was apprehensive.

'You were, as I thought, the ideal man to lead Sea Fencibles – and the taking of the Normandy privateer proved that.'

'But Captain Hoare —'

'Stuff Hoare! I hear he's claiming the credit, but my sources know better.'

Something jogged Anson's memory. The colonel's name had been mentioned by Commodore Home Popham when he was first briefed about the likelihood of future clandestine missions.

It was now perfectly clear. Colonel Redfearn was a key figure in anti-invasion intelligence.

'Anyway, I have more important matters to discuss with you.' The colonel handed him a document, explaining: 'It's a copy of a letter Home Popham wrote to Sir Charles Grey some time ago.'

Anson glanced at it and looked up questioningly.

'Yes, read it now. Take your time.'

Redfearn leaned back in his chair, massaging his forehead as Anson read the letter. The only sound was the loud ticking of a wall clock.

The letter set out Home Popham's assessment of the practicality of an enemy landing on the stretch of coast from the North Foreland in Kent to Beachy Head in Sussex. It dismissed the possibility of a partial attempt by the French as being likely to have only a limited effect, and went on to consider the conditions that would make a general invasion possible on the coasts within what he termed "the Narrow Seas".

The letter continued: "... it must also be considered what wind will permit the transports to sail out of every port in Holland, Flanders and France to the eastward of Havre de Grace, and at the same time insure the smoothest water on the coasts of England, because they can have no covering navy, and must very much depend on small vessels for the advantage of beaching."

A wind from East to East North East, the letter stated, would enable invasion craft to sail from French-occupied Holland for the southern part of Suffolk and Essex. From Sluys, Ostend, Nieuport and Dunkirk the same wind would carry them through the Queen's Channel and South Channel up the Swale past Faversham; and, the letter emphasised there were plenty of suitable boats in Holland and the turbot fishermen were as well acquainted with the coasts of Essex and Kent and the channels leading to the Thames as English pilots.

Anson turned to the marginal note and was surprised at the number of enemy-held ports listed: Gravelines, Calais, Boulogne, Etaples, Crotoy, St Valery – a name that gave him a jolt as he recalled the raid on the mole there in which he had been wounded and captured – Treport, Dieppe, Fecamp, and Havre de Grace, after which Home Popham had written: *"... distance from the above place to the S.W. coast of Kent and coast of Sussex from fifteen to twenty-five leagues."*

The letter continued with Home Popham's assessment of the invasion coast, concluding that the presence of the British fleet in the Downs was security enough against a landing between the North and South Forelands.

But it suggested that, significantly for Anson:

"... westward of Folkestone to the sea wall near Dymchurch there is a fine bay of six miles on which infantry may land at any time, and cannon and cavalry may be landed at half tide; and in many places ... it is so bold a shore that large ships may anchor within half a mile ..."

Redfearn held out his hand for the letter. He took a long hard look at Anson, as if weighing up whether or not he could be trusted with a piece of information of great sensitivity.

'There is something else you should know.'

'Sir?'

'This letter was written to Sir Charles Grey, who commands the Southern District. Other than him only a handful of people – those who have a need to know – have had sight of it—'

Anson knew of General Grey, who had made his headquarters at Barham Court, near Canterbury, just a few miles from his father's parish. Sensing that he was about to be lectured on the importance of maintaining tight security, he interrupted: 'Have no fear sir, I will keep it close to my chest.'

The colonel shook his head and replied gravely: 'I would expect nothing less. However, I regret to tell you that the detailed information in this document is *already* in the hands of the French.'

Anson was taken aback. 'The French, but how can that possibly be? Surely Sir Charles is totally trustworthy!'

Redfearn shrugged. 'That goes without saying. He is after all the very man charged with overseeing defence of the invasion route counties. What you need to understand, young man, is that the Admiralty, and no doubt General Grey's headquarters, tend to be gossip clubs in which a traitor – whether for ideological reasons or for money – can easily skulk while pretending patriotism and loyalty.'

'So there could be a spy at the very heart of the navy?'

'Or on General Grey's staff? Not necessarily. Others, in politics, the Treasury and elsewhere could have been aware of the letter and leaked a copy to the French.'

'But how can you be certain that it has fallen into their hands?'

Redfearn smiled wryly. 'I can be certain because I have been informed, through our own network of, shall we say *friends*, that the French have a précis of this letter annotated in part by the First Consul – Bonaparte himself – commenting on the assessments of likely landing beaches.'

'Good grief!'

'Grief indeed! And I am led to believe that other marginal notes are probably attributable to the officer in command at Boulogne.'

'So the traitor would have somehow got the document to them at Boulogne? But how? Smugglers?'

'Quite so, they are still running almost at will between the Kent coast and the Pas de Calais. For gold, such light cargo could easily be taken across to Boulogne on a routine fishing or smuggling trip. As you are aware from your own recent escape, the French positively encourage such traffic.'

Anson knew at first hand that security at the Channel ports was virtually non-existent but nevertheless it was something of a shock to hear that such sensitive news could so easily reach the hands of the French.

'The alarming thing about all this is that among those who handled the document was your predecessor.'

Anson was dumbfounded. 'Not Lieutenant Crispin?' He had never met the man but knew of his disappearance following an embarrassing incident, one of many, involving attempting to drill his men after having drink taken.

'Indeed, one and the same. I am led to believe he is now in Boulogne, drinking himself to death at the Frogs' expense, using his knowledge of our local geography to help them make their invasion plans – and interrogating smugglers and any prisoners they are able to take to monitor what we are up to.'

Horrified, Anson exclaimed: 'I'm appalled that a British sea officer would descend to such treachery!'

'Cheer up, my boy! Already the information in the letter is outdated and the important thing is that the French don't know that *we* know that *they* know.

Redfearn smiled at his own word-play that had clearly flummoxed Anson, and explained: 'All is not lost simply because the Frogs know this assessment of the likely invasion beaches. If they invade based on Home Popham's assessment they will be in for a few extra nasty surprises. I am told that in his marginal comments Bonaparte himself has actually confirmed that Home Popham was correct, saying things like: "This is the opinion of all the pilots." Flattering, don't you think!'

'So, if they don't know we are aware that they have seen this letter …?'

'And I am confident that they don't, so my reading is that when planning their invasion the enemy will take careful note of what the assessment says and react accordingly, expecting that we will be taking steps to counter landings in what Home Popham assessed as the most vulnerable spots and striving to surprise us elsewhere. I expect them to employ subterfuge – the French invented the word, after all – using feints in places this assessment mentions to disguise their true intentions.'

Nodding, Anson could see it clearly now. 'So they will attempt their main landings where they think we will least be expecting them?'

'Exactly, but we *will* be expecting them! Now, to the business in hand. You will be aware that Nelson has been appointed to command the anti-invasion forces in the Downs, with Deal as a focal point. We believe there are upwards of 75,000 men encamped between Flushing and Le Havre and already the French have at least a hundred shallow-draught barges on hand with many more on the way.'

'So the threat is very real, sir?'

'The government has let it be known that it fully expects the French are about to make an immediate decent on our coast. And so Nelson is planning raids on Boulogne aimed at destroying the greater part of the

French invasion flotilla before it sails. He first aims to soften up their defences with a bombardment and later mount a major cutting-out raid.'

Anson guessed what was coming.

'Now, before the bombardment I want you to arrange for Lieutenant Hurel to be put ashore in the Boulogne area. His main task is to make a detailed report on the effectiveness of the attack and what steps the French take to strengthen their defences. Such a report will be invaluable to Nelson when planning his follow-up attack which will not just involve a bombardment but will also aim at cutting out or destroying the outer line of vessels – and the landing craft within the harbour.'

This was exciting news for Anson and there and then he resolved to make sure he was in on the action himself.

'Hurel will have an important secondary task. I want him to make the French believe he has escaped from the hulks and bribed smugglers to drop him off on the French coast.'

'That has the benefit of being close to the truth, sir.'

'Indeed. He will be given various low-level intelligence – stuff he could well have picked up on his way through Kent – and when in Boulogne he will make contact with the military authorities, spin them his yarn, tell them what he has managed to find out and offer himself as an agent. He can offer to return to England. Not least I want him to try to find out who the spy is in our camp.'

'And if it *is* Crispin and if he's there?'

'Then I want him to be brought back, alive if possible – and that's where I trust you will be able to help spirit him away.'

For a moment Anson considered the enormity of the task he and Hurel were being set. 'Hurel will be putting his life at extreme risk, sir. Walking into the lion's den, so to speak.'

'Of course, but he is a brave man. Hurel is not quite what he seems. He has been posing as a republican, but in reality he is an aristocrat, and a royalist. He will not rest until he has done his utmost to bring down the foul republican regime that robbed him of his family. No, he is the Baron de ...' Redfearn hesitated. 'His real name must remain a secret between him and me, but I can tell you that he is rightfully the heir to a great estate complete with chateau, and lives for the day when he can avenge his family – and regain their lost lands.'

Anson did not reveal that Hurel had already confided this to him – and quite possibly every young lady he had met since departing the hulk.

'You, Anson, are required to put this officer ashore in France, stealthily and safely, mind, and accompany him and assist him in every way. I will let you know when to go. But not before it is appropriate for you to know.'

'I understand, sir.'

'I have chosen you for this mission because I know from the service you performed during the late mutiny that you are a resourceful young man – and that you have acquired some valuable knowledge of the Pas de Calais region following your capture and escape. You have some French, I believe, and no doubt many of your fencibles have a good deal of experience getting goods in and out of France – the so-called free trade?'

Anson's wry smile confirmed it.

'However, you are not to tell your men what you are about. Our coastal areas are alive with flapping ears and wagging tongues. If anyone – *anyone* – is told anything you can be sure it will be across the Channel like a rat up a mooring rope and the whole mission will be compromised. No, keep them in the dark. And keep Hurel under wraps!'

21

The Duel

Anson spent the night as Colonel Redfearn's guest at the castle and rode back next morning to Hardres Minnis, arriving at the rectory with a sore head as well as tender nether regions, vowing not only to moderate his intake of alcohol but to give up riding at the earliest opportunity.

As he turned into the driveway he was surprised to see Doctor Hambrook's pony and trap in front of the house attended by the young groom, Jemmy Beer.

He dismounted, handed him Ebony's reins and asked: 'What's afoot Jemmy?'

The boy scratched his head. 'Don't rightly know, Master Oliver, but seems the foreign gennelman what come with you t'other day has bin shot.'

Anson was stunned. 'Shot? Good grief! Is he dead?'

'Don't think so, sir, on account of when he come back with your sisters a-clutching of his arm and covered in blood he was laughing and joking – happy, like. That's all I know. Me dad sent me to fetch the doctor and told me to stay out here looking arter his pony.'

Anson nodded and hurried indoors where George Beer directed him to the kitchens. 'The doctor wanted a table to lay him out on, so we put him in here. Your mother didn't want to get blood all over the dining room ...'

Flinging the door open, Anson was astonished to see his sisters fussing around Hurel who was lying on the long kitchen table where the servants dined, his head pillowed by his blood-stained green velvet jacket.

'What on earth's happened?'

Elizabeth exclaimed excitedly. 'Monsieur Hurel – le Baron – has fought a duel and he's been wounded, but he's going to be all right, isn't he doctor?'

'A duel? Good grief!'

Doctor Hambrook, who had tended Anson following his escape from France, looked up from cleaning a wound in the Frenchman's shoulder. 'Merely a flesh wound. It's clean and should heal nicely.'

'But who, how ...?'

Hurel, basking in the admiration of the Anson sisters, grinned happily. 'An affair of 'onour, mon ami.'

Anne was bursting to tell the story. 'We took him up to the hall and while we were walking in the gardens with the Brax girls that yeomanry officer, the one who fancies Charlotte—'

'That oaf Chitterling?'

Elizabeth nodded. 'Well he rode up in his full regimentals.'

'He'd come to see her, to propose we think—'

'But Charlotte made eyes at Monsieur Hurel—'

'To make Dickie Chitterling jealous, and, well, he got very angry.'

Anson could picture the scene. The coarse, dissolute, preening peacock who was always throwing his substantial weight around and boasting of his martial prowess clashing with a French aristocrat equally picky about his so-called honour. And both, no doubt, egged on by the presence of Charlotte Brax, her sisters – and Anson's own romance-hungry sisters, even if the girls had not actively encouraged them.

'But what sparked this off?'

'Dickie Chiterling insulted Monsieur Hurel, called him a Frog and some other things we can't repeat ...'

'He said le Baron was an enemy of Britain—'

'And he challenged him to a duel!'

That was hardly surprising. Anson had had similar run-ins with the ghastly Chitterling.

'Le Baron kind of shrugged and said he would be willing to meet him at a more suitable time and place.'

'But Dickie Chitterling called him a coward for not fighting then and there. We think he expected him to back down.'

Anson shrugged. 'But he didn't!'

Hurel looked up and smiled at Anson. 'As I said, it was a matter of 'onour, mon ami.'

'Of course. But what did you fight with?'

'I would have preferred swords. I was a fencing master, you know. But this Chitterling 'ad pistols in his 'olsters'

'Loaded?'

'That man loaded them.'

'You had no seconds, no-one seeing fair play?'

Hurel raised his good arm dismissively. 'The ladies were there. And Mademoiselle – his amour ...'

Anne prompted him. 'Charlotte.'

'Yes, Charlotte. She made us march ten paces, turn and fire.'

Anson nodded. Knowing Charlotte as intimately as he did he could see how she must have deliberately provoked the row by sucking up to the Frenchman and how she must have revelled in having the two men fight over her. 'Don't tell me, Chitterling turned and fired first. Am I right?'

Hurel frowned. 'But 'ow did you know?'

'Let's say it was an educated guess based on previous encounters with this man. But tell me, did you return fire?'

Elizabeth intervened. 'No, le Baron dropped his pistol when he was hit.'

'And Chitterling?'

Anne blushed. 'He shouted at Monsieur Hurel to go back to France, but, well, he used a very strong swear word beginning with "f", but that was the gist of it—'

'And he shouted something about that teaching him to keep clear of Charlotte, and that if he clapped eyes on him again he would kill him. Then he snatched the pistol back, mounted his horse and rode off.'

Anson had no doubt that had it been a fair fight Hurel would have stood every chance of coming out on top, certainly if the Frenchman had been able to choose swords, but then Chitterling was never going to fight fair.

Everything he had heard reinforced his opinion that Chitterling was a bully and a coward. Turning and firing before his opponent was unforgiveable. But then there had never been a need for the so-called duel in the first place.

He also realised that it would not be long before news of the encounter would be the talk of the county. The ghastly Chitterling and Charlotte would make sure of that – he to enhance his reputation among his cronies and she to emphasise how easily she could stir men to violence.

And no doubt Chitterling would paint a picture of himself as upholder not only of a lady's honour but as a patriotic hero having winged a French prisoner whom Anson had allowed to roam the countryside frightening children and old ladies.

The whole thing beggared belief, but at least the Frenchman had not killed his adversary. If he had there would have been hell to pay and the whole mission would have been compromised totally.

Anson told Hurel to come to his room once he had been patched up and left him in the hands of Doctor Hambrook and his adoring sisters, noticing to his disdain as he went out that both were vying to mop the grinning Frenchman's brow.

Back in his room he pondered the situation. He would now have to find somewhere else to hide Hurel away until the time was right and arrangements could be made to get them across the Channel.

It was not something he had wanted to rush but now this had been forced upon him.

A knock on the door interrupted his thoughts. It was Hurel, his left arm in a sling and a broad grin on his face. He clearly seemed to have found the whole episode an amusing diversion and loved being the centre of the girls' attention.

Waving the Frenchman to an armchair, Anson raised his hands in frustration. 'I leave you here for a day, just *one* day, and what happens? You roam the countryside hobnobbing with half the local spinsters, make eyes at the biggest temptress for miles around and allow yourself to be challenged to a one-sided duel with the most pumped-up idiotic poseur in the neighbourhood.'

Hurel's grin froze. This was a steely side to Anson that he had not seen before.

'Has your mind become addled in the hulks? Did you think for a moment about the need for secrecy for our mission? Or are you just an idiot? And just in case you don't understand the language well enough, the French word for it is *idiot*!'

Hurel's grin faded away completely now and he took on a chastened look. 'Mon ami, I am very sorry, but this cavalryman, well, 'e was so insulting.'

But Anson was far from finished. 'The navy has gone to great lengths to enable you to disappear from the hulks and prepare for our mission, yet you have compromised yourself in such a way that the whole county will hear of this fatuous so-called duel within a few days.'

Hurel spread his good arm in a gesture of helplessness.

'You might just as well put a notice in the newspaper. In fact, news of this probably *will* appear in the news-sheets. Then what? Smugglers take

English newspapers to France – for a price. I daresay that's where the republicans get much of their intelligence.'

'Yes, yes. I can see that now and I am very, very sorry … vraiment désolé.'

'First you gave yourself away to a passing gamekeeper at Ludden Hall, and now this ridiculous duel. I hope you realise that I will now have to find yet a *third* place for you to hide up and try to advance everything before the world and his wife hear what we're about. What's even worse is the fact that you are now wounded and will be even more of a liability than you were before.'

Hurel endured the tongue-lashing and, clearly somewhat chagrined, protested quietly: 'My arm is not 'urt bad and I will keep what you call a low profile from now on, mon ami, I promise. Please do not be angry with me. The lady led me on—'

'Charlotte Brax? She's no lady. She's a scheming minx who eats men for breakfast and I can see how she will have played up to you knowing how it would irritate that idiot Chitterling. To him, all Frenchmen are the same. Even if I were at liberty to tell him why you are at large he would choose not to believe it.'

Anson shook his head and sighed. He knew he would have to seek out Charlotte and plead with her to persuade Chitterling and anyone else they had told about the so-called duel with Hurel to put a brake on their tongues in the nation's interest.

It would not be easy, not least because there was something else he had finally made up his mind to tell her – a message she would not welcome.

*

Anson rode up to Brax Hall, recalling that the last time he was there with his friend Armstrong there had been flaming torches lining the long lime tree avenue welcoming guests to the ball at which Charlotte had made such a play for him.

Leaving Ebony with a groom who appeared at his approach, he mounted the wide steps and pulled the bell chain beside the oak double doors framed by impressive ionic columns.

The butler emerged, bowed in recognition and directed Anson to the large summerhouse on a rise above the ornamental lake.

He walked slowly across the lawn rehearsing what he had to say to Charlotte, knowing only too well that she had the knack of discomforting him every time she opened her mouth and that if he allowed her to take the initiative he would never get his points across.

She was sitting on the summerhouse verandah at an easel, paintbrush in hand and attended by a maid who she immediately dismissed with a casual wave of her hand on his approach.

He assumed she was painting a view of the lake, but, however reluctant he was, his eyes were drawn to her plunging neckline rather than her watercolour.

Treating him to a triumphant smile, she put down her brush and exclaimed: 'Why, if it isn't the sailor home from the sea, or wherever you scuttled off to after out last … *get-together*! I trust that you've come to resume where you left off?'

Already she had managed to make him feel ill at ease. 'I, er, I …'

She asked mischievously: 'Still tongue-tied? When we were last together I felt you were summoning up the courage to ask me something?'

Anson winced. The brazen Charlotte was clearly under the impression that he had come to propose.

He cleared his throat. 'Miss, er …'

'*Miss*! I knew that naval officers were somewhat formal, but I seem to recall that you called me by rather more affectionate names when we were in bed together!'

'I am sorry. Of course I meant to say *Charlotte*. Look, the thing is, I have something of the greatest importance to discuss with you.'

Again she smiled triumphantly. 'You appeared to be about to propose just before you were so inconveniently called away. But here you are again and I am ready and waiting. Is it to be on trembling knee or would you prefer to do it standing up?'

For a split second he mistook her meaning, but then realised it was another of her wicked double entendres.

He stuttered: 'Propose? Oh, no! You misunderstand. I have just learned of the ridiculous duel that yeomanry oaf provoked and I've come to ask you to keep Monsieur Hurel's presence to yourself – and to ask Chitterling to do the same. Hurel is French, yes, but he and I are involved in a clandestine mission of the greatest national importance—'

She rose and pouted. 'Mission! What mission? So you are *not* here to propose?'

'What is all this about proposing? I have never, at least, I hope I have never given the impression—'

Charlotte sneered. 'Impression? *Impression*! You gave me more than the impression you wanted to marry me when you bedded me. You were willing enough to make an impression on me then.'

'But Charlotte, this has all got completely out of hand. I am simply, well, not ready for marriage, what with the war and all—'

She spun on him, angry tears in her eyes. 'Not ready! The war? Rubbish! You're just a pathetic excuse for a man, spineless!'

'Look, I am so very sorry if I have led you to believe that what happened between us was anything, well, lasting.'

She spat out spitefully: 'What a fool I must have been ever to think of marrying the likes of you? What are you anyway? You are pathetic – just a not-so-jolly Jack Tar who hasn't even got a ship.'

Anson was taken aback.

Her face reddened. 'What *have* you got? You despise Dickie Chitterling but *he* has expectations and he would marry me tomorrow if he could. He'll inherit thousands of acres but you're nothing but a jumped-up parson's son with no land and no prospects.'

'But you knew my lack of prospects when you led me on—'

'Don't forget that my father chooses who has the living of this parish and he could snuff out *your* father, your family, just like blowing out a candle.' She demonstrated with a wave of her small pudgy hand, pursing her lips and blowing 'Poof!' as if putting out a flame.

He frowned in astonishment? 'What on earth's brought this on? Why are you attacking me, when only a few days ago—'

'Only a few days ago you shied off proposing and pretended to be called away on urgent duty.'

'That wasn't pretence. I was sent for …'

She screwed up her face. 'Don't you see? I want you to *marry* me. You have tested the goods and seemed to like what you had. At any rate you were only too keen to come back for seconds. Now you can put your money where your mouth is.'

Anson was shocked at her directness. 'How can you threaten me in this way? How can you talk about turning my father out of his living?'

'Then marry me, you fool!'

'In the face of such threats? I did not mean to take advantage of you. But it wasn't, how shall I say, entirely one-sided. In fact it was you who made the running from the very start.'

Hands on hips, she looked him in the eye. 'Let's be clear, sailor boy, if you marry me you will be made for life on the dowry my father will put up, and let's face it, most men would kill to bed me whenever they like. I know Dickie Chitterling would.'

Anson had been discomfited by her forwardness at their last encounter – at all their meetings, come to that. Now he found her coarse and disgusting. The thought of being bought and paid for by the gross Sir Oswald Brax and becoming the lapdog of his spoilt, wayward daughter, who appeared to be rapidly acquiring the squire's unpalatable habits, appalled him.

What's more, he'd had his suspicions before that she and the yeomanry poltroon had history. Now he felt sure he was right and it was all too much. With as much dignity as he could muster he hissed: 'Then go to Chitterling. You deserve one another.'

Like a spoilt child, Charlotte frowned in anger, swung her arm and smacked him hard across the face.

Taken completely by surprise, he winced, stared at her, resisting the urge to strike back, then turned on his heel and walked quickly away.

22

Under Wraps

Summoned in haste to Hardres Minnis rectory, Hoover and Fagg arrived in Tom Marsh's pony and trap and were directed to the summerhouse where Anson awaited them.

He explained the predicament Hurel had foisted on him as a result of what he told them had been "a ridiculous so-called duel" with Chitterling.

'This means I have to find yet another place for Monsieur Hurel to hole up until we are ordered to make the crossing to France.'

Fagg shook his head. 'Ain't no use sending 'im down to Seagate, sir. You couldn't keep nuffink secret there – not fer five minutes.'

Anson agreed. 'No, I'd thought of that of course, but it wouldn't do. He needs to be kept out of the public gaze and chaperoned by someone who can keep a firm grip on him, and I have the very place in mind.'

Hoover put up his hand. 'I reckon the ideal place would be Fairlight. The signal station's off the beaten track, isn't it? And it strikes me Commander Armstrong would be great at keeping him in order – and entertained.'

'I had been thinking along the exact same lines. Commander Armstrong has the rank and clout to keep someone like Hurel in line – and he speaks very good French so they can while away the lonely hours gabbling together.'

He smiled at the thought. 'Besides, Armstrong lacks entertaining company and from what I've seen and heard of Hurel he certainly provides that!'

'Does the doctor reckon he's fit to travel?' Hoover asked.

'No, he'll need an eye kept on him for a few days by someone in the medical line.'

'Mister Shrubb?'

'Exactly!'

And so they hatched a plan. Hurel would be sent to stay at Wealden Bottom with the apothecary until he was fully fit, and then sent on to Fairlight.

He would travel in Tom Marsh's pony and trap, with Hoover accompanying him, armed and in uniform. That way he could deal with any over-inquisitive people – including the military – that they might encounter. Few would dare to argue with a sergeant of marines – and an American, what's more …

*

Hurel was alone in his room having eluded the Anson sisters following the severe dressing down he had been given for flirting and getting himself into the messy duel.

When Anson entered, the Frenchman looked up with a worried expression. 'You 'ave asked Mademoiselle Charlotte to keep silent about my, er, encounter with the fat cavalryman?'

Anson managed a hollow laugh. 'I think it safe to say that my diplomacy was such that she will now do exactly the opposite of anything I asked her to do! And if I were to approach Chitterling himself he would laugh me out of court and spread the word about you even wider.'

Crest-fallen, Hurel asked: 'So does this mean we must leave 'ere?'

'It does. You must leave tomorrow, wound or no wound. First I will send you to the home of Phineas Shrubb, an apothecary who has served in the navy as a surgeon's mate. He now looks after the medical needs of my Sea Fencible detachment. He will tend your wound until it is healed. His home is in a remote place and he will hide you away when anyone calls. My master-at-arms, Sergeant Hoover, will accompany you.'

'As bodyguard or jailer?'

'Both. Meanwhile I will write a letter to my friend Commander Armstrong who is in charge of a signal station further down the coast. I am sure he will agree to hide you there and when you are fully fit you and Hoover will go there.'

'Very well.'

'But from now on you must speak to no-one other than those I have named, certainly not to any young ladies. If you do I will happily kill you myself. Is that understood?'

Hurel noted the half smile on Anson's lips and agreed: 'Absolutely, mon ami!'

'Shrubb is also a Baptist preacher, so he may well attempt to heal your soul as well as your wound, and there will be no opportunities for horse racing, cricketing, card-playing, dancing or cockfighting!'

Not knowing of these Baptist taboos, the Frenchman was puzzled. He indulged in none of these pursuits, but in the circumstances he thought it best not to make some amusing remark.

'When you are transferred to the signal station you will find Armstrong more agreeable company. He lived in Paris for a time when he was younger and he is able to serve up good French wine, courtesy of the smugglers.'

'Thank you, mon ami. I will be on my best be'aviour.'

'Yes, you will. I shall warn Armstrong that while you are with him he must keep all females at bay so that you are not tempted to tell them your life story.'

Hurel assumed an only partially sincere crestfallen look.

'And as it is a naval station you must resume your admittedly thin disguise as a common sailor, doing menial tasks and obeying Commander Armstrong's every order. Is that also understood?'

The Frenchman now clearly *was* crestfallen and showed it sulkily with his habitual Gallic shrug.

But Anson had not quite finished. He fixed Hurel with his most withering stare. 'Lastly, remember to remain security-conscious at all times. Ideally, forget that you are French and stop gabbling on all the time!'

*

Before despatching Hurel to Shrubb's home to recuperate, Anson wrote a note for Hoover to deliver to Armstrong when they moved on to Fairlight:

"Dear Armstrong

Via my master-at-arms, I send to you for safe-keeping this French sea officer, Lieutenant Hurel. He is the royalist I mentioned during my visit who has been inflicted upon me by the chain of command because he is willing to undertake a mission over the other side when the time is right. His cover here is blown thanks to an unfortunate incident concerning a lady. Kindly keep him under wraps and pass him off as an extra lower-deck hand. Feel free to treat him as such. With your permission, Sergeant Hoover will stay with you to sheepdog him. Hurel speaks good English, almost without ceasing, and it would be wise not to expose him to female company of child-bearing age. Nevertheless, he should provide you with the amusing company your lonely post normally lacks. I will send for him when it is time for his mission. Grant me this great favour and I shall be even more in your debt.

*Yours ever
Anson."*

*

Hurel was duly delivered to the home of Phineas Shrubb in Tom Marsh's pony and trap with Sergeant Hoover in close attendance on Anson's horse Ebony.

What had originally been built as a smallholder's cottage with its part-flint, part-brick walls topped by a Kent peg-tiled roof, the peculiarly-named Mount Zion stood, appropriately, on a hill overlooking the hamlet of Wealden Bottom.

Tom Hoover had been there before and was happy at this – another opportunity to see Shrubb's daughter Sarah.

He helped Hurel down from the cart and up the slope to the cottage where the apothecary was waiting to receive them.

'This, Mister Shrubb, is Lieutenant Hurel. He is French but on our side, if you follow my meaning.'

'So you must be a royalist, brother?'

'Oui, monsieur, bien sûr!'

'And therefore of the Roman persuasion, I deduce?'

'Oh, no! I definitely prefer the ladies!'

Despite being a Baptist lay preacher, Shrubb was a man of the world. His time in the navy mixing with the inhabitants of the lower deck had seen to that.

'I believe you mistook my question, brother, and thought I was referring to certain alleged practices of the ancient Greeks, rather than the Romans. What I meant is that I deduce you are a Roman Catholic.'

Hurel looked puzzled, but for once remained silent.

It was left to Hoover to explain their presence. 'Lieutenant Anson sends his compliments and asks, no, he said *requests* that you take a look at this Frenchman's wound, well, only kind of a scratch really, and keep him here for a few days until he's fully mended – under wraps.'

'Wraps?'

'Yeah. Mister Anson says Lieutenant Hurel has a habit of drawing attention to himself and wants him to keep his head down on account of some forthcoming mission.'

Shrubb understood immediately. It must be some sort of cross-Channel venture. 'And you, Thomas?'

'Mister Anson said I'm to stay to help keep him out of trouble and stop him telling his life story to any young women he comes across.'

'Including Sarah?'

'Especially Sarah!' Come what may, Hoover clearly intended to protect *her* from the Frenchman's amorous wiles.

*

Having rid himself of the annoying Frenchman for a while, Anson returned to Seagate with Fagg and at the fencible building was greeted by Jacob Shallow who handed him a letter.

It was marked "Urgent for Lieutenant Anson, Seagate Detachment, Sea Fencibles" and he noted it was from Captain Matthew Wills at Chatham.

Puzzled, he broke the seal and read:

"To inform you that the French prisoner known as Citizen Bardet has escaped from the Medway hulks ..."

23

On the Run

Anson was surprised but not completely taken aback at news of the Frenchman's escape.

When he had met Bardet in the prison hulk the Frenchman had made no secret of his intention to escape. In fact he had boasted that he would make his get-away whenever it suited him and Anson could not conceal the hint of a smile at the man's effrontery.

He read on:

"Bardet and two other prisoners were found to be absent when a count took place last night and the subsequent extensive search of the vessel revealed that a hole had been cut on the lower deck just above the low tide water-line. It is believed Bardet and his companions effected their escape via this hole and that the timbers were then replaced and sealed using some form of glue or wax. There was nothing to indicate when the hole was cut but it can safely be assumed that by concealing it as they did, some of the remaining prisoners had the intention of using it again. The positioning of the escape hole was ingenious to say the least. Had it been above the high tide water-line it would almost certainly have been spotted earlier by the guard force. However, as it was under water for a good deal of the time it was easily missed."

Anson could understand that. When he had visited the hulk following Hurel's fake funeral he had noted the galleried walkway around the outside of the ship just above the high tide water-line. It allowed patrolling guards to inspect for escape holes, but *not* below the low tide mark.

"Having removed the escape hatch at low tide, the prisoners must have waited underneath the walkway until the sentries were temporarily elsewhere and somehow got ashore, probably at night. There was no sign of a boat being used, so it is assumed that the escapers used some form of flotation gear or simply swam ashore.

Despite an extensive search by the militia, Bardet and his companions, Cornacchia and Girault, are still on the run.

To state the obvious, they can be assumed to be making their way to the Channel coast to seek a passage to France, perhaps with the assistance of smugglers. Some of that fraternity are known to assist escapers.

There is nothing to indicate that Bardet has any knowledge of the existence of your current guest, but of course if seen there is every likelihood that he will recognise *him. You are advised therefore to take the greatest possible care to keep your guest out of the public eye until your own crossing is accomplished."*

At first Anson had been half amused on hearing of Bardet's audacious escape and had not thought through how it could impact on him and his own mission.

But now he suddenly felt sick and involuntarily exclaimed: 'Good grief!'

What if Bardet somehow already knew, or if he became aware that the whole Hurel death and funeral story was a complete charade?

If Bardet managed to get to France first he could warn the authorities and the world and his wife would be on the look-out for Hurel.

Anson well knew that the French were far from stupid, especially in the matter of intelligence. It would be amazing if Hurel was not interviewed about his "escape". The French would be only too well aware that valuable intelligence could be gained from escapers – especially those who made it back via Kent, an armed camp now that it was once again in the firing line as the gateway for would-be invaders.

How long before two and two were put together?

Anson recalled Hurel's encounter with the gamekeeper the day they arrived at Ludden Hall – and the reason they had had to up sticks and disappear to his father's rectory.

And then, far from keeping a low profile, the wretched man had just fought a duel and was no doubt fast becoming the subject of gossip among half the young ladies of Kent – including both Anson sisters and all three of the Brax girls.

So much for staying under wraps. Hurel seemed to have no sense of decorum or security, and if Bardet and his fellow escapers learned that he was still alive and at large, the game could well be up before it began.

Anson resolved to send a message to Hoover telling him to warn Hurel of Citoyen Bardet's escape and of the vital importance of keeping his whereabouts secret.

*

After several boring and frustrating days hiding out in the woods there was news for Bardet when he led his fellow escapers back to the farmhouse at dusk.

The farmer waved them to the kitchen table where their evening meal was laid out and while they were eating joined them, pouring himself a tankard of ale.

'That French bloke staying near Faversham, remember? You wanted to know more about him.'

He immediately had Bardet's attention. 'You 'ave discovered who 'e is?'

'That's right. He was staying with some old gent who's a bit eccentric, like.'

'Fou? You say 'e is mad?'

'Not mad exactly. Appears the old boy cuts up dead rats and whatnot to see what they had for their dinner. Lives in a big house near a village called Ludden.'

'And you say the Frenchman *was* staying with 'im?'

'Yeah. One of our contacts who delivers the newspapers thereabouts heard the servants mention a Monsieur Hurel, but seems he's moved on and we can't find out where.'

Bardet was taken aback. 'But that man is dead!'

'How d'you know?'

'He was in the same 'ulk, but 'e died and was buried on the mudflats – a place they call Dead Man's Island ...'

'Must be some other bloke with the same name, then. This one was with an English officer by the name of Anson, who's stayed with the old gent before.'

'Anson!' Bardet slapped his thigh.

His brain was working overtime. Anson was the name of the English naval officer with a livid scar and powder burn spots on his face who came on board the hulk to tell him personally of Hurel's funeral which he had claimed to have attended – and to return the dead man's few pathetic possessions.

He had wondered at the time why Hurel had been taken ashore to die in the first place. Why would the Rosbifs do that when they had never done such a thing before?

Then it all fell into place. Hurel's illness and funeral must have been faked – and the English officer's visit to the hulk must have been staged to convince the other prisoners that he was dead. Maybe, probably, this Hurel was a royalist – a turncoat. Apart from giving fencing lessons for small change he had certainly kept very much to himself on board the hulk. Perhaps he had agreed to work for the English and this was their way of spiriting him away and trying to convince his fellow prisoners that he really was dead so that he could undertake some mission against the republic.

Bardet cursed himself for not suspecting anything like this before. If the two were together and making for the coast, the likelihood was that they planning to cross on some spying mission. That made every bit of sense – a Frenchman who could move around with almost total freedom and an English sea officer who would of course know what to look for.

And the French coast with landing craft in every port was just twenty or thirty miles away.

Bardet smiled to himself. You had to hand it to the Rosbifs. They were cunning, sure enough, but they had reckoned without his own escape and the extensive intelligence network employed by the smugglers helping prisoners on the run – for a price.

And how foolish of them not to have given Hurel a false name …

The smuggler watched Bardet's reaction curiously. 'You think this other Frenchman and the officer he was with are up to something?'

Bardet nodded. 'There is, as you English say, more to all this than meets with the eye. If you can locate this Frenchman I can arrange for a large reward, monsieur, and if you can bring 'im to me in chains, an even larger reward. I would like to 'elp 'im to return to France.'

*

Young Tom Marsh urged his pony down the lane and brought it to a halt with a tug on the reins and a cry of 'Whoah, Nobby!' at the bottom of the rough steps leading up to Mount Zion.

Ebony, loosely tethered behind, immediately set about the cow parsley beside the gate.

Naming his hillside house after a site in the holy land was what Phineas Shrubb confessed was "a biblical conceit" of his. It was little more than a humble cottage but it did double duty as an occasional Baptist meeting house for the cure of local souls and as an apothecary's shop for the cure of their earthly ailments.

Sarah Shrubb was gathering bullaces from the fruit tree in the hedgerow and called down: 'Have you come for Sergeant Hoover?'

'Yes ma'am – and for the Froggie, I mean the Frenchman!'

She smiled and put down her basket, half-filled with the wild plums. 'I'll fetch them.'

Tom Hoover was splitting logs with an axe in the yard at the back, watched by Hurel who was sitting on a grassy bank having absolutely refused to engage in such menial tasks.

The American put on his jacket and went down to the gate, saving the crippled Marsh what would have been a long hop up the steps on his crutches.

'Time for us to go, young Tom?'

'Yes, sergeant. I'm to take the Froggie and Mister Anson said I was to bring his horse back for you to ride alongside, like.'

Hurel, his flesh wound from the one-sided duel with Chitterling now thoroughly healed thanks to expert treatment from Shrubb with his ointments, was demonstrably keen to be on his way.

As he had muttered several times to Hoover, nightly Bible readings, plain food after the culinary delights of Ludden Hall and the rectory, and having to hide in the small, dungeon-like cellar whenever villagers came seeking the apothecary's potions, were not his preferred amusements, even though life at Wealden Bottom was something of an improvement on the hulks.

It was different for the American. He had not experienced any form of home life since he had joined the marines. His father had been killed fighting alongside the British during the War of Independence, and now the patriarchal Phineas Shrubb was filling that gap.

As to Sarah, Tom Hoover could not take his eyes off her. She was plainly, almost puritanically, dressed, yet her wholesome good looks still shone through. She was gentle and caring, but intelligent and confident too. And the marine had fallen for her, hook, line and sinker.

Hurel was keen to be off and quickly gathered his few possessions.

He told Shrubb: 'It was kind of you to 'ave me stay 'ere, monsieur, but I 'ave to say I did not enjoy my imprisonment in your cave.'

'You mean my cellar?'

'I assure you, m'sieur, that in France it would be called a cave. I 'ave been in many, including the very large one at my family chateau. In France they were filled with many bottles and vats of delightful wines, but yours 'as only bottles of medicine for curing disorders of bladders and bowels. Not the kind of cave I am accustomed to.'

And, although he did not speak of it, the Frenchman had become increasingly frustrated by the fact that whenever he tried to engage Sarah in conversation or grasp her hand on some pretext or other, Hoover had appeared – his sheepdog and her guardian.

Nevertheless, Hurel thanked his hosts as warmly as he was able and strode off down the steps.

But Hoover lingered. 'Lieutenant Anson would wish me to express his thanks to you, Mister Shrubb.'

The apothecary smiled benignly. 'It was nothing. We enjoyed having *you* as a guest, brother.'

Hoover turned to Sarah, and Shrubb tactfully walked away.

'We, *I*, will miss you, Thomas.'

'And I, you, Sarah.'

'Until we meet again, then.'

He took her hand and squeezed it gently, then turned, musket slung over his shoulder and pack on his back, loped down the steps and mounted Ebony.

Hurel was already embarked in the cart. Tom Marsh flicked his whip and they set off.

As they rounded the bend in the lane the American looked back and raised his hat to Sarah, standing alone beside the house, waving farewell.

*

The wisdom of having an extension built at Armstrong's own expense became apparent with the arrival of Hurel and Hoover at Fairlight Signal Station.

The commander read the note Anson had penned and chuckled over the references to the Frenchman's garrulity and the need to keep him away from women of child-bearing age. Chance would be a fine thing, he mused: the only females seen around the lonely station were generally over-large examples out picnicking with husbands and broods of children.

'Welcome, mon vieux,' he greeted his guest. 'And you, sergeant. Of course I shall be delighted to accommodate you both. You may take over what were my quarters until I invested in the slightly more private addition you see attached.'

'Most gentil of you, monsieur. I am sure we will be most comfortable.'

'You may wish to revise your opinion after a night spent next door to my signalmen and dragoons who produce loud snores and other unpleasant sounds throughout the night – hence my extension. Oh, and then there's

Lloyd's tame jackdaw which has the habit of emitting blood-curdling shrieks from time to time, presumably when it is having a bad dream.'

'Most charming. Unlike we French, you English have such an affinity with creatures. My former 'ost, Monsieur Parkin, kept a great many of them, although of course they were mostly stuffed.'

Armstrong raised an eyebrow. 'Quite, quite. Now, mon vieux, I will not read you the Articles of War, but Lieutenant Anson clearly wishes me to lay down hard and fast rules for your stay, and here they are …'

Half an hour later Hurel was left in no doubt of the dire consequences he would face if he failed to keep a low profile, tried to engage passing females in conversation or committed a great variety of other offences.

The commander was most certainly affable and gentlemanly, but he was clearly also a strict disciplinarian when it came to members of his shore-bound crew straying from the straight and narrow.

24

The Presentation Sword

Eager to enjoy his hour of glory, the divisional captain entered the town hall early to find the mayor and town worthies still involved in a discussion about the need to remove a line of pigsties along the church wall – and to request another resident to remove a growing dunghill near the gun battery.

All eyes turned on the gallant captain, who, resplendent in his number one uniform, doffed his hat to the chair and was ushered by the town sergeant to a prominent seat at the front.

Acknowledging the distinguished visitor, the mayor apologised for the over-running of the meeting, due, he said, to 'complex matters of a sanitary nature.' The truth was that the pigsties belonged to one councillor and the dunghill to another, neither of whom was willing to remove them.

Now that Captain Hoare had arrived, the mayor was anxious to conclude council business and forced a vote. A show of hands put the two miscreants in the minority and the mayor was happy to announce: 'Both motions carried and that concludes our business.'

Hoare guffawed: '*Motions* carried? Haw, haw – most apt, what!'

There was a polite titter from those who caught his drift and he turned to beam at the growing number of townsfolk gathering in the public seats, there not so much for the coming spectacle but for the free refreshments that were to follow.

No-one noticed Sam Fagg entering and, for once, quietly taking a seat at the back.

The town sergeant banged his mace on the bench and demanded: 'Pray silence for His Worship the Mayor!'

Clearing his throat, Seagate's chief citizen rose to speak. 'Gentlemen, Ladies – I see there are a few present – we have one further item on our agenda today. A most pleasurable item, if I may be permitted to say so ...'

Hoare nodded smugly: 'You may, Mister Mayor, you may ...'

The townsfolk tittered again and the mayor continued: 'It is my pleasant duty to welcome to this historic chamber the gentleman known to us as the victor of the Battle of Seagate ...'

There was a suppressed snort from the back where Fagg was having difficulty stopping himself from having an apoplectic fit.

' ... the hero, I might say, of the hour. The man who put an end to the piracy of a notorious privateer out of Normandy that had been disrupting coastal trade along our coast for many a month.'

Hoare was smiling pompously, his pink puffy features positively glowing with pleasure.

The mayor was by now fully in his stride. 'In ridding us of this scourge of our coast, the gallant Captain Hoare and his men – good local men who answered the call to duty as Sea Fencibles – have earned our eternal gratitude and respect.'

Fagg smothered another hollow laugh that would have been lost anyway amid the 'Hear, hears' from those around him.

The irony of the fact that none of those 'good local men' the mayor had mentioned was present appeared lost on the gathering. The simple fact was that Captain Hoare had specifically asked that the fencibles should not be invited because he did not want to turn the occasion into "a vulgar brawl".

They had been told that they could attend the bun-fight afterwards which would be more in keeping for them, while he and the town worthies were feasting at the Rose.

The mayor continued: 'This body, representing as it does the townspeople of Seagate, has therefore voted – unanimously I might add – to mark this great victory with the presentation of a special commemorative sword.'

He indicated the object in question, lying on a blue velvet cushion on the bench before him.

'This, fellow councillors, gentlemen – and ladies of course – is the very sword, the finest work of both master cutler and engraver, at a cost of, well, never mind the cost ...'

'Worth every penny!' one of his cronies offered.

'Yes, worth every penny. It is suitably engraved: *"To the victor of the Battle of Seagate, Captain Arthur Veryan St Cleer Hoare, Royal Navy, from the grateful Mayor, Corporation and Townsmen."* And the engraving includes various patriotic and nautical symbols, a British lion, an anchor and whatnot.'

With that, the mayor was handed the sword on its pillow by the town sergeant and called for Captain Hoare to step forward.

'And so, it gives me the greatest pleasure on behalf of the town of Seagate to present you, sir, with this sword, a symbol of our deep gratitude for the great gallantry displayed by you and your brave fellows in capturing the Normandy privateer.'

There was loud applause from all but Fagg, who near choked at the travesty he was witnessing.

Hoare, however, was completely unfazed. It was as if he now believed that he truly *was* the hero who had captured the privateer and he had deluded the local hierarchy into believing it, too.

Accepting the sword from the mayor, he pulled it from its scabbard, peered at the inscription and announced to more laughter: 'Yes, Your Worship, you *have* spelled my name correctly!'

He slashed the air with it theatrically and pronounced it 'perfect for seeing off Frogs!' before returning it to the scabbard and attaching it to his belt.

'Your worship, town councillors, ladies, gentlemen. I thank you from the bottom of my heart for the honour you have done me in presenting me with this symbol of my victory over the French. It was not my first tussle with the enemy, gentlemen, ladies – nor, I earnestly hope, my last. In fact, just a few days ago myself and your mayor had the pleasure of firing from the Seagate Battery at another French privateer that had the gall and audacity to approach our coast. And we soon sent him packing, did we not?'

The mayor preened himself and thanks to the ensuing clapping and many 'Hear, hears' not all heard Fagg mutter: 'And sendin' that poor coaster to the bottom, eh?'

Hoare paused for the applause to die down before adding: 'I accept this sword, not only for the albeit leading part I played in the action against the Normandy privateer, but on behalf of all the brave fellows serving under me who did their bit, however small, on the day. And finally …'

But his last words were lost under the wave of applause which continued until a voice from the back shouted: 'Where's Lieutenant Anson and Coney, the impress bloke, eh? *They* was the 'eroes, wasn't they? Why ain't they 'ere?'

There was a pregnant silence as Hoare tried, but failed, to see who had called out.

He looked to the mayor. 'It seems we have a dissenter in our midst. But yes, the anonymous heckler has a point. Of course the officers mentioned did their bit, too. However, I prefer to think of this victory as my *team's* effort. It would be invidious to single out some for praise and fail to mention others. We were all, as it were, in the same gunboats ...'

'But that's just it, ain't it? You wasn't in the boats, was yer?' the hidden heckler countered.

The mayor was looking uneasy. The triumphal presentation ceremony was in danger of turning into farce. He rose and called to the town sergeant: 'Remove that man!'

But by the time the town sergeant had made his way through the spectators to the back of the chamber Bosun Fagg had slipped away.

*

One of the small pleasures of the Reverend Thomas Anson's life in his country rectory was the arrival of the much-respected county newspaper, the *Kentish Gazette.*

Each week, rain or shine, he sent one of the servants down to the end of the driveway to await the local carrier, Hezikiah Champion, who delivered it along with various household items ordered from Canterbury.

Occasionally, when the rector was expecting some particular piece of news such as new ecclesiastical appointments, he would go down to collect it himself.

However, of late he had given up that practice since his son Oliver had been damned with faint praise in the outrageous letter, reprinted in the *Gazette,* that Captain Hoare had written to the Admiralty following the Normandy privateer affair.

But the rector's righteous anger about that had faded over time and today he was not expecting to find anything of particular interest in the newspaper columns – or at least, nothing to annoy him. But he was wrong.

Coffee beside him and pipe in hand, he settled into his favourite armchair and scanned the public notices and war news, mostly reprinted from the *London Gazette.*

It was when he turned the page that his eye was drawn to an item of county news and the reviled name of Captain Hoare jumped out at him.

In disbelief, he read:

"It is with considerable satisfaction that we record the award by the Mayor and Corporation of Seagate of a handsome presentation sword to

Captain Arthur Veryann St Cleer Hoare of the Royal Navy to mark the successful capture of the Normandy privateer Égalité.

The enemy brig, of 12 guns, was boarded while attacking merchant vessels off Seagate last month and taken after a stiff fight by Sea Fencibles under Captain Hoare's command.

Presenting him with the suitably engraved sword, the Mayor referred to the heroic performance of the captain and the local Sea Fencibles.

Accepting, the hero of the hour said he was glad to have rid the coast of a ruthless enemy and modestly said some of the praise should go to his robust sons of the ocean who played their part in the action."

The Reverend Anson grunted with distaste, flung the paper down as if it were unclean and cursed loudly enough to draw the attention of his entire household.

His wife came to investigate, but he brushed her questions aside, stormed out of the rectory and marched down the driveway kicking stones.

'This,' he told himself, 'is a step too far! This charlatan Hoare must be brought to heel. The Admiralty must be informed, but how?'

25

A Proposal

Returning to the rectory, Anson was greeted by his mother, her eyes shining with excitement at some anticipated triumph. 'Oliver, you have a visitor, a most important visitor – Sir Oswald is waiting for you in the library!'

Anson experienced a most uncomfortable sinking feeling.

Squire Brax was indeed waiting for him, seated in a leather-bound armchair, glass in hand and a decanter at his elbow, florid-faced and portly as Anson remembered him from the welcome home dinner his parents had thrown for him on his escape from France – the dinner at which Charlotte Brax had first bewitched him …

'Ah, at last, young Anson – thought you might have got yourself becalmed somewhere!' Brax guffawed.

'Sir Oswald, what a pleasure!' Anson lied. 'How may I be of service?'

The squire laughed coarsely. 'Service is it? Yes, young man, you *can* be of service by marryin' me daughter – and then you can do as much servicin' as you like, eh? You catch my drift?'

Anson did catch his drift and was taken aback. 'Are you here on behalf of your daughter, sir?'

'You could say that. I'm here because Charlotte's a chip off the old block. I know what she wants and that's to be married before she runs to fat like her mother. And for some unknown reason it's you that she wants. So, I'm here to close the deal.'

Anson was appalled. Brax made it sound like a cattle market transaction.

'But, sir, when I last saw your daughter she made it very clear to me, very clear indeed, that she did *not* wish to marry an impoverished ship-less sailor, and I was very happy to withdraw from the fray in favour, she led me to believe, of Chitterling.'

He remembered only too well the stinging slap round the face she had given him and his unspoken relief at being free of her – or so he had thought.

147

The squire poured himself another glass. 'But that's the point! You need not be impoverished. That's why I'm here – to make you a proposal.'

Anson was astonished. '*You* are proposing, to me? On her behalf ...?'

'Call it what you like. What I'm proposing is a settlement, y'see? A generous settlement. You'll be well off and you can give up the navy altogether if y'like. I'll give you a lump sum on marriage, a sizeable lump sum, an annual allowance – and I'll settle a few farms on you. The income from those'll keep the wolf from the door. And of course you'll have *her*. Half the men in the county would give their eye teeth to bed her!'

The thought struck Anson that a good few of them probably had already, but he managed to button his lip.

Brax sank another gulp of wine. 'Well?'

Anson shook his head slowly. He was not for sale. 'I'm afraid, sir, that however generous your offer I cannot accept. Absolutely not.'

'Then you're a bigger fool than I took you for. Why the hell not? What have you got in your veins, blood or sea water?'

'I fear I would not make your daughter happy for long, nor she me. And I have no intention of giving up the sea, no matter how impoverished.'

'Look, I've got the figures written down here by my legal fellow – the farms, lump sum, annual allowance and whatnot.' Brax brandished a paper. 'Take this and think about it. Discuss it with your parents. *They* think it's a handsome offer. You'll get none better.'

Anson was even more discomfited to hear that Brax had been discussing what he regarded as private matters with his mother and father and declined the proffered paper. 'There is no point in me looking at any figures, sir. Your daughter and I have had a falling out from which there is no return – certainly not on my side.'

Brax laughed. 'Just a lovers' tiff! I'm sure it was nothing that a kiss, a cuddle and a handsome dowry won't put right. So let's shake on it, eh?'

Now even more determined, Anson shook his head sadly. 'The truth is, sir, that Charlotte and I are not suited and I deeply regret allowing myself to become involved with her in the first place.'

The squire's already florid features turned an even deeper red and he snapped: 'Is that your final word?'

'It is, sir.'

Brax snorted. 'So be it! Your father and especially your mother will find it hard to forgive you for passing up a union with my family. You're a damned fool and I'll waste no more time on you. My next stop will be the

Chitterling place – young Dickie will be cock-a-hoop. *He* knows a fine bargain when he sees one!'

And with that the squire threw back the remains of his drink, rose and stomped out without a backward glance.

26

Armstrong at the Admiralty

Commander Amos Armstrong strode across the Admiralty courtyard for the umpteenth time, feeling far less confident than the assurance his smart appearance indicated.

Thanks to Dragoon Dillon back at Fairlight Signal Station, his boots were polished to a high degree and his best uniform showed only minor signs of weathering – and that caused by foul weather on Sussex cliff-tops rather than at sea where he had spent minimal time of late.

His hair had been recently cut by a Pall Mall barber who had also given him his closest shave since his last brush with the French, and his wind-reddened face – also due to seemingly permanent prevailing westerlies – positively glowed.

He mounted the steps, entered the hallowed hub of the Royal Navy and was directed to the infamous waiting room by one of the intimidating porters whose chief mission in life appeared to be making visiting officers aware of their lowly status and keeping them away from the hierarchy.

The porter, who had a repetitive sniff, teased him: 'Back agin, sir? Still arter a ship, are we? Best join all the others then, heh, heh ...'

Before Armstrong could think of a suitable riposte he had been herded into the familiar limbo inhabited in the main by half-pay officers enduring the ignominy of half-life on the beach and seeking the holy grail of what false memory told them would be *real* life at sea.

He had sat among them a number of times before, waiting to see the appointers who he hoped would swap his present boring but arduous posting at his south coast signal station for a sea-going slot – *any* sea-going slot.

But this visit was different. This time he had not come on spec, cap in hand, to plead his case. Today, for once, he was answering a summons from Captain Wallis, who had sent him away with a flea in his ear last time.

While unemployed officer-watching in the waiting room, he recalled the time when he had sat there alongside Lieutenant Anson, who had since become his particular friend.

They had enjoyed a night on the town together and his brother officer had later secured him an invitation to a Brax Hall ball where he had met Anson's delightful sisters, or rather Elizabeth and the rather less delightful Anne.

But above all he had Anson to thank for breaking the boredom of signal station life by involving him in the ingenious plan to capture the Normandy privateer that had been plaguing the south coast, snapping up merchantmen as prizes.

Armstrong's reverie was interrupted by the sniffing porter who poked his head round the door and beckoned him.

The other waiting room occupants looked daggers at one of their number being taken, to their minds, out of turn. But Armstrong was delighted. Surely the fact that he had been summoned rather than calling on the off-chance meant that the appointers were going to offer him a better posting. And being hauled out of the dreaded waiting room in front of many who appeared to have taken root there must indicate something.

Captain Alfred Wallis, a short man with balding pate and sharp features, smiled as Armstrong entered his large office a few doors away from the waiting room. This, Armstrong thought, really *was* promising. He was not used to being greeted with smiles at the Admiralty.

'Ah, Armstrong, we meet again!' And, handing him a letter, the captain told him: 'Take a pew and read this while I sign a few documents, there's a good fellow.'

Puzzled, Armstrong sat, smoothed out the letter and read:

"To my Lord Commissioners,

To inform your Lordships of the successful taking of a French privateer off the port of Seagate by gunboats of the Special Sea Fencible Detachment under my command ..."

He did a double-take and looked up in surprise, but Wallis was engrossed in his paperwork. So this was why he had been summoned.

This was a report on the taking of *Égalité* by Anson and his jolly jack tars, but this was not his friend's style. Anson would never mention himself in the first sentence.

Armstrong read on, astonished at the tone of it – the references to its planning, the exaggerated casualties, the dismissive mentions of the role performed by Anson and Lieutenant Coney, of the Folkestone Impress Service, and the blatant lobbying for prize money. Needless to say, there was no mention whatsoever of Armstrong's own part in planning the privateer's capture.

He was therefore not one whit surprised to see the signature, that of Arthur Veryan St Cleer Hoare, Captain, Royal Navy.

Seething, he snorted, dragging Captain Wallis's attention back from his paperwork.

'You appear somewhat taken aback, Armstrong?'

'That I am, sir, totally amazed. Dumbstruck!'

'Quite a despatch isn't it? Some might say the stuff of legends!'

Despairingly, Armstrong put his hand to his forehead. 'Legends? Hah! I have to tell you, sir, that this despatch is more than a legend – it's a travesty, a complete travesty!'

Wallis did not appear surprised. 'Very well, kindly enlighten me.'

Armstrong took a deep breath. 'To the best of my belief this is not what occurred, or at least, not *how* it happened. It was Lieutenant Anson who conceived the plan to entrap the privateer and he was almost entirely responsible for the success of the operation. Not Captain et cetera et cetera Hoare!'

Wallis was clearly amused at the insertion of et ceteras in the place of Hoare's formidable middle names that claimed a dubious connection to West Country aristocrats. 'So you do not place too much credence in his report?'

'I do not, sir. Lieutenant Anson would be able to state the facts far better than I – as would Lieutenant Coney. I was merely involved in the planning, but they were there.'

Wallis smiled. 'I have this very morning interviewed Lieutenant Coney about his involvement in the taking of *Égalité.*'

'And, sir?'

'So now I merely require you to tell me what you know of the planning of the operation.'

Over the next hour Armstrong recounted how, after receiving a letter asking for any intelligence concerning a French privateer with a newly patched sail he had reported sightings enabling him to predict its likely reappearances. This in turn had enabled Anson to form a plan to use a merchant vessel as bait and lure the privateer into a trap so that the Frenchman could be boarded and taken by the Sea Fencibles.

Captain Hoare had not been involved in the planning or execution of the operation and, he understood, had arrived on board *Égalité* only when all was over bar the shouting.

Nevertheless, Hoare had been infuriated that Anson had returned the French officer's sword as a gesture of appreciation for calling upon his crew to surrender, therefore avoiding further bloodshed. And so Hoare had demanded it be handed to him and later encouraged the impression that it had been surrendered to him in battle.

Armstrong could not help himself ending with: 'It was a dishonourable act by Hoare yet now the man has the gall to claim the glory – and prize money. It's disgraceful!'

Wallis had listened attentively throughout without offering his own opinion, but now he asked: 'Have you kept the letter you received asking for intelligence of the privateer?'

'Why yes, sir, of course.'

'Can you recall whose signature it bears?'

Armstrong thought for a moment and his face fell at the recollection. 'Well, it was clearly written by Lieutenant Anson, but ...'

'But signed by the divisional captain?'

Screwing up his eyes and grimacing, Armstrong was forced to admit that it was.

'So it could be argued that Captain Hoare *was* involved in setting up this operation, could it not?'

Grudgingly, Armstrong conceded: 'I suppose it could be interpreted that way, sir, but—'

'But me no buts, Armstrong. I require only facts from you, not opinions. And, by the by, should prize money be awarded for this capture the divisional captain would be entitled to a goodly share of it, whether he was there or not.'

Armstrong nodded, though it pained him to do so. It was reckoned by some that a system under which senior officers far removed from the blood and guts of actions at sea were entitled to a far greater share than most who were there was patently unfair. But that was the rule.

A clerk entered and whispered something to Captain Wallis, who announced: 'I am summoned by their lordships on another matter. Is there anything else you wish to mention to me?'

'Well, sir, having had a sniff of action, albeit from the cliff tops, I should like to repeat my request for a sea posting.'

'Ah, your habitual request for a posting. I daresay I would have suffered from withdrawal symptoms had you not mentioned that. I cannot imagine why you fret so to leave your nice comfortable berth at Fairlight, but I will give it some thought and see what can be done for you.'

'Thank you, sir. I should be much obliged.'

As he left the captain's office Wallis called after him: 'You are to discuss the subject of our meeting with no-one. *No-one*, is that clearly understood?'

Armstrong left the Admiralty with his tail between his legs once again. After all his expectations there was to be no sea appointment, and, worse, it seemed that Captain Arthur et cetera et cetera Hoare would get away with his outrageous claim to be the only true begetter of the *Égalité* capture.

*

Anson was going over the future fencible training programme with Fagg at the Seagate detachment building when a dragoon messenger arrived from Dover.

It was what he had long been expecting: the go-ahead from Colonel Redfearn for his Boulogne mission with Hurel.

Fagg knew better than to ask outright and carried on making a list of new men for musket training, but Anson could not contain his excitement and burst out: 'This is it! All the beans are in a row at last and the Frenchman and I are required to cross the channel.'

The bosun pretended ignorance. 'To France?'

'Where else? We have a mission to perform connected to Nelson's forthcoming action aimed at frustrating the French invasion plans.'

Fagg wheedled: 'I thought it would be somefink like that. I can come wiv yer, can't I, sir?'

'In a word, no! I need you to stay here and crack on with training. Our boys could well be needed soon – one way or another.' Anson knew that if Nelson attempted some boat action against the French Channel ports, Sea Fencibles would almost certainly be required to take part. And if the enemy invaded across the short sea route the fencibles would be in the thick of it anyway.

'So 'ow are yer goin' across?'

'That's where you come in, bosun. I want you to help arrange a passage. But of course it must be discreet. This mission must not become the talk of the town because if it does we know that news of it will be across the other side in a flash – and the French could well be waiting to meet us as we go ashore.'

'Understood, sir. The best way, I reckon, was 'ow we came out of France.'

'Courtesy of smugglers?'

'Exackly, sir.'

'I had been thinking along the same lines. But do you mean the same boat – the *Ginny May* was it not?'

'Well, yes, we could try that smuggler cove, but 'e ain't bin seen around for a while. They reckon 'e's a Thanet man. Anyways, pretty well any smuggler would do. And of course, we've got a good few of 'em in the Seagate fencibles.'

Anson pretended astonishment. 'Good grief! Are you sure? I would never have believed that!' In reality he well knew some of his own men found a lucrative sideline in the free trading business, but turned a Nelsonian blind eye to it.

'They uses luggers like that one we come across in – smuggler-luggers they call 'em. Then there's the galleys like what they row across. With some good men at the oars they can cross in just five or six 'ours.'

'And not having to rely on finding the right wind?'

'That's right. They can go if there's ockered winds so long as it ain't too rough, or no wind at all. And they can dodge Revenue cutters and navy ships, no bother.'

'And the French, too, I would hope!' Anson could see that sort of manoeuvrability would be of great help to the smuggling fraternity.

The ability to outwit sailing vessels and swing into position to get off a carronade shot was one of his own detachment gunboats' greatest attributes – proven in the battle with the Normandy privateer. But the smugglers' row galleys would be faster and their comings and goings were tolerated, indeed welcomed, by the French.

'So how can we contact these smugglers?'

'Ah, that's the thing. I don't think you'd better be there, sir. It's the uniform y'see. If them lads see you comin' they might run a mile, thinking you wus from the Revenue or even worse, the press gang ...'

'So can *you* contact them?'

'Not personal, like, on account of not being from round 'ere. Not one that they'd trust, like. But I could get Sampson Marsh, or one of the others what's well connected local-like, to put a word out. Long as there weren't no danger of them being accused of smugglin', o' course.'

'Perish the thought! I think I can give them that assurance.' Anson felt sure he could ask for backing from Colonel Redfearn on this if it became necessary.

'They'd need payin' o' course and they'd want a darn sight more'n a King's shillin' apiece. It'd be a couple of guineas each, at least.'

'Very well, let's make it so. Kindly contact Sampson Marsh immediately and get him to have a word with his, er, contacts.'

'Aye, aye, sir!'

'And while you're about it send young Tom Marsh off to fetch Sergeant Hoover and the Frenchman back from Fairlight. We'll need to be ready to cross to France in a couple of days.'

27

A Family at War

Young Jemmy Beer raised his cap. 'Arternoon, Master Oliver. I'm to tell you your father wants to see you in the dinin' room soon as you get back.'

'Well, here I am, so if you'll kindly take Ebony off my hands I'll pop in there right away.'

To his surprise Anson found his parents and brother Augustine waiting for him. There were coffee cups on the table and they appeared to have been in conference for some time.

'Mother, father, Gussie, I gather you wish to see me?'

His elder brother bridled at the use of the childish version of his name that Oliver had used to annoy him since boyhood – and that riled him even more now that he was a minor canon at the cathedral.

'Kindly come in and shut the door behind you. What we have to discuss is not for the servants' ears.'

Puzzled, Anson raised his eyebrows. His father had not sounded this stern since he had hidden toads in his siblings' beds as an eleven-year-old.

He closed the door as requested, took a seat on the opposite side of the table to the other three and asked cheerily. 'What's happened? Has someone died?'

Clearly not amused, his mother took the lead. 'Your father and I – and Augustine – wish to speak to you about this nonsense over Charlotte Brax.'

So that was it. They were going to try to persuade him to change his mind and marry Charlotte because it would tie the Ansons to the wealthiest family in the district. It would have been what was known in the mating game as a brilliant match. And, to his mother, marrying off her offspring well was no game: it was a serious business.

But his brief affair with Charlotte was not something he wished to discuss with anyone, and certainly not with his parents. The fact that his detested brother was there sticking his oar in where it was not wanted was a further provocation.

Anson sighed. 'Look, this is, or rather was, a private matter. There was a brief dalliance between Charlotte and me, but we had a falling out and it's all over.'

Gussie snorted. 'A dalliance, hah!'

'Yes, that's all it was. I gather she has decided to marry that oafish nincompoop Chitterling. They suit one another and I wish them joy of it.'

'But Sir Oswald came to see you. To make you an offer ...' his mother protested.

'He made it sound like a transaction in a cattle market. If and when I marry it will be through choice, not because the price is right.'

'But an alliance with the Brax family would be of immense value to us — immense.'

'That's simply not going to happen. I have told you, Charlotte and I have had words and there is no longer anything between us. It should not have begun in the first place and now it's over, done, and I do not wish to discuss it further.'

His mother looked daggers and for a moment was uncharacteristically lost for words.

The rector, who had sat through the earlier exchanges with the same pained expression on his face that he wore when his piles were troubling him, joined the fray. 'My dear boy, arranged marriages among great families are perfectly normal, and in due time most couples invariably find that they rub along very comfortably together.'

Anson had to stop himself from smiling. It was Charlotte rubbing against him that had caused the problem in the first place. And to describe either family as great was something of an overstatement. The Brax family's wealth was inherited from a long line of bully-boy rural landlords while the Ansons' only claim to fame was a very distant connection, many times removed, to the circumnavigator and reformer of the navy whose surname they were privileged to share.

His father did not notice Anson's amused half smile. 'Yes, yes, the Brax girl is clearly greatly enamoured with you and she has her attractions.'

'Father, I have made my position clear and there is really nothing more to be said. I am afraid I will not stay to listen to any more of this and will go back to my detachment as soon as I have packed my things.'

Augustine Anson had been coiling himself like a striking cobra and now blundered into the debate, hissing: 'As usual, it's all about you, isn't it? Like the randy sailor you have obviously become, you've had your way

158

with this girl and are now running away from your responsibilities – running off back to sea!'

'Hardly back to sea, Gussie, although I wish it could be.'

'Don't dare to call me by that ridiculous name!'

Anson deliberately goaded him. 'Sorry, Gussie, I forgot. Now, if you'll excuse me, this conversation is over.'

'You poisonous brat! Don't you realise how upsetting this is for our mother and father? You have the opportunity to make a marriage with one of the most eligible heiresses for miles around – and a member of the Brax family at that. God help us if word of this gets to the Archdeacon! Have you forgotten that Sir Oswald holds the advowson for this parish, making your own father dependent on his patronage and goodwill?'

So that was what was really behind all this.

He got up to go but his father pleaded: 'Will you not reconsider, Oliver, for all our sakes?'

Anson shook his head. 'No. I am sorry that this matter has come between us, particularly between you and me, father, but I will not sell myself to the Brax family and I will not marry someone I do not truly love. It would be unfair to us both.'

His mother and Augustine exchanged looks. She nodded to him and, it seemed by prior agreement they had decided what action to take if they did not get their way.

Augustine spat venomously: 'If you will not do this one thing for us, the family, then it is our parents' wish that the generous allowance you have been receiving since you joined the navy is stopped forthwith and you are to get out of this house and never come back!'

Anson shrugged. 'So be it. Then there is nothing more to be said. I will leave immediately.'

At the door he turned briefly to see his mother and brother eyeing him with near hatred and his father with elbows on the table and chin resting on his clenched hands – a despairing, forlorn look on his face.

*

He went straight to his room, packed the few spare items of uniform he had kept there and put the rest of his belongings in his sea chest. It had his name painted in white on the lid and had been returned to the rectory by HMS *Phryne* after he was wounded and captured during the abortive cutting-out expedition in Normandy.

Seeking out George Beer, he explained that he was leaving forthwith and would send someone to collect his trunk.

'I know, Master Oliver, the word's already got round and I'm very sorry. All of us are. That Gussie, well … I can't find the words. Well, not polite ones, like.'

Anson had to smile. He knew that, like wooden walls, rectories have ears – and no doubt the butler Beer had been listening at the door.

He patted the old family retainer on the shoulder. 'You'll look after my father?' It was both question and plea, and Beer understood precisely what was behind it. The rector was a good man but no match for his waspish wife and their eldest son Gussie, who was thoroughly detested by all the servants.

Beer tapped his index finger to his nose indicating that he would indeed watch the rector's back.

Ten minutes later Anson had mounted Ebony, slung the uniform bag across in front of the saddle and crunched off down the shingle driveway.

He did not look back, but had a feeling that he was being observed – as indeed he was.

The rector was standing alone at his study window, despondently watching his favourite son riding out of his life, perhaps forever.

28

A Lesson in Economics

As he rode away, Anson thought back over the confrontation with his parents and brother. He regretted the breach with his father and asked himself if he could have handled things differently, but decided not.

He had surrendered to lust when Charlotte Brax threw herself at him, but he did not love her. The physical attraction had been intense, but after it had waned, as it most surely would, what then? There was no meeting of minds, nor friendly affection – merely lust.

Her appetites were such that he believed she would have looked elsewhere whenever duty called him away. He shuddered at the recollection of the hint she had given during their last bruising encounter that she had already given herself to the awful Chitterling – and who else?

No, he was far better off without her and after what had occurred there was no way he could have brought himself to agree to the marriage of convenience that the squire, his own parents and brother had tried to foist on him.

But now he had cast himself adrift from his family and there was no going back on that either.

This would be no great hardship to someone like him who had left to join the navy on the eve of his thirteenth birthday. True, he would miss the convenient and comfortable refuge of his room at the rectory. And he would feel the loss of the regular allowance his father made him, but then he had long felt uncomfortable about that. But he would not greatly miss his family. Having been away from home so much he felt he hardly knew them anyway.

Heading towards Seagate, he thought over the practicalities of his break with his family. No doubt Gussie would make sure the allowance was curtailed immediately. In fact, Anson told himself, he would do his utmost to pay back every penny of it that he had received over the years.

His room at the Rose would suffice as his sole base, but it did not come cheap.

Prize money from HMS *Phryne's* successful foray in the Mediterranean had dwindled to next to nothing. No wonder, he had shelled out a good deal of it during the escape from France, sprinkling gold coins around as if they were coppers.

The Admiralty expected its sea officers to make things happen, but – as Captain Hoare had reminded him – getting back money from the hammock-counters that one had spent on behalf of the service was harder than getting blood out of stones.

Since being appointed to command the Seagate detachment more of his money had gone on bribing dockyard men to cough up the guns and equipment they were due, paying for uniforms for his fencibles to wear at the Royal review at the instigation of Hoare, and suchlike. He doubted that he would ever get any of it back.

Not least, he had had to fork out more money for new uniforms for himself, and, of course, on buying Ebony.

His naval pay would barely cover his living costs and stabling.

On the credit side was the promise of more prize money for his part in the capture of the Normandy privateer, but that was still pie in the sky at present and might never materialise.

Pondering how to cut down his outgoings, he came to a sudden conclusion.

He had ridden a pony as a child but had rarely been on horseback since joining the navy and had long decided he would never make a horseman – simply hadn't got enough of a backside for it.

If he sold Ebony he would recoup at least enough to tide himself over and be able to send some of the allowance money back to his father.

So he took a diversion through the lanes and sought out Willie Horn who had sold him the horse.

Anson got down from Ebony with his backside tingling uncomfortably as usual after a ride of any distance.

Horn was leaning, clay pipe in hand, over his five-bar gate in exactly the same pose that Anson had encountered him before.

'Good day, Mister Horn.'

Horn sucked at his pipe, blew out a stream of smoke and asked suspiciously: 'I 'ope you 'aven't brought that there horse back to complain. Don't blame me if it don't suit. They says "buyer beware" and that there gelding was in fine fettle when it left 'ere.'

'No, no. I'm not here to complain about the horse as such. A noble creature, sound of wind and limb, like you said when you sold him to me.'

'That's right – exackly what I said when I let you 'ave him. Reluctant to let him go, I was, on account of him being a what-d'you-call noble creature. Sixteen hands of sweet-tempered beast is that, bought off a widder lady on account of her husband dying and having no further use for him.'

'Well, to get to the point, Mister Horn, sea officers are not what you might call natural riders and I've decided to give it up because it tortures my nether regions every time I get up on one.'

'So?'

'So I've come to offer you the opportunity to buy this horse back. A noble creature, I think you agreed?'

'You want to sell him back to *me*?'

'That's about the size of it. I think when you sold him to me you hinted that you had plenty of other takers.'

'Ah well, depends what you're expecting for him. Looking at him I'd say he's gorn downhill since you've had him – looks a bit scrawny in the withers to me. Now I give him a close look, he's more of a nag. Are you sure he's been looked arter proper? Looks a bit neglected to me – run-down, like.'

Anson protested: 'But I haven't done much mileage on him. The grooms at the coaching inn in town and at my father's rectory have taken care of him, and they've told me he's in very good nick.'

Horn ran his hand down the gelding's flanks. 'Hmm, I'm not so sure about that. Some of them grooms wouldn't know a donkey from a racehoss. Anyway, he's nothing like at what you call his peak like he was when I let you 'ave him.'

'So you aren't interested in buying him back?'

'Did I say that? No, I'd be prepared to take him off your hands at the right price.'

'You can have him for the price I paid you minus, say, six months' hire. It would be as if I'd hired him from you for that long and now he's coming back good as new.'

Horn laughed hollowly. 'You're what they calls a hoptomist. He ain't worth anyfink like that, now.'

'But you said he was a valuable horse, worth a lot of money.'

'Ah, that was then. This is now. I'd say that now, to me, he's not worth half what you paid. He's aged since then. Anyways, I'll be generous and offer you half, take it or leave it.'

Not being skilled in horse-dealing, Anson realised he might have been naive to bank on getting back more or less the full price that he had paid.

Nevertheless, he was annoyed to think that Willie Horn was about to dun him.

'Well?' the wily old man asked, puffing away on his pipe with the smug expression of someone about to make a highly favourable deal.

But Ebony chose this moment to whicker and rub his head against Anson's shoulder as if impatient to be gone.

That did it. In an instant Anson's mind was made up. There was no way he was going to sell his horse back to this old reprobate – certainly not for half what it was worth, no matter how poor the state off his finances.

He swung himself back into the saddle and to the old man's astonishment announced: 'Sore behind or not, I've decided I've grown too fond of this poor old nag to sell him back to you Mister Horn, so I'll bid you good day.'

And with that he turned Ebony and rode off, leaving Horn, his bluff called, leaning on the gate biting on his pipe so crossly that he snapped the stem.

29

Sparking Up the Fencibles

Anson was back at the detachment headquarters with Fagg, getting an update on the approach that had been made to smugglers who it was hoped would take him across to France, when an unwelcome visitor arrived.

It was the divisional captain, flush-faced and garrulous from another lengthy lunch with the mayor and his cronies.

Trying not to allow himself to show his intense dislike of the man, and determined not to let him in on the upcoming mission, Anson greeted him as politely as he was able.

'Still fostering good relations with the local bigwigs, sir?'

'Yes, yes, but this is much more important!' Hoare was clearly enthused. 'Nelson himself has written to me asking me to spark up the Sea Fencibles!'

'Written to you personally, or to all the divisional captains?' Anson asked innocently.

But Hoare failed to notice the sarcasm. 'Yes, Nelson himself! He tells me that of the 2,600 who've enrolled in the Sea Fencibles on the invasion coast under his command, less than 300 have agreed to service at sea, even in coastal waters. Disgraceful!'

Anson had assumed the dead-pan expression he had become accustomed to using during Hoare's rants.

'Nelson assures me that they, and I quote: "*shall not be sent off the Coast of the Kingdom, shall be kept as near their own homes as the nature of the service will admit and the moment the alarm of the threatened invasion is over, that every man shall be returned to their own homes*"'

'Really?'

'Yes, and he adds: "*I flatter myself that at a moment when all the volunteer corps in the Kingdom are come forward to defend our land, the seamen of Great Britain will not be slow to defend their own proper element and maintain as pure as our glorious ancestors have transmitted it to us, our undoubted right to the Sovereignty of the Narrow Seas, on which no Frenchman has yet dared to sail with impunity.'"*

'How typical of the great man to share such sentiments with you, sir.'

'Yes, yes! Quite so, Anson, quite so. I feel privileged indeed to be taken into his confidence in such a way ...'

'No doubt all the other divisional captains must feel the same, sir.'

But, again, Hoare failed to detect his subordinate's sarcasm. Instead, he was struck by a worrying thought. 'Good lord! It's just occurred to me. How many men in *my* division have volunteered for sea service? How many in your detachment, Anson?'

'I daresay most will if asked ...'

'Then ask away, for God's sake! Even you must see that this is the shark nearest the raft! How could I ever front up to Nelson if my own men haven't volunteered en masse?'

'How indeed, sir!'

'I must get on to my other detachment commanders forthwith!'

'I am sure that they and their men will be all ears, sir.'

Hoare snorted: 'Ears be damned – I need hands in the air, volunteering!'

*

Anson made his way to Sampson Marsh's fishmonger's shop and was ushered into the back room by the proprietor, who doubled up as the fencibles' petty officer responsible for gunnery.

'You have news for me, Mister Marsh?'

'I have that, sir. Sam Fagg asked me to look into arranging a passage for you and another gent over Boulogne way.'

'That's right. It's a hush-hush business and we can't afford any wagging tongues.'

'Just as well, sir, on account of the blokes who've agreed to take you across don't want no careless talk neither.'

'Smugglers?'

Marsh tapped his nose. 'Let's say, free traders.'

'How soon can they take me?'

'Tomorrow night. You and your oppo need to be at the Jolly Sailor at Capel around eight. You'll be contacted while you're there and taken down the Warren to a galley that'll be waiting for you.'

'Do I pay the crew?'

'No. These boys are going across on a regular run. Anyway, they know about you and that it must be some mission for old England. I'll sort out any payment due once you're safely back.'

'Good man!'

'Oh, and you'll need fisherman-type clothes. I'll get some to Sam Fagg – and a couple of pistols and a suitable weapon for Sergeant Hoover. It wouldn't do for you to be carrying any navy stuff, if you catch my meaning.'

*

Next day Hoover and Hurel disembarked from Tom Marsh's pony and trap stretching their aching limbs.

It had been a bumpy ride from Fairlight and there was barely room for them both and their kit in the small, chariot-style trap.

Fagg was waiting for them in the bar of the Rose and ushered them straight upstairs to Anson's room.

'Ah, Hurel, Hoover, welcome, welcome! I trust you had a stimulating stay at Fairlight and a good journey back?'

Hurel responded with his usual Gallic shrug. 'Your friend Commander Armstrong was a good 'ost, mon ami, but very strict about making me stay indoors when anyone came near the signals 'ut.'

'Quite right, too! Tell me, sergeant, did Monsieur Hurel behave himself? He was not compromised in any way?'

'He has not been compromised, sir. No-one other than the signals boys and dragoons knew he was there and he behaved very well, but I reckon I now know his life story from the moment he left the womb.'

Anson smiled. 'I thought that might be the case.'

'Luckily for the rest of us he and the commander spent a heap of time together gabbling away in French—'

'Capital! And did Armstrong entertain you well, Hurel?'

'Bien sûr, 'e is a very amusing fellow and obtains good French wine from the smugglers, but the cuisine is, well, not of the same standard – very English, I fear. For some strange reason 'e insisted on calling me "mon vieux" – yet, as you can see, I am still quite young. And another thing that was most disturbing ...'

'Oh?'

'It was the man Lloyd's bird, what we Frogs call "un choucas" – a pet jackdaw. In the night it uttered shrieks like some devil creature. It made me think of The Terror and of victims' screams as they were dragged to the guillotine.'

Hoover offered: 'That's true, sir. Sounded like a banshee. Commander Armstrong reckoned it has bad dreams.'

There was no answer to that and, the pleasantries over, Anson was anxious to get to the business in hand.

He sent Fagg limping back down the stairs to bring up a cold supper and beer he had ordered earlier, explaining: 'We cannot risk people seeing you dining in public, Hurel, so we will eat here in my room with Sergeant Hoover and then I am afraid we must revert to the pony and trap to get to our rendezvous and take passage for France.

It was said matter-of-fact, but all three knew they were about to embark on as dangerous a mission as they could imagine.

There could be Revenue men to dodge on their way to take passage in a smuggling vessel crewed by men they did not know they could trust. Then there was the Channel – sometimes benign, sometimes treacherous – to cross in the middle of the night to land on the enemy shore where they could quite easily be captured or killed.

It was a daunting prospect, but both Anson and Hurel had long awaited this moment and were anxious to make a start. Hoover would be along only to see them safely ashore in France, but would have to repeat the crossing again two nights later to pluck them off the beach – if all went well.

Anson had initially thought it inadvisable to take Hoover along at all. But he had relented, for the crossing at least. As the marine had proved during their escape from France, he was too valuable to be left behind. With Hoover beside him, Anson at least knew he would not have to watch his back constantly.

They ate in silence, each reflecting on the role expected of him, and when they had finished put on the scruffy clothes and boots that Sampson Marsh had borrowed for them from local fishermen.

Anson hoped their opposite numbers across the Channel were wearing something very similar. Sampson had assured him that was the case, and with Hurel's complete fluency, albeit with an upper deck drawl, and his own basic French, he hoped they could pass for fishermen.

Certainly the stinking sea boots should tend to keep inquisitive Frenchmen at bay once they reached the other side.

As soon as they were ready, Fagg led the way downstairs where he engaged the landlord and the few occupants of the bar in noisy conversation enabling the others to slip outside unobserved.

Young Tom Marsh was waiting. They threw their kitbags into the trap and Anson motioned Hurel to climb aboard. Marsh handed Anson a bag containing two pistols supplied by the smugglers who were to take them across to France and passed Hoover a longer weapon wrapped in sacking.

The marine examined it by the flickering light of the inn's lantern. It was a coaching carbine made by John Jackson of Cranbrook, and its brass barrel was a good foot shorter than the musket he was accustomed to using. He nodded. The carbine would be easier to handle in a cramped boat and – importantly – it was patently not of service issue.

Tom Marsh clicked his tongue to alert his pony, shook the reins and set off down the cobbled street with Anson and Hoover following behind on foot.

30

A Night Crossing

From the Jolly Sailor pub high up to the east of Folkestone beside the Dover road, a guide from the nearby hamlet of Capel first warned them to move as quietly as possible in case of patrolling Revenue men and then led the way down into the Warren, a jungle of stunted trees and dense undergrowth formed long ago by a giant chalk landslip and sloping down to East Wear Bay.

It was crisscrossed with narrow paths, some man-made, others worn by grazing animals, and without a light it would have been near impossible to find their way – unless you knew it like the back of your hand.

Their guide did. As a local lad he had played smugglers versus Revenue men here with his young mates. No-one had wanted to play the Revenue role, so sisters had to be drafted in for the purpose. Nowadays his free trading activities kept his eye in.

Anson and Hurel stumbled after him, frequently near tripping on brambles and low bushes, with Hoover trailing behind, nursing his carbine across his chest.

Carrying a bulky bag each did not help and halfway down Anson's foot snagged on a bramble and he fell heavily.

Hoover helped him to his feet and they resumed their descent.

As they neared the beach their guide hissed a warning for them to freeze and they crouched low catching their breath. Anson could hear him fiddling with a striker. Sheltered under the man's jacket, the flame flickered and it gave just enough light to see him ignite a thick stub of candle in a peculiarly-shaped lantern with a spout on it.

The guide swung it seawards and its purpose became clear. The spout funnelled the light towards those it was aimed at while not revealing the signaller's presence to anyone else.

It was a ruse used by smugglers to attract the attention of only those they wanted to attract. Not surprising, Anson thought – these men *are* smugglers.

Hurel's rasping breath revealed to Anson that after his spell in the hulks, being wounded by Chitterling and moving from pillar to post over the past few weeks, the Frenchman was still far from fit.

Ahead they could now hear the sound of waves breaking gently on the beach and the crunch of the shingle as they receded.

The guide ordered them to stay put and crept forward towards the shore.

Through occasional shafts of pale moonlight penetrating the cloud cover, a group of figures could just be discerned around a long row-galley drawn up on the foreshore.

After a few minutes the guide returned and squatted beside Anson. 'They're ready for yer, mate, but some of 'em's a bit nervous, like. They want me to remind yer that they're doing yer a favour, right? They don't want no come-backs, see?'

There was no need for him to explain. Free traders were quite naturally jealous of their anonymity and followed the principle that the less anyone knows the less they can tell.

Anson whispered: 'I'm navy – nothing to do with the Revenue. You can remind the boys this is for old England – and they'll be well paid. We don't care how else they earn their bread.'

The guide knuckled his forehead. 'Fair enough, mate. But yer just might recognise a few of 'em ...'

That, Anson thought, probably meant that there were some of his own fencibles among the crew, so he offered: 'No need for them to worry. It's too dark to see who's who. And anyway I'm terrible at remembering faces – and even worse at names.'

The guide laughed. 'I'll nip and tell 'em, mate, then they'll shove off. I'll whistle to let you know when they're ready and you lot will have to wade out and climb aboard, orlright?'

He left them and minutes later they heard the boat scrunching on the shingle-dotted sand as the crew heaved it down and into the water.

A low whistle and Anson rose, picked up his bag and told the others: 'This is it – you first, Hurel!' And they hurried down to the water's edge, with Hoover bringing up at the rear.

Hurel waded out and was pulled over the side by one of the oarsmen. Anson followed and once in the boat he took Hoover's carbine so that the marine could climb on board unhindered.

Anson noted that there were eight men at the oars and several more already in the thwarts – no doubt spare rowers to relieve the oarsmen.

As soon as the newcomers were settled, squatting in the thwarts, the bearded coxswain called softly: 'Dip oars, and pull ...' and the galley pulled away, leaving their guide standing alone on the beach and the sinister jungle of the Warren now well behind them.

Hoover, crouching beside Anson, gave him a thumbs up.

At last they were on their way back to France and after weeks of trying to keep him under wraps, Hurel's mission was about to begin.

*

Although the sea was a little choppy at times, the narrow, shallow-draught galley made the crossing in little over six hours.

The darkness had been kind to them, allowing them to approach the French coast without incident and both Anson and Hoover had taken spells at the oars to give some of the rowers a rest.

Not being haunted by the Fairlight jackdaw's nocturnal screeches and lulled by the lapping and slapping of the waves, Hurel had fallen into a deep sleep. In consideration of the ordeal the Frenchman was soon to face, Anson left him to what he hoped were sweet dreams.

Even if they had been spotted, the galley was ideal for the task. It was not only fast when rowed by a strong, experienced crew like this, but as long as conditions were reasonably calm it could be steered every which way, no matter what the wind – or if there were no wind.

As his bosun had explained to Anson, this gave it the capability of out-manoeuvring Revenue cutters, privateers or men-of-war – friend or foe. And it could be beached anywhere – as they were about to prove.

Despite the darkness, Anson thought a few of the rowers seemed familiar. Some of his own Sea Fencibles, no doubt. But this was a time for turning a blind eye – not for fingering poor seafarers turning a slightly dishonest penny.

In any event he did not see the evil in smuggling if it did not harm anyone. It put money in the pockets of poor men – and put fine French wines and brandy on dining tables up and down the coast, including his father's and even that of his particular friend, Amos Armstrong, helping to ease his lonely vigil on the cliff-tops at Fairlight Signal Station.

The Channel passage had given Anson the opportunity to study the weapons provided for him by the smugglers.

He had been warned that it would be unwise for him to carry his navy issue sea service pistols as in a tight spot in France their long barrels would have made them difficult to conceal – and, if caught, the official marks they bore would betray him as a British naval spy.

In the bag young Marsh had handed him were two smaller weapons. One was a .65 bore pistol with a nine-inch steel barrel and a reshaped stock – a light dragoon holster weapon much like those that Armstrong's cavalry messengers carried. Anson could just see faint traces of the Government markings to the centre of the lock-plate, a crowned GR and Tower on the tail. The King's proofs could still be clearly seen on top of the barrel. Heavy bruising on the stock indicated that the regimental markings had been deliberately removed, as had the butt cap. It had clearly been disguised for use by the smugglers and he wondered how it had been acquired. The other, lighter and more finely-balanced pistol was by William Bailes, of Tyburn Road, London, and almost certainly originally one of a pair stolen from some gentleman not quick enough to protect himself with them.

He loaded both, chose the cut-down light dragoon pistol for himself and handed the other to Hurel when he awoke. They would be needing them.

Just before dawn they heard waves lapping ashore and Anson could make out the vague outline of the French coast.

Far away to larboard they could just make out Cap Griz-Nez and nearer was another promontory that the coxswain told Anson was Cap d'Alprech.

They steered to starboard and in short order the galley ran up on a broad expanse of sandy beach where several men were waiting among outcrops of rock with crates and small barrels.

The coxswain turned to Anson. 'This is it, gents. You're just a few miles south of Boulogne. Best make yourselves scarce afore it gets too light. The Frogs patrol the dunes but it's a bit too early for them so you should be all right.'

He brushed Anson's thanks aside. 'We daren't hang around either. We've got some cargo to load and then we're off.'

The Frenchmen were already shouldering the casks and crates out to the boat.

The coxswain shook Anson's hand. 'We're getting paid for this, so we'll be back here, same place, at midnight in two days' time, right? We'll look for a light from this here spout lantern, but fire this flasher if the Frogs are on to you. If you're here and all's clear we'll take you back, but we'll not wait. Understood?'

Anson stuffed the lantern, tinderbox and the flasher – resembling a barrel-less pistol – into his kitbag. 'We'll be here.'

Hoover helped Anson and Hurel over the side, handed them their bags and wished them good luck.

The American whispered to Anson: 'I'll make sure these boys come back for you. There's a few of our fencibles among 'em.'

'I noticed!'

It was becoming lighter by the minute as Anson and Hurel waded ashore and crunched over the cockle and razor clam shells littering the beach.

They crouched among the rocks for a few minutes to catch their breath and get their bearings. Satisfied that the coast was clear, they left the rocks and made their way up to the sand dunes beyond. And, when they turned for a last look back, the party of Frenchmen had disappeared and the galley was already well out to sea.

Anson stopped his companion for a moment. 'Well, we're here, and now it's all down to you, Monsieur le Baron.'

The Frenchman smiled. 'Pas de problème, mon ami. Allons-y!'

'Yes, let's go!' And they set off into the dunes heading north for Boulogne.

31

Boulogne

It was mid-morning by the time Anson and Hurel made their way to the outskirts of the port. Little notice was taken of them thanks to their well-worn seaman's clothes and Hurel's perfect French. Whenever anyone drew near, he gabbled away about women and drink and Anson nodded as if he understood every word.

On the rising ground behind the cliffs of Cap d'Alprech, Hurel stopped beside a large house with paint peeling off the window frames, a small overgrown front garden and a broken wrought-iron gate.

'Nous sommes ici. Wait 'ere.'

Anson sat on a low wall trying to look as nonchalant as possible while Hurel disappeared inside the dilapidated house.

After a short time he reappeared and beckoned Anson from the door.

Inside, Hurel showed Anson upstairs to a front bedroom and announced:

'This is the 'ouse of Madame X.'

'Hicks? You mean Hicks?'

'No, no, not 'icks, X.'

'Oh, Madame X! You wish her to remain anonymous?'

'It is for the best, mon ami. She is an elderly friend of my family – a widow. She knows me from days gone by, before The Terror, but she does not know why I am 'ere. Nor does she wish to know.'

'But we must reimburse her for her trouble.'

'I 'ave given 'er some money for our stay 'ere and she is grateful. She 'as, what do you say, fallen on 'ard times. You will not know who she is, nor she you. So if the worst 'appens and we are caught we will say we broke in 'ere and that she knows nothing. Compris?'

'D'accord!'

Hurel smiled at his companion's French. 'What is more, Anson, I have told this lady that you are a foreign sailor in the French service who is a little fou – a tiny bit mad – from the sound of gunfire, and 'ave been known to bite people when disturbed. So she will not enter your room. Your food will be left outside your door.'

Anson laughed. 'You have chosen well, my friend. From here I can see part of the defensive line of ships – and in some detail thanks to this.' He tapped the small telescope he had carried concealed in an inner pocket of his trousers.

'Good! Soon it will be time for me to play the escaped prisoner, just back from the 'ulks with the 'elp of English smugglers.'

'It is not an act. All the above is true. Now, you remember what interesting snippets of information you are to pass on?'

'Of course.'

'And that the object of the exercise is not only to gain intelligence about the defensive line and the effects of Nelson's bombardment when it comes—?'

'Yes, yes!'

'But also to discover if Lieutenant Crispin is here, willingly or not.'

'And if so to see 'ow we could disappear 'im back to England.'

'Precisely. And when you return here—'

'I make sure not to be followed.'

'Good man!'

Hurel rested for a while before venturing out. Then they shook hands warmly and as the Frenchman left Anson called after him quietly: 'Bon chance!'

*

Anson settled himself down in a comfortable armchair beside the window, his feet up on the sill and telescope across his chest. There was a clear view across to the fortified old town – what Hurel called the "Haute Ville" – and the lower town, or "Basse Ville", and the harbour it dominated. Hurel could hardly have chosen a better viewpoint.

From time to time Anson raised the glass and observed the comings and goings down in the harbour – boats taking men and supplies back and forth, and occasionally a squad of blue-jacketed soldiers marching along the quayside, going on or off duty, he supposed.

At first he busied himself trying to draw a plan of the warships moored in a defensive crescent guarding the port. But it was not possible for him to identify them all by type and certainly not by name at this distance.

He had been taught the elements of drawing as a midshipman and had brought pencils and a leather-backed sketch book with him expressly for the purpose of making a plan of the French defences.

His mind went back to when he had watched the artist William Alexander at work recording the scene at the royal review of the Kentish volunteers at Mote Park, Maidstone, when more than 5,000 men had paraded and then feasted in the presence of the King at the expense of the county's Lord Lieutenant.

Anson had intended to purchase a copy of the resulting print, but due to the pace of events since then it had slipped his mind. He made a mental note to obtain one on return. It would be a fitting reminder of a great occasion – and, thanks to his chance meeting with the artist, a representation of a naval ensign would mark the tables his fencibles had occupied.

*

Hurel had left the house by a back door and waited, partly hidden by some bushes, until he was certain he was unobserved.

He followed an erratic route down to the harbour area where in his seaman's rig he passed unnoticed among the mariners – navy and fishermen – soldiery, and dock-workers thronging the area.

Entering a bar, he bought himself a carafe of wine and sat in a corner sipping it and listening to the chatter of off-duty soldiers – mostly fusiliers, he noticed – and sailors. They spoke of the Rosbifs being busy outside the harbour but appeared totally confident about the port's defences.

Then he had a bit of luck. One of the fusiliers announced he was due back on duty at the admiral's headquarters, downed his drink and left.

As unobtrusively as possible, Hurel followed suit. He dogged the soldier from a good distance, and to avoid suspicion stopped at one point pretending to get a stone out of his boot.

Eventually the fusilier unknowingly led the way to what was clearly the admiral's headquarters, in the ruins of a Roman lighthouse on the east cliff above the town.

Having waited until the man had reported for duty, Hurel presented himself to the guard commander who looked him up and down suspiciously.

Hurel assured him that despite his disreputable seaman's garb, he was a naval officer recently escaped from England and had important information for the admiral.

The young fusilier officer bade him wait in the outhouse that had been turned into a makeshift guardroom and went off to seek higher authority.

After a wait of some ten minutes that seemed to Hurel like ten hours the guard commander returned and ordered two of his men to conduct the newcomer to a nearby house.

A sentry stood at the door and one of the escorts approached him. There was a brief conversation that Hurel could not hear and then the sentry opened the door and he was hustled inside.

He was left standing in the hallway under the guard of the escorts while the sentry knocked and went into a nearby room, emerging a few minutes later to beckon him in.

Bookcases filled with leather-bound volumes lined the walls and behind the enormous desk that dominated the room sat a small, cadaverous, balding, middle-aged man wearing what appeared to be an officer's blue jacket.

After what seemed like an age the cadaverous incumbent looked up from the documents in front of him and examined his visitor and if he were some natural history specimen, polishing his thick spectacles but remaining silent.

Hurel assumed this was an intelligence officer, came to attention, bowed slightly, and announced himself as Lieutenant Gérard Hurel, a naval officer lately escaped from England, and repeated that he had important information for the admiral.

The intelligence man replaced his spectacles and, leaving Hurel standing, subjected him to a cross-examination: what ship had he served in, how was he captured, where was he held, how had he escaped – and how had he crossed La Manche?

Hurel had all the answers off pat and most had the benefit of being true. He explained that he had been held on a Medway hulk, escaped when taken ashore with a pretended fever, and made his way to the coast where he met up with Kentish smugglers.

These he bribed with money he had made from giving fencing lessons on board the hulk, and they had provided him with the seamen's clothing he was wearing and brought him across on a smuggling run.

He had grown accustomed to the smell of fish that enveloped him but noticed that the mention of the fisherman's clothes he was wearing prompted his interrogator into taking a small silver vinaigrette from a drawer and passing it under his nose. Hurel could not disguise a grin: the smell must be strong if it had to be countered with smelling salts.

As he gave details of his escape, the intelligence officer listened attentively, asking occasional questions and scratching notes with a quill pen.

Apparently satisfied that Hurel was bona fide, he came to the matter of the information his visitor claimed to have.

Hurel now launched into his story – that while arranging his crossing with the smugglers he had learned that Admiral Nelson was in the Kentish fishing port of Deal gathering a large flotilla.

He claimed that the smugglers had boasted to him that Nelson was planning to attack Boulogne with a bombardment due to start on the morrow and Hurel offered his opinion that the date had been chosen because it would be close to the third anniversary of the Battle of the Nile.

Warming to his story, Hurel described the make-up of Nelson's flotilla – frigates, gun-brigs, bomb-ketches and gunboats – and the fact that the admiral was now flying his flag in *Medusa*, a mere frigate.

The object of the coming attack, he said, was to cause maximum damage to the French defences, but not on this occasion to attempt to board their vessels protecting the port and cut them out.

After hearing him out, the intelligence officer, at last told him to be seated, rose, went to a side door and addressed an unseen man in the adjoining room: 'Monsieur Crispin, come in, if you please.'

*

The three sat, Hurel and Crispin on one side of the desk, the intelligence officer on the other.

There was another lengthy silence as the man took off his spectacles, blinked several times and polished the pebble-thick lenses once again.

Hurel realised that this was almost certainly a ploy intended to create a sinister vacuum that an unnerved person would try to fill by gabbling on and revealing more than he needed.

Crispin, pale, thin and sickly-looking, his fair hair long and straggly, sat toying nervously with the cuff buttons of his blue, French infantry-style jacket, his eyes darting between Hurel and the intelligence officer from time to time.

At last the intelligence officer replaced his spectacles and addressed both men in English: 'Lieutenant Crispin, this is Hurel. I am satisfied that 'e is a French naval officer recently escaped from England. With 'im comes confirmation of what we already know – that Nelson is about to bombard Boulogne.'

Turning to Hurel, he explained: 'Crispin is an English officer, but a republican who wishes to 'elp us fight 'is misguided countrymen.'

The two eyed each other fleetingly and Hurel detected a look of desperation in the Englishman's eyes.

'Now, Crispin, I wish you to take Hurel somewhere quiet where you can obtain from 'im every morsel of information that might be of use to us – about the prison 'ulks, the possibilities of organising escapes and the system the English smugglers use to 'elp escapers and bring them across La Manche.'

Crispin nodded nervously. 'Of course, colonel.'

The intelligence officer frowned at the revelation of his rank. 'And furthermore, I wish you to discover from 'im every smallest detail of the English anti-invasion forces 'e may 'ave seen or 'eard of on the English coast: naval vessels, troop dispositions, the precise positions of gun batteries – every smallest detail, you understand?'

'I do, monsieur.'

'Your report will be on my desk first thing in the morning. Good day.'

He removed his spectacles. The interview was over.

*

By coincidence, despite the wide choice of drinking dens in Boulogne, Crispin led Hurel to the same bar where he had listened in to the soldiery gossiping an hour or so earlier.

The Englishman indicated a corner table, well away from prying ears, and a large glass of what appeared to be calvados was brought immediately by a skivvy. Crispin was obviously known here.

The girl looked enquiringly at Hurel and he ordered red wine.

Sipping it, he watched Crispin gulp back his glass of spirits and put his hand up for another.

The Frenchman made the first move. 'I will give you what information I can for your report, monsieur. In fact, I will 'elp you write it if you wish. But first, may I ask 'ow you come to be 'ere?'

Crispin, his hand shaking perceptibly as he lifted his second glass, bit his lip. 'It's a long story ...'

*

Several refills later, Crispin was in full flow. Hurel had wheedled the full story out of him – how he had been undermined and incriminated in a blackmailing scam by his own bosun at the Seagate Sea Fencible detachment, and found relief only in drink. When a certain highly secret letter had come into his hands he had decided to escape in a smuggling vessel to France, using it as a bargaining chip to start a new life.

But this drink-fuelled escape had turned into a nightmare. He was now firmly in the clutches of the sinister bespectacled officer he referred to as "pebble-eyes" and deeply regretted betraying his country.

Almost in tears, he said he hated being used as a stool-pigeon to help interrogate captured fellow-countrymen and admitted to his sympathetic listener that he would give anything to be able to return home, no matter what the consequences.

Another drink, and Hurel felt it was safe to tell him: 'Mon ami, I know someone I think could 'elp you. But first, allow me to 'elp you with the report the colonel has demanded. We must use our imaginations to paint 'im a picture that will make 'is brain ache!'

32

Turncoats

Day-dreaming at first, Anson had soon dozed off, awaking some hours later, he guessed, as it was now growing dark outside.

Feeling hungry, he remembered what Hurel had said about the old lady providing him with food, but that she had been warned not to enter the room because of his alleged madness.

Sure enough, there was a plate of cheese and ham, a bread baguette and a jug of red wine outside his door.

He carried it in, made use of the chamber pot under the truckle bed and washed at the washstand with its bowl and pitcher of water. The old lady had even provided a towel.

Refreshed, he tucked into the food and scanned the harbour as he ate. But it was too dark now and all he could make out was a confusing jumble of lights. He told himself there was nothing further he could do this night. It was time to stand down the watch until dawn.

Taking off his jacket, he wedged the back of a chair under the doorknob and lay down on the bed, his loaded pistol beside him.

Wondering how Hurel was faring, he lay awake for a while hoping that Nelson's bombardment would come sooner rather than later so that he could escape the claustrophobic room which made him feel like a prisoner in solitary confinement.

*

He awoke with a start. Someone was tapping on the door. He froze. What if Hurel had been captured and talked? Supposing someone else had noticed the strangers entering the house and informed the authorities? But no, they would not come knocking quietly on his door – they would have kicked it open.

It *was* Hurel.

Exhausted, he slumped in the armchair and Anson passed him the remains of the wine.

'You look done in.'

'Mon ami, I am trés, trés fatigué as we Frogs say – exhausted! All day I 'ave crept around pretending to be on some official business or other.'

'Did you get near enough to see what preparations the French, sorry, I mean the enemy, are making?'

Hurel nodded. 'The port is defended by a line of twenty-four brigs and gunboats anchored across the 'arbour mouth.'

'How are they secured?'

'I could not see for certain, but I presume by ropes.'

'What about shore batteries?'

'I counted ten, all of 'eavy guns although I was not able to get close enough to see the calibre. I joined a group of gunners smoking their pipes near one of the batteries to ask for directions and 'eard them joking that they might as well smoke next to the ammunition store because the powder is so weak it would not explode if you emptied your pipe in a barrel of it!'

'Really? Do you think there was any truth in that?'

'Perhaps, but I cannot be sure. They might 'ave been what you English call pulling my legs.'

'Were you able to discover where the headquarters are?'

'There is a ruined Roman lighthouse on the east cliff, above the town, where there was a lot of activity. I followed a soldier who was going on duty there.'

'But it's a ruin?'

'Nevertheless, it is Louis-René de Latouche-Tréville's 'eadquarters ...'

'*Admiral* Latouche-Tréville?'

'One and the same. And if 'is 'eadquarters are 'ere, Boulogne is clearly the centre of the invasion forces.'

Anson agreed. 'The admiral would naturally wish to be at the centre of things.'

'I know of this man. Like me 'e was an officer in the royalist navy. I did not serve under 'im myself but knew 'im by reputation – 'e has a good strategic brain and 'as been cunning enough to survive the revolution and serve on in the navy and prosper since then, when others lost their careers – and some were parted from their 'eads.'

'Then he is a formidable opponent?'

'Bien sûr. Not only 'as 'e survived, but 'e is admired by all as the only French admiral who appears to be able to stand against Nelson with any 'ope of success.'

'If only we could get to him ...'

'We cannot. I tried, but was, 'ow do you say, fobbed off and questioned by an intelligence officer.'

'You stuck to your story?'

'I did and 'e appeared to believe me. Then, encroyable …!'

'What?'

'This colonel of intelligence introduced me to Lieutenant Crispin and sent us off together to prepare a report on escaping from England and British anti-invasion preparations!'

'Crispin! Here? Good grief!'

Hurel smiled at the reaction to his news. 'It was easy to get 'im drunk and 'e told me 'e is disenchanted with republican France and would give anything to go 'ome. I 'ave taken the liberty to say that after the bombardment I will take 'im to see a contact, a 'orrible scar-faced English smuggler who might be able to arrange it.'

'That's me, I take it?' Anson frowned wryly at his description.

'Exactly – and I 'ave told him 'e must bring a plan of the 'arbour and the defending ships, details of the landing craft being built, the damage Nelson's bombardment causes and anything else 'e can acquire.'

'Good man, Hurel!'

Anson was delighted. The thought of being able to take Crispin back to England and with him information about the Boulogne defences that would be of great value to Nelson in planning a cutting-out raid made all the risks they were taking worthwhile.

He asked: 'What will you do now, Hurel?'

'I will return to the admiral's 'eadquarters and offer to go back to England with the smugglers and spy for 'im.'

'But how do I know that you—?

Hurel was there before him. 'So 'ow do you know that I am not a double agent, or about to become one? You don't, mon ami, but this is a matter of 'onour – and trust.'

Somehow Anson knew now that he *could* trust this man – this minor aristocrat who had lost all in the revolution yet served on, awaiting his chance to play his part in ousting the republicans; this skirt-chasing, proud, sometimes vaguely ridiculous character who was prepared to risk all for his cause. Yes, it all came down to a question of honour and trust.

He held out his hand and the Frenchman grasped it. 'Je suis d'accord, Hurel – honour and trust!'

Anson sensed his companion was close to shedding a tear.

'This mission has confronted me with old ghosts, mon ami. I admire Latouche-Tréville greatly for his professional attributes, but I do not admire 'is politics. In order to survive 'e 'as changed from royalist to republican. We are both from similar backgrounds, both from royalist families. But, sadly, 'e is now a traitor in my eyes.'

'A turncoat, like Crispin?'

'Exactly. But I believe 'e will think I am like 'im, willing to blow whichever way the wind blows. He will believe me.'

'But if you are not able to see the admiral?'

'I have told Crispin when and where we are to rendezvous, so I will meet 'im as planned and if all is well I will bring 'im 'ere and we can 'ide up until it is time for us to rendezvous with the smugglers.'

'Will you rest here until the bombardment starts?'

Hurel smiled. 'No, there is a young ... well, a lady I know from the past. Boulogne was my 'ome port, you see? I will seek 'er out and 'old 'er 'and if she is frightened by the noise of cannons.'

'Good man, but I hope she likes the smell of fish! Now we must await the bombardment, assess its effect and report back to England with Crispin and as much intelligence as he can bring us. Simple, isn't it?'

But they both well knew it would be nothing of the kind.

Again, Anson wished the Frenchman 'Bon chance!' and fell asleep soon after he left.

But he awoke with a start at the detonations of many cannons. The bombardment had begun.

33

"Nelson Speaking to the French"

At five o'clock in the morning, *Medusa* had sailed past Boulogne – just out of range of the shore batteries – trailing a line of bomb vessels and gunboats. The British flotilla then closed to within a mile of the French floating cordon and opened fire.

The cannonade from the bigger ships accompanied by heavy fire from the bomb vessels and gunboats was soon being countered by the French ships and shore batteries.

All day and well into the evening the bombardment and counter-fire from the defensive line of brigs, gunboats and shore batteries continued, covering the crescent of French ships and the harbour in toxic clouds of smoke.

At his observation post beside the window Anson could see nothing and snapped his telescope shut. It would be a long, frustrating day and he looked forward eagerly to Hurel's return.

Across the Channel on the famous white cliffs above Dover, watching crowds of spectators were calling the gunfire that could be clearly heard "Nelson speaking to the French."

*

After a few hours Anson couldn't bear not knowing what was going on any longer. His room had become a prison. All he could see from the window was a blanket of drifting smoke covering the harbour and all he could hear was a cacophony of detonations. There was nothing to indicate whether or not the defensive line of French vessels was still intact and he felt totally impotent.

What if Hurel had been taken – or killed? Either was a real possibility, and if the worst had happened Anson would have to stay in hiding and try to make it to the rendezvous alone without being able to assess the effect of the bombardment.

His report would be useless and all the effort put into mounting the mission would be wasted.

There was only one course of action: he must leave the comparative safety of his room and go down into the harbour; that was the only way he could find out what was happening.

His scruffy seaman's rig should not attract attention, especially in the smoke, and the noise was such that he could avoid speaking to anyone. If challenged, his schoolboy French should get him out of trouble – especially if he posed, as he had during his escape after the Normandy raid, as a Flemish sailor in the service of France.

The old lady was nowhere to be seen and he was able to slip out of the house unnoticed.

The streets leading down to the harbour were almost deserted, no doubt because the populace was taking sensible precautions and taking shelter during the bombardment.

Nelson had specified that his bomb-boats were to "throw shells at the vessels, but as little as possible to annoy the town." But the inhabitants were not to know that.

Through the thick smoke Anson could see the flames from a fire evidently caused by a stray shot and on the street corner several men were pumping up water and filling leathern buckets.

Perfect! He ran over to them, grabbed a filled bucket and hurried towards the harbour. In this inferno no-one was going to take the slightest bit of notice of a man heading for a fire carrying a water bucket.

Down in the harbour, men were bustling around, some like him carrying buckets, others bringing away casualties on stretchers and many soldiers being organised, he supposed, ready to counter any attempt by the British to land.

Explosions continued every few minutes and from the heights around the town came the echoing return fire from the French shore batteries.

Men were fighting another fire in one of the harbour-side buildings that had been hit but the amount of destruction appeared to be limited.

He paused at the water's edge and strained his eyes seaward, trying to make out what effect the British bombardment was having on the defensive line of French vessels – the object of the raid. But the smoke was too dense for him to see anything except for a few boats bringing casualties ashore.

There was nothing more he could learn here until the bombardment ceased and the smoke cleared. Meanwhile he risked capture so, with reluctance, he decided to make his way back to Madame X's house and hope for Hurel's safe return.

As he walked back, still carrying his water bucket, he noticed two large horse-drawn wagons parked in the comparative safety of a back street.

Curious, he made for them, nodding to the two drivers who were standing beside one of them smoking clay pipes as if everything was normal and the British flotilla was not hammering the harbour.

He sat on a nearby fish crate and took out the bread and cheese he had in his pocket, and, chewing on it, he took a closer look at what the wagons were carrying.

To his surprise their loads were chains – great coils of large-linked, and no doubt extremely heavy, chains.

*

Soon after wading ashore from a Kentish lugger just south of Boulogne, Bardet and his two fellow escapers had heard the cannonade and counter-fire begin.

It came as no surprise. The Whitstable smugglers who had brought them here had warned them of an imminent attack but had not been fazed by it. No-one, friend or foe, was going to bother with the comings and goings of a fishing boat while *that* was going on.

On the way over, Bardet had been told that they were not the only ones landed near Boulogne in the past day or so. The lugger skipper had confided: 'It were a Folkestone galley, we hear. They put a Frenchman and some English bloke ashore close by where you're landing.'

To Bardet, the most likely explanation for that was that this was Hurel from the hulk who had supposedly been buried on Dead Man's Island, but he now knew was very much alive. And the Englishman with him could well be the officer who had reported on the fake funeral and had been staying with Hurel at Ludden.

As they trudged along the foreshore towards Boulogne, Bardet put two and two together. The probability was that Hurel and his companion were on some sort of spying mission, no doubt connected with the bombardment now taking place.

If they were to be captured it was vital that he reported to whoever was in charge of intelligence in Boulogne, and as soon as possible.

He hurried Girault and Cornacchia along and the three soon entered the town, now seething like a disturbed ants' nest, with some fighting fires down in the harbour and others bringing casualties from the defensive line of ships.

With some difficulty, Bardet managed to discover where the headquarters were and there he sought out the officer in charge of intelligence.

In the same room where Hurel had been interrogated the day before, the colonel adjusted his spectacles and stared at Bardet for several moments, making the normally supremely confident Citoyen fidget uncomfortably.

The colonel indicated the young man seated beside him. 'This is Lieutenant Crispin. He is an English navy officer. You speak English, do you not?'

Puzzled, Bardet replied: 'I do, but …?'

'Very well. Crispin is, shall we say, now on our side, but 'is French is not good, so we will use English. Now, you have just arrived from the shores of perfidious England and the 'ulks? How?'

Bardet shuffled his feet. 'My escape was arranged through a bribed guard. My comrades and I got out through a hole cut in the side of the vessel; we swam ashore and were picked up by a gang in league with smugglers.'

'Ah, yes, the Whitstable escape line. I have 'eard of this. In fact many others before you 'ave used the same people. They are apparently very good at what they do and are most discreet on account of the fact that they would prefer not to be 'anged as traitors aiding and abetting the enemy – us.'

Bardet nodded.

'And your passage back to France?'

'All organised by the smugglers – for a price.'

'Smugglers – ah, yes, my friends the Kentish smugglers. They believe in free trade you know. And they are a most useful source of information. They bring me everything from the English newspapers – full of poisonous propaganda, half-truths and lies, but sometimes also a little gem of information – to Steel's navy list, a most useful document and freely available. Such trusting, naive people, these Rosbifs. Doomed to defeat, of course.'

Outside, the din of bombardment continued. The colonel took off his spectacles and polished them with a small cloth. 'And what can you tell us of Nelson's activities – other than the dreadful noise he is currently making?'

'Monsieur, I know little of Nelson's plans, but I do know he 'as sent spies here and I believe they may be 'ere in Boulogne, right now.'

Suddenly animated, the intelligence officer demanded. 'And do you know who these spies are?'

'One is French, a man named Hurel, and 'e is with an English naval lieutenant called Anson. They, too, came over with smugglers.'

The colonel looked up in surprise and Crispin blanched. They exchanged a questioning look.

'Hurel? Are you certain?'

'As sure as I can be, monsieur, yes, he was a prisoner on the same 'ulk as me. The Rosbifs faked 'is death and I believe 'e must be a royalist who 'as agreed to work for them. The smugglers told me he was seen with the naval officer *after* we 'ad been told of 'is funeral.'

'So it appears we have a suspected royalist agent accompanied by an English navy spy at large here. So what could be the reason for that? To report on our invasion preparations, certainly – the number of barges et cetera – and what damage Nelson is doing to our defences.'

Bardet nodded.

'Now, Bardet, would it surprise you that this Hurel was in this very room only yesterday, telling me tales of 'is own escape and giving me supposed intelligence of Nelson's anti-invasion plans?' He reached for a document. 'This is a report this Hurel 'elped Crispin to write.'

Bardet was truly astonished.

The intelligence officer turned and squinted at Crispin. 'You were with Hurel for some time. Did you discover where 'e is staying?'

Crispin cleared his throat nervously and thought quickly. He had arranged to meet Hurel again in little over an hour, so lied: 'No, Monsieur, but we are to meet again this evening.'

'Bien! Then Bardet, here, and his two men will accompany you.'

Near panic, Crispin protested: 'But that will spook him!'

'They will follow at a distance. Bardet is the only one who knows what both Hurel and this Lieutenant Anson look like.' The colonel rose. 'Come, Bardet, I will introduce you to the officer of the guard and 'e will provide you with some weapons and fusiliers to back you up. I want both these men taken – alive – and brought back 'ere for interrogation. Is that clear?'

They went out leaving the panic-stricken Crispin alone. He put his head in his hands for a moment and then, mind made up, he shuffled through the papers on the colonel's desk, stuffed what looked important down his jacket and left hurriedly.

*

Within the hour Crispin was back in the drinking den where the day before he had unburdened himself to Hurel.

By now the intelligence officer would have realised he had made off with the stolen documents, so he was on the run. He was known to frequent this bar, but it was the only link he had with Hurel and the possibility of escaping the living hell he had allowed himself to be sucked into.

All he could do now was pray that Hurel arrived before Bardet.

From Nelson's flotilla targeting the harbour area and the opposing gun batteries on the heights around Boulogne, the fire and counter-fire continued, sometimes intensive, sometimes spasmodically.

At least, Crispin thought, it drew attention away from him.

To steady his nerves he ordered a stiff brandy and nervously clutched a bag containing a few possessions he had just had time to collect from his billet – and the stolen papers.

He had another drink, and then another before the hour passed.

At last Hurel entered, looked around and made his way to Crispin's table at the back of the bar.

Hurel held out his hand, but Crispin rose and stuttered: 'We must go – now!'

Puzzled, Hurel shrugged and followed the Englishman from the bar. On the way out Crispin flung some coins on the counter and muttered: 'Au revoir.'

Outside, as they walked away from the drinking den, he explained: 'We must get away from here and off the streets immediately. I have stolen some papers from the intelligence colonel and a Frenchman called Bardet knows you are here—'

Taken aback, Hurel exclaimed: 'Bardet? Citoyen Bardet! But 'ow?'

'He escaped and came across with smugglers – like you. He's told the intelligence people that you're with a naval officer called Anson. Is that true?'

Hurel nodded. There was no point in denying it.

Crispin looked around. 'For God's sake let's get off the streets! Bardet's been given soldiers to help find you – *us* – and they could be here any minute.'

There was no time to think it through. Crispin could be laying a trap to catch both him and Anson, but Hurel was fairly confident the Englishman was telling the truth. He was clearly rattled, scared almost witless in fact – and when they halted briefly in a doorway to let the dust settle after a stray cannonball hit a nearby building, Crispin opened the bag he was carrying.

A tantalising glimpse of official-looking documents, including one that appeared to be a plan of the port defences, was enough to convince Hurel and he led the way through the back streets to the safe house.

*

Lying on the bed, Anson had let his mind wander over recent events. All this had resulted from attending Hurel's funeral that never was. The Frenchman had been exasperating at times, and trying to keep him under wraps and eventually getting him across to France had been an exceedingly tricky business.

And now the longer Hurel was away, the more Anson became convinced he had been taken, forced to talk – and perhaps even already executed as a spy.

One thing was certain. This time the Frenchman would not end up being buried on the God-forsaken mudflat of Dead Man's Island, that dismal place in the Medway haunted by the cries of curlew sounding like the uneasy spirits of the dead.

Not least, what Anson had seen of the bombardment did not encourage optimism. Some of the ships had been damaged but the masts of landing craft were clustered just as thickly as before in the harbour. And although it was not yet over, it seemed to him that in effect the raid was going to fizzle out in failure.

What's more, seeing the wagons loaded with chains had worried him. If they were used as he guessed they might be, the follow-up cutting-out expedition he knew Nelson was planning could well end in disaster.

His musing was interrupted by sounds of the front door slamming and hurried footsteps up the stairs.

Cocked pistol in hand, he flung the door open. 'Hurel! Thank God! And this is …?'

'I 'ave brought you a visitor, Monsieur Crispin.'

Before the two could exchange a word, Hurel explained: 'Crispin 'ere has stolen some important documents and wishes to return to England with us. But by now the intelligence people will be on to me and Crispin. Another escaper named Bardet has arrived from Kent and spilt the peas—'

192

'Beans!' Anson was deliberately trying to play the situation down, but the mention of Bardet had alarmed him. The Citoyen would be able to recognise them both.

Hurel shrugged. 'Ça ne fait rien, as we Frogs say. Peas or beans, it doesn't matter! They will be seeking us now and we must leave immediately!'

Anson ushered them into the bedroom and, uninvited, Crispin sank onto the bed, clearly already shattered.

Holding up his hand to hush Hurel, Anson urged him: 'Calm down, mon ami, and tell me, were you followed here?'

'No, they will go first to the bar Crispin frequents and try to pick up our trail from —'

'But there is no trail, and so there is no need for us to leave here until it's dark. Then, thanks to the bombardment, we stand a good chance of giving them the slip and reaching the rendezvous in time to meet up with our smuggling friends.'

Hurel considered. 'You are correct, of course. We Frogs 'ave a tendency to become over-excited, I'm told. Yes, we can rest 'ere and I am sure our 'ostess can find us some food. I 'ave not eaten today and 'ad a busy night at the 'ome of my lady friend, so I am trés fatigué. And Crispin 'ere is also very tired.'

And three parts drunk, Anson reckoned, but kept the thought to himself.

Food and some wine were produced and Crispin drank while Hurel and Anson ate. Then they rested up as best they could until it began to grow dark.

Before they left, Hurel went into a huddle with the old lady, no doubt pressing some more money on her and explaining as much as he thought wise about what was afoot.

He told Anson: 'Unless they are watching as we leave they will never connect 'er with us. I 'ave told 'er that if the authorities do question 'er she must say that some men broke in, tied 'er up, stole food and slept in this room.'

Then, with Hurel in the lead and Anson bringing up at the rear, they left quietly by the back door and made their way through winding alleys towards the outskirts of the town heading for the rendezvous.

34

Brotherly Love

After dinner at Hardres Minnis, Augustine Anson sought out his father in the library.

He found the rector deep in thought about next Sunday's sermon – or rather once again wondering which one to copy from his printed book of such pontifications and tweak for local consumption.

'Ah, father, so this is where you're hiding!'

'Oh, it's you, Augustine. It's too early for bed and you find me pondering my next sermon. With Nelson at Deal and expected to make some further show against the French after this bombardment of Boulogne, I thought I might try something martial. If there is some action, your brother Oliver could well be involved.'

Augustine hurrumphed. 'I thought we had agreed that after his refusal to marry the Brax girl his name would not be mentioned in this house.'

The rector protested weakly: 'That was said in the heat of an unfortunate family spat. Surely we should not go that far. It was merely a disagreement after all.'

'Spat? Disagreement? It was treachery! Firstly he embarrassed us all by bringing a Frenchman here – and a papist for God's sake! And then he had the opportunity to secure this family's future prosperity through marriage to the richest heiress this side of the county, yet shied at it!'

The rector flinched at the tirade.

'And now you've had the ignominious task of reading the banns for her marriage to that oaf Chitterling. The whole thing beggars belief!'

'At least the squire has been kind enough to allow me to officiate at the wedding. To me that's a sign that he'll not take his revenge for Oliver's refusal by freezing me out of my parish.'

Augustine snorted. '*My* future father-in-law, the archdeacon, has already been asking me if some sort of scandal is behind all this, and at all costs I must keep it from the ears of Podmore, the incumbent at Nether Siberton.'

'The skeletal fellow with the annoyingly loud voice?'

'Well, yes, admittedly he is rather slim and has a penetrating vocal delivery, but that's ideal for sermons in his large church. Worshippers tend to congregate at the back of the nave, but I'm told his voice still penetrates there. He saw my sisters at a Cathedral service. I introduced them and he has led me to believe he is interested in Anne.'

'And you think he would be a good match for her?'

'Indeed. He has a good living, he's highly ambitious and it's thought he could be a bishop or dean one day.'

The rector nodded appreciatively. In the present circumstances it would be good to marry off his younger daughter to a fellow clergyman in a wealthy parish with a rich tithe income. Pity about the bellowing, he thought, but after all no-one was perfect. He confessed: 'Does Anne return his interest?'

'She is aware and is not averse, I believe. Mother and I will have to arrange things carefully, exposing him to her gradually as it were and making her aware that by marrying him she would become mistress of a substantial household and first lady of his parish. The first step is to invite Podmore here for dinner, but if he hears about this Brax business it could spook him.'

The rector knew that Augustine and Anne were two of a kind and marrying for status and comparative luxury would not put her off a match with a man like Podmore, loud and skeletal or not.

He asked: 'So you'll not progress the match-making as yet?'

'Not until after Charlotte Brax is married off to Chitterling and the fuss about her and Oliver has died down. To tell the truth I'd be more than happy if my wretched brother were to be killed in whatever this action of Nelson's is. At least we could hold our heads up – and, after all, the memorial plaque is still in the church. As I have said to you before, all we would need to do is to get the mason to alter the date of death!'

The rector was shocked. 'I do hope that was meant to be a joke. I entreat you not to make light of all this with base humour, but then I suspect that in saying such things you are actually serious …'

35

Run for Home

Having spent several hours on a fruitless search of the bars and streets of Boulogne, Bardet and his men realised they were on a wild goose chase. Their quarry had obviously gone to ground.

Short of a house-to-house search which would require many more men, there was virtually nil chance of finding Hurel and Crispin, who had probably long since joined the English naval officer wherever he was hiding.

On the way back to report to the intelligence officer, Bardet tried to place himself in the fugitives' shoes. Having so recently been on the run himself, he reckoned they would be intending to get out of Boulogne as soon as possible.

The bombardment and resulting confusion gave them the perfect opportunity to slip away – and they would realise that if they delayed until the situation got back to normal there was a danger that a full-scale search could be mounted.

So where would they go? Almost certainly they would head back to the beach most regularly used by the smugglers and hide up in the dunes until the next run.

And so, when he was ushered into the intelligence colonel's office to report that he had failed to find any trace of the missing men, he was able to offer a plan.

*

Crouching in the sand dunes, Anson strained his eyes seaward. Nothing. He was now beginning to question whether he had found the right rendezvous point – and at the correct time.

Hurel whispered: 'Can you see anything, mon ami?'

'Not much, but I'm fairly sure that headland behind us is Cap d'Alprech.'

'Oui, and these rocks, they are the same, 'ow do you say, *formation*, as where we landed, are they not?'

Anson had thought the same, but the dunes and beach were otherwise featureless and might there not be similar rock formations, as Hurel called them, elsewhere?

They went to ground among the rocks and Anson fished in his kit bag and pulled out the spout lantern and tinder box the smugglers had given him, lit the candle and pointed the spout seawards.

If the galley crew were anywhere near they would look for a pinpoint of light that would tell them all was well ashore.

There would be no need, he hoped, for the flasher – the barrel-less pistol he also had in his bag that could be used to emit a blue flash to warn an incoming boat if the landing site had been compromised.

But, he wondered, would the small focused point of light from the spout lantern be visible from a boat anyway?

Crispin lay back against a low rock. Unfit as he was from excessive drinking over a long period, the trek to the rendezvous had exhausted him. He asked, weakly: 'Are you sure they'll come for us?'

Anson lied: 'Of course. We're just a bit early.'

But as he spoke, shouts from the dunes back towards Boulogne made all three freeze.

Crispin croaked: 'My God, they're after us! What can we do?'

Anson peered back out to sea. And suddenly there it was – a galley heading straight for them. His signal had been spotted and rescue was at hand. He grinned. Why had he doubted? The smugglers knew their business.

A swift calculation told him that judging from the shouts of the men approaching through the dunes it would be only a matter of minutes before they arrived. And the row galley? Maybe about the same.

They could run down the beach and wade out to the approaching boat, but the moon was already up and they would most certainly be spotted. In any event, Crispin was unfit, exhausted and would never make it.

The options were limited. They needed to let the smugglers know where they were, but as soon as they revealed themselves their pursuers would zero in on them.

The shouting was getting closer and Anson made his mind up. He rose, aimed his pistol in the general direction of their pursuers, cocked it and fired. The chance of hitting them was remote, but the sound of the shot might make them think twice and take cover. And the flash and bang would have let Tom Hoover and the galley crew know exactly where he was.

He turned to Hurel. 'Help me with Crispin. We must get down to the water – now!'

They helped Crispin up and, supporting him each with an arm over their shoulders, dragged him down the hard-packed sand.

The shouts from their pursuers told them that they had been spotted immediately but ahead Anson saw that the row galley was negotiating the last of the breakers only a few yards from the beach.

But ashore it was an unequal race. Encumbered as they were, Anson and Hurel could make only slow progress, giving their pursuers the advantage.

Half a dozen French infantrymen, followed by Bardet and his two henchmen, appeared from the dunes, fanned out and doubled towards them shouting excitedly.

It was a stark choice – abandon Crispin and go flat out for the boat or stay with him and risk almost certain capture, wounding or death. And if Hurel was taken alive he would no doubt face a firing squad.

But everything changed in an instant. From the boat came the flashes and bangs of a ragged volley. One of the pursuing infantrymen fell, screaming and clutching his gut.

Anson mouthed: 'Thank God!' The smugglers had seen what was happening and come to their aid.

The volley had won him precious seconds and he urged Hurel on over the last few yards.

In the boat it was Tom Hoover who had orchestrated the covering fire – and it was a ball from his carbine that had felled one of the Frenchmen.

The American resisted the temptation to reload. It would have been difficult anyway in the crowded boat. Instead he left the weapon in the thwarts and vaulted over the side.

He waded through knee-deep water to where Anson and Hurel, both completely blown, had dropped Crispin at the edge.

As they fought for breath several musket balls screamed past. Now over the shock of the volley from the boat, the pursuers had got their act together. The infantrymen had dropped to one knee to present a lower profile, and were firing, reloading and preparing to fire again.

Hoover grabbed hold of Crispin, pulled him up over his shoulder and turned back to the boat.

The crackle of musketry continued and a sound like a punch and a cry told Anson that Crispin had been hit.

Reaching the boat, Hoover heaved the wounded man into the thwarts and was joined in the water by several of the crew. They helped Anson and Hurel climb aboard and shoved the galley back down the beach.

Several of the smugglers had reloaded and their returned fire put the Frenchmen off their aim.

Some of the rowers were already in action, dipping their blades and straining hard, and gradually they pulled clear of the beach as the remaining crewmen clawed their way back into the boat.

Anson was so used to being in command in situations like this that he shouted: 'Keep low, boys!' before remembering he was merely a passenger for this escapade.

He looked back to see the Frenchmen running down the beach with a figure he recognised at the rear – Bardet.

Pulling his pistol from his belt, he tried to reload, but the oars were sending sprays of seawater over the sides of the galley and his hands were shaking so from the effort of getting Crispin down the beach that he fumbled it and gave up.

Hoover, trained to reload in any conditions, was more successful. He raised his carbine and took aim at Bardet, now only some thirty yards away up the beach.

But Anson shook his head. Killing one more Frenchman was not going to solve anything, and he had a sneaking admiration for Bardet's successful escape from the hulks and for managing to track down Hurel.

The American got Anson's drift, raised his weapon and fired what was now merely a warning shot well above the heads of their pursuers.

As the galley gained seaway, the Frenchmen stopped at the water's edge and gave up the chase.

Turning for one last look, Anson saw Bardet remove his hat and could have sworn that it was raised in salute.

*

Mid-Channel, halfway between the country of his birth and the enemy he had betrayed it to, Lieutenant Crispin, one-time commander of the Seagate Sea Fencibles turned spy and traitor, was dying.

The musket ball that hit him as Hoover was carrying him to the boat had caused a devastating gut wound from which it was immediately plain no-one could possibly recover.

Anson crouched beside him in the thwarts and tried to make him as comfortable as possible, putting pressure on the entry wound to try to stop the bleeding, but it was a losing battle.

Crispin lapsed in and out of consciousness and when his eyes opened for a moment Anson leaned forward to speak to him, although words were unlikely to give him any comfort at such a time.

Nevertheless, it was worth a try. 'Crispin. Can you hear me?' The wounded man's eyes flickered. 'We're making good progress and in a few hours you'll be home.'

His response was barely audible. 'Home, yes, please take me home. My gut hurts so.'

'It won't be long,' Anson lied.

Crispin's mouth was working but Anson couldn't catch what he was trying to say so he whispered in his ear: 'Try to speak up a bit.'

It registered. Crispin's eyes fluttered open again and he said, quietly but quite clearly now: 'I know I'm dying. I didn't want to be a traitor, you know. It was the drink. It took over my life ...'

'I understand.'

'By God, I need some now! Is there any in the boat.? '

'Sorry, no, but anyway it wouldn't help you now. Is there anyone you want to be told what's happened to you? Your parents?'

Crispin gave a slight nod. 'My poor parents. They'll be wondering what's happened to me since I left Seagate. Will you tell them?'

'Where do they live?'

'Their address is in my notebook, in my pocket here.' He felt for it but the effort was too much for him and he screwed up his eyes in pain.

Anson found the notebook and assured the dying man: 'Of course I'll tell them and I'll report that you had been on a mission fighting the French and died at sea.'

Anson thought he detected a half smile on Crispin's lips and a muttered 'Thanks.'

The wounded man was clearly sinking fast, but made one last effort, asking: 'You won't put me over the side, will you?'

'No, we'll take you home.'

Blood appeared on Crispin's lips and his body convulsed and went limp.

Hoover, taking a turn at an oar, looked across questioningly. 'Has he gone?'

Anson nodded. 'Yes, he's gone, but we'll take him home.'

*

The smugglers needed little persuasion to take the galley into Seagate. Several of them lived there anyway and they trusted Anson when he told them that if the Revenue or anyone else challenged them he would confirm that they were on an official Sea Fencible mission. If necessary, he promised, he would create retrospective paperwork stating that they were all fully signed-up fencibles.

However, they would be getting a good deal more than a shilling for this night's work.

The galley's approach had been sighted from the gun battery and Fagg was waiting for them at the harbour accompanied by Phineas Shrubb and his daughter.

But there was no patching up for them to do as everyone had come through without a scratch – except for Crispin.

Exhausted and ravenously hungry, Anson led Hurel to the Mermaid for bacon and eggs.

He had shaken hands with each of the oarsmen, telling them: 'Thank you all, whoever you are!' This especially amused his own fencibles among the crew, but it meant that the worst-kept secret of their free trading sideline was safe with him.

Hoover had grim work to do. He sent the Mermaid potboy to fetch George Boxer, who handled the detachment's administration and in civilian life was an undertaker. There was a burial to arrange.

Over breakfast Anson quizzed Hurel as to what he wanted to do now that his mission was over.

'Your friend Commander Armstrong told me that if such a situation arose he would introduce me to some émigré French friends of 'is 'oo are taking the 'ealthy waters at a spa somewhere called Tunbridge Wells. They are royalists, of course, and apparently would be willing to 'ost me.'

'What an excellent idea! Tell me, are there some *female* royalists with them and do they all tend to talk almost without stopping?'

'Mais oui! But I think this is some sort of pathetic English 'umour that you are teasing me with. Very amusing. If I was not so very fatigué I would laugh out loud, but for now all I can manage is a small grimace ...'

'Touché, mon ami!' Anson clapped him on the back, dislodging a slice of bacon from the Frenchman's fork.

'By the by, I am extremely glad that you survived your mission. It would have been most irritating if it had been you and not Crispin who died in the boat.'

'No more than irritating?' Hurel asked sadly.

Anson laughed. 'Well, don't forget that I've already attended your funeral on Dead Man's Island and I'm damned if I wanted an encore!'

Events had proved extraordinarily tricky since Hurel came into his life. Nevertheless he would miss the Frenchman when he departed for the healthier waters of Tunbridge Wells.

36

The Chain of Command

Anson had visited the small Cinque Ports town of Deal before, firstly to board the store-ship waiting in the Downs anchorage for a favourable wind to sail down-Channel and carry him to the Mediterranean to join the frigate HMS *Phryne*. And later, after his return from France, he had visited his two fellow escapers in the small naval hospital there.

Its many boatmen and fisherman not only served the many ships that gathered in the Downs but no doubt continued their favoured more lucrative pastime of smuggling.

He knew that not many years since, soldiers had been sent to destroy the Deal luggers and galleys suspected of smuggling.

However, these free traders were descendants of the Cinque Ports men granted – by royal charter, no less – the right to import goods freely in return for their services in defence of the nation before the emergence of the Royal Navy.

There was no way, therefore, that men of independent spirit like these were going to be put off carrying on with what they regarded as a sacred right.

And now, since the outbreak of the war with France, no-one was going to stamp out what had become an essential cross-Channel trade.

The French wines and brandy that graced many a table in Kent, including that of Anson's clergyman father, came courtesy of the men of Deal and their like along the Channel coast – as did a good many other luxury goods.

Now the town was busier than ever, with marines and soldiery at every turn and a forest of warship masts in the anchorage.

Anson had gone there having been told at Dover Castle that Colonel Redfearn had left to call on Nelson's staff – no doubt to discuss intelligence matters concerning the forthcoming operation.

Clearly the written report Anson had prepared for the colonel following the bombardment of Boulogne would be of the utmost importance, seeing that it was first-hand news of the effect of that raid and the state of the French defences.

In it, he had expressed his concerns: that the bombardment had caused little damage, the defensive line of vessels was still largely intact and, most importantly, that he suspected the French had by now secured them with chains, making them pretty well invulnerable to a boat attack.

For what it was worth coming from a mere lieutenant, he had recommended that if the proposed cutting-out raid was mounted, some of the boats should carry blacksmiths with tools capable of breaking chains.

His vital task now was to get his report into the hands of Colonel Redfearn who could then brief the admiral's staff in detail.

He walked down to the beach intending to look for a boat that could take him out to the flagship and was confronted by an extraordinary sight.

Among the many ships in the Downs anchorage he could see a frigate he guessed was HMS *Medusa* from the steady succession of all manner of boats circling around her.

Anson was astonished. He had never seen the like before and could only imagine that Nelson's fame had drawn sightseers from far and wide who had paid the Deal boatmen good money to take them out. It seemed that the world and his wife wanted to catch a glimpse of their great naval hero.

*

From his cabin in *Medusa* the object of their attention was writing to his lover, Emma, Lady Hamilton, complaining of the goldfish bowl scrutiny he was under from his admirers.

Nelson had achieved undying fame through his great victories – Copenhagen and Aboukir, the Nile. He had sought fame and at first enjoyed it.

But now ...

He wrote: *"The Mayor and Corporation of Sandwich, when they came on board to present me with the Freedom of that ancient town, requested me to dine with them. I put them off for the moment but they would not be let off."*

And he complained to Emma of the attention *Medusa* was receiving because of him: *"Oh! How I hate to be stared at! Fifty boats, I am told, are rowing about her this moment to have a look at the one-armed man."*

*

On shore, as Anson approached a row of ships' boats drawn up on the beach he grimaced on seeing a figure well-known to him in conversation with one of the coxswains.

'Dear God, no! The last person on earth I wished to see.'

It was his divisional captain – the portly, cherry-cheeked, be-whiskered social-climber and stealer of others' glory, Captain Arthur Veryan St Cleer Hoare.

With heavy heart Anson crunched down the beach and waited. Hoare, busily engaged in negotiating for a boat to take him out to the flagship, failed to notice his underling at first.

But then, as the coxswain knuckled his forehead to settle the passage, Hoare turned and stared at Anson in astonishment.

'What on earth are *you* doing here? I heard a rumour that you'd gone to France on some pretended mission or other.'

'It was an official mission, sir, initiated by the commodore.'

'Home Popham? But he's gone!'

'Nevertheless, sir, I acted under orders from Colonel Redfearn, his successor in intelligence matters.'

'I was not consulted and did not authorise you to go, so it could not be an official mission.'

Anson sighed. The last thing he wanted was to get into an acrimonious debate with this poltroon. 'Look, sir, as a result of my reconnaissance over the other side I have information of the utmost importance. It affects the operation that's about to take place and I must see Colonel Redfearn so that he can present my report to Lord Nelson or someone senior on his staff.'

Hoare fumed. 'Get back in your cot, Anson. Who do you think you are? *I* am your superior officer. You report to *me*. In turn I report to the admiral. That's how it works. It's called the chain of command.'

'But Colonel Redfearn—'

'Redfearn be damned! Hand *me* your report.'

Anson struggled to keep his temper. 'Look, if Lord Nelson attacks the French line of ships defending Boulogne it could well end in disaster. I believe they cannot be cut out because by now they are chained together. I have seen the chains.'

'Chains fiddlesticks! Do you really think that Nelson is going to call off a raid of this magnitude just because one lily-livered junior officer thinks the Frogs might have chained their ships together? I hope they have. If they cannot manoeuvre they'll be sitting ducks, well, sitting *Frogs* anyway, ha, ha!'

Anson bridled at the suggestion of cowardice, but kept his cool. 'It's not only the chains. They have strong anti-boarding nets, too.'

'Most helpful of the Frogs to give us climbing aids – it'll make it all the easier for our men to board them, eh?'

Anson despaired. The way Hoare had taken the news of the chains did not fill his 'underling' with confidence.

The man clearly did not understand the importance of this intelligence. It would be difficult, if not impossible, to cut the French vessels out conventionally. Axes would be fine against ropes, but not metal. To Anson it was as simple as the paper-scissors-stone game he had played as a child. In the grown-up version that was about to be played out, using axe blades against iron would be like tackling stone with scissors.

And if the assault boats went equipped only to cut hemp cables the whole raid could turn into a fiasco.

Hoare had certainly misunderstood the netting. Far from helping boarders, it would catch them like fish in a trawl and they could be shot or stabbed as they tried to cut their way through.

Did he need to spell this out to his superior officer? Anson thought that maybe he did. Hoare had never attempted to board an enemy ship, nor fought hand-to-hand.

He ventured persuasively: 'Look, sir, the point is that the boarders will need special equipment to cut their way through the netting – and to break the chains. If they don't they will be snared like rabbits and easy prey for the defenders – and any that do get through won't be able to break the chains to cut out the French ships. The whole operation will be in vain and many lives will be lost. It's as simple as that. It's all here in my detailed report, addressed to Colonel Redfearn.'

Hoare sighed theatrically. 'The point you are missing, Anson, is that what will be required is not special equipment but good old British guts!'

'But you *will* be sure to give my report about the chains and netting to Colonel Redfearn?'

'Enough, Anson. Give it to me. I have said I will pass on whatever needs to be passed to the admiral.'

Anson had grave misgivings but reached into his jacket for his report and the package containing the French intelligence officer's papers stolen by Crispin.

'Then please also pass him this. It includes a sketch plan stolen from the French showing their defensive line and the types – and names – of all the vessels. It also shows the existing shore batteries and the new ones being built.'

Hoare snatched the report and package from his hand and stuffed it down his own jacket.

'Now, Anson, to more important matters. I have been asked to provide two fully-manned gunboats for the raid. Nelson has yet to be convinced of the usefulness of Sea Fencibles, so I intend to demonstrate it to him.'

'Two from your division?' Anson queried.

'No, both from Seagate.'

'None from Folkestone, Hythe, et cetera?'

'No, I have decided to give Seagate the honour of providing both. You have the new gunboats and your men are accustomed to working them – the men from the other detachments are not.'

Anson's patience was now paper thin. 'So if the raid goes wrong, as it surely will unless full account is taken of the netting and chains, the widows and orphaned children will be confined to one area – Seagate?'

Hoare gave him an icy stare. 'Once again you border on the insolent, Anson, and for a proper officer you are far too lily-livered and emotional about your men. They are mere harbour rats, ten a penny.'

Anson seethed but held himself in check.

'By the by, the admiral requires an officer to command each boat.'

'So you will be coming yourself ... sir?

'Love to, of course, but I have bigger fish to fry, as you'll hear. No, I have ordered Lieutenant Coney of the impress to command one of the Seagate boats and you'll take the other.'

Anson knew Coney well. He was a good man, despite the universal unpopularity of his job.

'Did he not volunteer?

'Volunteer? This is the navy, not a democracy. We do as we are told, not pick and choose like a bunch of amateurs!'

Anson had heard that before, not least from a former captain, but coming from Hoare it grated.

'Knowing Matthew Coney, I feel certain he would have volunteered if given the opportunity.'

'Pah!'

Hoare's dismissive snort angered Anson and he snapped: 'For someone given the opportunity to win glory you are surprisingly reluctant yourself!'

Hoare spat: 'Watch your tone – and have the decency to call me si*r*! As to glory, I have more than enough – the *Seraphim* affair when I saw off a Frenchman that far out-gunned me, and the battle, well, now the *battles* of Seagate as the townsmen are calling them. No, Anson, this is an opportunity for younger men yet to make their mark and win their spurs. I think I have earned my place alongside Nelson in his flagship to liaise and advise him on Sea Fencible matters, don't you?'

'I see … *sir*.' The pause before 'sir' was long enough to make it sound insolent, which Anson fully intended it to be. 'So you'll be in *Medusa*?'

'Alongside Nelson.' Hoare smirked. 'Wait ashore here and I'll send you your written orders. Study them carefully and brief the men accordingly. I want no cock-ups from the Sea Fencibles while I am at the admiral's side.'

Hoare turned to the nearby boat and called to the coxswain: 'Send one of your oarsmen to help me aboard.'

The coxswain motioned a burly sailor to attend the captain. Hoare ordered him to bend over like a schoolboy about to be caned, and mounted him to be piggy-backed through the surf to the boat so that his boots did not get wet.

Anson could scarcely believe what he was seeing. He shook his head in disgust, turned and walked away.

*

Later, back in his room at the Rose, Anson opened the sealed orders that had been handed to him after a long wait on the beach at Deal.

Following his own mission to Boulogne with Hurel, there were no real surprises. He was only too conscious that, with Nelson commanding the anti-invasion forces, great things were expected of him as the hero of Copenhagen and Aboukir if he were to be the saviour of the nation.

Anson was aware, too, that His Majesty's ministers, believing that an army of 75,000 soldiers was encamped between Flushing and Le Havre, with more than 100 shallow-draught barges already available and twice as many more built or on the stocks, had allowed it to be leaked to the newspapers that they "fully expected the French would make an immediate descent upon the island."

It would not be sufficient merely to deter invasion. Nelson was expected to pre-empt it – and that meant carrying the fight to the enemy.

After the largely ineffective bombardment of Boulogne it did not take a genius to fathom that the admiral would need to stage something far more dramatic.

Hence a second attack on Boulogne, but this time cutting out the ships moored off-shore, as the orders stated: *"... until the whole flotilla be either taken, or totally annihilated."*

The plan was for boats from the ships of Nelson's squadron and from the Sea Fencibles, to be formed into four divisions under the command of a captain, each of about fifteen boats armed with howitzers and carronades. A fifth division of large lugger-rigged flatboats would give supporting fire with eight-inch mortars.

The main force was to launch a frontal attack on the moored ships – the sailors boarding with cutlasses, pikes and tomahawks, the marines armed with musket and bayonet.

At the same time, two boats from each division were to pull through the enemy line to cut their cables. Any prizes that could not be brought out to sea were to be burned.

37

Wedding Bells

The ivy-covered, flint-walled 12th century church of Saints Cosmos and Damian was bedecked with flowers within and a crowd of villages had already gathered outside, anxious not to miss the event of the year.

There had not been such comings and goings there since the memorial service two years earlier for the rector's son, the late Lieutenant Oliver Anson, Royal Navy, who had subsequently turned out not to be late after all but a prisoner in France.

Even after his escape and return home the memorial plaque recording, prematurely as it turned out, his death in action on the Normandy shore had for whatever reason remained in the church.

It was well known among parishioners that his unloving elder brother Gussie had cynically suggested that in the interests of economy it be left where it was, covered with a curtain, so that the date of death could be altered "when the time comes".

But today was not one for memorialising. It seemed that a good half of what passed for society in the county had headed there, along with many of the local yokels for whom such an event was a rare – and free – spectacle.

Rich or poor, all were agog to witness the marriage of Squire Brax's eldest daughter Charlotte to Richard, known as Dickie, captain of the local yeomanry troop but, more importantly, heir to the sprawling Chitterling estate consisting of a score of large productive farms, a great many smallholdings and hundreds of acres of valuable woodland.

It was to be a joining of the county's two wealthiest families and to all outward appearances it was a match made in heaven.

The groom certainly thought so. He was getting a rich, exceptionally pretty – indeed voluptuous – wife who had already allowed him to sample the coming delights of the marriage bed, to his complete satisfaction.

She had also made it quite clear to him that once the knot had been tied and she had presented him with the necessary heir and a spare she reserved the right to do her own thing with whom and whenever she chose. She had told him: 'Don't ever forget, I'm a Brax – not some mare you can tame with a bridle and bit! You'll answer to my father if you annoy me.'

Chitterling knew that was no idle threat. No-one thereabouts would willingly get on the wrong side of her fierce father, who was not only a rich and powerful man, quick to anger, but a tyrant who dictated his own version of the law as the local magistrate and enacted it in draconian fashion.

On the upside, Charlotte had indicated to her future husband that she did not much mind what *he* got up to after they were wed. His womanising and gambling could continue as long as it did not come home to roost with her.

There was only one cloud on the horizon. Charlotte heartily wished she was marrying someone else. Not *anyone* else, but one and the same naval officer whose memorial plaque graced the church where the wedding was about to take place: Lieutenant Oliver Anson.

She had been instantly attracted to him on his return after escaping from France following the abortive cutting-out raid in Normandy and had made a play for him, successfully using all her physical charms to reel him in.

He had succumbed – what man wouldn't? And she had done her very best to force him to propose, but, in retrospect, she could admit to herself that she had rushed her fences and scared him off.

The fact that his father, the Reverend Thomas Anson, was officiating at her marriage to someone else rubbed more salt into the wound.

But she hid her chagrin and went along with the fiction of blushing bride eagerly marrying the man of her dreams. Except that in her case blushing was most definitely a thing of the past.

Chitterling, despite never having faced anything more dangerous than an unarmed fox or pheasant, arrived on horseback and in full regimentals, accompanied by a fellow yeomanry officer who was to be best man.

They were followed by a score or more from the groom's own Pett Valley Troop of the South Kent Yeomanry, mainly drawn from the sons of his family's tenant farmers.

Resplendent in high-plumed helmet, the chubby-cheeked, red-faced groom, was showing the beginnings of a paunch only just restrained by his tightly-buttoned, elaborately-brocaded blue jacket and scarlet waist sash that was riding up slightly under the strain.

His extravagant outfit was completed with vivid red stripes down his overalls, highly polished riding boots and spurs, and at his side hung a magnificently-hilted silver-sheathed, but as yet unused sabre.

For the occasion he had abandoned the chestnut mount common to the Pett Valley Troop and instead drew envious glances with his magnificent grey, a wedding present from his father.

Groom and best man stood, two peacocks showing off their finery, at the church porch posing like conquering heroes, with Chitterling acknowledging tenants and others he knew who had come to gape.

Then, as Sergeant Sam Noad – an ex-regular dragoon and the only real soldier in the volunteer troop – lined up the men as an honour guard, the groom and best man strode into the church, spurs jingling, and marched noisily down the aisle to take position at the front.

Once seated, Chitterling turned to peer back at the full pews, nodding and smiling to those he knew like a politician seeking votes.

The Anson sisters were there with their mother, he noticed, but there was no sign of their naval brother. Pity, he thought, to the victor the spoils – and it would have been good to have been able to rub that jumped-up sailor's nose in it for sniffing around Charlotte Brax when she was so obviously well out of his price range.

The un-blushing bride-to-be arrived on her father's arm attended by her younger sisters and swept up the aisle, every bit the swan followed by her cygnets.

But for Charlotte there were no smiles to left or right.

Acknowledging her soon-to-be husband, who with his best man had risen to his feet, with a nod, she stared ahead and remained so as they took the final steps to matrimony.

Their responses were loud and matter-of-fact. This was no love match. A lust match perhaps, and certainly what amounted to a business merger between two great land-owning dynasties.

Rings were exchanged, the rector declared them man and wife and Chitterling took his bride's hand and led her like a prize mare down the aisle.

As they swept out of the church under the crossed sabres of the Pett Valley Troop's guard of honour, one of Chitterling's men was cheeky enough to comment: 'Good for you, Master Richard. Come mornin' they'll be another little trooper on the way for sure!'

Chitterling guffawed, but his bride remained silent, appearing not to have heard the remark. But she had.

And the truth was, she knew that she was *already* expecting – hence going through the marriage ceremony at the earliest opportunity. But she had no idea whether the child, if male, would be a little trooper – or sailor.

*

During a lull at the lavish Brax Hall wedding breakfast that followed, the groom, having already imbibed copiously, found himself alongside the rector.

'Dull service, old fruit, but I s'pose you've got to rattle through all that "ordained by God and let no man put asunder" stuff to make it legal, eh?'

The Reverend Anson winced, but could not immediately think of a suitable response. Chitterling poked him in the chest and demanded: 'By the way, that naval son of yours – the uppity fellow who attacked me on the way to the Mote Park review – what's he up to these days. Off playin' with his harbour rats, is he?'

The rector started to stutter a reply but Chitterling had already spun on his heel and, spurs jingling, moved on.

The rector was left feeling humiliated. Oliver had spurned the squire's offer of a generous settlement if *he* had married Charlotte. In itself this would not have been a problem and he could understand why his son had shied at such a flighty, spoilt and headstrong partner.

But as rector he himself was in thrall to the Brax family who held the advowson of the parish and were therefore able to dictate who would be the incumbent. This put him firmly under the squire's thumb. And now the awful Chitterling, who clearly hated Oliver, would also be able to exert *his* malevolent influence.

Added to that was the Reverend Anson's feeling of discomfort and guilt at allowing his wife and Gussie to sway him over the business of Oliver's refusal to marry Charlotte Brax which had opened a wide rift between him and his favourite son.

All told, he had a feeling of depression and foreboding, heightened by rumours from the coast that, following his bombardment of Boulogne, Nelson was about to mount some great operation against the French.

It was common knowledge that Nelson's flotilla had returned to Deal, where there was now feverish activity and the naval yard had begun to collect oared sea-going boats. This could mean but one thing – there was going to be an attempt to cut out enemy ships. But where? And although he had no idea where Oliver was, he had a strong premonition that he would be involved and that it would not end well.

38

Volunteers to a Man

Anson summoned Fagg and told him to call for volunteers to man both gunboats.

Fagg laughed. 'That's sorted then!'

'What do you mean?'

'Take it as they'll all volunteer, sir.'

'How d'you know?'

'I'll *tell* 'em. I'll just 'ave t'say: you, you and you! They'll volunteer orlright!'

'No, no, no. That won't do at all. This isn't the proper navy. They're not pressed men. They'll need to be willing volunteers. Lord Nelson would not wish to include unwilling men.'

'Look, sir, it's like this: what wiv Nelson and you, too, well, you're both what they call lucky orficers. So don't you worry, sir, they'll all follow 'im anywhere – and you, 'specially if there's a whiff o' prize money.'

'More like a strong whiff of gunsmoke! I doubt there'll be many prizes, if any. The admiral has made it clear that any enemy craft we can't easily winkle out must be burnt where they are.'

'Whatever, the boys'll volunteer orlright.'

'Nevertheless, Lieutenant Coney will be bringing some of his men and we have more in the detachment than we need to man the two boats, so we'll only take real volunteers, is that clear?'

'Aye, aye, sir.'

'And I'll check that they are truly volunteers, so there'll be no pressing unwilling men, is that understood?'

'Aye, sir.'

'Oh, and another thing – only you and Hoover are to know the true objective.'

'Boologny?' Like many a Man of Kent, Fagg was completely unable to pronounce the name of the French port correctly although they lived only just across the Channel from it.

Anson corrected him, not for the first time. 'Yes, Boulogne. But the men are not to be told until after we are at sea. This is meant to be a surprise attack. With Kentish smugglers going back and forth to France all the time someone is sure to leak the target. So let 'em think it's going to be Flushing, Dunkirk, the Normandy ports, or whatever …'

'So I'm to tell 'em it's not Boologny?'

'If anyone mentions Boulogne, remind 'em that Nelson's already bombarded the Frogs there and smashed a lot of their invasion barges, so more than likely we're off to attack somewhere different.'

They discussed how many they would need to man the boats, with spare oarsmen to ring the changes during long hauls rather than risk blowing the men.

Anson announced: 'I'll take Hoover and Sampson Marsh as gun captain. And you and Lieutenant Coney can have Minter. He's good with the carronade. And take young Tom Marsh. You won't find a stronger rower anywhere along the coast.'

That was certainly true, but Anson's real reason for splitting Sampson and Tom Marsh was to try to avoid too great a loss in one family if things went pear-shaped and one of the boats was lost.

*

Later, Fagg sought out Anson in the Mermaid where he was finishing his supper and reported that the boats were ready, that the blacksmith Ned Clay and his mate had turned up with their bags of tools as requested, and that the rest of the men were gathered.

'Good. I'd best let them know what's what. They must be all agog.'

'You could say that, sir. There's bin orl sorts of rumours – everyfink from invadin' France to Gawd knows what!'

'Very well, let's go.'

The men stopped talking and there was an expectant hush as Anson entered the detachment building, Fagg preceding him shouting: 'Gangway for the orficer!'

They were all there: Sampson Marsh, the fishmonger turned gun captain; his crippled nephew Tom, the unit's best oarsman on account of his upper-body strength resulting from a lifetime of hopping around on crutches; Boxer, the undertaker; Hobbs; Minter; Heale; Oldfield; Hogben; Shallow; Longstaff; and others who had been with him since he took over and had already seen action.

There were new faces, too, some no doubt having heard some sort of operation was pending and anxious to be involved. All hoped that whatever it was would turn out to be another triumph like the taking of the Normandy privateer which was still the talk of the town – and for which it was rumoured those involved would receive a substantial share of prize money.

Anson looked around, nodding to key men like Sampson Marsh and Joe Hobbs, a cobbler by trade and the detachment's best coxswain, who grinned back, clearly flattered to be acknowledged.

He was delighted to see that Phineas Shrubb, who had seen plenty of action as a surgeon's mate during the American war, was among the volunteers to go. The apothecary-cum-Baptist preacher would, he knew, prove his worth tending anyone wounded in action and it comforted the men to know he would be there to patch them up.

The bosun called the men to order and Anson addressed them: 'Right men, it's like this. Admiral Nelson is now down at Deal commanding the anti-invasion forces – including us ...'

There was a murmur of approval. Every man jack had heard of Nelson and knew of his winning reputation following his great victories at Copenhagen and Aboukir. Being included among those the great man commanded made them proud.

'... appears he's got something important to be done and the navy and the Deal and Dover men can't handle it without our help ...'

The men laughed. There had always been rivalry between the Channel ports and the Folkestone and Seagate men, he knew, had long been convinced they were better than their neighbours at just about everything.

'We'll be taking the boats and Lord Nelson wants an officer in each, so I'll be in *Striker* with Sergeant Hoover. Lieutenant Coney has kindly volunteered to command *Stinger* and will be bringing along some of his men. Bosun, you'll be with him.'

There were some apprehensive looks. They were well aware that Coney was in charge of the local impress service, and normally the Seagate men avoided anyone associated with the press gang like the plague. But now some would be sharing a boat with them.

Anson noted the uneasy looks and made use of them. 'It'll be handy because if any of you don't do your duty the press gang boys can row you straight off to a receiving ship afterwards!'

There were muted laughs. The thought of being pressed into naval servitude was no laughing matter, but they felt sure Anson didn't mean what he'd just said. Or did he?

'Now, I want volunteers for the boats – *just* volunteers mind, no pressed men. This could be a hazardous mission so I don't want married men with children – nor newly married men.'

Fagg held up his hand and to renewed laughter asked: 'What abaht them like me as ain't married as such, well, not churched like, but might 'ave lots of orfspring what they don't know nuffink abaht?'

'Very amusing bosun, but of course *you* will be considered to have volunteered as a matter of course. We need you.'

The bosun grinned. 'Thank you very much, sir, 'appy to oblige.'

'The boats are ready?'

'Aye, ready, sir.'

'Good, then we'll make our way down to the harbour and rendezvous with Lieutenant Coney and his men. When we get there I want to see only those who wish to volunteer. Fathers and anyone not wanting or unable to go for whatever reason must fall out on the way. There'll be no come-backs. I will choose from those still with us when we get to the boats.'

He watched as Fagg ushered out the volunteers and one man caught his eye.

'You can fall out Heale, you've already sacrificed two fingers for the King.'

Heale protested: 'Plenty more where they come from, sir. Anyhow, I'm bustin' to go – to get revenge for me fingers, like.'

'Very well. But hang on firmly to the rest of your body parts this time.' Ned Heale was a good man, keener than ever to have a go at the French after being wounded in the battle with the Normandy privateer, and Anson was happy to take him.

'Mister Boxer?'

'Sir?'

'I wish you to be in charge of the rear party. I know you would give your eye teeth to come but I need you to stay here in charge of things and look after the rest of the men – and the families of those who go, if need be.'

'But, sir—'

'No buts, Mister Undertaker, it's an order. Oh, and please take a note of the names of those chosen to go. Once we have gone kindly inform their families. Tell them we hope to be back, I think, in a few days. Now, let's go!'

As they walked down to the harbour Anson singled out Clay. 'You know what you and your mate must we do if ...' he corrected himself,'... *when* we get on board an enemy?'

'Look for mooring chains and break any we find, sir?'

'That's right, but these will more than likely be pretty hefty chains.'

'Every chain has a weak link, sir, and I'll find it.'

'Good man, but be under no illusion. You'll be doing it under fire. It won't be quite the same as knocking out a piece of iron back in your forge.'

'I'll cope, sir.'

'Good man, Clay, I'm sure you will.'

*

The two gun-boats, *Striker* and *Stinger*, were of a new type trialled by the Seagate detachment. Clinker-built row galleys, each had a slide for'ard extending back to the third thwart for mounting a 12-pounder carronade and, aft, were pairs of throle-pins to accommodate eight oars a side.

The slide for the carronade was pivoted at the fore end so that it could be elevated or depressed, and on rollers at the after end for training it to starboard or larboard.

The detachment had used these boats to great effect in two skirmishes with the Normandy privateer, resulting in its capture, after a hail of splinters sent on their deadly paths by a carronade ball had killed and wounded many of the Frenchmen.

Now, with all oars manned, they cut through the swell with ease as they passed Folkestone heading for the Downs anchorage.

The row was easy-paced to conserve energy, and Anson and Coney did nothing to discourage the good-natured banter between the two boats.

When *Stinger* fell behind a wag aboard *Striker* called out: 'Oughta rename your tub *Slug* not *Stinger*!'

The offended crew put in a spurt, passing *Striker* with the rejoinder: 'Who're the slow coaches now? You couldn't catch a tart in a brothel!'

And so it went as they passed Dover and headed for Deal.

From way off, the 12-mile-long anchorage appeared like a forest of masts. It was sheltered four miles out by the notorious Goodwin Sands, graveyard of many a ship over many a century – victims of the shifting sandbanks that could make a fool of any pilot.

Here, Anson knew, East Indiamen and traders of every shape and size, passenger vessels and warships gathered to await a favourable wind to head up into the North Sea or down-Channel into the Atlantic.

The forest of masts turned into a flotilla of naval vessels. Nelson's flagship, the 32-gun *Medusa* lay at its centre, flanked by several other frigates, gun brigs, bomb vessels and gunboats of every type, and, to his surprise, even a few Revenue cutters.

39

Band of Brothers

Coney ordered Fagg to ease off, allowing Anson to lead the way.

Their approach had been noted and a burly young lieutenant hailed them with a speaking trumpet from a jolly-boat that had clearly been co-opted as flotilla sheepdog.

'What boat?'

Anson cupped his hands to his mouth: 'Sea Fencibles, from Seagate.'

The lieutenant consulted a list. 'Do your boats have names?'

Anson cleared his throat: '*Striker* and *Stinger.*'

'Say again?'

'*Striker* and *Stinger!*'

'Commanded by?'

'*Stinger* by Lieutenant Coney, *Striker* by me. Anson's the name.'

They were close enough now for the lieutenant to dispense with his loudhailer. 'Lieutenant Anson? Are you any kin to *the* Anson?'

The usual question, the usual answer. 'Only very distantly I'm afraid.'

'You are nevertheless most welcome to Admiral Nelson's proposed outing to enjoy the delights of Boulogne. Perfect for a run ashore at this time of year, I'm told ...'

The boats drew level and the lieutenant briefed Anson on what lay ahead.

After being towed across, both boats would be in the second division commanded by Captain Parker.

Anson had not met Edward Parker, but had certainly heard of him as a great favourite of Nelson who was reputed to refer to the young man, only 23, as "my child" – which most believed indicated the admiral thought of him as the son he never had.

Certainly Nelson's "little Parker", who had left command of a sloop to serve as the great man's aide-de-camp, was being given the chance of glory that most ambitious officers – Anson included – would literally be willing to die for.

Once in position outside Boulogne, Anson learned, the attacking boats would be joined by as many marines as they could squeeze into the thwarts and when the signal was given the crews must follow the directions of the lead boat of their division and row like hell for the French line.

They were to board the nearest French vessel, take it, cut its moorings, tow it out of the defensive line and take it out to sea.

'So y'see, nothing much to it, is there?' the lieutenant quipped.

Anson laughed. 'Everything will be fine just so long as we can break the Frogs' chains, eh?'

But the sheepdog lieutenant had already turned his attention to another arrival, shouting through his speaking trumpet: 'What boat?'

*

In his great cabin, before leading the flotilla down-Channel towards Boulogne, Nelson was again writing to Lady Hamilton:

Medusa, *Deal, 15th August, 1801*

"As you may believe, my dear Emma, my mind feels at which is going forward this night; it is one thing to order and arrange an attack and another to execute it. But I assure you, I have taken much more precaution for others, than if I was to go myself ... After they have fired their guns, if one half of the French do not jump overboard and swim on shore, I will venture to be hanged ... If our people behave as I expect, our loss cannot be much. My fingers itch to be at them."

*

A few hours' sailing away, his adversary Rear Admiral René-Madeleine La Touche-Tréville was expecting another attack after the earlier bombardment.

During the afternoon he was alerted to increased activity among the British ships patrolling offshore. And now, in addition to the 74-gun HMS *Leyden*, to which he had become accustomed, a newly arrived frigate appeared to be the centre of attention – *Medusa* and Nelson!

Reports from spies, smugglers and fishermen who traded scraps of intelligence along both coasts, and news from escaped prisoners had already reached him stating that the English admiral was now flying his flag in the frigate.

At first he had doubted what he heard, but now he felt sure it was true. Through a glass he could see that *Medusa* was accompanied by two other frigates and around them were many flatboats, barges, cutters, gunboats and other small craft.

It was certain indication of a coming assault. And the only way to attack Boulogne was via the defensive cordon of 24 ships moored across the harbour mouth.

It would have to be a night raid otherwise the shore batteries would decimate the attacking boats and he knew that when it grew dark the French gunners would fear hitting their own ships.

And, he judged from the increased activity he had witnessed, it would be this very night that the British would attempt to board, cut out and tow away vessels from the cordon protecting Boulogne.

Confident he knew exactly what to expect, he turned his mind to his defences. Since the earlier bombardment he had reinforced the defensive line with bigger ships. More soldiers had been sent on board so that each vessel was defended with both musketry and grapeshot, and patrol boats were deployed by night to give early warning of an attack.

All down the line heavy netting had been rigged to be hoisted after dark to repel boarders, and loaded small arms and sharpened cutlasses were placed in racks, readily accessible at the first sign of an assault.

But his ace card was the mooring system he had devised. Keels were moored with chains and – crucially – linked to one another so that individual vessels could not be cut out.

The Rosbifs would not be aware of this. So the axes they would bring expecting to cut hempen cables would be useless. It would be like attempting to cut bone with a butter knife.

He gave orders for a full alert to be mounted and the crews of boats anchored ahead of his cordon were instructed to fire off musket warnings at the first signs of the attack.

It would be a busy night and the Rosbifs were in for a deadly welcome with no chance of success.

*

During the crossing there had at first been much ribbing among *Striker's* crew, acting like schoolboys on an outing.

But, towing in a line of other boats in the frigate's wake, they had soon fallen silent, those yet to see action speculating as to what it would be like and every man-jack wondering if he would come through it unscathed.

Anson himself had been able to think only of the chains that he believed now held the French defensive line together. Had Hoare informed Colonel Redfearn, or Nelson himself? If he had, how was it planned to break the links? And if the admiral did *not* know what awaited the attackers, would the raid be a complete disaster?

On arrival off Boulogne, he had been concerned that his dark thoughts could be transmitting themselves to those around him, so forced himself to smile and say cheerily: 'It would be good to have a song to give ourselves a lift, boys. *Heart of Oak* would be the very thing, but Lord Nelson might be trying to take a nap and wouldn't thank us for giving him a wake-up call.'

That had raised a nervous laugh.

'But if we can't sing, there's nothing to stop us hearing a bit of Shakespeare ...'

'What, poetry, sir?' asked Longstaff. 'I can recite a poem about a young tart from Deal if y'like ...'

'Thankee Longstaff, and most entertaining it would be, I'm sure. But I had in mind something a little more inspiring. Can you all hear me?'

Hoover ordered: 'Silence fore and aft and listen up to Mister Anson!'

Anson waited for silence. 'This is from Shakespeare.'

'Shake 'oo?'

He ignored the joker. 'It's something he wrote in his play about King Henry the Fifth. I think it's appropriate to the business we're about.'

Heads were turned to him.

'His army was about to face the French at a place called Agincourt. His men were heavily outnumbered and this is what he said to inspire them.' Anson cleared his throat:

"From this day to the ending of the world,
But we in it shall be remembered;
We few, we happy few, we band of brothers;
For he today that sheds his blood with me
Shall be my brother; be he ne'er so vile
This day shall gentle his condition;
And gentlemen in England now a-bed
Shall think themselves accurs'd they were not here,
And hold their manhoods cheap whiles any speaks
That fought with us upon this day."

Anson had chosen to omit the mentions of Saint Crispin's day in case some of the men got confused and thought he was talking about his – now *late* –predecessor.

223

For a moment or two there was total silence as the words sunk in – until a voice piped up: 'So what 'appened then? Did they beat the Frogs, sir?'

Anson joined the laughter and confirmed: 'Yes, after hearing words like that of course they beat the Frogs!' But he dearly wished he could feel as confident as he hoped he sounded.

But the mood *had* lifted and the joker Longstaff got to work. 'Now we've been hinspired, like, 'ow about that poem of mine?' he offered. 'It's about a young floozy from Deal, what'd do anyfink for a square meal …'

But Hoover reined in the laugher. 'Don't forget, boys, the flagship's nearby and the admiral's got more on his plate than listenin' to a bunch of schoolgals like you gigglin' at silly rhymes.'

They simmered down and Hoover whispered to Anson. 'I didn't mean *your* words, of course, sir. They were spot on.'

'We can thank the Bard of Avon for them, not me.'

'Yeah, but it's knowing when to repeat them that counts.'

*

By early evening off Boulogne, all the remaining ships' boats were hoisted out and dropped astern to join those already towing behind. And all boats were now fully prepared, with oar blades and throle pins muffled, grappling irons, axes and other assault equipment loaded.

Finally, red-jacketed marines swarmed down into the boats to join the boarders already crouching in the thwarts.

To mark friend from foe, seamen chosen for boarding parties put on white belts borrowed from the marines, and were issued with newly sharpened cutlasses, half pikes, tomahawks, and loaded pistols and muskets.

By eleven o'clock the heavily laden boats of all four assault divisions were ranged astern of their commanders' boats, loosely linked by ropes to keep them together lest the strong currents split them up, and looking like strings of ducklings following their mothers.

Anson felt the familiar tension he had known before other raids, reminding him of St Valery-en-Caux in Normandy and the abortive cutting-out expedition from HMS *Phryne* which had led to his capture.

The tightening in the gut was all too familiar, but this time it was somehow magnified. For the first time he was experiencing an almost overwhelming foreboding that this was going to end in defeat, despair – and death.

It was a moonless night and he concentrated hard, staring through the gloom to where he had last glimpsed the flagship.

Nelson had ordered six lighted lanterns to be hung over the side of *Medusa* as the signal to pull for shore and suddenly they appeared.

Anson croaked: 'There's the signal, men!' and *Striker's* coxswain ordered: 'Dip oars and give way!'

The admiral, Anson knew, would be watching from the deck of his flagship and Anson was not alone in feeling that the great man was with them in spirit – had wished to be with them in the boats.

Indeed, the challenge to be used if the boats became separated was 'Nelson' – the response 'Bronte', a reference to the dukedom the admiral had been awarded for his part in suppressing the revolt in Naples two years earlier.

As the boats pulled away, aboard *Medusa* Captain John Gore's log recorded the moment with a terse laconic line: *"At 11.30 the boats proceeded to attack the enemy's flotilla."*

40

Boulogne in Chains

In pitch darkness, the variable currents swept the boats towards the French line.

But some were swept faster than others and in *Striker* Anson had little idea where they were or where they were heading.

It appeared that the assault force had been dispersed almost immediately, and to avoid collisions some boats had cast off the ropes that had held the divisions together.

Striker's coxswain Joe Hobbs shouted: 'Do y'want me to cut loose, sir?'

Anson hesitated. If they lost contact with Captain Parker in the lead boat there would be no chance of coordination – just chaos.

Gun flashes were now lighting up the night sky and already the bark of cannon and carronade, accompanied by the roar of mortars and the sporadic crackle of musketry, was deafening. But at least the flashes gave him occasional glimpses of Parker's boat.

'Cut loose? No! Mark Captain Parker's boat in the flashes and keep after him at all costs!'

'Aye, aye, sir!' The coxswain shouted at the oarsmen: 'You 'eard what Mister Anson said. Row like buggery after the lead boat!'

To watchers on board *Medusa,* gun flashes showed that the currents appeared to be carrying both Somerville's and Jones's divisions past the enemy line. But as to being able to fathom out how the assault was progressing, Nelson and his officers might as well have been in the Outer Hebrides.

The currents had favoured the second division and a particularly bright flash revealed an anchored brig directly ahead – the *Etna* – flying a commodore's pendant and veiled in netting.

Striker, now in close contact with Captain Parker's flatboat which was still accompanied by a barge and cutter, was hailed by a lieutenant. 'The captain requests you to attack the French ships at the northern end of the line to create a diversion while we board this brig.' Anson could not help laughing. The navy could be absurdly polite, even at a time like this.

He shouted: 'Will do!' and ordered his coxswain to steer to starboard, warning the boarders – some of his own fencibles and the embarked marines – to stand by.

Looking back, Anson glimpsed Parker standing in the bows of his flatboat, sword drawn, at the head of his men. It was a heroic gesture – no more than he would have expected of Nelson's favourite.

He could see the flatboat bumping alongside the Frenchman and immediately Parker and his men attempted to board, but the strong netting, triced up to her lower yards, baffled them.

And as they continued their attack a blast of grapeshot and musketry cut through them and Parker and many of his men were thrown on their backs in the boat, all either killed or wounded.

Anson watched, impotent, as Parker's surviving men scrambled up the ship's side only to be enmeshed in the netting. It was an uneven struggle, painful to watch.

French infantrymen were crowded on the brig's gunwhale, firing their muskets and then stabbing the British sailors and marines struggling at the nets with their bayonets and pikes.

Those attackers who grabbed the bulwarks to heave themselves aboard had their hands axed with tomahawks.

Anson cried out in frustration as he saw one brave soul run through with the French captain's sword as he clambered over the top of the netting. But as the Frenchman seized the boarder by the hair and dragged him to the deck he, himself, was stabbed in the shoulder by the dying man.

Parker's boat drifted away, full of dead and wounded. But *Striker* and several other boats from his division had by now managed to reform to attack further up the line.

The night sky was lit up like some malicious, death-dealing firework inferno, and Nelson's grand plan was meaningless now to the men in the boats. Their world had shrunk to their own boat, the thirty or so men who inhabited it, and whichever enemy vessel they struck first.

Only the detonations and gun flashes were universal. And the smoke – it was everywhere.

Striker closed on a dark shape, lit spasmodically by the gun flashes, looming up directly ahead.

Anson yelled: 'Keep low boys! But his voice was drowned by the deafening, reverberating cacophony of dozens of great guns, carronades and mortars, and the accompanying angry crackle of musketry.

A volley of musket balls buzzed overhead and there was now no need to urge the men to keep down. The instinct to survive had seen to that. The oarsmen rowed with lowered heads and the boarders crouched even lower in the thwarts.

Miraculously, it seemed, no-one had yet been hit and at last they bumped alongside the boats already attacking the French ship – another brig.

Already the other crews were attempting to board, but they were being forced back by the determined defenders. Anson knew he had to make an instant decision. He could join the others struggling to board the brig, in which case his men would have to wait their turn to get close enough, or he could seek another target.

He chose the latter and ordered the coxswain to make for the next ship in the French line.

Gun flashes lit the sky like lightning strikes and through the dark and drifting clouds of smoke another vessel loomed up ahead. Anson stood up, waved his sword, and shouted: 'This one's ours men! Get alongside!'

The rowers pulled with increased power and closed on what Anson took to be another brig lying side on to the harbour entrance.

There were shouts aboard the French vessel as the coming danger was spotted and a few blue-jacketed figures could be seen peering at them through a heavy screen of netting, waiting to shoot or bayonet boarders.

Hoover had seen the danger. They would be sitting ducks once enough Frenchmen had lined the deck above them. He shouted into Sampson Marsh's ear: 'Elevate the gun *now*, for pity's sake!'

Marsh nodded and worked the pivot just as *Striker* smacked against the side of the Frenchman and slewed to starboard so that, more by luck than judgement, the carronade was pointing up and along the deck.

Hoover yelled: 'Fire!' and Marsh touched the slow-match he had been cradling in a leather bucket to the powder and there was a deafening bang accompanied by screams from above.

He had loaded grapeshot.

Anson wiped the sweat from his eyes with the back of his hand and peered at the deck above. The Frenchmen who had been waiting to do execution had disappeared and the thick rope netting was in tatters. The grapeshot had done its work.

He shouted: 'Stand by to board!' Grappling hooks were flung up, some catching what remained of the netting, and Anson clamped his sword blade between his teeth and grabbed the nearest rope.

Hoover was beside him and several of the marines and fencibles detailed as boarders and armed with pikes and tomahawks were already clambering aboard the Frenchman.

But on board the brig the surviving fusiliers and sailors had recovered, reformed and were preparing to fire at their attackers.

Anson let go of the rope and rolled onto the deck to find a French fusilier standing over him, musket in hand, preparing to bayonet him. His sword fell from his teeth, cutting the side of his mouth. And the absurd thought struck him: 'First blood to me!'

As the Frenchman arched to plunge his weapon down, Anson pulled the sea service pistol from his belt and shot his adversary in the gut.

He stooped to pick up his sword but as he rose another Frenchman rushed at him clearly intent on bayoneting this Rosbif officer. He stepped back to avoid the wicked steel and before the Frenchman could strike again a pike whacked his musket aside.

Anson glanced sideways. It was Hoover, now in the act of clouting the defender round the head with the flat of his pike.

As the man crumpled, Anson nodded his thanks and the American grinned, his teeth startlingly white against his cork-blackened face, and moved on.

Stumbling over a wounded defender, Anson made for a cluster of Frenchmen who were in the act of reloading their muskets.

Another boat had bumped alongside and now the boarders were beginning to outnumber the surviving Frenchmen.

He was conscious that Hoover was still beside him, pike in hand, and together they pushed forward shouting encouragement as more of the marines and fencibles clambered aboard.

Anson hoped the oarsmen had obeyed orders and stayed in the boat. They would be needed for towing out this prize – or escaping when it became necessary to withdraw.

A ragged line of French soldiers had formed amidships and fired a volley which brought down two of the marines from *Striker* and at least one of the fencibles – Anson could not see who.

Hoover had discarded the pike and picked up the musket dropped by one of the fallen marines. He took aim and shot down one of the defenders, and several other boarders were also kneeling and firing.

Two more boats had banged alongside and more boarders were joining by the minute. He saw the unmistakable figure of Bosun Fagg wearing his tall, black-lacquered hat and waving a cutlass.

In the chaos, *Stinger* had been cut off from the rest of Parker's division and while manoeuvring to find a target Fagg had chanced upon *Striker* and ordered his coxswain to row to support their Seagate comrades.

Anson shouted: 'Where's Mister Coney?'

'Wounded, sir. I'm in charge now!'

'Good to see you, bosun – we need you!'

Judging that there were now enough boarders, Anson, blood streaming down his jaw from his accidentally self-inflicted wound, waved his sword shouting: 'Up and at 'em, men!' and charged at the remaining Frenchmen.

Several more of the enemy fell and the rest threw down their weapons and raised their hands.

The attackers gave a ragged cheer. The vessel was theirs.

Anson shouted to Fagg: 'Get the axes – and Clay and his mate!'

The bosun nodded and bellowed down to the boats. 'Look lively and 'and up the axes. And get a bleedin' move on – we ain't got all blurry night!'

The axes appeared and willing hands grabbed them.

'Locate the mooring cables – and the ones to the ships astern and ahead!'

The men did not need telling twice and it did not take long to locate them thanks to the gun flashes, incoming and outgoing, that were now almost continuous.

But, as Anson had feared, the shout went up: 'Chains! The Frogs have used chains!'

Nevertheless, axes were swung and sparks flew as the men tried severing the moorings, cursing loudly as they did so.

'Mister Clay!'

'Sir?'

'You've got your tools? Good, then get to it and break these damned chains!'

Clay and his mate hurried aft and Anson passed his hand over his eyes which were stinging from the thick powder smoke.

Fagg appeared at his elbow. 'Even with Clay's tools they ain't goin' to be able to break them chains. If we'd got all the time in the world, maybe, but we ain't got a cat's chance wiv all this going on.'

As he spoke, musket fire crackled from the ships moored end to end with the brig now that the French realised it had been taken.

Anson had only seconds to decide what to do. It would not be long before the superior forces either side of them would sweep the brig's deck with musketry – or, worse, with grapeshot from their cannons.

If Clay and his mate could not break the chains quickly there was no prospect whatsoever of cutting the brig out and towing her away.

Nor, he cursed, did they have the means to set the vessel on fire.

Worse, French boats were bringing more soldiers from the inner harbour and they were about to board the vessel's shore side.

Hoover's shout made the decision for him. 'The other boats are pulling away!'

Anson realised that there was no choice: they had to withdraw – and rejoin their own boats immediately or risk certain death or capture.

He had no idea what was happening elsewhere. His world was now the few yards he could see on the deck of the French ship.

He shouted above the din: 'Back to the boats, men!' and, with Hoover at his side, began prodding a small group of prisoners towards the large hole in the boarding nets.

Musket balls from the ship astern were screaming across the deck, and Anson knew that if they did not leave immediately the rest of his boarding party would be wiped out – dead meat.

He crouched low and dashed for the side. Hoover was leading the way, prodding the French prisoners with his bayonet. They would be required back in England for intelligence.

As the marine forced the Frenchmen down into the boat, Anson looked around to check that he was the last to leave. But as he prepared to jump he saw a French officer rise from behind a mast and aim a pistol at him. Something struck his shoulder, spun him round and he staggered and fell into the boat, striking his head on the thwarts as he landed.

The coxswain was desperately trying to man the oars, but there were gaps where rowers had disobeyed their orders and followed the boarders attacking the lugger – or had been hit by musket fire where they sat.

Hoover shouted: 'Hobbs! Put these Frogs to the oars. They'll row if the men behind 'em show them a cutlass!'

The coxswain grabbed the nearest prisoner and shoved him towards an abandoned oar, shouting 'Allez, allez!' Two more were pressed into service but he motioned the fourth, who was clutching an ugly head wound, to crouch in the thwarts.

Anson was on his back there, bleeding profusely and near fainting from the pain.

Hoover shouted to the coxswain: 'Let's get the hell out of here or we're all dead men!'

41

"Row Like Hell!"

Joe Hobbs had needed no encouragement. He and the nearest rowers cast off the grappling irons and pushed against the side of the French vessel to free the gunboat from its embrace.

Once clear, he yelled: 'Dip oars and row like hell!'

After a few chaotic moments, with the prisoners all awry, the rowers achieved some sort of rhythm and pulled slowly and awkwardly away from the cordon of French ships.

As they did, a curtain of mortar fire from the British flotilla came arching overhead and found targets all along the enemy line.

Hoover crouched over Anson and put his mouth to the officer's ear. 'Are you hurt bad, sir?' But Anson could only shake his head weakly. 'What about our boys?'

'Dunno yet. Two or three have been hit at their oars—'

'The boarders?'

'I saw several marines and one or two of our men fall but some got back wounded.'

'Mister Shrubb?'

'He's already working on them. I'll get him to take a look at you.'

Anson shook his head. 'No need. I'll be fine—'

'I gotta disagree with you there. Just look at all the blood …' He unbuttoned the officer's jacket but when he tried to take it off Anson winced at the pain and fainted.

When he came to he was still lying in the thwarts but his head was now pillowed on his own bloodied jacket, his left shoulder swathed in bandages and Phineas Shrubb was kneeling beside him.

The intensity of gunfire and counter-fire had slackened and musketry had ceased. At least they had made it out of small arms' range.

'Mister Shrubb,' he croaked, 'how long have I been out?'

'A good while. It's the loss of so much blood, you see? Sergeant Hoover saved you. He used his own shirt to plug the wound and stop the worst of the bleeding.'

'I'll make a note to buy him a new one—'

'You'll be making no notes for a while, and I'm afraid we had to cut your jacket off …

'No matter, it was only my second best.'

'But the good news is that I've fished the pistol ball out along with a bit of splintered bone. You've also acquired a nasty cut alongside your mouth. It'll require stitching but that's best left to my daughter to work on once we're on dry land.'

'So I'll live?'

'I see from your other scars that it's not the first time you've been wounded. Yes, you'll live, God willing …'

'What about the men?'

'Two of our fencibles and a marine dead in the boat, a dozen with wounds of some sort, several serious. One will most likely lose a leg and another an arm, but the butchery will have to wait until we're ashore. Oh, and one of the captured Frenchmen has a very serious head wound. I fear he won't make it.'

'Thank you, Mister Shrubb. You'd best attend to them, but can you send Sergeant Hoover to me?'

The American appeared at his side. 'Back in the land of the living, sir?'

'Barely. I feel very light-headed and the pain seems to come over me in waves, but Shrubb tells me I'll live. Can you put me back in the picture?'

'The firing seems to be tailing off and one of our ships, a frigate I think, has just taken us in tow. I reckon we're already heading for the Kent coast. But the boys say they'll row back and have another go if you want.'

'How many have we lost?'

Hoover hesitated as if he was unwilling to impart bad news to someone in Anson's weakened condition. 'I make it eight or nine from our two boats missing from the boarding parties, most of them marines we'd embarked. Several of 'em were killed, I saw, but at least some might just have been wounded and taken prisoner. We've got four of theirs, by the by.'

'And Shrubb tells me we've three dead in the boat – and a good many wounded?'

'Correct. We didn't put the dead men over the side. Phineas reckoned you'd want to take 'em home for a proper burial.'

234

Anson nodded. It was what he wanted. 'How many of them are our own boys?'

'Fencibles? Most of 'em did as they were told and stayed at their oars, but no-one knows what happened to Rogers. He's not here now, that's for sure.'

'And?'

'Hogben's dead, hit in the head by a musket ball I reckon, and Brooke lost an arm and has just snuffed it – bled to death.'

Wincing from the pain of his wounds as well as this sad news, Anson muttered hoarsely: 'I'm sorry to lose them – all good men. I'll take a look at the wounded when I've caught my breath.'

'No, sir. Mister Shrubb says you're to stay still.'

Anson tried to sit up but a wave of pain engulfed him and he sank back, eyes closed and teeth gritted.

When the pain subsided he whispered: 'We didn't do very well, Tom. The raid, I mean, and there's not much glory in defeat.'

It was the first time the American could remember the officer calling him by his first name and he was touched. He shook his head slowly. 'The boys were brave enough and we went for it, but it appears the currents sent the other boats every which way. I reckon some of them didn't get anywhere near the French ships, and, like us, those that did couldn't break those damn chains.'

'Clay broke one before he was wounded, but maybe the other boats didn't have blacksmiths' tools—'

'And there's no way you can bust a chain with an axe.'

'My eyes are stinging, Tom. Can you …?'

'Sure.' Hoover found a clean remnant of his discarded shirt, dipped it over the side and wiped the blood, sweat and burnt cork from around Anson's eyes.

'Thank you, Tom. I just hope Hoare *did* warn Nelson about the chains and it wasn't that that caused this disaster. Hurel and I risked our lives getting that information. If Hoare's to blame for this fiasco I swear I'll kill him.'

Hoover made to respond but then noticed that Anson had drifted off once more.

*

The return to the Downs anchorage was a blur to Anson and it was Hoover who saw to all the arrangements – sending the wounded to the naval hospital at Deal, and handing over the surviving French prisoners.

He also prepared the returns of casualties and details required by the admiral's staff to enable them to piece together the full picture of the action.

The American handled it all with the help of Boxer, who had come over from Seagate with Sarah Shrubb in anticipation.

There was conveyance of bodies to arrange, too – Boxer, the undertaker's daily business. And he excelled at it.

On Phineas Shrubb's instructions, his daughter stitched Anson's torn face as neatly as if she were embroidering a sampler. 'You will have a slightly lop-sided smile,' she told him, 'but otherwise you will be as handsome as ever.'

For the first time in many an hour he exercised that smile, lop-sided or not, although the pain from stretching the stitches discouraged him from repeating the exercise.

42

Aftermath

A young, fresh-faced marine came seeking the Seagate boats and Hoover quizzed him: 'What d'you want, son?'

'There's a gent asking after a Lieutenant Anson. He's got a young lady in tow, sergeant.'

Hoover assumed this could be Anson's father and perhaps one of his sisters. 'Bring 'em along, lad. You'll probably get sixpence for your trouble.'

'Thanks, sergeant.' And indicating Anson, he asked: 'That's him is it? Wounded is he?'

'That's him – and as you can see for yourself he's been in the wars.'

'Right, only the old gent asked if I could find out if he's dead or alive, so I'll tell him he's just half dead, shall I?'

Hoover raised an eyebrow. 'Make that half *alive*, son. Don't want to upset his next of skin, do we?'

But it was not the Reverend Anson and one of his daughters, but Josiah Parkin and his niece Cassandra who returned with the young marine.

They were horrified to see the state Anson was in, lying on the shingle by the beached boat, his head pillowed on his bloodied jacket and blood seeping through the bandages around his shoulder.

His face was still smeared with blood and cork-black, and he was deathly pale. The stitches in his face wound had pulled one side of his mouth into a clownish grin.

Parkin could not help exclaiming: 'Dear God! What on earth's happened to you, my dear fellow?'

Cassandra fell to her knees beside him, tears in her eyes, and put her ear close to his mouth to hear him murmur: 'I had a bit of a set-to with some Frenchmen – and they came off best.'

She took his hand, but quickly dropped it, concerned that any movement might cause him pain, and resorted instead to gently wiping cork-blacking and dried blood from his face.

Hoover told the old gentleman: 'We heard someone was looking for the lieutenant, sir. Thought it might be his father.'

'The Reverend Anson? No, no. I am acquainted with him, but, no, I don't believe he is here. I am an old friend of poor Oliver. We heard some action was afoot and that the Sea Fencibles were involved. The whole county is awash with talk of Nelson and his exploits. So we came to Deal to discover what had become of Oliver, here.'

Hoover nodded. 'We're waiting right now for the surgeons to tell us where they're going to take him – probably the hospital if it's not already full.'

'So he has just been left here – on the beach without medical attention?'

'Our surgeon's mate, Mister Shrubb, and his daughter have been looking after him, but there's a good many dead and wounded so they've had to move on to help others.'

Parkin was beside himself. 'Look, sergeant ...?'

'Hoover, sir, master-at-arms of the Seagate Sea Fencibles.'

'Ah, Hoover! I thought I recognised the trace of a New England accent. Lieutenant Anson has spoken of you as his most trusted man. Look, Sergeant Hoover, my niece and I have taken rooms near where the admiral has had some of his wounded officers taken. Please help me to take Lieutenant Anson there where he can be looked after properly.'

Cassandra looked up, her tear-filled eyes pleading, and Hoover turned to a group of the Seagate men who were listening in.

'You heard, men, this gentleman's a friend of our officer and he's got somewhere better'n the beach to take him. Double away and find a stretcher and if you can't find one get hold of a sail and we'll carry him on that. Be quick about it now!'

A sail it was. They folded it to stretcher length and Hoover supervised as they lifted Anson on it with great care.

'Now, when I give the word, lift away together and follow this gentleman and lady to their accommodation. Ready? Gently now – lift!'

Once in the sail, Anson whispered to Hoover: 'Tom, you'll look after Ebony for me?'

'Sure I will.'

Parkin, who had been watching anxiously, shook the American's hand. 'Thank you, sergeant, I am greatly obliged to you, as I'm sure Lieutenant Anson will be.'

He turned and led the way with the temporary stretcher-bearers following behind and Cassandra trailing, clearly distressed, alongside the wounded man.

*

That night, as the British ships lay anchored off Deal, the rest of the wounded were sent ashore to hospital, the less serious cases to lodging houses. Nelson rented rooms in Middle Street for his particular friends Parker and Lieutenant Frederick Langford.

And as the fog of war began to clear, fuller details of what had occurred emerged.

Captain Somerville's scattered division had managed to reform and launched a ferocious attack on *La Surprise* which was resisted just as fiercely.

Captain Cotgrave's division had attacked a brig but as his own boat bumped alongside, French sailors heaved a cannonball over the side crushing some of his men and smashing through the bottom.

A third division was swept past Boulogne by the tide and could not attack for another three hours – then took a brig, found that she was unmovable and, when daylight came, the boats were driven off by gunfire from other French ships and from shore.

The last division was carried so far past its objective that it never went into action.

It had been a decisive defeat. Nothing had been accomplished and the cost was heavy with 18 officers and 172 seamen and marines killed or wounded in the boats.

The admiral sat in his cabin beside the curved row of windows across the stern of *Medusa* and wrote to the First Lord of the Admiralty:

"I am sorry to tell you that I have not succeeded in bringing out or destroying the enemy's flotilla moored in the mouth of the harbour of Boulogne. The most astonishing bravery was evinced by many of our officers and men ...

We have lost upwards of 100 killed and wounded ...

Dear little Parker, his thigh very much shattered; I have fears for his life."

*

Funerals of the other young officers were held in Deal and crowds gathered to watch Nelson following the coffins with tears on his lined cheeks.

The admiral was unfairly criticised for not accompanying the boats himself and a pensioner was quoted as saying: "Tho' I daresay everything was done that could be done without him – had he gone in, the boats, the chains and all would have come out along with him."

The Naval Chronicle printed a single verse:

"Exult not, France, that NELSON's vengeful blow,
Has not, as usual, thy destruction gain'd;
Say what you will, this truth the world must know,
Altho' unconquer'd, you were left enchained."

It was true, as Anson was later able to console himself – that despite fighting off the attack the French remained well and truly bottled up in Boulogne, prisoners there of their own making.

Captain Parker was to linger on for more than a month. At his funeral six captains bore his coffin through the streets of Deal and Nelson followed, weeping.

*

The room was familiar. It was where Anson had first stayed while convalescing at Ludden Hall from a fever during the mutiny and again when he had brought Hurel here just a few weeks ago. Weeks that seemed like months.

But now there was something different about the room.

Two large coloured prints of naval battles graced the walls alongside the antiquarian pictures that were there before, and there were two pretty vases of wild flowers, one on the washstand and another on the window sill. Cassandra's work, he guessed.

He dozed and when he awoke again she was sitting by his bed, a book on her lap.

'Mister Anson – Oliver. So you are awake at last?' It was the first time she had addressed him by his first name.

He was conscious of a throbbing pain in his shoulder and when he tried to speak one side of his mouth wouldn't function as normal.

She noticed his puzzled look and said softly: 'You have stitches in your face. When they're taken out you will be able to speak normally – and without pain.'

He managed to croak: 'You brought me here from Deal?'

'Uncle Josiah arranged it. You lay there mostly unconscious for two days, but then we thought it best to bring you home. The navy know where you are and so does your family.'

'And my fencibles?'

'Yes, and your fencibles. Now, the doctor is in the study with my uncle and left strict instructions that he is to be called the minute you awake.'

The doctor examined him thoroughly and appeared satisfied with Anson's condition.

'It is plain that you have been through the wars, young man, but your shoulder wound shows no signs of mortification. I daresay it will exhibit some stiffness for years to come, but so be it. I suppose this is the kind of thing you must expect if you insist on continuing to put yourself in mortal danger.'

Anson managed the ghost of a smile.

'As to your face, well, it's as neat a piece of needlework as I've seen and all being well the stitches can be removed in a day or two.'

'Obliged to you, doctor,' Anson whispered huskily.

Doctor Hawkins nodded benevolently. 'Now, you'll need lots of bed rest and, I think, only liquid food until your face is healed. Chicken soup would be capital. But first we must get you cleaned up.'

'Oh, no!' Anson thought, remembering his earlier convalescence at Ludden Hall.

And yes, it was the redoubtable Emily, she of ample girth and hint of a moustache, beaming at him, gap-toothed, from the doorway, pitcher of water in hand and flannel and towels over her arm.

Helpless as a baby, Anson could do no more than to submit to another bed-bath at the work-coarsened hands of the sometime nurse and layer out of the dead of the parish.

43

The Weakest Link

Captain Hoare crossed the Admiralty's cobbled courtyard with a spring in his step.

Word of his successes against privateers had reached their lordships, he knew. He had made sure of that himself.

And now, being alongside Nelson himself during the raid on Boulogne surely added to the kudos he had earned.

Could they be about to offer him a more prestigious and salubrious posting, or perhaps a decoration? Captain Arthur Veryan St Cleer Hoare, Commander of the Bath, had quite a ring to it.

Being kept on tenterhooks in the infamous waiting room was an occupational hazard but he was nevertheless relieved to be summoned forth after a relatively short sojourn.

Hoare was ushered in to find Captain Wallis, whom he knew, seated behind a large desk with a rear admiral who was not known to him. Neither greeted him, and, unusually he thought, the admiral did not introduce himself.

He waited, a little apprehensive. He had expected that this summons must be to do with official recognition for the capture of *Égalité*, but the cool reception had sparked a flickering doubt.

After seconds that seemed like minutes, the admiral asked abruptly: 'Hoare?'

'Yes, sir, *Captain* Hoare.'

'Be seated.'

'Thank you, sir. May I ask—?

The admiral ignored his half-asked question and barked: 'You know Captain Wallis, I believe?'

Hoare directed a rictus grin at Wallis but got no reaction. 'I do, sir.'

'He – *we* – have some questions for you concerning the taking of a privateer operating out of Normandy. *Égalité* was it not?'

'Yes, sir, I had the honour of …'

'And is this a copy of the report you subsequently sent to their lordships?' The admiral slipped a sheet of foolscap across the desk.

Hoare scanned it quickly. 'It is, sir.'

The admiral turned to Wallis. 'Ask away.'

Wallis cleared his throat and asked: 'Captain Hoare, to what degree if any were you involved in planning this operation?'

'From start to finish ...' Rattled, Hoare almost called Wallis 'sir', but conscious that although his questioner was his senior they were of the same rank, so refrained.

'Elucidate.'

'Well, I er, I wrote to request signal stations along the coast to pass me intelligence of the privateer's movements.'

'*You* wrote?'

'Indeed, the letter bears my signature.'

'Was it not Lieutenant Anson whose initiative this was, and who drafted the letter for your signature?'

'I dispute that. The captain of a ship or establishment is deemed responsible for everything that occurs under his command, is he not?'

Wallis brushed aside the question. 'And who formed the plan to lure the privateer into a trap, made such arrangements that were necessary with Commander Armstrong at Fairlight, and so forth?'

'All this took place under my command.'

'Not *at* your command?

'It was as I said, *under* my command. Surely a captain cannot expect to know precisely what every bilge rat is up to ...'

Wallis exchanged a knowing glance with the admiral. 'Let us now turn to the capture itself. Were you there?'

Hoare looked from one to the other nervously. 'As my report says, I was present to take the surrender of the French officer. I have his sword still.'

'But you arrived *after* the fighting was over, did you not, and found that the Frenchman had already struck and surrendered his sword to Lieutenant Anson?'

'The wretched Frog still had his sword!'

'Is it not the case that Anson had given it back to him as an honourable gesture because the French captain had ordered his men to lay down their arms to avoid further unnecessary bloodshed?'

Hoare spluttered: 'That uppity fellow Anson has engineered this! It's nothing but a stitch-up!'

'No, *Captain* Hoare, Lieutenant Anson has not seen fit to challenge your account, preferring to remain silent on the matter. However, Commander Armstrong, Lieutenant Coney – and the French officer himself, who is now a guest of His Majesty in the Chatham hulks – have been interviewed in depth—'

'You'd take the word of a Frenchman?'

'Over yours, yes. It is clear from what all three have told us that your version of what occurred before and during this whole affair is a gross exaggeration, sir, at the very least.'

Hoare's mouth worked but no words came forth.

Wallis continued: 'You took no part in the planning or execution of this operation. What's more when it was all over you thought fit to reprimand Anson for carrying it out behind your back.'

'Yes, yes, it was rank insubordination!'

'Nevertheless, although you had not been involved you took the credit and passed yourself off to the local mayor and anyone else who would listen as the hero of the hour?'

Hoare stammered: 'N-no, you don't understand, I …' He looked pleadingly at Wallis. 'Look, is this any way to treat a fellow captain? You besmirch my honour.'

The admiral held up his hand to stop Captain Wallis's questioning and took over himself, staring Hoare down with a piercing glare.

'Honour be damned!' Captain Wallis has my full authority – their lordships' authority – to put these questions to you. And it is plain that your report of the *Égalité* business is a total misrepresentation of what occurred.'

'I protest!'

'It is also a fact that since the *Égalité* affair you have managed to sink one of our own merchantmen rather than another privateer that was attacking it?'

'It was merely a coaster, and you cannot make omelettes without—'

'Omelettes? Are you completely deluded? And to cap it all we are informed that you have hoodwinked the town worthies and persuaded them to present you with a sword of honour to recognise your so-called victories.'

Hoare put his hand to his forehead, for once speechless.

'You, sir, are a disgrace to the navy. You should be court-martialled and drummed out of the service.'

The admiral paused to let his words sink in before demanding: 'Well, what d'you have to say?'

Hoare looked up, red-eyed and despairing. 'Anson betrayed me, sir. He kept what he was up to from me. I should have been kept in the picture. He, well, it's plain that he was trying to grab the glory for himself. I just wanted to put him in his place. I've sensed from the start that he's never liked me.'

The admiral shook his head. 'Fortunately the service doesn't rely on who likes who. Has it not occurred to you that your lieutenants get on with things without consulting you because you are seldom available? You are too busy hobnobbing with the local bigwigs, enjoying the social scene and whatnot, are you not?'

Hoare protested: 'I take the view, sir, that becoming part of the social scene is of considerable importance on the invasion coast.'

'What view you take is of no interest to me whatsoever, *Captain* Hoare. Were it not for the fact that your report has been Gazetted and those dim-witted locals have presented you with that ridiculous inscribed sword, you would surely be court-martialled.'

He tapped a copy of the *Kentish Gazette* on his desk with the report of the presentation circled in ink. It had been sent to the Admiralty with a note briefly outlining the bare facts of the privateer incident by some-one signing themselves "a well-wisher".

Hoare cringed.

'Yes, you should be court-martialled. However, such a step would not only expose and punish you, but it would also bring disgrace upon the service. It would make the navy into a laughing stock at a time when we need to enhance its reputation as saviours of the nation, not to be portrayed as a bunch of clowns.'

The admiral picked up another file and opened it. 'Are you aware of a Colonel Redfearn – and his role?'

'Y-yes.'

'This is a report from him stating that intelligence was reported to you of the French installing strong anti-boarding nets and chaining the Boulogne flotilla together so that their ships could not be cut out during Nelson's recent raid.'

Hoare blanched again.

'It states clearly that you were made aware of this before the raid and yet did not relay the information to Colonel Redfearn, or indeed, Lord Nelson, although you sailed with him in *Medusa* and had every opportunity to do so. What's more, the colonel states that papers taken from the French in Boulogne before the raid and handed to you failed to reach him until after the event. Is that the case?'

Hoare put his head in his hands. 'All preparations had been made. Nelson would have thought me lily-livered if I had tried to stop the operation on account of a few chains.'

Wallis shook his head slowly. 'Have you not heard of the chain of command? You should have done, because *you* are the weakest link in it! It was not for you to pick and choose what to tell the admiral. If Lord Nelson had been in possession of the information about the chains he could have acted accordingly.'

Hoare protested weakly: 'But I believed I was acting in the best interests of the service ...'

The admiral favoured him with a look of disgust. 'Best interests? You say you thought you were acting in the best interests of the service but as a result many men were killed or maimed and the operation failed!'

'But—'

'What's more, you were in possession of a plan of the French defensive line and the positions of shore batteries – a plan obtained at great personal risk by two very brave officers, and yet you chose not to pass it to Colonel Redfearn or Nelson.'

'I, er, forgot about the sketch. It was in my jacket, but, well, it was only on the way back that I remembered it,' Hoare admitted weakly.

Shaking his head, the admiral closed the file in front of him.

'Sadly we cannot court martial you for the reasons I have already outlined. However, it would be improper, totally improper, for you to remain as divisional captain. Too many within and outside the service know of these matters. So we must look to your next posting. You are a West Countryman, are you not?'

Despite his dejection, Hoare sensed a lifeline was being thrown to him and could not resist boasting: 'I am indeed, sir, and related to some of the foremost families in Devon and Cornwall.'

'Well, it has pleased their lordships to create a post that will suit you down to the ground: resident naval officer in the Isles of Scilly. Charming scenery and a wonderful climate, I believe, although a trifle windy much of the time – off the Atlantic, you see. You will remain there until we can think of a way of ridding the navy of you altogether without attracting attention.'

Hoare's horror-stricken expression said it all. 'But the Scillies are the farthest west you can go, totally cut off from civilisation—'

'Precisely. You put it far better than I could. Personally I would have sent you to Muckle Flugga or even Botany Bay. Either would have been more in keeping with your offences!'

'But—'

'But nothing. You will need to keep an eye out for enemy shipping passing by, arrange the replenishment of the odd ship that touches the islands for watering and that sort of thing, but I understand the duties are minimal. The social life of which you are so fond probably lacks a little sophistication, so I do hope time doesn't hang too heavily. At least you will be far enough away to avoid doing the navy any further damage.'

Hoare's mouth had dropped open and stayed open long enough for circling flies to begin taking an interest.

'Of course, if you'd prefer not to take on the Scillies challenge you can go on half pay and remove yourself somewhere a little more lively. Tunbridge Wells, Bath or Buxton spring to mind. Well what's it to be?'

The devastated Hoare had been well and truly painted into a corner. After a brief hesitation he muttered almost inaudibly: I accept, sir – the Scilly posting I mean. But, sir, may I—?'

'May you what?'

'May I be permitted to keep my presentation sword?'

The admiral snorted: 'I suppose the burghers of Seagate or whoever they were would start to ask questions if you handed it back, so you'd better keep it as a reminder of a *less* than honourable episode in your naval service.'

No doubt, the admiral thought, Hoare would soon be showing it to any movers and shakers he might encounter in the Isles of Scilly and portray himself as a hero no matter what had just occurred. But no matter, he would be got rid of once and for all as soon as convenient to the service.

'Now you may go. But before you leave the building Captain Wallis here will make the necessary arrangements for your delightful new posting.'

Totally crushed, Hoare made to go, but at the door the admiral stopped him.

'Oh, one last thing. Among the papers Captain Wallis will get you to sign is one relinquishing any claim whatsoever to any prize money that might accrue from the capture of the Normandy privateer *Égalité*. It would be more fitting if those who actually spilt blood in that enterprise did not have to share with the likes of you.'

44

Convalescence

After a few days the doctor pronounced Anson recovered sufficiently to be helped to a seat in the garden to enjoy the late summer sunshine.

One of the maids set up a small table beside him and Cassandra served tea and biscuits. 'No need to tap them,' she assured him mischievously. 'They are completely weevil-free!'

He managed a genuine smile – rare since the raid. 'I fear you have been consorting with rough sailors to have learnt of such things, Miss, er, sorry, Cassandra. Refined ladies should not be aware of the gory details of seamen's eating habits.'

She laughed – a charming natural laugh that raised his spirits. 'Tut, tut, Mister Anson, you are the only rough sailor I am acquainted with, so you are entirely to blame if I am turning into a Jolly Jill Tar!'

But a look of concern wiped her smile away when she saw him wince and clutch his shoulder.

'It still pains you?'

He nodded, eyes closed until the wave of pain subsided. 'Just a little. You are guilty of making me laugh and when I try to laugh my wound catches me out. But please don't stop – I can do with all the amusement I can get.'

She took his hand. 'I'm sorry. The very last thing I want to do is hurt you. Uncle and I thought we had lost you and now we'll do whatever it takes to make you well again.'

'I could not be in better hands.'

'You must know that my uncle is very fond of you. He regards you as the son he never had, just as he treats me as his daughter.'

Anson had a sudden dark thought of Nelson and young Edward Parker, but tried to keep the mood light by quipping: 'I hope that doesn't make us brother and sister?'

She blushed and quickly changed the subject. 'He took to you from the first time he brought you to Ludden Hall when you were taken ill on the stagecoach.'

It had been at the time of the mutiny at the Nore and Anson looked back with affection at the happy days he had enjoyed while convalescing as the guest of Josiah Parkin.

'Then, when you went off to sea, he so often mentioned you and wondered how you were faring. And it was a great thrill when he received what was left of your stuffed birds!'

They exchanged smiles and he noticed she still had her hand on his.

'He had, well, we *both* hoped that when you returned from the Mediterranean you would come to see us. We didn't realise at the time that you were a prisoner in France and then so very busy with your Sea Fencibles capturing that Normandy privateer. Then it was such a thrill for my uncle when you turned up with that French officer, Lieutenant Hurel.'

'Was it a thrill for you, too?'

She blushed again. 'Of course, although le Baron was perhaps a little over-attentive. But then you were snatched away from us again so quickly. I am coming to believe that the only way we can keep you here is to make sure you are ill or wounded first!'

There was a crunch on the gravel and she drew her hand away. 'Ah, Uncle Josiah, I was just telling Mister Anson that the only way we can be sure of keeping him here is if he is sick or hurt, as I believe they say in the navy.'

Parkin chuckled. 'My niece has a point, Anson, but I am delighted to see you looking a little better. Cassandra's company is clearly more effective than medicine in your case. However, I believe cook wishes to have a word with her about suitable restorative meals for you, and there is something I wish to discuss, so ...?'

Cassandra took the hint and went off in search of cook.

Parkin took her place on the garden seat and gave Anson a searching look. 'You are well enough to discuss a matter of some importance, I trust?'

'I am, sir.'

'Well, it concerns your relationship with your family.'

Anson shook his head sadly. 'That is not a matter for discussion. It was a family affair to do with a proposed marriage of convenience that I rejected.'

'Ah,' Parkin nodded understandingly. 'I did wonder.'

'As a result of that I have broken off all connection with my mother and father – and my elder brother, although I will maintain a link with my sisters, well, with Elizabeth at least – perhaps through a particular friend of mine.'

'But you are aware that I know your father as a fellow antiquary, and through that connection he has been in touch with me seeking a reconciliation with you. That is what I wish to discuss.'

'No, sir. I know you act out of friendship and for the best reasons, but it is all too raw. To add to the problems, I have had a falling out with Sir Oswald Brax over the same private matter. My father is in thrall to him because he has the advowson, and the squire may well exact revenge through him if I don't absent myself.'

'Do you say you will never be reunited with your father?'

'Perhaps one day. But our relationship can never be as it was before this marriage business.'

'Meanwhile?'

'I am going to write to my father regarding the allowance he has been giving me since I joined the navy. I intend to repay him. Heaven knows, if Sir Oswald Brax ousts him from his living he will need every penny.'

'I am sure he will not lose his living. But where do you plan to live, and how will you support yourself?'

'I have a room at a coaching inn convenient to my Sea Fencible detachment. As to money, well, sea officers are not in the service solely for the fun of it. They do pay us, too! And there is the matter of prize money, in which I have been moderately successful.'

Parkin protested: 'But a room in an inn is not a home.' He clasped his hands under his chin and leaned forward, looking earnestly at Anson. 'You have become a dear friend to both me and my niece. This could be your home.'

*

After dinner Cassandra left the men to their port and, feeling much better than he had since his arrival, Anson sat back and addressed the old gentleman.

'I have been giving thought, sir – considerable thought, to the matter you proposed to me.'

'About making Ludden Hall your home when you are not off with the navy or with your Sea Fencibles?'

'Indeed. I am most grateful to you, sir, for the kind thought behind your offer.'

Parkin smiled. 'It would give my niece and I the greatest satisfaction were you to accept, my boy.'

'Well, sir, for reasons you well know, I cannot, will not, go back to my father's rectory, at least, not for the foreseeable future.'

'So?'

'Since we first met, when you rescued me after I fell ill on the coach, well, we have become close. We have shared interests.'

Parkin smiled: 'Romans and rats?'

'Indeed, I would dearly love to join you in digging up evidence of the former although I can't bring myself to enjoy dissecting the latter! You, and Cassandra, have been kindness itself, particularly since you came to my rescue again after the Boulogne raid.'

'Then ...?'

'But however much I might wish to, I am afraid I cannot accept your offer to make my home here.'

The old gentleman's face fell. 'Why ever not, if it is your wish as well as ours?'

'The truth is, I find myself growing fond, extremely fond, of your niece.'

Parkin smiled again. 'I am delighted to hear that. I had hoped that the two of you ...' But he left what he was thinking unsaid, not wishing to tempt providence.

Instead, he looked earnestly at his guest. 'So there is no impediment. This shall be your home and should your fondness for Cassandra, which I am certain is reciprocated, mature let us say, well, that would be my dearest wish.'

'But, sir, there *is* an impediment. I fear I have compromised myself elsewhere and am unworthy of your niece.'

Parkin held up his hands. 'I feel I know you well enough to say that there is nothing you could have done to make yourself unworthy of my niece. On the contrary. But come, the maids are waiting to clear the table, so let us adjourn to my study with the decanter and you can tell all.'

As they left the table, the old gentleman added: 'Since for the time being at least you find yourself unable to discuss such things with your father, please regard me as serving in loco parentis.'

And so they adjourned to Parkin's study and, with the help of the contents of the decanter, Anson poured out his heart. As he unburdened himself, his host sat back in his favourite armchair paying close and sympathetic attention, with only the glass eyes of his collection of stuffed creatures looking on.

At length his host rose, poured Anson another drink and told him quietly: 'This Charlotte Brax is clearly an exceedingly scary lady, if that is the right word for her, but had you not heard of her marriage?'

'Marriage?' Anson was astonished.

'No, of course you won't have heard. It must have been while you were off to Boulogne. It was reported in the *Kentish Gazette*. She married some yeomanry fellow ... at your father's church, come to think of it.'

'Not Chitterling?'

'Yes, I do believe that's the name.'

'Good grief! So she is, well, no longer on the hunt for a husband.'

'No, it appears she has found one. But look, my dear boy, you must not let this business with the Brax woman worry you further. You are not the first to allow yourself to be ensnared in such a way.'

Anson looked up at him questioningly.

'As a young man on my grand tour I was similarly lured into ... well, that's another story. But in your case surely there is no longer a problem. The minx has married the yeomanry fellow. So you are free of her! And you have no lasting feeling for her?'

'None but revulsion. But I still feel that I have behaved dishonourably and that I must tell Cassandra.'

'Nonsense. She need not and should not know. You are a man of honour but you are a sea officer, and, being a sensible girl brought up to be open-minded, she will assume as a matter of course that you are a man of the world – a man of, let's say, experience ... In fact, she is so sensible about such things that I believe she would be somewhat disappointed if you were not!'

'But, sir, after what I have told you about Charlotte Brax I hope you don't for a moment think that I would behave anything but honourably towards your niece. She is not only beautiful and intelligent, but pure and ...'

'My dear fellow, I trust you completely. There is no need whatsoever for you to give me assurances.'

Anson felt a huge wave of relief and did not demur when Parkin poured them both another glass.

'Now, we'll forget all that nonsense and discuss important matters such as moving you to a bigger room, sending to the rectory for your things and so forth.'

'I am eternally grateful to you, sir. But before I settle in too comfortably now that I am on the way to being mended, both physically and mentally thanks to you, I must get myself back to Seagate and my duties with the Sea Fencibles.'

Parkin protested: 'But you are *not* fully mended. Doctor Hawkins mentioned to me that he is concerned about the wounds you have suffered – even before Boulogne. He tells me you were lucky to survive and fears that if there is a next time you may not be so lucky.'

'It is all part of being a sea officer and at least, unlike Lord Nelson, I have managed to hang on to all of my body parts.'

'But will you please at least consider giving up the sea altogether before it is too late and we do lose you? I have more than enough money, far more than enough, to make your life comfortable. We could pursue our shared interests, and travel – with Cassandra of course – when the war ends, as surely it must. Our own grand tour: Paris, Venice, Rome – just think of it! And perhaps on return we three could put our minds to tackling some of the many social injustices that plague our country, and this county in particular.'

'You are most kind, sir, and most persuasive, but I will not be a drain on your purse. I can and will contribute my share. Also, perhaps you do not quite understand what drives us in the navy?'

'Adventure – the lure of the sea?'

'Why yes, but it is more than that – far more. It is every midshipman's dream to pass for lieutenant, and each lieutenant's ambition to become a captain – and a post captain at that. Every sea officer's dearest wish is to command his own ship and I am no different. Then there is flag rank to aspire to ...'

The old gentleman put up his hands in mock surrender. This was a debate he was not going to win.

But Anson was not yet finished. 'You see, as long as there is an enemy of Britain afloat anywhere in the world, we are driven to follow our profession.'

Parkin smiled indulgently. 'I feared you would say something of the sort, but at least consider delaying your return to duty until you are properly fit.'

Anson shook his head. 'No, I have been absent too long and there will be much to be done, not least to ensure that the other Boulogne raid casualties and the families of those who died are being looked after properly.'

45

The New Divisional Captain

Sam Fagg was holding forth to the landlord in the Mermaid. 'It's a treat to sit quiet wiv a jug of ale now we got them blurry funerals out the way. Can't abide funerals, I can't. All that weepin' and wailin' – it drives yer nuts!'

The landlord was sympathetic. 'Could have been worse, I suppose. What did you lose, five was it?'

'Fencibles? Three, all from Mister Anson's boat and 'e was quite bad hurt hisself. Hogben stopped a musket ball in the 'ead. Brooke 'ad 'is arm chopped orf when he tried to get through the netting and bled to death. Poor old Longstaff 'ad his 'ead split right open by a Froggie wiv a tomahawk. The boys used to say 'e 'adn't got no brains, but he 'ad. You could see 'em, all dribblin' out.'

The landlord winced at the thought, trying not to think of the tapioca pudding he had eaten with last night's supper. He swallowed hard and grunted: 'The going of him won't do my trade no good. He was one of my most regular regulars, he was.'

Fagg nodded. Longstaff had been a serious toper all right. He remembered the man getting rotten drunk at the review of the volunteers by the King at Mote Park and having to restrain him and hide him in a wagon.

'Yeah, 'e was a drinker orlright, but on the raid 'e showed he 'ad guts as well as brains – 'e carried on tryin' to cut through the Froggy nettin' even after some French matelot stabbed 'im and then split 'is 'ead open like a melon. Just wouldn't let go, see? Mind you, 'e was proberly 'alf cut, but there you go. That's guts for you whatever way you sees it.'

'How did you go on, in your boat?'

'We wus shoved off course by the current, but we managed to join up wiv Mister Anson and 'is lot and get right up close and personal with the Frogs. One of the impress lads and three of the marines wiv us copped it.

256

Mister Coney stopped a musket ball, but 'e'll live, and a couple of our fencibles wus wounded.'

'How about Tom Hoover?'

'Orlright – 'e wus in the other boat. Come out of it wivout a scratch. Mister Shrubb and 'im saved Mister Anson's life by all accounts. Nah, Tom's orlright for an American. Right now 'e's orf with Shrubb and his daughter, visitin' the wounded. Whenever she appears 'e's orf escortin' 'er round and whatnot. Wouldn't surprise me if 'e didn't pop 'er the question one of these days.'

Fagg grounded his tankard and the landlord answered the signal by drawing another draught of ale.

'But, o' course, the big noos is that old porky face ain't around no more.'

'What, Captain Hoare?'

'That's 'im. Appears 'e went along wiv Nelson in the *Medusa* to hadvise 'im. Can ye beat it? I wouldn't let 'im hadvise me pet dog if I 'ad one, which, thank Gawd, I ain't!'

The landlord asked gingerly: 'Is that why the raid didn't quite ...'

'Don't mind yer words, mate – just say it. It was a effin' disaster, excuse me French.'

Fagg swigged his ale. 'Anyways, since then 'oare's supposed to have got called to the *Hadmirality* and no-one's seen 'ide nor 'air of 'im since. All I bin told is that 'e's bin replaced.'

'Not promoted, surely?'

'Gawd 'elp the navy if they're kickin' 'im upstairs to be a hadmiral 'imself. Wouldn't put it past a lying, cowardly git like 'im to talk 'em into it, though, just like he talked your daft mayor into givin' 'im that presentation sword. If I'd 'ad my way I'd 'ave stuffed it right up where the sun don't shine!'

The landlord agreed. He had not been in favour of using rate money on such fripperies when there were plenty of more pressing local issues to fund, getting rid of the town's extremely smelly and growing dunghills being just one.

*

Back at the Seagate detachment Fagg soon worked himself into a tizz, supervising some unemployed Sea Fencibles who, for their King's shilling a day, were only too willing to titivate the place ready for inspection by the new divisional captain – and for the return of Lieutenant Anson.

257

The bosun chivvied one of the fencibles who had the temerity to rest on his broom reversed. 'You there, Bishop, put yer back into it! I told yer to sweep the place up, not move the blurry dust from 'ere to there and back agin and doze orf when yer feel like it!'

Bishop obliged by putting the broom back into action and disturbing a pile of dust he had gathered earlier.

As the clean-up continued, Tom Hoover reported back from visiting the wounded and handing each a shilling as a day's pay. They were not strictly entitled to the money but had surely earned it by putting their lives on the line at Boulogne.

The American had wanted to dish out more of the navy's money, but had heeded Boxer's warning that if some of the men, incapacitated though they were, had been given more than the minimum per day it would disappear very quickly down the town's pub urinals.

Fagg gave the working party another blast and winked at Hoover. 'I'm just what they calls encouragin' them. To be honest wiv yer, Tom, I'm all out of sorts meself. I effin' dread clappin' eyes on this new divisional bloke. What if 'e's—?'

'Out of the same mould as Hoare? For sure there couldn't be more than one of *him*, could there?'

'That's just it. Supposin' 'e is? After all what's 'appened I can't see Mister Anson puttin' up wiv anuvver bleedin' 'oare. What wiv bein' wounded bad and all, if anuvver bad-un turns up 'e might decide to chuck it in. I would, if it was down to me. I'd get out and run a pub ... or buy a chicken farm. Anyfink not to 'ave to serve under anuvver pompous effin' idiot like 'oare!'

His tirade was interrupted by Tom Marsh who had been lurking around outside as lookout to give early warning of the new divisional captain's arrival.

'Right, you lot!' Fagg ordered, not unkindly. 'Stop fannyin' abaht and disappear out the back wiv them brooms and whatnot. I want this place lookin' shipshape and it won't while the likes of you lot are pussy-footin' around makin' the place look untidy. If the noo divisional bloke sees you lot 'ere 'e'll fink 'e's wandered into a looney bin!''

Hoover shot him a glance and held up crossed fingers as the door swung open and the new divisional captain entered.

*

Anson was deep in thought throughout the journey from Ludden Hall down to the coast in Jeremiah Parkin's coach.

Already the last time he was at Seagate sorting out the men to go on the Boulogne expedition seemed like an age ago.

Some of those men he had selected to go were now dead and buried, others wounded, in some cases maimed for life. Although he well knew that fault for the failure lay elsewhere, he could not help feeling responsible. They were, after all, his men.

And, with the prospect of having to continue to serve under the dreaded Hoare, who from the outset had given him more grief than help or guidance, he had never felt the loneliness of his junior command more keenly.

Worse, he felt he could no longer defer to Hoare. The divisional captain had long since forfeited his loyalty. And if it was true, as he believed, that the man had failed to pass on the warning about the chains securing the Boulogne flotilla, then he deserved to be court-martialled – and shot.

No, his mind was made up. He could not, and would not, serve under the man for another minute. Anson knew he must confront Hoare once and for all, and, if there was no other course open to him, he was prepared to call him out.

He stepped down from the coach and told Dodson to seek water and feed for the horses at the Mermaid before steeling himself for the coming encounter with his despised superior officer.

*

Bosun Fagg, his foully smoking clay pipe clenched in his teeth, was waiting at the entrance to the detachment building and greeted Anson with a wide grin.

Knuckling his forehead in salute, he chortled: 'Back from the dead agin, sir, eh? Them Frogs must be wonderin' what they 'ave to do to knock you orf yer perch permanent-like! Mind you, you've gorn very thin, more like a skellington ...'

Despite his black mood, Anson could not suppress a smile. 'Thank you, as ever, for your solicitude, bosun. Is all well here, and has Captain Hoare arrived?'

Fagg's grin widened. 'Captain 'oare? Why, no, sir, you're a bit what they calls be'ind the times – 'e's been posted orf to somewhere called the Silly Islands, 'e 'as. Right place for 'im, if ye arsk me. Nah, but the new bloke's arrived and 'e's waiting for yer inside, checkin' the books and runnin' 'is fingers over the furniture to see if 'e can find any dust, I 'spect!'

Anson's mood had lightened at the news of Hoare's departure and the thought of him trying to social climb among the tiny population of the Isles of Scilly. But, nevertheless, he sighed as he entered the building, preparing himself to meet his new master.

After the bright autumn sunlight it was dark inside and he paused to adjust to the dim light from the few high windows. The naval officer sitting behind the solitary desk rose from his chair and even in the gloom Anson recognised a face he knew well.

'Armstrong? Good grief! What are you doing deserting your nice comfortable signal station?'

His friend beamed. 'Welcome back to the land of the living! And I've not deserted, mon vieux, perish the thought. I've been posted at last!'

It was then that Anson spotted the shiny new epaulette on his friend's shoulder – a captain's epaulette.

Armstrong was the new divisional captain for the Sea Fencibles ...

*

With much hilarity, they left Fagg in charge and adjourned to the Mermaid where Armstrong ordered the landlord to produce his very best bottle of wine and hang the expense.

The publican emerged from the cellar blowing a thick layer of dust from a bottle that no doubt pre-dated the war, the glint in his eye indicating great satisfaction as he worked out how much he could charge for it.

Armstrong tasted it, pronounced it excellent, and called on the landlord to produce a second bottle of the same, telling Anson: 'Always keep some of your forces in reserve ready to join battle when required, mon vieux!'

The new divisional captain's delight at his escape from his cliff-top signal station and longed-for promotion, and Anson's heartfelt pleasure in having seen the last of the dreaded Hoare and welcoming his particular friend, promised a long and convivial evening.

But, as they reminisced and Armstrong regaled Anson with his plans for greater use of the several Sea Fencible detachments – including Seagate – now under his overall command, they did not notice a stranger enter the bar-room.

Short and thickset, with powerful shoulders, tattooed neck and a nose that had clearly been broken several times, he had the look of an old sailor washed up on an alien shore – not an unusual sight in the Channel ports.

And, with his coat collar turned up and his hat pulled down low over his scarred forehead, the landlord failed to recognise him as an old regular from a couple of years back.

The newcomer took a seat in a dark corner and signalled a serving girl to bring him a tot, raising two fingers to make it a double.

With the Mermaid's best wine already taking effect, the brother officers were so engrossed in their convivial conversation that they failed to notice that they were under close surveillance.

After being ambushed and coshed by some of the men he had exploited, handed over still dazed to a press gang in Rye, and enduring a long absence as an unwilling inmate of one of His Majesty's ships, Billy MacIntyre was back in his old stomping grounds.

He blamed Anson, who had uncovered his lucrative false payroll and blackmailing scams, for his fall – and for being pressed back into the navy to serve on the bottom rung of the ladder, unable to reveal his true rank and past service lest he be accused of desertion.

The late, but not lamented, bully-boy bosun of Seagate Sea Fencibles, was a deserter now sure enough, having taken the opportunity to disappear when the ship-of-the-line he was serving in docked at Chatham for repairs.

Unnoticed by the other drinkers, least of all the two officers who were reminiscing happily as the landlord uncorked their second bottle, he knocked back his rum and signalled for another.

And, while he waited, he fingered the razor-sharp knife in his belt and plotted revenge.

Historical Note

Nelson's two attacks on Boulogne in 1801 actually happened in much the way described in this story and the words attributed to him are all his own.

They come courtesy of the late, great Nelson expert and national newspaper naval and defence correspondent Tom Pocock, whom the author knew well during his time as an Admiralty – and later Ministry of Defence – information officer.

However, Lieutenant Anson, his family, friends, comrades in arms and enemies, are, of course, entirely fictional, as is Seagate, located in the author's imagination somewhere to the west of Folkestone, and time-spans have been adjusted slightly to fit the story.

Armstrong's lonely signal station at Fairlight in Sussex has long since disappeared, but the beach where Anson and Hurel landed, at Equihen-Plage, just south of Boulogne, is much the same as it must have been in 1801, although it is now used by sand yachting enthusiasts rather than smugglers.

The Sea Fencibles most definitely existed and would have played a key defensive role, especially along the Kentish coast, had the many-times-threatened French invasion taken place. Nevertheless, this Nelson-era 'Dad's Navy' was involved in various skirmishes with French privateers and Nelson did encourage them to serve afloat.

Thanks are due, again, to Tracy-Leon Barham, Esquire, and Colonel Robert Murfin for their expert advice on weaponry and smugglers' signalling devices of the day.

The hulks were only too real. An officer incarcerated in one on the River Medway later reported to the French Government that "it is in these floating tombs that prisoners of war are buried alive." Many died and were buried on nearby mudflats – including the sinisterly named Dead Man's Island, and recent erosion has exposed the remains of some of the unfortunates buried there.

Rochester's Guildhall Museum's display, where children are shown how to make straw-work boxes and fluffy rats – can give only an impression of the horrors of imprisonment aboard the hulks.

Small wonder that a good many of the prisoners sought to get away, often using the escape route centred on Whitstable that actually existed – again, much as described.

In 1801, Nelson was given command of Britain's anti-invasion forces, assembled a squadron which first bombarded Boulogne, and later mounted a major boat attack in an attempt to cut out the French flotilla defending the port.

Adverse currents and Admiral Latouche-Tréville's seaman-like precaution of chaining his vessels together foiled Nelson, who promptly accused the French of behaving dishonourably by doing so.

It did not take long for the French to celebrate what they claimed as a victory with a song that translated as:

"Off Boulogne,
Nelson poured hell-fire!
But on that day, many a toper
Instead of wine, drank salt water
Off Boulogne."

Many, like Anson, initially considered the raid an ignominious defeat for the assault force. But, on reflection later, he revised his view.

The reality was that the Royal Navy's ships continued to rule the waves and were masters of the Channel while the French remained locked up in their ports.

And the Naval Chronicle countered the enemy's boasts with its own piece of doggerel:

"Baffled, disgraced, blockaded and destroyed ...
The Gallic Navy a skeleton remains,
And as a scare-crow is now employed,
To frighten babies as it hangs in chains."

It was true that the chains that had saved Boulogne enchained it still. And for the French the possibility of mounting an invasion of England was as remote as ever – for the present.

But Oliver Anson, distant kinsman many times removed of the great circumnavigator and reformer of the navy, will be called to action once again along with his oddball Sea Fencibles.

About the author

David McDine, OBE, is a Deputy Lieutenant of Kent and a former Royal Navy Reserve officer and Admiralty information officer.

He is the author of *Unconquered: The Story of Kent and its Lieutenancy*. His fiction output includes *The Five Horseshoes*, his debut novel in the *Animal Man* series, and more recently his popular historic naval fiction series featuring Lieutenant Oliver Anson. His first novel in that series, *The Normandy Privateer*, and its prequel *Strike the Red Flag,* are also published by Endeavour Media.

If you enjoyed *Dead Man's Island*, please share your thoughts on Amazon by leaving a review.

For more free and discounted eBooks every week, sign up to our Endeavour Media newsletter.

Follow us on Twitter and Instagram.

Made in the USA
Middletown, DE
17 April 2018